A mystery with substance!
— C.E.

An easy read and moves along logically to an entertaining climax. Your writing and your story are strong and engaging. It kept me turning the pages.
— E.S.

Enthralling. Ingenious. Thrilling. I look forward to reading more Rett Swinson installments.
— C.S.

This was a solid mystery with some twists and turns.... Rett is a dynamic character and I liked watching her find her way. This was an enjoyable read and I look forward to the next book in this pleasantly charming new series.
— Dru's Book Musings: www.drusbookmusing.com

I thoroughly enjoyed Eric Lodin's first novel. Soft Hearts has all the ingredients mystery fans love: a solid plot with ample suspects, vividly portrayed characters who feel both familiar and fresh, just enough hints of romance to make the reader want more, and a conclusion that is satisfying in multiple ways. But most of all, Soft Hearts has Rett Swinson, an outstanding leading lady with intelligence, humor, and zero tolerance for injustice. She's spent a few months wondering what to do with her future after her husband deserted her for a girl half his age. But when the nastiest woman in the neighborhood is murdered and homicide cop Daryll Schmidt recruits Rett to ferret out local secrets, she throws herself into the task with a new purpose. Readers will cheer for Rett as she solves a murder while discovering her own strength and independence, and they will want to see her in action again and again.

    –Sandra Parshall, *Agatha and Daphne Award-Winning author of the Rachel Goddard mysteries*

SOFT HEARTS

A RETT SWINSON MYSTERY

ERIC LODIN

For my family,
who has loved me through it all.

Though the day of my destiny's over,
And the star of my fate hath declined,
Thy soft heart refused to discover
The faults which so many could find

—*Lord Byron, "To Augusta"*

PART I

DRAGON

But this is human life: the war, the deeds,
The disappointment, the anxiety,
Imagination's struggles, far and nigh,
All human; bearing in themselves this good,
That they are still the air, the subtle food,
To make us feel existence, and to show
How quiet death is.
—*John Keats,* Endymion

Ask My Students:
-*What are some of "imagination's struggles"?*
-*What does it really mean to "feel existence"?*
-*And is a quiet death any consolation?*
—*entry in Professor Wanda Hightower's notebook*

CHAPTER 1

NEEDLESS NECESSITIES

Lydia Schmidt, the crusty old bird who lives across the street, knocked on my door one late October morning, stirring me from my hangover doze to tell me her Taurus wouldn't start and seeing if I'd give her a lift to her quilting club.

Back when Allan and I were operating our real-estate development company, you wouldn't catch Harriet Swinson sleeping in on a weekday. By seven I'd already be at the office running numbers or checking the work of contractors in one of our subdivisions. But this was the tenth month of our separation, and I was chin deep into the dark routine of a bottle of wine each night.

Here's why: My husband and his twenty-something real-estate-agent mistress, KayLeigh Rider, had moved into a brand new house in one of the subdivisions Allan and I had built north of Raleigh. Meanwhile, I remained in the home where we'd raised our college-aged daughter, in the historic downtown neighborhood where Allan recently revealed he'd never wanted to live in the first place.

Had anything about our marriage *not* been a charade?

Lydia chose to wait outside and smoke in her baggy, red NC State Wolfpack sweats while I threw on some jeans and a turtleneck sweater, splashed some cold water on my face, and ran a wet brush through my neglected, split-end curls. I silently cursed my bathroom mirror for adding lines to my already 42-year-old expression, as if my recent hard living was all its fault. *This must be how wicked witches are born.*

I donned big sunglasses to cover the bags under my eyes and met Lydia at my Camry. She stomped out her cigarette in the gutter and off we went.

It turned out that Lydia got her daily quilting fix just a mile away in a nearly abandoned strip mall in East Raleigh where an A&P and a Kmart thrived back in the 1970s. Now, it seemed like the Retail Center That Time Forgot. Behind the building ran a two-story embankment swarmed with thick layers of kudzu reaching up to a row of rundown houses. In other directions loomed ramshackle apartments and sad, decaying church buildings. Talk about seeing better days.

The sign above the double glass doors announced "Needless Necessities" in hand-painted cursive. For a second I'd misread it as *Needles* Necessities, as though we'd arrived at a syringe-exchange program for intravenous drug users. The glass in one of the doors was cracked and covered with brown packing tape. Near the door, a vandal had spray-painted black squiggles that looked like demonic spaghetti.

I didn't have the heart to tell my neighbor that her hobby spot was a complete dump.

I could have just dropped Lydia off and come back an hour later to pick her up, but it's not like I had anything better to do, so I followed her across the moonscape parking lot. Inside I removed my sunglasses, expecting to find a cavernous community center with a half-dozen bridge tables and a soda machine stocked with R.C., Tab, and Mr. Pibb. What confronted me instead was quite a feast for the eyes.

Filling the space between the front wall and the front desk were more than a dozen sizable blue bins, the kind a daredevil might ride over Niagara Falls. Each bin featured a different random item at a discount price. One bin held plastic hats for 50 cents each. Another featured framed photos of perfect strangers. Yet another advertised "Funky Plastic" at $1 per pound. Along a wall, shelves bulged with boxes of sports trophies, calendars, picture frames, and empty tennis ball tubes. On the top shelf perched a stuffed guinea hen.

And this was just the center's *foyer*.

"Good morning, Lydia!" said the short Black woman standing behind the main counter. Around my age I guessed, she sported lovely, thickly braided black hair; but what first caught my eye was a life-like tattoo of a little boy's face peeking above the neckline of her red blouse.

Without pausing her stride, Lydia rasped, "Jasmine, meet my pal Harriet, goes by 'Rett.' See you both in an hour or so." She practically sprinted into a side room where I could see a group of women working their needles above cloth stretched across wooden racks.

Jasmine smiled at me as she came out from behind the main counter. I hated happy people these days. My therapist thought I needed to lighten up. "A cynic," she said (meaning *me*) "is someone who recognizes the cost of everything and the value of nothing." Who did she think she was—Socrates? I had insisted this wasn't about me being cynical. It was about my life going from pretty okay to becoming a complete shit-show.

"Caught you looking at my tattoo," Jasmine said conspiratorially. "That's my student-athlete, Russell. I could sing his praises all day, but I'll spare you for now. May I help you find something?"

I wasn't inclined to chit-chat with retail help these days. I certainly wasn't used to talking about breast tattoos. I changed the subject.

"What exactly is this ... place?"

Jasmine did a little Vanna White "ta dah" move with one of her hands. "This here is the Needless Necessities Arts and Crafts Emporium. We have a little bit of everything for sale, most of it donated, as we are a nonprofit. All our inventory ends up in art instead of the landfill. Are you an artist?"

I could have mentioned how I'd been a fine arts major in college, specializing in painting—botanicals, to be exact. But I had not been near an art-supply store since graduation, and wasn't even sure where I'd stored my bulky easel after we moved to Raleigh nearly two decades ago. I shook my head.

"I just came to give my friend a ride to her quilting group."

"Well, if you are ever interested in a class, we do host a number of them—macramé, needlepoint, stained glass. The painters meet four days a week. In fact, there's a lesson going on right now." She led me toward another doorway just beyond the quilting room where I poked my head in. A dozen adults sat in front of easels doing work I immediately pegged as amateurish. Jasmine said, "I'm going to enroll Russell soon. He likes to weight train, but I tell him he needs to be more well-rounded if he's going to get into college."

The class was being led by a young, scrawny, and heavily tatted female instructor who, to my horror, saw me gawking and paused her lesson to ask if I wanted to join them.

"No, thanks," I said, and I quickly backed out of there.

"Take some time to explore the center," said Jasmine. "No one in the history of the Qrazy Qwilters has ever finished early, I can assure you of that."

I thanked her and began making my way down the main hallway, ducking into a small side gallery empty of people, where the most expensive piece cost ten dollars and wasn't any better than what the painting students were doing. When I turned to leave, blocking my only way out was a middle-aged woman with short, curly brown hair and red-framed glasses. "Welcome," she said. I glimpsed the woman's name tag: *Sally Field, Founder*. She must have seen me looking, because she quickly interjected, "I'm Sally Field. I'm not the actress, but I am the founder of this center. We'll have been open a year in December."

I thought how my divorce would be final then, too.

"This was a dream of mine for many years," she continued. "My mother was an artist, and Needless Necessities is a tribute to her." Her eyes became misty. "Excuse me." She pushed past me and began straightening the gallery's paintings.

Feeling uncomfortable at the woman's display of emotion, I returned to the hallway and followed it to a warehouse-size fabrics area showcasing rolls of cloth and racks of patterns, yarn, and thread. I didn't sew, so I kept walking past the fabric into another large hall where the aroma of paints struck me hard. Immediately I was transported to the undergraduate studio at East Carolina University, where I had spent hours at a stretch with light, color, and canvas.

I don't know how long I stood there day-dreaming before I was interrupted again.

"Excuse me." It was a different Black woman, this time a customer who looked to be in her thirties. She held up a pink tutu. "My niece wants to put her name on this for Halloween. Do I have to sew it on, or can I paint it on?"

"Sorry," I said. "I don't work here." Heck, I didn't work anywhere anymore.

"My mistake," the woman said. She started to leave.

"Wait," I said, stopping her. "Acrylic paint should work fine on fabric; you just have to let it dry for a day or two to set." I remembered all those paint-ruined clothes I'd had to throw away after college when I married Allan and began helping him in real estate. At the time it had felt like shedding an old skin. Now I was beginning to wonder if I'd lost something essential.

"Oh, good," the woman said, her eyes brightening. She began scanning the paint rack for the color she wanted.

"You know," I said, as the woman browsed, "I used to help make my daughter's Halloween costumes. She's in college now."

"I bet you're so proud of her."

I didn't mention how Stephanie was shunning most of my phone calls lately. She was resentful of the divorce, somehow blaming me, even though her father had been the one who'd cheated. She'd always been a Daddy's Girl, but it was still surprising, and it still hurt.

The woman finally settled on a color. "Thank you for your help."

"I hope your niece has a nice Halloween," I said.

Her expression fell. "Me, too, but so few families in our neighborhood give out candy anymore," she said. "I don't know why."

I offered, "If you're looking for another neighborhood to trick-or-treat in, keep Woodmont in mind."

"I know where that is. Over near the cemetery, right?"

"That's right." In fact, my house practically backed up to Woodmont Cemetery, one of Raleigh's oldest.

"We might try that," she said. "Thank you so much."

After the woman left, a voice behind me said, "Well done." It was Jasmine. She looked pleased, as if I'd passed some sort of test. "I sure wish we had someone who could monitor the paints part-time. Someone who can serve customers like that lady— and keep the huffers away."

"The who?"

"Sometimes we get ne'er-do-wells who just want to sniff the paints and model glue."

I guess this place served only the best.

Right then my own hangover headache began to throb. "I could really use a cup of coffee," I said. "Is there a café nearby?"

"No, but I'll see what I can do. By the way, when was the last time you painted?"

I cocked an eyebrow. "Who said I liked to paint?"

"No one had to." Before I could respond again, she retreated to the back of the hall where I imagined the staff room to be.

Hearing some raised voices from back in the fabrics area, I went to investigate. I came upon a plump, middle-aged white man with a bushy mustache and an oversized toupee who had ambushed Sally "Not the Actress" Field in the open and was now chiding her. "I'm sorry, I can't give you another extension," he said.

Sally stood her ground. "Look, Mr. Simms, I'm trying to raise an advertising budget. If I can do that—"

"I've got a prospective tenant who might want to lease this space for warehousing," the man interrupted. "Now, I agreed to give you until November 15 to provide the ten thousand dollars in back rent you owe. That's just a few weeks away."

Just then Jasmine reappeared next to me holding two steaming hot mugs. I took one from her gratefully—the words on my mug screaming COFFEE FIXES EVERYTHING!—as she rolled her eyes at the conversation before us and muttered, "Good thing for him my Russell ain't here. My boy doesn't like bullies one bit."

The landlord, oblivious to the small audience he'd attracted, responded to Sally, "Why don't you sell something like jewelry or designer clothing that will bring in some real cash?"

"Folks can already buy those things at Crabtree Mall or Cameron Village," Sally said.

"Sure, but you can get every one of *these* things"—he gestured at the store's wares as if they were nothing at all—"at the Wake County Dump."

"You've made your point, Mr. Simms."

"Just trying to be helpful," Simms said. In the process of leaving, he shot a glare at Jasmine and me that could have killed infants and the immuno-compromised.

I tried to think of something that would lift the dark cloud left in the landlord's wake. "Cheer up, Sally," I said. "Here, I'll buy this." I put my free hand on a vintage sewing machine rising from amidst the many spools and patterns.

"That's just for display," Sally sighed. "What we really need is more volunteer help around here. Between working the cash register and processing donations in the back, I'm going nuts."

I hadn't seen a lot of cash register action up till now. But it did seem unrealistic for two people to be responsible for so much square footage.

"Rett would be a wonderful volunteer in the painting supplies section," Jasmine interjected. "She's a painter herself."

I sputtered, "Oh, I haven't really—"

"Perfect!" Sally cut in. "Jasmine can orient you tomorrow. Right, Jasmine?"

"Of course. Russell is going fishing with his daddy tomorrow, so I can come in," Jasmine lifted her mug as if we were sealing the deal with a toast. The two devious ladies were smiling at me so pleasantly I could only stare at them mutely. What in the funky plastic had just happened?

Before I could argue, Sally said, "By the way, Jazz, the computer's inventory software is down again."

"I'll grab some index cards from Stationery," Jasmine said in her can-do manner.

"As for the back rent," Sally added, "we need a plan. We've only got three weeks to get that together." She slumped back against the mountain of fabric, as if inviting a cloth avalanche to cover her up forever. "Maybe it was a mistake to open this center in the first place."

I don't know what got into me next. Maybe it was the caffeine jolt. Or maybe all the wine I'd drunk over the past few months had caused some serious brain damage. In any case, the successful co-founder of Swinson Development opened her big mouth. "Just a suggestion, but why don't you make your little gallery available to some serious local artists and charge commission?"

Sally looked at me like I had two heads. "We can't take money from starving artists."

"But a commission structure is how most galleries operate," I argued.

She grunted. "Well, it's not how we operate *here*."

"Okay," I said, switching gears. "Have you tried hanging flyers at the local art colleges?"

Sally shrugged. "We don't serve a lot of college students."

Which had been my point, of course. Like Charlie Brown, I was about to make a run at the football again when Sally threw up her hands and said, "I need to call the bank and see if we have anything left in our line of credit." And with that she walked away.

Jasmine sensed my frustration.

"Give it some time. I'm sure she'll come to value your opinion eventually."

I thanked Jasmine for the coffee—which was quite decent actually—and for the encouragement. On the drive home, I bitched to Lydia about how I'd been roped into volunteering *and* had my sound business advice rejected.

"Sally can be a real pill sometimes," said the transplanted Midwesterner. "But she is the founder. She has a right to be stubborn, I guess."

I gritted my teeth. "Well, this founder can be stubborn, too." It was true. Every year Allan and I would spar over what to do with our company's profit. He usually wanted to distribute the gains as income and spend it on luxuries, while I preferred growing a company nest-egg so we wouldn't have to borrow so heavily for our development projects. Fortunately for me, Allan never liked to argue, and over the years our business had built up a sizable kitty of nearly $20 million. How to split the assets of the business was likely to be a sticky issue in our divorce settlement.

I told Lydia about the landlord cornering Sally and demanding his money. "Your quilting club might want to start looking for another place to meet."

"Nuts! But this place is so close to my house. That really chafes my rear!"

"At least I won't have to volunteer there for very long," I muttered.

"Speaking of volunteering," said Lydia, "I'm going to need your help setting up for the Halloween block party again this year."

But Halloween was more than a week away. Right this minute, I was still obsessing over how I would argue for my ideas the next time I saw Sally.

At my orientation the next morning, before I could even share the first new business idea with her, Sally came rushing toward us, blurting, "I know what we'll do to make up the rent! We'll host a bake sale right here at Needless Necessities on November 15th. It's the day the rent is due—and it happens to be my birthday, too."

Somehow I managed not to laugh in her face. "You owe ten grand. Just how many cupcakes do you expect to sell?"

"Not cupcakes, silly. Pies! We'll combine a pie-baking contest and auction with a Fall art show where artists can sell their work. We won't take a penny in commission, of course." Was she actually trying to torture me? "Rett, I'm counting on you for a pie."

I said, "I have a cold pie recipe that involves Cool Whip, nuts, and pineapple chunks. It's called Million-Dollar Pie, but I don't think you'll get more than ten dollars for it."

"Then make three," Sally countered. "And help me recruit ten other bakers. Oh, this is going to be fabulous!" Before I could quibble, Sally was off telling anyone who would listen all about her perfect pie plan.

I couldn't freaking believe it. This precious tribute to her mother was a damn sinking ship.

And she was counting on me to help save it? Talk about desperate.

I frowned and turned to Jasmine. "If I come through with some pies, do you think she'll finally start to listen to some sense?"

Jasmine smiled. "Don't worry. Things usually have a way of working out."

Sorry to break it to you, Sister, but the mug was wrong. Coffee can't really fix everything. Or maybe Jasmine with her star-athlete-student son just didn't have much to worry about.

Over the next week I continued to drive Lydia to quilting as I volunteered at my station. Helping this and that customer with paint supplies was mindless, something I could have done in my sleep. I still had no desire to pick up a brush and embarrass myself like the students in the paint class, though this volunteer gig did serve the purpose of getting me out of bed before noon.

I hadn't recruited the first pie, though. A bake sale just seemed so pointless.

Then on Friday morning the prospective new leaser sent some workmen to verify the cubic footage of the center. "What do they plan to store here?" I asked the man measuring near me.

"Styrofoam containers," said the guy. "You know, for fast food."

Are you kidding me, Sally? You're going to let this place fail so that someone can store the most destructive artificial shit known to mankind? That stuff has a half-life of a billion years.

Fine. I'll get your precious pies. Then, when your tribute to your mother—the same person who so thoughtfully named you Sally Frickin' Field—totally implodes, I can say I told you so. I won't do it for you, or even for Jolly Saint Jasmine, but for my neighbor and fellow crab-apple Lydia, who needs a place to quilt. Maybe I'll do it, too, because it will take my mind off my shitty life for a while. If that's cynical, so be it. At least I'm not crazy.

Needless Necessities was as insane as its name.

CHAPTER 2

A HALLOWEEN MURDER

Each year our neighborhood celebrates Halloween with a block party at my cul-de-sac that begins where two streets meet at a right angle. I wasn't feeling festive, but I put on my big-girl pants and helped Lydia—cigarette dangling from her lips—pull several card tables from each of our basements and set them up in one long row. We took our time as we worked, allowing us to take in the neighborhood's vibrant swaths of fall leaf color.

Woodmont was a historic neighborhood with a large number of Victorian homes. Though most of the houses had undergone renovation if not a complete remodel, there had been serious efforts by many to preserve much of the original architecture. But, for me, Woodmont's main draw was its giant oak trees, with every home enjoying the shady canopy of at least one century-old beauty. Surely Allan must be feeling at least a bit nostalgic for Woodmont these days as he settled into a practically treeless subdivision with his young tart.

As we were draping our tables with black and orange coverings, a black police cruiser rolled up and stopped in the center of the cul-de-sac. The intimidating Dodge Charger belonged to

Lydia's forty-something son, Darryl, a homicide detective just like his late father. On the weekends that Darryl needed child-care for his nine-year-old son, Charlie, Lydia happily let her grandson bunk down in Darryl's boyhood bedroom. Darryl was my age. Divorced these past two years, he lived with his son in a small house on the north edge of town not far from Charlie's mother and the boy's elementary school.

Darryl pulled two sawhorses from the car's massive trunk and placed them at both entrances to the cul-de-sac. Darryl had grown up in Woodmont but had moved out long ago to attend NC State. He stood over six feet tall, with dark brown hair neatly trimmed and a tad of gray showing along the sides. In the throes of my own break-up, I was curious to learn how Darryl had coped with his divorce, but I felt shy to ask. Instead, I resorted to saying something incredibly dork-like.

"Nice weather today," I said.

"I sure don't miss the humidity," Darryl said. "I love being able to see the details of the leaves on the trees."

Could he see every wrinkle on me? The Mulligans, whose home was centered along the cul-de-sac, had transformed their garage into a haunted house. As their fog machine revved up in their driveway, I wished for some of the mist to waft over and give me cover.

Charlie asked his dad if he could change into his costume.

"Sure. I'll come with you. I've got to help your grandma move some food outside." After a courteous nod to me, he followed his boy.

The Mulligans' spooky soundtrack revved up featuring howls, wails, and shrieks. Neighbors began arriving with blood punch, crypt-keeper finger pretzels, eyeball cookies, and enough chips, cupcakes, hotdogs, and hamburgers to get us through a zombie apocalypse. Seeing children run around in their Halloween costumes took me back to when our daughter was a little girl and all the fun we had decorating the house in spooky things and dressing her up for trick-or-treating. I had called Stephanie this morning to see if she might be coming to the annual party, but once again she'd let my call go to voicemail.

I was feeling sorry for myself and was considering ditching the party altogether when a friendly face, the Reverend Jim Thompson, arrived with Ben, his old and docile black lab. The pastor was a quiet, tall, slightly heavy-set man of Irish heritage with fringes of white hair sneaking out from beneath a Durham Bulls baseball cap.

I liked Jim well enough but tended to bond more closely with his wife, Nancy, who played the role of Slightly Naughty Wife of a Preacher Man. After Jim and I had greeted one another, I asked, "Where's Nancy and her Halloween pie?" Jim and Nancy didn't have children of their own, but over the years they had treated all the neighborhood children like honorary nieces and nephews. They could have made a pretty penny if they'd charged us parents for the meals and treats they'd served our kids over the decades. Every Halloween, Nancy baked a pie (sometimes more than one) that was completely to-die-for. I'd been planning to ask her to bake something for the Needless Necessities fundraiser, but hadn't yet.

Jim said, "She sent me up ahead, said a 'watched crumble never cools.'"

"My grandmother used to say, 'A watched pot never boils,'" I said. "Maybe it's an Eastern North Carolina thing." Like me, Nancy had been raised between Raleigh and the North Carolina coast.

"Speaking of," said Jim, "is your ECU student going to make it tonight?"

"Too busy with school work," I said, hoping I wouldn't go to hell for fibbing to a minister.

"Pastor, how you been?" called another neighbor. Jim politely tipped his cap to me and stepped away.

Several of the adults were drinking beers or wine out of Solo cups. I was tempted to get my own cup of wine, but I had always thought of Darryl as a strait-laced guy. Would he break out his badge and enforce Raleigh's open container laws? Probably not, but I also didn't want to come off like a lush. Anxious as hell, I paced, trying to distract myself with the various children's costumes.

A ghastly mob was chomping down on the goodies. There were zombies, witches, and ghouls—but also a Mario Brother, a hot-air balloon, and a girl-sized taco ironically enough eating one of Lydia's famous bratwursts. Charlie returned having changed into Spiderman. My favorite costume was worn by one precocious lad, perhaps twelve, who had a woman's nighty over his sweat pants and a t-shirt. The garment contained stickers with the words "Super Ego," "Ego," and "Id."

"What are you dressed as?" I asked.

The boy's deadpan answer: "A Freudian slip."

"Ha! Good one!"

As for the adults, a few did dress up. One man wore a frightening Frankenstein mask. He kept tapping people on the shoulder until they turned around, then he'd snarl loudly to startle them. While I was keeping Creepy Frankenstein Guy in my line of sight, someone else entered my periphery. I wasn't the only one to make note of Nancy Thompson's arrival. Like air travelers jockeying to be first to board a flight, everyone pressed forward for a sample of this year's special dessert.

"Don't crowd now!" shouted Nancy. "There's enough for everyone to get a taste!"

Nancy seemed more careworn than the last time I'd seen her, the wrinkles in her face more pronounced, her permed, gray hair a tad more frazzled. I had to remind myself that many of the old timers in Woodmont were becoming quite elderly. A few older couples had already transitioned out of the neighborhood into townhomes, while others had moved into assisted living facilities or nursing homes. As I watched this almost diminutive woman with slightly shaky cinnamon-powdered hands peel the tinfoil lid off her dessert, it was like glimpsing my own future—and a Halloween chill went down my spine.

"There. I hope you all find it tasty," said Nancy, stepping back to let the vultures descend on her crumble. She needn't have worried. Everyone was already melting over the smell. First in line was Skip Green. As chair of the Woodmont Culture Committee, Skip often organized the neighborhood's food-centered events, which also included the Woodmont Chocolate Fest each spring.

Emulating Paul Hollywood of the *Great British Baking Show*, Skip spooned a sizable pile of the crumble onto his black-cat paper plate and took a deep sniff. "Smells delightful!" He took a large bite with his plastic fork and closed his eyes. "Oh, heavenly!" I took my own bite and sighed. Let the little goblins have their cupcakes with mile-high orange frosting. Skip and I tacitly agreed: apple was the true taste of autumn.

"It's the cinnamon that's the key ingredient," Nancy offered. "Hey, Rett, how are you? Have you seen my darling Jim?"

My mouth full of crumble, I pointed with my fork, then quickly swallowed to ask if she would bake something for the Needless Necessities fundraiser. "It's a really wonderful cause for artists and crafters," I explained cheerily. Heck, if I was going to help with a bake sale and pie contest, I might as well fully embrace my inner dork.

Nancy agreed to bake a pie or two for the event, and I promised to share more details in the coming days.

Having wolfed down their dinners, a motley crew of monsters now lobbied their parents to let them trick-or-treat.

Though there was still plenty of light outside, an early start suited Woodmont's safety-minded parents. A mother insisted they convene for a group photo first.

"Go on, Son, get in the picture," Darryl said. "Your costume looks great!"

Spiderman moped over to where the other kids were posing.

Darryl lingered. Did I catch him casting a glance my way?

My heart quickened a little as I narrowed the space between us. Ostensibly off-duty, Darryl wore brown shoes, khakis, and a brown leather jacket over a light blue button-down. Not particularly fit and maybe a bit overweight, he nonetheless seemed like someone comfortable in his own skin—something I'd always found attractive in a man. "What are you dressed up as?" I asked, "an undercover superhero?"

He chuckled. "I figured my mug was ugly enough I could go as myself."

Darryl wasn't ugly at all. Yes, he sported a fairly thick five-o'clock shadow—but it was after five by now. I liked that he stood a head taller than me without seeming intimidating, even though I suspected a holster and gun were hidden under his leather jacket. Lydia told me he even carried one to the grocery store, because one never knew when an off-duty detective might have to spring into action.

I let his self-deprecating joke slide by. "It's good to see you," I said. "Your mother talks about how much you've been working lately."

"Yeah, the population of Raleigh keeps growing, but the number of the police isn't keeping up."

I looked for another way to connect besides a city-tax conversation. "Want a piece of Nancy Thompson's crumble?" but I had to backpedal when I noticed the dessert had already been completely devoured. "Sorry. Too late."

"It's okay," he said. "This fat paunch doesn't need any more calories."

The photoshoot finished, shouts went up from the children:

"Let's trick-or-treat!"

"Yeah!"

Charlie ran up to Darryl. "Can I go with the others?"

"Are there lots of moms and dads going?" Darryl asked.

"Yes, sir."

Darryl scanned the group. "Okay," he said, "but only if you promise to stay with Mrs. Mulligan and Mrs. Pitts. They're leading the group this year."

Spiderman nodded vigorously.

"Go have fun," Darryl said. "I'll meet you right here when you've circled the block."

Spiderman ran to catch up with the others.

"I wonder if they'll go to the Dragon Lady's house this year," said one of the mothers remaining behind.

"You mean Wanda Hightower?" said another mom, squinting as she peered down the block in the direction the children were traveling. "I doubt it. The front of her house is looking pretty dark."

Wanda Hightower had been part of the neighborhood way longer than me. A long-time English professor, she had never been overly social, but it was only in the past year or so that she'd developed a reputation as an unpleasant, even malevolent hermit. Some of us had tried to intervene in a random act of kindness that had not gone well, something no one liked to talk about. In any case, I doubt anyone seriously expected Wanda to take part in any Halloween fun this year.

The parade was a cue for several of the adults at the party to rush to their homes and assume treat-dispensing positions. Fortunately, the children were moving away from my home and Lydia's; there would be plenty of time to chat-up Darryl some more before the horde of candy cravers made it all the way around the block to our houses.

"Are you and Charlie staying in Woodmont this weekend?" I asked him.

"Just tonight. Charlie's mom is taking him in the morning to visit his other grandparents in Greensboro."

"It must be hard giving up your boy half the time."

"It is, though I have to admit, it forces me to be more intentional during the times we're together." It was attractive to see a dad being so attentive toward his son. "How's your daughter?" Darryl added. "Haven't seen her in a while."

Nor had I. "Oh, she's fine. Her sorority keeps her busy, even if schoolwork doesn't."

Darryl smiled. "I can relate. I was in a fraternity. Were you a sorority girl?"

"GDI," I said. He looked confused, apparently unfamiliar with the "G-D independent" acronym. "Let's just say I was an arts geek."

Before I could say anything more, a couple of the older boys from the trick-or-treating group came rushing back toward us. "Mom!" cried one. "You have to see this! It's so creepy!"

"Yeah!" shouted his friend. "It's at the Dragon Lady's house!"

"What are you talking about?" asked the first boy's mom. "Did Ms. Hightower put something scary on her porch?"

"Come see for yourself," the second boy said. "We don't want to spoil it."

Before they could leave, everyone's attention was drawn to one of the chaperone mothers running our way, holding her daughter's hand while calling out for her husband, who stopped his conversation with the other dads to run and meet his wife. Out of breath, the wife muttered something to him I couldn't quite make out. But Skip Green was close enough to hear. Whatever was said caused him to cover his mouth with his hands.

"What's going on, Skip?" the Rev. Thompson asked as Skip rushed over to us.

"It's Wanda Hightower. Apparently, some of the older children went to trick-or-treat at her front door."

His voice wavered:

"They found her face-down on the front porch with a knife in her back—dead!"

CHAPTER 3

AFTERMATH

Perhaps thinking he might confront an assailant escaping on foot, Darryl pulled out his pistol and ran down the street toward Wanda's. I hopped in my car and drove in the other direction in order to square the block and intercept the main group. Parking my Camry hurriedly, I quickly found Spider Man and pulled him aside. Charlie wasn't surprised when I told him his dad would be busy for the rest of the evening.

"Someone got kilt, I bet," he said.

"Yes," I said. "Someone lost their life. But let's not scare the other children."

But word of the murder had already traveled by text to the chaperone group. I huddled with the moms, who were reluctant to cancel trick-or-treating despite the tragedy. I'd witness similar thinking a few years later when the COVID pandemic threatened to keep kids home, yet their parents still found a way. Maybe the whole point of Halloween was to help people laugh in the face of death. This night the Woodmont mothers decided it would be safe to continue so long as the group only

24

approached the homes of people we knew and wrapped things up before darkness fell.

"Do you want to visit a few more houses with me before heading to your granny's for the night?" I asked Charlie.

He nodded. I kept both eyes glued on him as he visited the remaining homes.

Once we'd squared the block, Charlie ran inside his grandmother's house to count his candy in the kitchen. Lydia was sitting in the den smoking, her cigarette jittery. She had learned about the murder the same time I did but had seen Darryl again when he came back a little while later for his car and forensics kit. He had told her that there was no sign of an assailant, though officers were on patrol looking for anyone suspicious.

She appeared to blink back tears. "Wanda Hightower, killed! I can't imagine anyone around here who'd do that. Wanda was a piece of work—heck, a few people around here definitely resented her—but no one deserves this."

She saw that I was trembling, too. "You sit down," Lydia said. "I'm going to get some iced tea. Want some?" What I really wanted was a glass of wine, but Lydia didn't drink, and she was from a part of the country that had missed the memo about adding sugar to tea.

"No, thanks," I said. "Just water, please."

I sat on her clean but time-worn sofa. Once Lydia returned with our drinks, we began to compare notes about Wanda, someone I didn't know well despite living three doors down from her for nearly two decades.

I did know that Wanda and her husband had divorced not long after their daughter and son graduated from high school. The children would be in their thirties by now. The son was a musician who toured in a band with his father, while his big sister worked at a corporate job in Charlotte, perhaps in banking.

"I've worried about Wanda for some time," said Lydia.

"Ever since…"

"Even before that." We were referring to an occurrence back in September that left a blot of shame on our otherwise drama-free neighborhood—an occurrence we had tacitly agreed not to speak about.

Outside it had grown fully dark. "Are the doors locked?" Lydia asked suddenly. I hopped up and checked.

"All locked," I said. "Do you think any other trick-or-treaters will show up?"

"If word has gotten around, I doubt it."

"You've lived in Woodmont a lot longer than I have," I said. "Can you remember another crime like this?"

She took another drag of her Virginia Slim. "There was a suicide by an elderly widower before you moved here. He was the biggest grump you ever met. You wonder why he didn't do it a lot sooner and spare us the misery."

I looked at her disapprovingly.

"Listen," she said, "it takes a grump to know one." She put out her cigarette in her ashtray and lit another. Lydia was a pack-a-day smoker. I didn't like breathing exhaust, but it wasn't my house.

"When do you think Darryl will be back?" I asked.

"How long is a piece of string?"

"You won't want to stay here alone until he gets back. I'll stay with you."

"Oh, I'm not scared."

"Maybe I am."

"Then stay, and we'll have a slumber party."

We both chuckled at that.

"You can have the guest room," she said. "Darryl can sleep on the couch. He got used to couch-sleeping while being married to that gold-digger." There had never been much love lost between Lydia and Janice, her son's ex.

"Tell me how you really feel, Lydia."

"Stick around and I might."

I told her I needed to grab a few things from across the street. As Lydia protectively watched me through the window, I stepped into the night. A chilly breeze pried at my sweatshirt's collar and made my teeth rattle. In the cul-de-sac, a small group of adults sat in lawn chairs, warming themselves around a portable campfire. Down the block, police lights blasted the front of Wanda's home like a stage, while additional lights were trained on a newscaster standing in the street talking to a camera person next to a TV van. Soon, everyone in the city would know about the evil visited upon our quiet neighborhood this Halloween night.

I dashed to my home and gathered a few clothes and toiletries, making sure I flicked on the porch light as I left.

When Lydia let me in again, I noticed she'd made a quick change into her nightgown. Charlie could be heard upstairs drawing a bath.

"Good thing Darryl was at the block party," I said, settling into the couch again. "I bet he'll crack this case in no time."

"Darryl is clever. And cute, too. You two should spend more time together."

"Are you playing match-maker, Lydia?"

"So sue me if I like to see good people happy. Do you have anything against being happy?"

I weighed my words carefully. "My therapist says I don't think I deserve to be happy."

"Sounds like psychobabble to me. Do you buy that?"

"I actually think I'm numb from everything that's happened with Allan. My feelings seem pretty distant." A million miles away, if you must know. "Don't you ever have trouble naming your feelings, Lydia?"

"I know when I'm pissed off—which is most of the time." She followed the statement with a deep, raspy laugh. "I know when I'm happy—when I'm gardening or quilting. Or if I'm sad. That's when I'm just sitting around thinking about the past. Consider yourself lucky if you don't feel much."

We were interrupted by a knock at the door. We froze, and after a few seconds, we heard the scamper of steps leaving the porch. I tiptoed to the front door and peeked through the blinds.

"Trick-or-treaters," I whispered. "Four of them."

"They might not know about the murder," she said, quickly adding, "Oh, heck, maybe you can catch them before they leave." She put out her cigarette and scrambled to her bowl of candy, while I flicked on the porch light, opened the door, and called to the children to come back.

The first thing I noticed was the children were Black. Though we had a few Black families in Woodmont, I did not recognize these kids from the party. Then I noticed that the littlest girl wore a pink tutu with her name clearly imprinted in purple: *Shauna*.

I blurted out, "Hi, Shauna! I love your costume. I think I met your aunt the other day when she was shopping for it."

The other three looked at Shauna, who looked at me like I was from outer space. I instantly regretted putting her on the spot.

"Shauna's our cousin. She's shy," said the oldest girl, dressed as Wonder Woman.

"It's okay to be shy," I said. "Did you all get some good candy tonight?"

"Oh, yeah!" said one of the boys, a pirate.

"Say, 'Yes, ma'am,' Curtis!" retorted Wonder Woman, who I took to be an older sister to the boys.

"Yes, ma'am," the little pirate corrected himself. "Lots of candy." He lifted his nearly full bag and patted it, smiling.

"Is the party still going on?" said the other boy, a Pee-Wee football player who seemed a bit older than Curtis.

"The block party?" I asked. "No, that was over a while ago."

A squad car zoomed past the house and away from the neighborhood, followed immediately by another.

"Dang! What up with the po-lice?" asked the older boy.

"See, I told you!" Wonder Woman said. "I told you I heard po-lice."

"Did someone get hurt?" asked the tallest boy.

"I don't know all the details," I said.

"Did someone get SHOT?" asked Curtis.

"Hush!" said the big sister. "That's not polite."

"I just asked!"

"I'm not sure what all happened," I deflected. "Here, take a few extra pieces of candy."

Throughout the banter, Shauna had remained quiet, stealing the occasional glance behind her. Only tentatively did she step forward for the extra piece of candy.

"Now, you all should probably head home," I suggested. "Do you live nearby?"

"My mother is picking us up," said the eldest, as she started to lead the others away.

"Shauna's auntie?" I asked.

They nodded.

"Tell her I said hi. If she asks, just tell her we met at Needless Necessities."

There was a round of muttered thank-yous as the group trickled to the street. They seemed about to head in the direction of the police hubbub when Wonder Woman thought better of it and led them in the direction from which they had come. I saw the light of a cell phone that she pulled from her bag.

I closed the door and turned off the porch light. "Do you mind if we call it a night?" I asked my friend.

"That's fine. Darryl has a key. We shouldn't wait up."

"I'm not kicking your son out of his bedroom. I'll take the couch."

"It's up to you. I'm not going to twist your arm."

But the thought of Darryl arriving to find me sleeping in his mother's living room made me feel equally uncomfortable, so I decided I would remain awake—and fully dressed—until he arrived. I didn't want to wait alone, though, so when she went to bed I grabbed Lydia's key from her kitchen and—after locking the door behind me—rushed back to my house a second time to fetch a comforting sidekick. A full-bodied merlot.

Back at Lydia's I had time to kill, so I left another message with my daughter's voicemail, not saying anything about the murder. I watched a report about it on WRAL, but when they didn't have any new information I changed the channel to *Forensic Files*. I'm not sure how many episodes I watched before the details of the show's murders began to run together, so I changed the channel to some wacky reality show about women who go out of their way to give birth in the wild, far from medical help. It was about that time I must have dozed off.

The front door opened, jolting me awake. Instinctively I looked at my phone; it was nearly 1 a.m.

Darryl must have sensed I'd been asleep. "Mom texted me that you'd be staying," he said in a hushed tone. "I didn't mean to disturb you."

"I'm in your boyhood home," I said. "That means I'm disturbing *you*." I was talking normally now. I tried not to sound as tipsy as I felt. Hopefully he would just think I was tired.

The detective certainly seemed dog-tired. "I'm glad you're staying here. I'd worry about anyone alone in their house tonight." He closed and locked the door behind him. "Is Mom asleep?"

"It seems not even bloodcurdling murder can keep her up past nine," I said. "Sorry, I didn't mean to be disrespectful to the dead. I'm just wore out. But you've got way more reason to be exhausted. Was the crime scene very bad?"

"Bad enough," he said. "Excuse my manners. Would you like something to drink?"

"I've got some water, thanks." I always drank a ton of water after wine, or I would wake up too hungover to function.

I heard Darryl toss his keys on the kitchen counter and fill a glass of water from the faucet. While he did that, I lightly slapped my face several times to bring color to my cheeks.

As I'd hoped, he brought his drink to the living room and sat in the chair across from me.

"You were at that crime scene a long time," I said. "Find many clues?"

He shrugged. "Sometimes you don't know what's relevant until after you've interviewed a lot of people and revisited evidence from the scene."

"That makes sense," I said. There was silence for a moment as we both drank our waters. I was ready to turn in, but I wanted to keep the conversation going. "I didn't know Wanda as well as I would have liked."

Darryl said, "I barely knew her. Her kids were, like, eight and ten when I left for college."

"I always thought of Wanda as quiet, introverted. I guess how you'd imagine a professor to be."

Darryl set his glass down and pulled from his pocket a small notebook and ballpoint pen, one that had several colors a person could choose from—black, red, green, or blue. He chose a color and made a note.

"When do you think she was killed?" I asked.

"Coroner says within a half hour or so before the kids found the body. The blood on the porch was still wet." He seemed suddenly to realize again who he was talking to. "Sorry, I shouldn't be running my mouth."

"That's okay. I'm not squeamish. I watched hogs being slaughtered every winter by my uncles when I was a little girl."

"That's right. You're from the Land of Pork."

That was an understatement. There are so many pig farms in Eastern North Carolina that there was literally a beauty pageant where the girls *wanted* to be crowned Miss Piggy.

"Was it true what that boy's mother said," I asked, "that Wanda was stabbed in the back?"

"Yes, and right through the heart, too, by the looks of it. She couldn't have lasted more than a few seconds after a cut like that. At least there's that blessing. You hate to imagine the victim suffering." He asked, "Do you know anyone in the neighborhood who would have wanted to harm her?"

I picked my next words carefully. "I'm sure she upset a neighbor here and there, but I doubt she had any violent enemies." I took a sip of my water, then said, "Please tell me you at least found fingerprints on the scene."

The detective tapped his pen on his notebook as he thought aloud. "You were with me setting up the party beginning around 4:45, right? The body was found at around 5:45."

"Sounds about right." Then I added with a smile, "Are you trying to eliminate me as a suspect? How do you know I didn't sneak away from the party and come back later?"

"Oh, I would have noticed if you'd sneaked away."

So, he *had* been looking my way. Maybe he was just trained

to be observant. But there was also the possibility that he was interested in me.

I hoped he didn't see me blush.

"If I share a few facts of the case with you," the detective said, "you can't tell anyone, you understand? This is the most puzzling homicide I've seen in a while, and we're already stretched thin at the department."

I nodded. I was used to this, a gift from my mother. People had always told my mom things. She was nonjudgmental, patient, and a saint for putting up with my dad's extreme anxiety all these decades. I was none of those things—least of all a saint —but I had inherited her unassuming, inviting expression. I didn't always like the burden of a person's confidence, but sometimes, I suppose, it came in handy. Like now.

"Disclaimer," I said, "I've watched plenty of crime shows in my life, but I can't say that very much stuck."

"That's okay. I've watched millions of hours of football and still couldn't name all the positions if you paid me." He glanced at his notebook. "You asked about prints. We didn't find any initially, but I've got an officer securing the scene overnight. We'll send someone in the morning first thing to do some more dusting. It's a big house."

"Aren't there any on the knife?" I said hopefully.

"Not from what we could tell, but we'll take a closer look in the lab."

"What sort of knife was it?"

"A carving knife. It could have come from the deceased's kitchen. But we can't be sure yet, because none of the knives in the kitchen seem part of a matching set."

"Did the murderer drop a matchbook? That's what always happened in *Perry Mason*."

"This ain't TV. There was a notepad with one name scribbled on it: 'Otis.' The handyman, I assume. Know him?"

"Of course. Everyone in Woodmont knows Otis." Otis was a retired auto mechanic, a Black man in his seventies who did a lot of work for the neighborhood's residents. Otis had rehung more than one door and had pressure-washed my front walk more times than I could count.

Darryl continued. "We did find a rubber swim cap near the body, which is a little odd, because the deceased was dry and fully clothed when we found her."

"Do you think she was killed as part of a robbery?" I asked.

"That was my first thought for something like this, but her purse was visible in the den, her wallet still inside the purse. A couple of nice guitars seemed untouched. The only thing possibly 'missing,' I guess, was a pear from a half-dozen fancy golden pears you can order online. But the deceased's daughter is due to meet me at the house tomorrow afternoon to try to see if anything valuable is missing from the house and whether this might be a robbery gone bad."

"That would be Angela."

"That's right. She didn't react much when I called and told her. I think she was in shock. She's on a business trip on the West Coast. I couldn't get hold of the son. He's supposedly in Asia playing concerts or something with his dad."

"Daniel. I think some of the teenage girls in the neighborhood had a big crush on that boy." Swooshy skater hair. Electric guitar. What could be more thrilling?

He asked, "What did you think of the ex-husband? Messy divorce?"

"Not sure. Paul always seemed like a cold fish to me."

I knew I shouldn't ask too many questions, but wine made me talkative. "Are you sure the murderer was inside the house at some point?"

"Not sure. There was a pane of glass in the front door that had been broken, big enough for a small hand to have reached in and opened the door. But there were no shards of glass lying inside or outside. Strangely, there were glass shards in the kitchen just inside the back door—but no broken panes there."

"Signs of a struggle?"

"Not clear that there were, really. Of course, someone could have tidied up after the murder."

"Maybe he hid on the porch and surprised her."

"That ivy on the porch trellis could hide a person. She was wearing thick wool gloves when she was killed, so we do suspect she meant to go outside at some point."

"But wouldn't we have heard a scream?"

"How could we tell the difference between a scream and the haunted house music in the Mulligans' garage?"

"Good point."

"I would have thought someone living on the street would have seen someone. Did *you* see anyone suspicious at the party?"

I thought for a moment. "There was this one creepy dude. Remember him? He was dressed in a Frankenstein mask scaring people. I was going to ask others who he was, but that's about the time Nancy Thompson distracted me with her apple crumble."

Darryl turned another page in his little notebook. "I don't remember Frankenstein. Describe what he looked like."

"He was tall, maybe six-two. Aside from the mask, he wore a red flannel shirt, overalls, and hiking boots that were mostly covered by his pants."

He made some notes. "Tomorrow I'll ask some of the other neighbors if they recognized him. If he was an outsider, that's definitely suspicious."

"Were you able to find any witnesses at all?" I asked.

"We did talk to some trick-or-treaters from outside the

neighborhood. They were just leaving the neighborhood after dark when we questioned them."

A light bulb went off. "I wonder if that was the group that came here! The youngest was named Shauna. And, one of the girls called one of the two little boys 'Curtis.' I'd say he was six or seven, just comparing him to your boy."

"That's them. They said their relative dropped them off around the time of the block party. They hadn't been to Woodmont before and found themselves in the alleyway."

The alley Darryl was talking about ran behind the homes on my side of the block and separated our neighborhood from Woodmont Cemetery. A tall, chain-link fence prevented people from using the cemetery as a cut-through. Still, the alley had always felt to me like the least safe feature of our neighborhood.

Darryl continued.

"The littlest girl said she saw someone in the alley wearing a dragon costume. It could have been the killer himself either approaching or leaving Wanda's house, or it could have been a witness who saw the killer. Do you remember anyone at the party dressed up as a dragon?"

"No," I said, "but a group photograph was taken. I'll bet at least one of the moms is still up." I texted several of the moms and, a moment later, had the photo. "What's your number? I'll text it to you."

A second later we were each squinting at our copies of the photo for signs of a dragon, with no luck.

Darryl turned off his phone. He looked at me curiously. "What are you doing in the morning? I need to interview everyone on this block to see what they might have seen or heard. Problem is, I moved out of this neighborhood more than twenty years ago. With one or two exceptions, I don't know the folks here anymore. I'm thinking it might help if you came with me on the interviews. You could provide me some background about each neighbor in advance. And, with you there, maybe the neighbors would feel more comfortable opening up."

"Why not use your mom? She's lived here longer."

"Take my mother to work? I'd never live that down at HQ."

I thought about it. "Are you deputizing me, Detective?"

"Not officially. But, in a way, I guess so."

Interviewing witnesses sure would be an interesting way to spend a Saturday morning. While I was at it, I could ask more of the neighbors if they would donate a pie to Needless Necessities' absurd fundraiser and get Sally off my back.

"You've got me till eleven," I said, remembering how I'd agreed to volunteer at the center then. "Is that enough time?"

"Plenty," he said. "Now, I think it's about time I turned in. I'll get my stuff out of the guest room so you'll have a place to sleep."

"Oh, no," I insisted. "I'm sleeping on the couch."

But he wasn't having it, and no amount of protesting did any good. A moment later Darryl had returned downstairs holding a short stack of clothes and a robe.

I grabbed my own things and started heading toward the stairs, but Darryl stopped me with a word of caution.

"Watch that bottom step. It's cracked. Otis was going to fix that this week, but I guess he didn't get around to it."

I noted the broken step. Even with my hands full—and my head still wobbly from the wine—I was able to grip the bannister higher, put my foot on the second step, and pull myself up.

"Good night," I said. "Thank you for letting me stay. I won't wear out my welcome."

"Are you kidding? You're a breath of fresh air in this smoker's den."

He sounded like he meant it.

CHAPTER 4
BLOOD OATH

When I awoke, Darryl was in the shower, unable to see me emerge from the guest room in my morning less-than-glorious. Charlie was already multi-tasking with his tablet and the TV. I was amused to see him watching an old Scooby-Doo re-run from my childhood.

I let Lydia know I was heading across the street. At home I got right down to business, hopping under the water and washing my shoulder-length rat's nest. I blow-dried my hair and even took the time to use a curling iron in several places to deliver some form to the chaos. Getting my hair done placed second only to shopping in terms of activities I despised. If I'd enjoyed self-grooming more, might Allan have remained true?

I decided I shouldn't look too dressed up for this errand. So, I donned blue jeans (my bespoke pair from Raleigh Denim), a plaid shirt, and gold, leaf-shaped earrings to accent the season. Finally, I added a bit of lipstick and blush.

"I would have noticed if you'd sneaked away."

Back outside again I paused to look at the morning paper. My father had always referred to the *News & Observer* as the *News & Disturber*. This morning he'd be spot on, for right beside a feel-good feature about a downtown fire department doing a breast-cancer fundraiser was this troubling double-bolded headline:

Halloween Homicide Rocks Woodmont

Parents and children trick-or-treating Friday night in one of Raleigh's most historic neighborhoods were shocked to discover a woman on her porch dead of a stab wound. Police are treating the death as a homicide.

The crime took place during the annual Halloween block party in Woodmont, less than a mile from the heart of downtown Raleigh.

The victim, Wanda Lorraine Hightower, 62, had worked for nearly 30 years at Wake Tech Community College as an English composition and literature professor before retiring over the summer.

Her supervisor, English Department Chairman Gary Roland, said he was shocked to learn of her death.

"Wanda was a vital part of this institution for nearly three decades. She taught thousands of people, young and old. Our thoughts go out to her family and friends who are grieving right now."

Police Chief Randall Paine said there are no suspects in custody. However, police are hoping a trick-or-treater may have seen the assailant.

"We'd like to question someone who was in a dragon costume who we consider a person of interest," said Paine. "Anyone with information about a person matching that description should contact the police department."

Though it seemed to be the best lead that the police had to go on, I wondered if finding someone dressed as a dragon on Halloween might be futile.

When I returned to Lydia's, Darryl was downstairs lacing up his shoes.

"There you are," he said. I like to think he let his eyes linger on me a little after asking if I slept okay.

"Like a dream. I just feel bad you had to endure that couch."

"Better than the couch at the station. I've caught winks there more times than I can count."

"Not all glory being a detective, I guess?"

"How about *none* glory." He stood up. "You sure you want to do this?"

"It'll be fun. Besides, I need to collect some pies."

The confused look on his face was priceless.

"You don't want to know," I said.

"Gotta work today, Dad?" asked Charlie, looking up from his tablet and TV show. Turned out the "ghost" terrorizing the town was a mechanized swamp monster after all.

"Yeah. Have fun with your gramps and grans today. Your mom is picking you up soon, so go get ready. I'll see you tomorrow night, okay?"

"Okay," Charlie said. "Love you."

"Love you, Son."

Charlie stood and the pair shared a hug.

On the front porch, feeling a little nervous, I asked, "Where to first?"

"Let's start with the deceased's direct neighbors on either side," he said.

We began with the home of Skip Green and his husband, Stuart, men both in their fifties who (as I shared with Darryl) had moved next door to Wanda about five years ago. Skip was a state lobbyist for an environmental organization. Stuart was an IT executive who had started his own small company from the ground up, sold it, and now helped run the merged venture. I told Darryl how Stuart wasn't nearly as much fun as Skip, but that he was rock steady and the first person I always reached out to if I needed help with my home internet connection.

Stuart was in the front yard raking leaves. As Darryl approached him, I paused on the sidewalk to allow the pair some privacy. My gaze was momentarily drawn to the veritable army of thick, white beetle grubs gnawing on fallen acorns that had been cracked open by the shoes of neighborhood walkers.

Darryl beckoned me to rejoin him.

"You sure?" I asked.

"It's fine."

Stuart seemed grateful for a break from raking. Turns out Skip wasn't home; he'd gone to a local candidate breakfast, leaving his husband to handle the leaves.

Stuart didn't have much to tell. During the party, he said, he had been working overtime helping his crew install ethernet at a new school being built. "I missed the party and all the excitement, I guess."

"I think Skip ate enough Halloween treats for both of you," I said.

"That sounds like my honey bun," Stuart winked.

I wondered if Darryl might feel uneasy talking with Stuart. Back in college, easily half of my fellow arts majors were out of the closet. I had always felt comfortable moving between my artsy-fartsy world and Allan's Old South universe. Maybe too comfortable, for I had learned to ignore comments by Allan and his friends that were unkind to gay people.

"Was there anything suspicious you saw happen at Wanda's house any other time?" Darryl asked.

Stuart shook his head. "Wanda's been more or less a hermit lately. She didn't used to be that way, but I guess she lost her job at the community college over the summer and just kind of became more and more reclusive after that."

"The paper this morning said she'd retired," I said.

"That's probably right, then," said Stuart.

"Did you hear a different reason for why she became unemployed?" asked Darryl.

"I heard rumors through Skip—he's got ears everywhere—but nothing I'd feel comfortable repeating." I respected Stuart for his discretion.

"You said Ms. Hightower became a hermit," said Darryl. "When did you last see her in the flesh?"

"Oh, gosh. It's been a few months, I'd say."

Darryl acted surprised. "You're her next-door neighbor, yet you haven't seen her in months? Didn't you at least see her leave for errands?" I gathered by Darryl's line of questioning that he was trying to sketch out a picture of Wanda's life—her routines, her habits, her relationships.

"I think she had most things delivered. There were always UPS trucks and such."

"Would she at least go to the street to get her mail?"

"This is an old-fashioned neighborhood. She has a mail slot in her front door. Our house has one, too."

"I'd almost forgotten some of the houses still have those," Darryl said. "Besides the post office and delivery trucks, did you see anyone else visit?"

Stuart scratched his head. "Her daughter every couple months. That's about it. I'm sorry I'm not much help."

Darryl looked at his notebook, as if searching for a last, helpful question. "Anything that would indicate any strife between the deceased and anyone else?"

Stuart threw me a quick look.

"Not that I can think of at the moment," Stuart said quickly. "But I think that Skip will be able to tell you more. He's tapped into, well, pretty much everything. Isn't he, Rett?"

"Most definitely," I said. "Do you know when he'll be back? I need to ask him a favor." Even if Skip was better known for *eating* pastry than baking it, I'd still ask him for a pie.

"Within the hour, I'd guess," he said. "Just look for his little banana."

Stuart grinned at his own joke, for every frequent visitor to Woodmont was well aware of the yellow vintage Triumph convertible roadster Skip drove.

While Stuart went back to raking his yard, Darryl and I walked in the direction of Wanda's house. Police tape still blocked off Wanda's entire property, so I expected him to usher me to the next house. Instead, Darryl stopped me and drilled an accusing look into my retinas.

"What aren't you telling me?"

I tried to swallow but couldn't. Then came the choking noise I always make when I get caught in a serious deception.

"You and Stuart exchanged a look back there," Darryl said. "What's going on?"

"I'll tell you," I said. "But first: notice anything different about Wanda's house from the others on the block?"

The house itself sat up a little from the road—a two-story Victorian with peeling white paint and a long, wooden front porch mostly secluded by a trellis covered in sickly brown vines. Darryl's eyes scanned the home and its calamitous yard.

"Until seeing it just now in the broad daylight, I didn't really notice how bad everything looked. Especially the yard."

There was no grass, nor much of anything else.

"If you think the yard is bad now, you can't imagine what it looked like a couple of months ago. Actually," I took my phone out of my pocket, "Skip sent everyone 'Before' and 'After' pics."

I expanded the first photo for Darryl. "Here's 'Before.'"

The detective's left eyebrow went up. The photo showed hedges overrun with grape vine, out of control weeds like crabgrass, Japanese stiltgrass, clover, briars, and periwinkle, not to mention clumps of liriope crowding out most of the lawn.

"You can't even see the steps to the front porch," Darryl said. "Isn't there a homeowner's association here? I know my dad always acted like there was. He cut our grass, like, every other day."

"Neighborhoods this old don't have associations," I said. "Now, here's the 'After' pic."

I swiped my screen to the left. Taking the place of the overgrown lawn was a designed landscape with mulched beds, newly planted azalea bushes, and neatly trimmed hedges. A small garden of pansies sat front and center in the sunniest part of the yard.

"That's gorgeous," he said. "Are you sure it's the same house?"

"This was just about five weeks ago. Several of the neighbors waited until late at night and sprang into action. They worked under a full moon. By the time the sun rose, they'd transformed the entire front yard."

Darryl squinted at something in the photo. "What's this?" He used his fingers to magnify a sign: *Surprise, Wanda! Signed, The Neighborhood Elves.*

"Well, she must have been dang surprised, all right." Now he looked at the yard in front of us. "What happened?"

"Wanda happened. The next night she destroyed everything the group had done. She pulled up the azaleas, knock-out roses, and mums; sawed down the bushes that had been trimmed; scattered the mulch from the beds. She even managed to dig up a Japanese maple and toss it into Skip's yard."

The detective shook his head. "And what was your hand in all this? For that matter, what was my mother's hand?"

"Your mom and I didn't work in the yard, but we contributed

dollars. So I guess we were just as culpable as everyone who actually did the sprucing up."

"I guess I'm wondering who the ringleaders were."

"Definitely Skip Green and Eleanor Foster, along with Brad and Gail Norris across the street. Those four were the most eager to improve her yard and home."

"They must have been pretty upset by Wanda's reaction."

"I only spoke with Skip afterwards, but I'm sure you're right."

Darryl took a final glance at the elves' work before handing my phone back.

"I'm sorry I didn't tell you sooner," I said. "I didn't want to sound like I was tattling on others, including your mother."

"Mom wouldn't take to anyone meddling in her own flower beds."

"Skip swears that the Wanda he knew would have appreciated the gesture. He'd worked with her on a neighborhood festival several years ago. I don't think anyone thought of Wanda's wild yard as how she wanted it to look."

Darryl shot me an I-hear-you-but-I don't-necessarily-agree-with-you expression. "Okay. Now that we're square, let's move on."

We rapped on the Fosters' front door. I had asked Darryl if he really wanted me around for this interview, given that he already knew Phil and Eleanor from decades ago. "Maybe give us a little bit of space," he said, "but don't go too far. I don't think I can tolerate Eleanor for very long on my own."

For sure, Eleanor was the more notorious of the couple. Originally from Texas, the aging socialite had been writing for years about high-society individuals and events in a *News & Observer* column called *Mint Julep*. Though some might consider *Mint Julep* hoity-toity, it did bring publicity to some worthy causes.

Eleanor's personal cause was preserving the historical

homes and properties of Downtown Raleigh. "George Washington Slept Here" went only so far toward curbing the enthusiasm of downtown developers. But that didn't stop her from attending zoning board meetings in town and putting up one hell of a fight.

Thank God none of Swinson Development's projects had ever had to go head-to-head with Eleanor.

A moment later the door opened a crack. "Come on in," muttered a woman's voice. Darryl and I exchanged a puzzled look as we stepped inside and found Eleanor attempting to lie down on her couch while balancing a large ziplock bag of ice on her forehead.

"Eleanor, what happened to your head?" I asked.

"I fell," she said, pronouncing it *FAY-ull.* "By the way, nice to see you, Darryl. It's been a while. Help yourselves to some sweet tea or water in the kitchen, then come sit down." For Eleanor, "down" had two syllables: *DAY-own.*

I wondered if Darryl was asking himself the same thing that I was. Did this high society dame injure herself in a struggle with Wanda? As the detective took a seat across from her, I moved toward the kitchen, crossing the spotless and opulent living room with its refinished oak floors, oriental rugs, period furniture, velvet drapes, and well-cared-for ferns and ficuses.

From the kitchen, I could still hear their conversation:

"We didn't see you at the block party, Mrs. Foster."

"I meant to go, but I was running behind, rushing to make my Green Slime Goo. *Guaco-MOH-lay.* I sort of slipped on an avocado pit that had fallen on the floor. The whole time during the party I was laid up right here."

"Ouch! What do you mean 'sort of' slipped?"

Her voice lowered a bit. "You're gonna laugh."

"Try me."

"I didn't see the pit fall off the counter, but I did notice it rolling on the floor. I was wearing my reading glasses and really couldn't tell what it was. Darryl, I thought it was a big-ass bug! I turned to run and lost my footing. *Blam!* Hit my head on the sink cabinet."

Darryl said, "You must really have been in a lot of pain to miss the party. I see you there every year."

"I know. Philip was disappointed to miss it, too, and he had to cancel his golf outing this morning to run get me more Advil. He'll be back any minute."

I returned to the family room with two waters. As I placed one of them on the side table near Eleanor's head, I crouched to ascertain what Eleanor could see of Wanda's front walkway from the couch.

She couldn't have seen much. Someone standing in Wanda's yard would have to be quite tall to appear in Eleanor's line of sight.

"Thank you, dear," Eleanor said. I offered the other water to Darryl, but he waved it off, and I went over and sat with it in a chair by the window.

Eleanor continued, "I thought these things only happened in small towns on *Dateline*—not in Raleigh." She pronounced it the old-fashioned way: *rally*. "And definitely not in Woodmont. We look out for one another here. We care for one another. We—"

"Redo other people's yards when the grass gets too high?" interrupted Darryl.

Her eyes narrowed. "That yard is one thing, Detective. The home's *structure* is quite another: peeling paint, rotting wood, ivy damage. Probably termites, too! It's like watching Rome rot very, very slowly. I was in that home forty years ago, and it features the most marvelous fireplace mantle, hand-carved, in the shape of a fire-breathing dragon. Do you know the storied past of that house? It was a speakeasy in the Twenties, a haven for whiskey runners. Some of the most deplorable outlaws in the county played poker there, including..."

While Eleanor droned on, my phone buzzed. Hoping it might be Stephanie, I excused myself to the kitchen again. Unfortunately, it was just a text from Jasmine at the center:

-CUSTOMER'S PAINTING WON'T DRY. COMPLAINING WE SOLD HIM A BILL OF GOODS!! HELP!

I imagined someone like Mr. Simms was giving Jasmine a difficult time. Yes, Jasmine's sunniness got on my nerves, but she didn't deserve abuse. I couldn't type a response fast enough:

-He's painting with oils. Could take days or weeks to dry. Point him to a subscription to Painterly Magazine. *Oh, and tell him to be nice, we're a nonprofit.*

Jasmine's response came right away:

-LOL. OKAY!

Had I really typed "we"? I must be going crazy.

When I returned to the living room, Eleanor was still in full house-history monologue mode. Darryl looked to me for help.

"Eleanor," I said, interrupting her while taking my seat again, "maybe you can tell Darryl if you think anyone wanted to do Wanda harm."

"Hah!" Eleanor exclaimed. "Half the neighborhood was furious after she pulled up all the flowers and bushes we'd planted. But murder her? *Naw.* Really, people pitied her. Her divorce, losing her parents, then her job. After that she became a hermit. Why, I haven't seen her face in so long."

Darryl asked, "Know anyone who *would* have seen her?"

"The UPS man. Maybe you should talk to *him.*"

I watched Darryl scribble something in his notebook. "Did you see anyone come or go from Ms. Hightower's house yesterday?"

"As I told the officer who came by here last night, I was laid up right here on this couch." She turned her head and looked at me. "You know, Rett Darlin', I was hoping we'd give Wanda's house a nice new paint job, but after that fiasco with her yard—"

"Mrs. Foster," Darryl cut in. "By chance did you *hear* anything unusual? Maybe you heard someone next door cry out?"

"Phillip was upstairs taking a shower, and I was either in the kitchen or on this couch. We didn't hear a thing."

"Do you listen to music while you cook?"

"I do not. There's no telling what recipes I'd foul up if I did."

Darryl said, "You know, Mrs. Foster, I think I'd like some of that tea you offered after all."

Eleanor started to get up.

"No, ma'am," insisted Darryl. "You stay here and rest a minute. Rett, will you come to the kitchen and help me?"

"Sure."

As we rounded the corner to the kitchen, Darryl touched my arm lightly and whispered, "I need you to do me a favor. Here in a bit, go next door to Wanda's. Step onto the porch and call my name. Then give that porch a really good thump with the stick end of the broom that's over there. Make it count. Can you do that?"

"I think so."

He found the tea pitcher on the counter, poured a glass, and tried to get ice from the fridge's dispenser. It made a slight whir, but no ice came out. Eleanor shouted from the other room. "That thing's been broke for years! You got to reach in and use your hands!" *HAY-uhnds.*

"That woman's got good ears," Darryl muttered. "In a minute we'll see just how good."

"Look," I whispered. I pointed to a wooden knife block from which one member of the set was missing. We found the missing knife—the smallest paring knife—lying in the sink, dirty. The set's carving knife was still firmly in place in the block.

Darryl winked at my observation and led us back to the family room. Before we could sit, Darryl announced in an off-hand way, "Ms. Swinson, could you do something quick for me?"

"What's that, Detective?" I responded, as if playing Elizabeth Taylor to his Richard Burton.

"One of my officers thinks he left his flashlight on Ms. High-tower's porch early this morning. Will you please go next door and see if you can find it while I finish my interview with Mrs. Foster?"

"Certainly." I paused. "But the police tape—"

"That porch has been gone over with a fine-toothed comb. Just step under the tape."

I hurried out the door and cut through the Fosters' lawn. Though badly in need of raking, it still looked a hundred times neater than Wanda's battered wasteland with its dried-out clumps of potting soil and dead hedges lying about like tumbleweeds.

The porch, which had been painted green many years ago, was vacant aside from some wicker porch furniture and a broom. A derelict-looking ceiling fan collected spider webs. In the late afternoon, with the sun far behind the home, thanks to the vast trellis work and ivy, the porch would have been an easy place for someone to lurk unnoticed. I noted the broken window just to the left of the front door. There was no screen or storm door—such things weren't a thing when these houses were built a hundred years ago.

Between the welcome mat and the first step was a ruby-red stain the size of a dinner platter. Clearly there had been an attempt by the authorities to clean up Wanda's blood after their investigation. However, because the paint on this part of the porch had worn away long ago, the blood had seeped into the cracks of the unprotected wood.

And nothing in the world was going to get that stain out.

I remembered the time my younger brother, perhaps nine, had used his pocket-knife to cut an inch-long gash on the back of my right hand. He and all his cool friends had done it to their own hands in order to become "blood brothers," and I'd shown some interest. He promised it wouldn't hurt the least bit, so I let him do it.

"Now," he'd said, as the blood pooled up and a scream threatened to escape from my lips, "swear something you'll do for me." I blurted out something about cleaning the mud off his sneakers. That promise—or the pained tears he saw welling in my eyes—seemed to satisfy him.

But he'd misled me, and I never felt close to my brother again after that day.

The loneliness of blood.

"Wanda," I whispered above the porch wood's terrible mark, "I will find out who did this to you. I swear it."

CHAPTER 5

BROKEN WINGS

"Detective Schmidt!"

I gave the porch a strong whack with the stick end of the broom—then gagged as a small cloud of dust erupted from its bristles. Coughing, I leaned the broom where I had found it and ran off the porch.

"Did you find the flashlight?" Darryl asked, as I barged into Eleanor's home and living room.

"No, just a palmetto bug," I fibbed, clearing my throat. "I tried to hit it with a broom."

"I hope you killed it!" Eleanor exclaimed. "They try to come inside this time of year."

"Thanks for looking for the flashlight," Darryl said to me. "It probably just rolled under his seat in the squad car."

Eleanor lowered her voice. "I just now thought of something, Detective. What if there's a treasure in that home, some stolen loot hidden or buried by some old Prohibition whiskey runner —and his ancestor came last night to claim it. Surprised by Wanda, he lashed out!" It sounded like a Scooby-Doo episode.

"That's an interesting theory, Mrs. Foster. But if there was hidden loot from the 1920s, don't you think whoever left it there would have come to claim it a lot sooner than now?"

"You're probably right," she said, her voice returning to its normal tone. "But stranger things have happened in the old homes of Raleigh. For example, did you hear about—?"

The front door opened and Phil Foster walked in. Phil, in sales all his life, never met a stranger. Though nearly twenty years older than Allan, he reminded me of a more genuine version of my soon-to-be ex-husband. There had been talk over the years of him having a wandering eye, but I'd always thought the rumors stemmed from him being married to someone most people couldn't imagine enduring for twenty minutes.

Phil gave a firm handshake to the detective. "Good to see you again, Darryl, despite the present circumstances." He saved a friendly nod for me. "I see you both got drinks. Ellie, I got your medicine. Sorry it took me so long. I ran into Scott Willis and we chatted a bit." He took a pill bottle from the Walgreens bag he was carrying.

"Thank you, Sweetie," Eleanor said. "Fortunately, I've had these lovely guests to distract me from my personal misery."

Phil said, "Poor girl slipped on an avocado pit. Now that's a new one."

Eleanor sat up and used her water to wash down several Advil as Phil sat down at the far end of the couch near his wife's feet.

"We're going over the events of yesterday afternoon, Mr. Foster," said Darryl. "Do you recall seeing or hearing anything unusual next door?"

Phil thought about it. "It was probably around 5:15. I was upstairs, just getting out of the shower, when I heard a thump and Eleanor cried out. I ran down and found her on the kitchen floor, dazed. I called her sister, who's a nurse. She said as long as the lump swells out, that's a good sign. If it makes a dip, it could be what the doctors technically call 'drain bramage.'

"Ha, ha, ha!" Eleanor mock laughed.

"So, you missed the party entirely?" Darryl asked.

"Didn't even think to finish the dip. Just stayed put."

"Did you receive any visitors around that time?"

"Not until about 5:45 or so, when we got our first group of trick-or-treaters—a whole bunch of kids at once. It wasn't long after that we heard a ruckus, and then the first squad car appeared. That's when I stepped outside to see what was happening. The police tape had already gone up—you work fast, Detective—and I saw you studying the body on the porch."

"Phil came back and told me, 'Ellie, I think Wanda Hightower had a bad fall.' We didn't know at that point she'd been murdered, though."

Darryl interjected, "Do you know anyone who would have cause to kill Ms. Hightower, or anyone who had a strong grudge?"

Phil shrugged. "No one was very happy about her home's upkeep. But that's no reason to murder anyone."

I wanted to agree with him, but then I remembered an old TV commercial from my childhood: an advertisement for a collection of volumes about the Wild West that included the story of John Wesley Hardin, who (the announcer declared in a gravelly twang) "once shot a man simply for snoring." Could Wanda's killer have been as cruel and cold as that?

Eleanor asked Darryl, "Have you talked with Wanda's daughter? She never looked very happy when she was visiting. I always wondered if that house was just as much of a disaster inside as out." She looked at her husband. "When one house has bugs, they can spread to other houses."

"Oh, Honey, we have our house sprayed."

She was resolute. "That house is just filled with bugs, I'm

certain." She was looking directly at the detective, angling for confirmation.

"We didn't see evidence of an infestation, Mrs. Foster," Darryl assured her.

Darryl probed a bit longer around Wanda's comings and goings, with nothing of insight revealed. It seemed that Wanda was as much of an enigma to her next-door neighbors as she was to everyone else.

As we were leaving, I leaned down to Eleanor and said, "I hope you start feeling better soon, because I need your help." I quickly explained about the pie event and asked whether she could contribute.

"Rett, dear, if I can keep from killing myself in the kitchen, you can have *two* pies!" she said. "Ha, ha, HA!"

"That was interesting," said Darryl, as we left the house.

"Do you really think one of them might have killed Wanda?"

"I'm less interested in them as suspects than as witnesses," Darryl said. "We proved that Eleanor would have heard an attack on Wanda's front porch. I watched her face while you ran our little experiment, and she definitely reacted when you thumped the porch."

"But you can't *see* much from that couch," I said. "When I delivered her water, I hunched way down and looked."

He smiled. "I watched you do that. I was a little worried your back might get stuck in that position."

"Ha, ha, HA!" I laughed. "What do you think all of this means?"

"If they are telling the truth, it means that the murder likely happened at the same time that Eleanor had her accident. That would put the time of death at about a quarter after five. That's in line with what the coroner thought likely."

We crossed the street to the home of Sheila Perry and Maxine White. I knew the couple well. Maxine ran a counseling practice out of her home—and I was one of her clients. Maxine had agreed to keep our therapist-patient relationship on the down-low, as I didn't want the neighbors talking—nor did I want Allan's lawyer hassling Maxine for information if our divorce ever got nasty. I didn't know what Darryl thought about therapy. I wasn't obligated to tell him who my therapist was and didn't plan to.

Darryl rang the bell, and a second later Sheila's slim, tan, attractive face appeared as she cracked the door. "Can I help you?"

"Hi, Sheila," I said. "I've got Detective Darryl Schmidt here with me. The detective is talking to everyone about the murder last night."

"We don't have any information about that," Sheila said, her words nervous, clipped.

Maybe this was my chance to prove my worth to Darryl. "Can we at least come in and talk?" I asked.

"Hold on," she said, abruptly shutting the door. The door opened again a second later, but Sheila still blocked the way. "Could you come back later? Maxine isn't decent."

Darryl gave me a look like I was failing.

"Sheila," I said, "may I come in for a moment? Just me?"

She thought about it. "Fine."

She let me in and closed the door behind us, locked it.

"What the heck is going on?" I asked.

"Follow me." She led me deeper into the home. Along the way we passed two of the couple's three dogs and one of their four cats. Saying Sheila and Maxine were animal lovers was an understatement. Besides the traditional cats and dogs, their backyard was a veritable petting zoo with numerous chickens and goats. Maxine, in addition to helping humans with their mental health, also hosted goat yoga, while Sheila worked as a vet tech. I was a regular recipient of their surplus chicken eggs, which always seemed tastier than the ones from the grocery store.

We found Maxine—fully dressed, I might add—lying on top of a half-made bed. She held a tablet in her right hand. Her other hand was hidden beneath a blanket next to her.

"What exactly is going on, Maxine?" I demanded. "Lydia Schmidt's son is on the front porch waiting to talk with you two. In case you've forgotten, he's a homicide detective."

Maxine looked to her partner. "Should we trust her, She?"

Sheila nodded. Maxine withdrew her arm from the blanket. In the center of Maxine's cupped hand sat a live creature of some sort.

"Oh, my gosh!" I said, jumping back. "Is that a bug?" Eleanor's fear was contagious.

"No. It's a hummingbird," said Maxine. "We found him on the ground in the backyard this morning. Speckle was sitting there licking his whiskers, trying to figure out whether he should put salt on his tail or just eat him raw. It appears to have a broken wing."

"Max, we've got to hide that bird right now!" Sheila urged. "There's a fricking cop at the front door!"

I looked at them both like they were crazy. "What's the big deal about a little hummingbird?"

Maxine sighed. "It's illegal to keep a migratory bird. Massive fines. And Sheila could lose her license to work with animals."

This certainly would explain Sheila's skittishness.

Maxine continued, "The bird will die if we don't do something. I've been researching the care and feeding of hummingbirds. For the next several minutes I think he'll be okay in my sock drawer. Take your time letting the copper inside, Sheila. I'll be there in a sec."

While Sheila went to stall Darryl a bit longer, Maxine opened a drawer and gingerly lay the bird inside. "I actually don't know if it's a 'he,'" said Maxine. "All I know is that it's a Ruby Throated Hummingbird who should be well on its way to Central America by now."

"Can you nurse it back to health?" I asked.

"I can't, but Sheila might be able to." She closed the drawer. "Now, no word of this to the authorities—not a breath!"

I had just come clean with Darryl about the makeover of Wanda's yard—and already I was inserting another secret between us.

A few minutes later, the four of us had settled in the couple's homey family room amidst their many curled-up dogs and cats. Sheila and Maxine told Darryl they had been at a Halloween party last night with some friends in nearby Cary, returning home around nine to find their block abuzz with news trucks.

"How long have you known Ms. Hightower?" Darryl asked.

Maxine sighed. "We met when we moved here about four years ago. Wanda learned I was a therapist and a practicing Buddhist. She'd come over and we'd assume lotus positions in the backyard and meditate—or attempt to."

"I didn't know Wanda was into meditation," I said. "I've been meaning to try it." Translation: the times I'd tried, I'd gone right to sleep.

Maxine smiled. "Unfortunately, professors and other intellectuals can have a difficult time meditating. Letting go of your thoughts doesn't sound like a cure for anything if you rely on your analytical brain every day for your livelihood. In that way, thinking can be like drugs, or drinking. We remain attached to our crutches."

I exchanged a glance with Maxine. In our sessions, she and I had talked a lot about anxiety, how I had come by it naturally from my father and that my recent drinking was surely an effort to medicate it. She had encouraged me to stop, saying it would help me get closer to my feelings and work through them. But I didn't think I was quite ready to get rid of this particular crutch.

"Were you Wanda's therapist?" Darryl asked Maxine.

"Ha! No. Wanda once said to me, 'First, the Christians took the mystery out of God, then the psychologists took the mystery out of human beings.' Detective, I find that there are two kinds of people in the world: those who are desperate for certainty, and those who are far more comfortable with life's mysteries. Wanda was definitely in the latter camp. She considered herself an atheist, but she still liked to quote the poet Emily Dickinson, who wrote, 'I dwell in possibility.'"

Darryl said, "Sounds like you two spent a good amount of time together."

"When we first arrived in the neighborhood, yes. Not so much the past couple years. Though I'll say last year around this time we did manage a couple of short conversations over tea. As I recall, she seemed very anxious and aggravated."

"About what?" Darryl asked.

"Her workplace, state politics, anybody she'd see out and about. She thought her daughter worked too hard, and she rarely saw her son after he started touring with his father professionally. I just think she had become extremely angry and bitter. I take it you told the detective about the gardening incident this fall, Rett?"

"I did." *Uh, just not right away.*

"Then you see what I mean, Detective."

"Actually," Darryl said, "I can totally understand why someone would get upset having others work in their yard without permission."

"Of course some people would—but not Wanda. At least not

the Wanda most of us knew back in the day. She would have seen it in the light of a gift, even if she didn't like it. The Wanda we knew would not have shown rage—even if she *was* angry. No, I think her anger had very little to do with the yard specifically. If it hadn't been the yard makeover, it would have been something else. Just my theory."

"Were you part of the yard project?"

"No. In September I was tending to my parents' move to a retirement home, and I just didn't have time for much else. I might have kicked in some dollars, though, if I'd known about it. I know Skip. He wouldn't have moved forward with the project if he didn't think Wanda would appreciate it."

"I'd never have gone along with it," Sheila cut in. "Manicured lawns are a menace." She seemed so adamant, it caused Darryl to lean back a little in his seat.

"Sheila is a naturalist," Maxine explained. "She even refused to kill insects for her bug collection in college biology."

Sheila added, "The professor wanted us to put perfectly healthy bugs in a cyanide kill jar. I couldn't bring myself to do that, or even put them in the freezer to die alone in the cold dark. Instead I found insects that were already deceased. It took a lot longer, but I completed the assignment and got closer to nature in the process."

I could tell that Darryl didn't know what to make of Sheila, who could come across as a sort of nature girl, awkward in the realm of humans. She had been a patient of Maxine's many years ago until ethics required the therapist-client relationship to end so a romance could ensue. I had not asked Maxine why the two had not married; that seemed a step too personal.

Darryl at last shifted his focus to Sheila. "What can you tell me about Wanda?" His question was almost intimate, the way a friend might pose it. But Sheila's eyes widened, perhaps her thoughts, like mine, rushing to the tiny creature behind the wall who was nestling its beak among socks and bras.

Maxine put a calming hand on Sheila's arm. "It's okay." At her partner's touch, Sheila's blood pressure seemed to go down.

"She gave us a book once," Sheila said.

"Ah, yes," Maxine said, going over to a built-in bookcase and returning with a coffee-table volume which she handed to Darryl. "It's all about Highclere Castle, the real-life setting of *Downton Abbey*. Somehow Wanda picked up that we both love the show. We're determined to visit there some day."

Darryl glanced at the book briefly before handing it to me. I flipped through some of the pages. The lovely grounds matched the beauty of the manor itself. I turned to the inside cover where there was an inscription I read aloud:

> *"To be happy at home is the ultimate result of all ambition,*
> *the end to which every enterprise and labor tends."*
> — *Samuel Johnson*

> *For Maxine and Sheila,*
> *Best wishes for a long and happy life in Woodmont.*
> *Regards, Wanda Hightower*

"What a thoughtful housewarming gift," I said.

"That was Wanda," said Maxine. "She was very considerate. I'm going to miss her."

"When did you last speak with Wanda?" Darryl asked.

"Probably early in the spring," Maxine said. "I tried to reach out this summer when I heard she'd left teaching, but she never returned my calls."

A sound like cymbals reverberated from the back of the home. The sound was familiar to me, but Darryl's eyebrow went up in mild alarm.

"The neighbor children love to ring our Chinese gong on the back porch," Maxine said. "We don't mind if they visit the animals, but, Sheila, you might make sure they don't leave the gate open again. The last time that happened, our goats nearly made it to Skip's flowers."

Sheila used the opportunity to excuse herself, and the interview ended.

When the two of us were alone again outside, Darryl asked, "Is Sheila always so squirrelly?"

"Sheila's an animal person—*not* a people person. As you heard, she literally wouldn't hurt a fly." I knew I should probably tell him about the hummingbird—but I rationalized Darryl wouldn't want to be put in the position of enforcing a law that would have such oversized consequences.

As the detective placed a call to the host of the Halloween party that the couple said they'd attended, I texted Maxine to ask if she and Sheila would donate a pie or two to the fundraiser, as both women knew their way around a kitchen. Right away I got back a thumbs-up and a pie emoji.

Darryl ended his call. "Their alibi checks out," he said, "but I do wonder what our friend Sheila might be hiding."

Next door to the couple and directly across from Wanda lived Bradford and Gail Norris. A for-sale sign in their home's yard featured both their photos and the slogan, "The Norris Team — At Your Service!" I shared with Darryl what many of us on the block knew, that Brad and Gail had signed a contingency contract for a new house just north of town on Falls Lake. However, selling their Woodmont home had been proving difficult due to Wanda's eyesore of a home.

Brad invited us in and seated us before going to fetch his

wife. I'd worked with a number of agents over the years and generally found them pleasant but hard to get to know. The Norrises were extreme in that regard, a suspicious veneer of non-controversiality covering everything they said.

Brad returned to the sitting area with Gail, a trim, attractive brunette smartly dressed and impeccably coiffed. She had the patience to grow perfect nails and this morning wore a smart navy-blue dress jacket and skirt. We stood when she entered the room. She greeted us solemnly and added, "Isn't this the most awful thing?"

"It is," I said. "I think you both know Lydia who lives across the street from me. This is her son, Darryl, who is a detective. He happened to be at the party, too, when the children found Wanda."

Gail turned to Darryl. "I do know your mother, and she is precious. How is she?"

"Shaken by the murder like everyone, but okay. Why don't we all sit down? This shouldn't take very long." We all sat.

Darryl and I both remembered seeing Brad at the block party. Darryl asked him when he had arrived.

"A little after five, probably. I brought 'Blood Punch' made from fruit juice and ginger ale, with a few fake eyeballs made from peeled grapes and raisins to float around. It's always a hit with the kids."

"And you, Gail?" asked Darryl.

"I had to run and do a showing while it was still light out. The housing market is *crazy* in Raleigh all over again." She was right. I had no idea how the average family could afford to buy a home in the more attractive school districts, with the average price creeping toward a half million dollars.

Whether or not Gail had been visiting with a client could certainly be checked out. If you want to track a busy agent's movements, just cross-examine her cell phone. Darryl wrote down the name of the client for later follow-up. "You two have a straight-on view of Wanda's porch. Did you see anything suspicious before you left your home?"

Both shook their heads.

"What about after the party?"

Brad answered, "I rushed ahead to be in place for the usual trick-or-treaters. Kids move fast when candy's on the line. I didn't happen to look over at Wanda's porch."

"That house is quite the eyesore," Darryl said. "A lot of people were upset by it. Could you tell me about that?"

Brad looked at me like we had a family secret between us, for the Norrises had easily bankrolled half of the makeover cost.

By way of explanation, I said, "We just spoke with Eleanor Foster."

"Poor Eleanor," Gail interjected. "She's been fretting about that house for years. And it would have been such a lovely house if Wanda had kept it up. Such great bones." It made me uncomfortable under the circumstances to hear Wanda's house compared to a skeleton.

Darryl continued, "Did either of you think that sprucing up Ms. Hightower's house might increase the marketability of your home?"

Brad shrugged. "We knew she wasn't working anymore and just wondered if she lacked the funds to keep it up. We were hoping if we made her yard look pretty, she'd take us up on an offer to paint it, too."

"How did that make you feel, when she tore up her newly landscaped yard?"

"We felt terrible," Gail said. "We thought we were doing a good thing. We all did, didn't we, Rett?"

"Yes," I said. I resented her for, however subtly, spotlighting my involvement.

Darryl asked, "Did you talk with her after the makeover?"

"Brad and I both tried. We even sent her a note of apology, with no response. I still feel bad, but don't you think we could be forgiven for planting a few flowers in her yard?"

"Do you two still plan to move to Falls Lake?" I asked.

"Only if we can sell this house in the next sixty days," Brad said. "Otherwise, our contingency contract will fall through. Too bad. It's getting harder and harder to find lakefront property."

"And this crime won't help," Gail added. "Woodmont has always struggled being so close to downtown and the homeless population. I'm afraid Falls Lake may have to wait, Brad, until news of this dies down."

"You're probably right," Brad said.

And Gail probably was right, but still I could not shake the notion that this couple stood to benefit from Wanda's death. It all depended on what Wanda's heirs decided to do with the house. Almost always the heirs fixed up the place and sold it.

I wished I could rule out the couple as suspects.

One thing was for sure: I wasn't interested in any pies they might bake.

CHAPTER 6

A VENGEFUL THREAT

The attorney couple who lived in the arts-and-crafts home on the other side of the Norrises hadn't shown themselves at the block party and still didn't appear to be home. I knew they owned a home in the mountains near Blowing Rock. Darryl took down their names for follow-up, and we crossed the street again to visit with my next-door neighbors —the Rev. Jim Thompson and his wife, Nancy—who lived in a split-level built in the 1960s. "Just so you know," I said, "Skip didn't ask the Thompsons to help with Wanda's yard. I think it's because they're older and live on a minister's income."

Darryl had known the Thompsons as a boy. I was glad we were visiting them, as I hoped there might be some surplus apple crumble Nancy had held back from serving at the Halloween party. That would more than make up for skipping breakfast. Nancy greeted us warmly ("I spotted you two making the rounds!") then led us through their cozy den and into the kitchen where she was cooking a late breakfast. Gospel music played on the radio: *"Will the circle be unbroken? By and by, Lord, by and by..."* Their sweet old dog Ben lay flopped on the floor, snoozing.

"Where's the Reverend?" Darryl asked, glancing at his watch. It was past ten.

"Still in the bed," she said with a frown. "Jim has always been a night owl. Besides, he's still recovering from the flu, which he had just a couple weeks ago. But he's a typical man. He won't be able to resist the smell of bacon and eggs."

Soon coffee was joined by heaping plates of eggs, bacon, and toast, with plenty of spreadable options available on the lazy Susan: butter, jam, honey, apple butter, and Nutella. The biscuits Nancy pulled out of the oven seconds later couldn't have been more pillow-like, and we each received a small bowl of grits with a side plate of grated cheddar. No wonder the kids in the neighborhood always managed to find their way into Nancy's kitchen over the years.

Nancy insisted we start eating while she put together a plate for herself. We hadn't eaten two bites of our meal when we heard footsteps on the stairs. Jim greeted Darryl with a firm handshake and gently touched my shoulder so I wouldn't bother standing. The pastor was neatly dressed in blue jeans and a flannel shirt, but sported a terrible case of bed head.

"Oh, Jim, your hair!" Nancy exclaimed. "You look like you slept in the clothes dryer."

"No one told me we were having guests, or I would have put on my baseball cap." He took a seat at the table with us. Nancy put her plate in front of Jim and began to clean up from her cooking. Jim said, "I'll be retiring next year from Ardmore Memorial Christian Church, where I've pastored for nearly thirty years. If you want to know the secret of staying in one church home for that long, it's a woman who is good with people and *great* with food."

"You behave," Nancy said with a wink. It was the sort of well-worn, easy-going love I had hoped to share with Allan in our later years.

I said to Jim, "You didn't tell me last night that you'd had the flu."

"It will knock a guy out," he said. Then a gloom came over his expression. "No doubt you're here about Wanda."

"Yes, sir," Darryl said. "Did you see or hear anything yesterday, before you came to the party?"

Jim shook his head. "No, unless Nancy did."

"I wish I had," Nancy said from the sink. "I can actually see pretty far down the street from the windows in the den, but I was here in the kitchen."

"Did Wanda suffer long before she died, Detective?" Jim asked. "That thought has bothered me."

"We'll get the full autopsy report later today and know more then," Darryl said, "but I suspect she died nearly instantaneously. Tell me, did you two have many dealings with Ms. Hightower? I can't remember if you were close."

Nancy said, "Jim invited her to worship with us many times, though she always declined. I always thought of her as standoffish. I don't know. Just sort of kept to herself. I haven't seen or talked to her in months and months."

Darryl nodded and turned to Jim. "When was the last time you saw Wanda, Reverend?"

"'Saw' her?" Jim thought for a beat. "The very last time I 'saw' her was the night before last. I guess technically it was Halloween, because it was around 3:30 in the morning. I noticed her silhouette in her upstairs window, presumably her bedroom. I'm often walking the dog around three or four in the morning when the newspaper gets delivered. If I see Wanda's newspaper on the sidewalk, I'll throw it on her porch or put it in her mail slot. A lot of the old homes around here still have them."

"I'm aware," said Darryl.

"Of course. I keep forgetting you grew up here. Anyway, every now and then I'd also drop in her mail slot something inspirational. I've seen depression in my parishioners from time to time. They think that if they are faithful they should have a brighter outlook. But the causes are often chemical. At the very least they need to stop being so hard on themselves, change the tape that plays in their head."

"Sounds like cognitive therapy," I said. It was a term I'd learned about in sessions with Maxine.

"That's right," Jim said. "I call it 'self-talk,' because many in my church are suspicious of psychology."

"Jim's congregation is very traditional," explained Nancy. "For example, they discourage their children from going to college after high school, worried they will be corrupted by the world. That's a little too conservative for my taste, but they are good people. And they absolutely adore Jim. Jim treasures them in return, don't you, dear?"

"I do. Some of them are quite simple in their faith, but it works for them. And that can be quite refreshing."

I'd grown up Southern Baptist and still had many happy memories of church picnics, hymns, and soulful prayer meetings. That said, I didn't miss my home church pastor's judgmental sermons and the self-righteousness and hypocrisy of so many church members. I'd visited a couple churches in Raleigh after 9/11 and again after the 2008 economic crash, but both times something kept me from going back with regularity.

"So, you think that Ms. Hightower suffered from mental illness, Reverend?" Darryl asked.

Jim shrugged. "I'm not a psychologist, but becoming a shut-in is one way a depressed person can act. All I know is that we didn't see her for months. And, a couple weeks ago, even her mail slot stopped working."

"What do you mean?" I asked.

"It just wouldn't open. I tried to put the newspaper through the slot like normal one morning, but it was like it was stuck. I came back in the afternoon and knocked and knocked, but she wouldn't answer then either. I thought I might be able to help her—"

"Don't be so hard on yourself, dear," Nancy said as she finally sat with her own plate of food. "You meant well and that's what counts."

"What about you, Mrs. Thompson?" asked Darryl. "I remember while I was growing up how you were always baking things for people on the block. Did you ever bake for the Hightowers?"

Nancy shook her head. "They were sort of an odd family. I just think about that boy's *hair*. How in the world did he *see* anything? And the father, Paul. Not a friendly man at all."

Jim nodded in agreement. "Paul was a dark character. I always thought of him as overly focused on his musical career. You never saw him playing outside with his children." Jim cleared his throat. "Sorry to be judgmental. Nancy and I never could have children, so maybe we were a little sensitive to families that didn't show affection to their kids in the way we would have. I'm sure that Paul Hightower loves his children in his own way, but those children just seemed to have gloomy natures."

"What about Ms. Hightower?" asked Darryl. "Was she friendly to children?"

"Very," said Jim. "Kids loved her."

"I suppose so," agreed Nancy, though less enthusiastically. "Oh, I'm not trying to speak ill of the dead. It's just you live on a block with someone for decades, it would be nice if you could chat with them, trade recipes—*something*. But, people are different, and that's okay."

The doorbell rang. While Jim went to answer the door, Nancy snuck a peek and clued us in that it was one of the parishioners from Jim's church, probably there for an impromptu counseling session. We heard Jim greet the woman and invite her to sit down in the den area to talk.

I asked, "Don't they require more privacy? We can leave."

"Don't worry about that. Jim's counseling sessions are always in the open. That's something that he learned from the Reverend Billy Graham. A minister should never be alone with a woman, that way she can't accuse him of any funny business later." At "funny business" Nancy did a little shake of her hip that made me giggle.

Darryl closed his notebook and drained the rest of his coffee. We both thanked Nancy for the breakfast.

As we moved through the family room, trying not to disturb Jim on the way out, my phone vibrated. I paused just long enough to read yet another text from Jasmine:

-CUSTOMER LOOKING FOR A HORE HAIR BRUSH

"Hore"? A reflex chuckle escaped me, catching the attention of Jim, who politely stood to introduce us to his parishioner. Her name was Gwen, and whatever concern had brought her for counseling didn't appear to be related to depression, judging by her pleasant demeanor.

While everyone else small-talked for a moment, I began quickly texting with Jasmine:

-lol Do you mean HORSEhair?

-SORRY! HOW CAN I TELL DIFFERENCE BETWEEN A HOREHAIR BRUSH AND A FAKE BRUSH? I MEANT HORSE HAIR! LOL

-Only one of them whinnies. Seriously, it's hard to tell the animal hair brushes from the synthetic ones. See if they can come back later. I will separate the brushes later today.

I put my phone in my pocket. The others were still chatting, so I paused to examine the Thompsons' his-and-her desk spaces just a few feet from one another. Several crafts and paintings of Nancy's caught my eye, as well as framed photographs of her posing with others for the camera: in the front lobby of the North Carolina Museum of Art, holding butterfly nets in a field of lavender, and standing in front of the Colosseum of Rome—to name just a few.

"You probably aren't acquainted with my 'continuing ed' corner," Nancy said, breaking from the others to join me. "The Senior Center at Wake Tech has a hundred courses and travel tours for geezers like me. I just discovered it last year."

"Are you taking any classes now?" I asked.

"No, but Jim is taking me to Washington, D.C., in December. We're going to visit all the sites. That will be an education in and of itself."

Darryl, overhearing her, said, "My boy will be going to D.C. with his fifth grade class next year. He's already talking about it. He wants me to chaperone."

"I chaperoned the D.C. trip when Stephanie went in the fifth grade," I said. "Exhausting, but so worth it."

Between the couple's two desks hung a magnificent quilt. "Did you make this, Nancy?" I asked. "I don't remember it."

"I made it years ago. It's been on our bed. Just felt like hanging it up."

"Needless Necessities has an active quilting club. You might enjoy it."

"Is that the place with the pie thing you told me about?"

"Exactly. Darryl's mom is active in the Qrazy Qwilters there."

"Then maybe I'll go and check it out sometime."

Seeing how much fun Nancy had with her many hobbies made me long for my own. The urge to take up painting again had grown stronger with every visit to Needless Necessities, but I still felt a wave of anxiety whenever I thought about picking up my brush. My technique would be terrible after so many years. And who cared about pictures of flowers these days? That was a simpler time in my life, one that now seemed to belong to a different person.

Between Nancy's workspace and the door was Jim's desk, which featured several books on the Bible: concordances, histories, and Greek and Hebrew dictionaries. Above the desk hung his 1983 diploma from Sanders Theological Seminary in Chicago. Scattered about, too, were a number of artifacts: a canteen, a military beret, several medals—even a grenade.

"Don't look now, Pastor," said Gwen cheerfully, "but someone else has entered your museum."

Jim said, "Rett knows I'm a World War buff. Those wars are what shaped so much of our nation's modern history."

"God was truly on our side," Nancy said.

"Amen!" added Gwen.

We thanked the couple again for the breakfast and said our good-byes.

"Do you think that was a waste of time?" I asked as we left down the front walkway. "Aside from the delicious meal, that is."

Darryl shrugged. "The pastor gave a fuller picture of Wanda's mental state. If she was depressed and shut-in, it makes me skeptical that she would answer her front door for a stranger, especially if she wouldn't even answer it for a neighbor."

"Maybe she stepped out to grab her mail and was ambushed."

"I found a bunch of mail stacked neatly on her kitchen table."

"Maybe the perpetrator moved it?"

"Possible, or it could have been delivered through the mail slot—which was clearly functioning yesterday, despite what the pastor said just now."

"Was Jim fibbing about that?"

"It would be an odd thing to fib about. We can easily check

with the postal carrier to verify there was a time it wasn't working."

"Maybe she stepped out to grab a package which couldn't fit through the slot?"

"I can have someone check with the various shipping companies to see when packages were delivered." As he made a note in his little pad, there was the sound of an engine revving. We both turned our heads and watched a yellow roadster roar up Skip Green's driveway.

His little banana.

By the time we got to Skip, he was at the front of his house crouching between two exquisitely manicured bushes. When he stood back up, he looked visibly annoyed. I asked him what the matter was.

"Dang weeds! Here it is November and we haven't had a proper frost. Seems the warmer weather hangs around later and later each year." He noticed Darryl. "I'm sure you want to talk with me about Wanda. Come on inside."

Darryl said, "Right here is fine." I got the strong sense that Darryl was ready to get these neighborly interviews over with. "I saw you come and go from your home during the party." Maybe he was thinking that Skip could have left the party just long enough to murder Wanda before returning again.

Skip didn't take offense. "I'm head of the Woodmont Culture Committee, so I help organize these events. I brought out some decorations for the tables, and I contributed some punch and some cookies. I made several trips back and forth to my house."

"You acted pretty shocked when you learned of Ms. High-tower's death," Darryl said.

"It just seemed so surreal, especially in Woodmont. The biggest problem we normally have is homeless people rummaging in our cars for loose change."

"Do you know anyone who would have held a grudge against her?"

Skip looked at me. "Don't worry," I said. "He already knows."

"So you told him about that little incident?" Skip asked. He turned to Darryl. "I guess if anyone bore a grudge, it was me. I don't know what all Rett told you, but it was one fine mess."

"I heard you were pretty angry."

"Pissed off is more like it! I had everything so organized. We had the people. We had the materials. It was supposed to be like one of those makeover shows in which the family jumps for joy and Tiny Tim gets healed at the end. Only in this episode, the family goes on a screaming rampage and burns the house down. It was worse than that time I thought I had enough votes for a bill, then some rookie legislator farts and everything goes fubar. I'm not very good with surprises."

"It seems Wanda wasn't either," said Darryl.

"She used to seem very kind and sweet," Skip said.

"Didn't you two work together on Chocolate Fest one year?" I asked.

"Yes. About five years ago. And we worked very well together."

"People change," I offered.

"Do they?" questioned Skip. "Because I've never really seen anyone change. They just become *more so*. That's something my grandmother used to say, and I think she was right. No. I was lured into a false sense of who Wanda was. The whole time she was a mean, selfish witch, and I just didn't notice. That's the only thing that explains it."

He raised a finger, as if remembering something.

"She called me, you know, just before she went outside and tore everything up. She wanted to know who was involved in the project. I thought she wanted to know who she needed to *thank*, so I gladly read her the list of everyone who had contributed.

Then she said, 'Speaking of *dirt*, I have dirt on each and every one of you moonlighting gardeners! You all better watch your backs!' and then she just hung up."

Darryl and I looked at one another.

I asked, "Did you tell the others she said that? Because I sure don't remember you telling *me* that."

"No, I felt bad enough having organized something that flopped so badly. I didn't want to give everyone a conniption."

Darryl asked, "Do you know what 'dirt' she might have had on people? Do you think she had dirt on you?"

Skip let out a guffaw. "Detective, I'm an out gay man in Southern politics, so I really don't think there's anything my elderly next-door neighbor could embarrass me with. As for the others on the block, I can't say. I guess anything is possible."

CHAPTER 7

A SURPRISE ATTACK

Skip's revelation was a bombshell. The notion of Wanda threatening revenge—and claiming to have blackmail power over others—opened up a whole new avenue of consideration. Darryl asked Skip to text us the names of everyone who had contributed to the makeover project. After obtaining the promise of a pie from Skip, I started across the street with Darryl.

Darryl wanted to know if I believed Skip when he said he didn't tell anyone about Wanda's threat.

"I do," I said, "but what if Wanda contacted people directly?"

"Then we've suddenly got a lot more people with motives."

We stopped in front of the home of Cynthia Roberts, Lydia's next-door neighbor. Darryl asked, "Weren't Wanda and Cynthia Roberts good friends once?"

I nodded. "They used to share walks, but I haven't seen them together in a while." I reminded Darryl that, like Wanda, Cynthia was an English professor, though at the much larger NC State University. "I know Cynthia was on sabbatical in England last year. Your mom watered her plants for her, though she hired a landscaping company to mow her yard."

Noting Cynthia's car in the driveway, we knocked on her door, but she didn't answer. "Perhaps she's sleeping in," I said.

"I'll leave my card," Darryl said, and placed it in the crack of the doorframe. "I'll ask Mom to let me know if she sees her out and about."

"I'll do the same," I said.

Darryl smiled and put out his hand, which I automatically took into mine. "I really appreciate your help today."

"Even if I did keep you in the dark about our neighborhood's greatest sin?"

He smiled extra at that and squeezed my hand warmly. I was sad a second later when he let go. "It's nearly impossible for groups of more than two to keep conspiracies quiet," Darryl said. "In fact, most of the time the police crack cases because we're tipped off by someone who knows who did the crime."

"Do you think that could happen this time?"

"Chances are, yes."

A police car pulled up in front of Lydia's. The lone officer was about to head up Lydia's walk when he saw Darryl and headed our way instead.

"Everything okay?" Darryl asked the officer.

My phone buzzed. I saw it was from Jasmine, but whatever she needed could certainly wait. I'd be heading to the center in the next half hour.

The officer stopped in front of us and looked at me uncertainly.

"She's fine to listen," Darryl said.

The officer said, "Something strange happened a little while ago. I was making my rounds in the alley behind the victim's home, when I saw an elderly Black gentleman loading up some junk from the neighbor's house."

"Which neighbor?"

He pointed to Skip and Stuart's house.

"Probably Otis," I said. "He's always coming by for that sort of thing. I always assumed he sells it for scrap."

"That's what I figured he was doing," the officer said, "but when the gentleman saw me rolling up behind him, he jumped in his truck in a hurry. Drove past a bunch of houses—and some pretty good throwaway junk, I'd reckon. I kept a distance but still followed him. He rounded the block and parked at your mom's house, Detective, and zipped inside, carrying his toolbox. When I knocked on the door a little while later, your mother answered. Wouldn't let me in to talk with him, which is her right, of course. So I left. That was about thirty minutes ago. When I came back just now, I noticed the gentleman was gone. No offense, Detective, but they were both acting pretty cagey."

"I'll ask her about it and contact Otis as well," said Darryl. "Thank you."

Before the officer turned to leave, Lydia burst out of her front door carrying her quilting gear. She called over her shoulder as she crossed the street, heading straight for my car, "Are you driving, Rett? We're gonna be late." Her Taurus was out of the shop, but we had continued carpooling to and from the center.

Darryl called out, "Mother, just a second, I need to ask you—"

"I've got no time to yack, Darryl! Rett, aren't you volunteering today? If not, I'll drive myself."

I shouted, "I can drive us, but I think your son wants to ask you some—"

"He can talk to me later!" she snapped as she disappeared into the passenger side of my car and slammed the door.

Darryl raised an eyebrow and muttered. "I guess it's true what they say: quilting waits for no man!"

~

On the way to Needless Necessities, Lydia was quiet, and I was preoccupied, too. I mulled the events and conversations of the morning. So far, only the Norrises stood out to me as true suspects. But could an eagerness to sell their house really drive one or both of them to murder Wanda?

Perhaps there was a different motive on the part of someone in Woodmont, like the desire to cover up a secret that Wanda was prepared to reveal.

Or could it still be some psychopath on the prowl on Halloween?

Bothering me for a different reason were a few of the inane things I'd done and said in front of Darryl. I had made a promise to Wanda to find her killer, but I didn't know the first thing about investigating homicides.

There's the mirror in your bathroom—and then there's the one you carry with you, everywhere you go.

We parked. As Lydia proceeded into the center, I lingered to phone Stephanie. When she didn't pick up, I left a voicemail mentioning the murder. I had been running out of unique messages to leave on her voicemail—and this one was certainly unique. As I watched my phone for signs of a call back, I told myself I should give her some space, but lately that space had become the width of the Grand Canyon.

Maybe children didn't like taking sides when their parents divorced, but Stephanie had wasted little time in siding with Allan. She seemed to buy his arguments that I just wasn't appreciative of how hard he had worked to save our marriage, that I had ignored his emotional needs for over a decade. I felt helpless, because everyone seemed to know about Allan's unhappiness in the marriage except me. What was worse, an amazingly high number of otherwise sensible adults seemed to buy Allan's song and dance that everyone should feel sorry for him now that he was losing his spouse and business partner at the same time.

Allan charmed people in that way. It was easy to fall under his spell. Even I found myself feeling sorry for him. After all, his family had been devastated after his older brother committed suicide at age sixteen for reasons that were never understood. His mother became a pill-popper, while his dad became a workaholic. Allan, at age twelve, had not only lost an older brother, he'd lost his parents, too.

But that didn't excuse what Allan had done.

The most hurtful aspect was the extent to which Stephanie had taken to Allan's mistress. Apparently, KayLeigh Rider had superb fashion sense, sported a complexion to die for, and was a consummate professional who offered great tips for building one's personal brand. The woman certainly had beauty-queen looks. Her hair remained straight in a way we curly-heads have always envied. And that skin tone was no joke—it allowed her to tan but never burn. If Ariana Grande ever went to real estate school, she might graduate as KayLeigh Rider.

My therapist told me that college-aged children of divorce tended to have a harder time coping than young children like Darryl's son. The last thing I wanted on my hands was a depressed college student who was failing her classes, withdrawing from friends, or contemplating self-harm.

Let her get closer to her dad, I reasoned. Let her find in KayLeigh the sibling Allan and I never gave her.

But I'd keep trying to reach her. It was all I knew to do.

To get to the paints section, I had to pass through the fabrics area where the checkout counter was located. Today, the register was being tended by a petite, college-aged girl with shoulder-length blonde hair. Something seemed off about her, and I moved a little closer, only to discover she was posed absolutely stock-still with her head lowered. Then I saw that pinned to the front of her black turtleneck shirt, like Wall Street's version of a tacky Christmas sweater, were a dozen or more five-, ten-, and twenty-dollar bills.

"Excuse me, Miss," I said. "Are you okay?"

The girl didn't respond. She continued to stare at the counter as if attempting to set it aflame with her gaze.

"You won't get her to talk, ma'am," said a young man's voice.

I turned to find a tall, red-headed boy holding a mop and bucket. Like the girl, he seemed to be around college age.

"What in the world is she doing?" I asked.

His forehead crinkled. "Something about the inter-spacial—"

"Inter*stitial*," piped the girl. I turned quickly, but I wasn't fast enough to catch her breaking her pose.

"Right," said the boy. "Wo is 'examining the *interstitial* space between buying and owning.' She calls this particular work 'Capitalist Limbo.' You see, she's stuck in the middle of a purchase, which often makes buyers uncomfortable." He bent to whisper in my ear, "A lot of Wo's work is about making people uncomfortable. Just ask Sally about Wo's last big show."

"What happened at her show?"

"It—well, better ask Sally. It's kind of a girl thing."

"Okay," I said, still whispering. "What did you say your friend's name was? 'Wo?'"

"Have you heard the word 'woke'?"

"I'm not sure..."

"It sorta means 'super smart about things in society like racism and sexism.' That's why she goes by 'Wo K.' Get it?"

I had my doubts that anyone who called themselves woke was, in actuality, woke.

"And your name?" I asked in normal volume.

"Washington Monroe Henry. Most folks just call me Wash.

And, here I am—washing!" He pumped the mop twice in its bucket.

Judging by his accent, I gathered that Wash was from the eastern end of the state same as I was. I told him my name and that I was raised in Goldsboro.

"Well, shit fire and save matches, Rett! I'm from Tick Bite! That's just around the corner from Goldsboro!"

"Yay! We might be cousins," I said, trying not to sound too sarcastic. I lowered my voice again. "Does your friend often do these sorts of things?"

"Yep. She's a design major at State. We met one day when she needed manure for one of her performances. I'm an ag major, and she came by the testing station where I was trying pigs on different diets. Spoiler alert—she got her manure!"

I detected a glimmer in his eye. By gosh, this country boy was in love. And why wouldn't he be? His classmate was cute as a button, if a tad unusual.

"I'm curious," I said, "what did she do with the manure?"

"She set up a food stand outside the student union's burger restaurant, put up a sign that said '100 Percent Animal Product' and sold manure burgers. It made quite a stink, you might say. Well, she wasn't actually selling manure burgers. If someone called her bluff and bought a burger, she'd hand them one with a plant-based mixture she made up."

"Tempeh," peeped Wo. Again, I wasn't fast enough to turn and catch her lips moving.

"Right," said Wash. "Tempeh. Looks like crap, and kind of tastes like crap, too, but it's technically edible. Anyway, her point was to show that animal products are really gross and shouldn't be eaten. Wo is a vegetarian."

"Vegan," she corrected.

"That's right. Vegan. Anyway," continued Wash, "the burger place got Campus Police to shut her down. But they weren't even the health department, so it's not like they had jurisdiction, and students sell food on the Brickyard all the time." He actually seemed upset that someone took offense to his friend's poop exhibit. This boy must really be infatuated.

I had been worried that Needless Necessities wasn't going to make the month's rent. Now I wondered how it could possibly survive another day with its checkout girl totally checked out.

Not. My. Problem.

"I gotta go," I said. "I'm working the paints."

"I have to get back to work, too. This store ain't gonna mop itself."

Traffic in the paint section was slow. At some point Sally dropped by to grill me about my progress recruiting pie-bakers. I told her I'd found four so far.

"I knew you could do it. Keep going!" she said, before proudly prancing away.

Jasmine had observed the whole exchange. She handed me a steaming mug that announced YOU GOT TROUBLES? I GOT TIME. "Girl, you look like you've lost your best friend. What's on your mind?"

I could have mentioned our neighborhood's murder, but that wasn't what was really bugging me right now. Jasmine's truth-serum coffee—a hundred times better than break-room coffee was supposed to taste—prompted me to tell her all about my estrangement from Stephanie and my separation from Allan. I even admitted that I'd been lying around the house drinking way more than I should.

"You don't have a drinking problem so much as a *purpose* problem," she commented once I'd finished the whole sordid story. "Besides, surely you've got friends you can lean on who are way more loyal than your husband."

"I guess I do," I said. "But they're all really busy people."

"They can't be too busy for you. Reach out to them! We

always should remember where we came from, but it's even more important to remember *who* we came from. That's what I always tell Russell. 'Remember who you came from.' He gets it. He's a sharp boy. All his teachers say so."

Speaking of friends, Lydia showed up to fetch me a little earlier than usual. She looked especially worn out. I thanked Jasmine for her time and handed her my empty mug.

"You're really good at this coffee thing," I said. "Ever thought of opening your own café?"

Jasmine spread out her arms. "This is my café!" Off my skeptical look, she admitted, "Well, I guess I *could* use a new coffee maker."

Inside the car, Lydia leaned her head back and closed her eyes. I wanted to ask her about Otis's visit that morning, but even more than that, I was curious to know more about her son. Did she think Darryl was open to dating? I didn't want to give her any false hope, and I wasn't sure I was ready to date myself. Heck, my divorce wasn't even final. But it was thrilling to think about dating again. It had felt good to spend a couple of hours with a man.

Upon our return to the neighborhood, Lydia seemed to be asleep, so I gave her a shake to wake her. When she roused, she looked at me confusedly, her face oddly contorted, as if half her face had been squished against the side door—but it hadn't.

"Are you okay?" I asked.

She moved her lips, but only a sort of grunt came out.

"Lydia? What's wrong. Something's not right." Her expression looked almost desperate. Alarmed, I got out and went to the other side of the car, but she wasn't able to respond to me.

I spotted Cynthia Roberts walking rapidly to her car from her house.

"Cynthia, quick! Please call 9-1-1!"

To my great shock, Cynthia completely ignored me, got in her car, and drove away.

Had everyone suddenly gone insane?

I opened the back door of my car, grabbed my purse from the backseat, fished out my phone, and dialed 9-1-1 myself.

The dispatcher's voice came on the line immediately. "Nine-one-one. What is the nature of your emergency?"

"Please help!" I cried. "I think my friend is having a stroke!"

CHAPTER 8

"A PRIMAL SYMPATHY"

The paramedics arrived. One interviewed me while the other rapidly checked Lydia's vitals. I followed the ambulance in my car and called Darryl, who arrived at the ER just after doctors had used a CAT scan to confirm a blockage in Lydia's brain and rule out any bleeding. To combat the stroke's clot, they put Lydia on blood thinners and aspirin, then watched her closely to make sure surgery would not be required.

At four o'clock we were told she would be spending the night in the ICU. We wouldn't be allowed to see her. The hospitalist advised us to go home and check back in the morning.

As Darryl walked me to my car I told him that, despite our big brunch, the adrenaline of the past few hours had made me famished all over again and that I planned to go home and make a sandwich.

He wouldn't have it. "Seeing as how you helped me with the morning's interviews and saved my mother's life today, why don't you let me do something for you for a change? I'll grab some dinner for us and meet you back at Mom's house."

I knew that letting me pay for half our meal wasn't an option for this Galahad. And, I sure wasn't going to offer up my kitchen, which had been a complete mess for months.

After a hot shower and a glass of wine, I was feeling halfway normal again. That's when I received Darryl's text saying that he was on his way with our meal.

To get to Lydia's I had to pass by Cynthia's. I noticed her car was back. Rather than remaining miffed at her earlier strange behavior, I mostly just felt confused. I went to the front door and knocked. No answer. I tried the door. Finding it unlocked, I pushed it open.

"Cynthia?" I called. "Are you home?"

From the doorway I could see her on her living room couch, rousing. A bottle of Bulleit rye whiskey lay on its side on the coffee table in front of her, half consumed.

"Hello?" she said distantly as she tried to sit up. "Who's in my house?"

"It's Rett," I said, taking a step inside. "I was worried something was wrong just now, so I let myself in."

She sat up and held her head in her hands.

I said, "I wanted to let you know that Lydia had a stroke."

"Out..." she mumbled.

"Are you sure you don't need some help?" I asked.

She became emphatic: "Out. Out!"

"Okay, okay," I said, backing out the door but being sure to lock it before pulling it shut.

As I tried to make sense of the encounter, a familiar vehicle pulled in front of Lydia's home. It was Otis Jones, his beat-up pick-up filled to the brim with various metal junk.

I walked to the passenger side where the window was down.

"Hello, Ms. Swinson," he said. "How are you?"

"I'm okay, Otis. How are you?"

"Fair to middlin'." He looked past me toward Lydia's home. "How is Ms. Schmidt doing? I heard she's under the weather."

"How did you hear that?" I asked, but I thought I knew. Darryl had probably called him to ask about the events of the morning. "Lydia's stable," I said. "They'll let us know more in the morning, but they're positive she had a stroke."

"I'm sorry to hear it. Very sorry to hear it." His expression had turned gloomy.

"Do you know if anything in particular might have upset Lydia? You saw her this morning."

"Yes, I did see her." I could tell he didn't really want to talk about the morning incident with the police officer, so I shifted tactics. "Do you have need of all this metalwork in your truck? We could probably use some of it at Needless Necessities." I told him about the center and where it was located.

Otis said he was familiar with the place but had never stopped to check it out. "I use scrap for projects," he said. "Come to think of it, I'm running out of room in my shop and need to clear some things out. I'll bring some things by."

"That's great," I said. "By the way, when you were rummaging behind Wanda's house this morning, did you happen to—"

"Gotta go," he said suddenly and sped off.

He had been looking in his rearview mirror. As his truck turned the corner, Darryl's department-issued Dodge Charger pulled up in its place. The detective stepped out holding two plastic bags of Outback Steakhouse.

"What did Otis want?" he asked.

"He was asking after Lydia. I don't know if it was my questioning or you showing up that scared him off."

"Odd."

"By the way, I spoke to Cynthia. *Also*, odd. I'll tell you about it over dinner."

In Lydia's kitchen I set the table. I had resisted the temptation to bring a bottle of wine from my home, as that felt a little too date-like. But I did pick out wine glasses for our ice waters.

As Darryl unpacked the steaks, baked potatoes, mixed veggies, and Bloomin' Onion from the packaging, I thought about how little first responders typically got paid. Steak dinners weren't an everyday thing.

"This looks bloomin' delicious," I said.

"Dig in, Mate," he smiled. Turns out we were both famished, and for a while we didn't speak as we stuffed our mouths.

"You must be exhausted," I said after a while. "And your poor mom."

"Life rarely goes as planned," he said. "We'll see tomorrow if there's any damage to her brain. One thing's for sure: she's going to have to stop smoking."

"That's not going to be easy on her."

"It's not going to be easy on *us*. Get ready. My dad had to quit smoking after his cancer diagnosis, and my mom quit for a while, too, for solidarity. It was like living with a couple of cats in a sack." He shook his head and took a bite of steak.

"I remember your dad. Gruff guy, but a good man."

"Thanks," he said. "I miss him." He cleared his throat and drank some water. "So, you were able to talk with Cynthia?"

"I let myself in, but she threw me out. Judging by the whiskey bottle, she'd pretty much tied one on all afternoon."

"Doesn't sound like Dr. Roberts. She always seemed super straitlaced to me."

"It's strange. She didn't seem to hear me when your mom collapsed and I asked her to call 9-1-1. She sort of looked through me. She must really be mourning the loss of her friend."

"And her former professor."

"What do you mean?"

Darryl turned to a page in his trusty notebook. "Cynthia was a graduate student at NC State at the same time that Wanda was a professor there. In fact, Wanda was on her graduate committee —which I guess means that she was sort of an advisor to Cynthia."

"I've had a number of friends in grad school," I said. "Wanda probably advised Cynthia on her thesis if she was a master's student, or her dissertation if she was a Ph.D. student."

"That makes sense. Cynthia was finishing up her Ph.D. about the time that Wanda left to teach at Wake Tech." He closed his notebook. "All that came from a random database. Seems odd that one would leave a large university like State to teach at a community college, don't you think?"

"Unless you decided you liked teaching a lot more than research. But it is worth checking out. Any other revelations you feel comfortable sharing? Have you found your 'dragon of interest' yet?"

"Not yet. Honestly, I'm beginning to think this crime was pulled off by a specter."

"What about the autopsy?" I asked.

"She died the way we thought. A single stab wound to the back and through the heart. The coroner found one thing interesting: irritation to her nose and eyes and throat. Not burns, but close to it."

I remembered the swim cap. I asked, "Could the burns be caused by hot water or steam in the shower?"

"If so, it was quite a while before she was killed, because the home's two showers weren't the least bit wet or damp. We checked."

"Maybe hot water from a sink?"

"That's more likely. My roommate in college used to make steam in the dorm bathroom sink as an acne remedy. Either way, it doesn't seem particularly relevant. Maybe toxicology will show us something, but that usually takes weeks."

Darryl appeared distracted. "What's bothering you?" I asked.

"Otis didn't have much to say when I phoned him earlier. He insisted he came by because Mom wanted him to take a look at her freezer's ice maker. But that thing's been broken for years—like Eleanor's, now that I think about it. Did Mom say anything to you?"

"No, and I didn't ask her in time. Sorry."

Darryl shook his head. "I've known Otis practically my whole life. Half of our house—heck, half the neighborhood—has his fingerprints on repairs of everything from washing machines to fence gates. I just wonder if he discovered something important back there in the alleyway. I can't imagine Otis being wrapped up in any of this, but if he's trying to protect someone..." His voice trailed off.

"Who?"

He shrugged. "I don't know."

"Not to change the subject, but how is Charlie? Did you call him to tell him about your mom?"

"I did. He was very sad to hear his grandma is sick, but I thought it better to be honest with him. Parenting is exhausting —but I guess you know that."

"My only girl is grown and off to college. I guess I should worry less, because now if she gets in trouble with the law, it's all on her."

Darryl smiled at that, and I detected an opening. "If you don't mind me asking, what happened with you and your ex-wife? My husband and I are separated right now. We'll be divorcing soon."

"Sorry to hear it. It's nothing I'd wish on anyone."

"It happens."

"In my case, it was divorce or the Poor House. Janice was spending all our money, plus money that we didn't have. Shop, shop, shop. I honestly believe she couldn't help herself."

"Your mother called it 'gold digging.'"

"I wish there were gold for Janice to dig up. I did have a small settlement from a wreck I sustained chasing a drunk driver about five years ago. That was going to be the start of Charlie's college fund. She spent it, and I lost all respect for her."

I was about to share something Maxine had told me in one of our sessions. But should I?

Yes, I should. There was just no way I was going to get involved with someone who didn't see the benefits of therapy. Allan never would consider sharing his thoughts with "a damn stranger," as he always put it.

Ladies and Gentlemen, do not worry about the people who go to therapy; worry about the ones who won't.

So I took a deep breath and said, "My therapist says that marriage can't handle resentment for very long."

Darryl didn't miss a beat. "Your therapist is spot on. I just hope when my son's older that he won't resent me for divorcing his mom."

"I think he looks up to you too much for that."

His expression softened. "What about you?" Darryl asked. "Did having an empty nest have something to do with your break-up?"

"No, I think we were broken from the beginning. I was living on the surface, where Allan has always lived. I was never myself with Allan, not really. I thought I was being what he wanted me to be. In betraying myself, I'd betrayed the relationship. Maybe it wasn't as bad as an affair, but it was a form of cheating, too."

"That's pretty deep."

"Psychobabble, your mother might call it."

"I just don't meet many people who can put into words what they're thinking the way you just did. Maybe it's because I hang out with a bunch of crotch scratchers and knuckle draggers."

The image made me giggle. "That can't be true."

"You'd be surprised. Sometimes the stereotypes are completely accurate."

"Actually," I said, "I think most people are deep, but it's painful to plumb those waters. Even now, it's hard for me to get back in touch with something I'd call my real self. Too much anger in the way."

"I still get angry at Janice," Darryl said. "Fortunately, like you did, I saw a therapist. And he helped a lot."

"He helped you get over your anger?"

"Well, he made me realize that every person has different genes, different experiences, different brain chemistry. I finally accepted the fact that shopping was Janice's way of finding peace and comfort. Yeah, it's a destructive method of coping, but we all do things to feel better. At least by understanding that, I was able to stop hating her."

"Besides," he continued, "if you think about your anger all the time, over the course of time it just crushes you. It steamrolls your whole life."

I smiled.

"Something funny?" he asked.

"It's just that someone else in this room is pretty deep, too," I said.

He blushed a little, then got serious again. "How do you deal with your anger toward Allan?"

"I don't," I said. "I drink."

The revelation surprised even me. I felt myself getting choked up and became quiet. I waved my hand by way of apology and tried to drink some water.

Faster than most men move, Darryl pulled his chair to my side of the table and put his arm around me. He just made himself present, a simple gesture I'd never witnessed Allan express, ever.

"I'm sorry," I whispered. "Thank you. I'll be okay."

"I know you will," he said confidently. "We both will." I wasn't so sure he was right, but my heart responded to his optimism with a small leap before he moved back to his side of the table.

"Of course, you can probably guess what I'm going to ask you next," I said.

"What is that?"

"Did you meet with the deceased's family today?"

He chuckled. "Nothing can distract you from this case for long, can it? I'll talk with Wanda's daughter tomorrow. She's flying back to Charlotte from California tonight on the red-eye."

"And what about the ex-husband and son?"

"They're still in the Far East playing classical guitar. I guess there's a market for that sort of thing outside the States, but I can't imagine anyone making a living doing that here."

"Did you talk to them?"

"Yes. I learned neither had talked with Wanda in quite a few months."

"Maybe you'll learn something from the daughter," I said.

"I hope so."

Here we were, eating take-out while talking about divorce and murder. That couldn't classify as a fun time together, could it?

Then why was I already wanting to spend more time with him?

Come morning, the doctors moved Lydia out of the ICU and into a private hospital room. I was eager to see her, but Darryl, who had arrived before me, met me at the door and ushered me down the hall to talk in private.

I asked, "Is she okay?"

"I just wanted to prepare you. She's conscious and alert but..."

"But what?"

"She's been trying to talk, but the words won't come out. She can't write either. The doctor seems to think the language center of her brain was affected. It's like she tries to communicate—then just shrugs and gives up."

"Does she at least understand others?"

"She sure understood when the doctor told her she'd have to quit smoking. She wasn't happy about that one bit."

"Is her speech the only thing affected?"

"They think so. They might even release her tomorrow and start rehab on Tuesday. She'll have to do rehab most every day for several weeks."

"Be honest," I said. "Would it be best if I waited until she got home to see her?"

"Probably. She needs to rest. When she does return home, her Cousin Doris, who lives in Garner, has agreed to come sit with her during the days and get her to rehab."

Lydia had told me about Doris, the widow of Lydia's cousin, a man who had followed Lydia and Karl down to Raleigh from Wisconsin in the sixties and married local. He'd passed away some years ago. But, like Lydia, Doris had never remarried. According to Lydia, Doris wore her widowhood like a badge of honor.

"Isn't this the cousin known as 'Boring Doris'?" I asked Darryl.

He smiled. "Yes, but I'm hoping that for everyone's sake Mom will overlook that. Doris just wants to be of some help."

"And I'll be glad to cook dinner for your mom and stay with her every night until she recovers," I said.

"Wait, Charlie and I can—"

"No, you can't, Darryl. Your work hours are unpredictable.

And Charlie's school is close to where you live now. I'll be glad to stay nights and even some days that Doris can't. I know your mother well. Maybe I can anticipate some of her needs even if she can't speak."

"Now I'm the one who's speechless. You're a saint, Rett."

But I didn't want him to see me as a saint. I wanted him to see me as a woman.

As Darryl returned to his mother's side, I walked, lost in thought, through the myriad hallways back to the parking deck. Somehow I felt Lydia's condition was an extension of what had happened to Wanda. Not literally—I didn't think that someone had laced my friend's iced tea with poison—but the two events seemed connected in a way that I didn't yet understand.

I sat in my car without starting the engine, an entire Sunday ahead of me and a deep reluctance to spend it in my empty house. I found myself waxing nostalgic for Allan's manic weekend presence with its constant free-flow of music, food, flowers, and friends. Without its official social chair, the house felt airless, dead.

The phone rang. Speak of the devil. I allowed my ex-husband's call to go to voicemail. The message was classic Allan, all cheery and rushed:

"Hi, Rett! We're having that party on Saturday afternoon to celebrate ten years of the firm and raise the cash we need to move forward on the over-50 condo project. Hoping you can still be there. Pencil in Saturday, four till seven, at the new house. Thanks. Let me know what time you plan to be there, okay? Hope you're having a great day!"

I'd totally forgotten about the investor party, which was something we often did to kick off our projects. It happened to coincide with a company anniversary—a bittersweet celebration indeed. To communicate confidence to our investors, I'd be expected to make nice in front of everyone. I had yet to confront

KayLeigh, who, as the project's primary agent, was sure to be at the party.

It was a good thing I hadn't yet pulled out of the hospital, because just thinking about the party sent my blood pressure through the roof. If I didn't find something else to focus on really quick, I might just have a stroke myself.

Instead of heading home, I drove south, winding my way past downtown toward a place I hadn't visited in a long time: the main campus of Wake Tech, where Wanda Hightower had worked for nearly three decades before her death.

The main campus had been renovated of late and featured a massive student center. With some effort I located the English department and the office of Gary Roland, its chair. Roland's door was closed and no one answered when I knocked, but I rounded the corner and found the English department office with its door wide open.

A slender, short, moderately handsome Caucasian gentleman of about fifty sat at a round table with several stacks of papers.

"You seem to be reading the modern equivalent of *Moby Dick*," I said.

The man looked up from his work and smiled weakly. "I have to make freshmen turn in their term papers in October if I'm going to get them read and graded by Christmas."

I told him my name and that I was a neighbor of Wanda's. "Are you Gary Roland, by any chance?" Except for the two of us, the departmental office was empty.

"That's me. Please, have a seat."

I sat down across the table from him. "Isn't it unusual for a department head to be grading papers for freshman comp?"

"We're short staffed. Our newest instructor quit in the middle of the term."

"Would that have been Wanda's replacement?"

"Indeed," he said. "Wanda is missed in more ways than one."

"That's why I'm here," I said.

"To grade papers?"

I nearly laughed at that. "No, I'm trying to figure out what happened to her." I watched his face carefully as I added, "The newspaper article yesterday stated she retired, but everyone acts as if she was fired."

Roland studied me closely, trying to gauge my intentions. My whole adult life, people had tended to unload their personal thoughts and feelings on me. I guess I appeared harmless to most people—and Roland was no exception. "It's no big secret," he said at last. "Wanda had some difficulties last year. She did come very close to being fired."

"What happened?"

Seemingly grateful for a break, he leaned back in his chair. "About a year ago, Wanda started becoming irascible in meetings. It seemed that just about anything and everything would set her off. I tried to sit down one-on-one to talk to her about it, but she stormed out of those meetings, too. After a while, we both decided she would remain home and call in. Meetings went much smoother that way—especially when she decided to stop joining them altogether."

"When was that?"

"Around Christmas."

"And then the spring semester?"

"Come spring semester she missed a number of her classes. That became unacceptable."

"But you didn't let her go?"

"Once HR got involved, they persuaded her to retire instead. It didn't make a lot of difference to me."

"Any clue what caused her to turn so—"

"—ornery? Wanda was always very tightly wound, her mind going a million miles a minute. She was absolutely brilliant. You know, she didn't always teach at our little community college. She actually taught at State for a while."

"I heard that. Do you know what caused her to leave there?"

He shrugged. "I can only presume she had a meltdown back then that was similar to this one. Why there would be three decades of time between mental breakdowns, I can't begin to guess."

"Is there anything else that struck you as strange about her behavior?" I asked.

Roland thought for a moment. "When we needed her head-shot for the school website last December, everyone else sent in a nice portrait. But not Wanda. She sent in a photo of a stack of books."

"How odd."

Roland chuckled. "She was a clever woman in many ways. That was part of her charm—until it just wasn't charming anymore."

He said, "Follow me. I'll show you something."

Roland led me further into the English department office to a corner table. "This was put together yesterday by a couple of her colleagues." On the small table sat a shrine of sorts that included an heirloom china vase holding a single white lily. Next to the vase was a lovely, framed photograph of Wanda from a younger time, perhaps when she first came to Wake Tech.

Beside the photograph was a verse in a matted frame:

From "Ode on Intimations of Immortality"
By William Wordsworth

Though nothing can bring back the hour
Of splendour in the grass, of glory in the flower,
We will grieve not, rather find
Strength in what remains behind

In the primal sympathy
Which having been must ever be;
In the soothing thoughts that spring
Out of human suffering;
In the faith that looks through death

I had never cared much for poetry, but this seemed beautiful to me, and I said so. "Didn't Wordsworth also write that poem about the ancient mariner I read in high school?"

"No, but his friend Samuel Taylor Coleridge did."

"I'm struggling," I said, still regarding the poem, "to find 'soothing thoughts' in the wake of Wanda's death."

"It will take time," said Roland. "I think everyone here had a soft spot for her. She was an adamant atheist, but I daresay she was one of the most spiritually grounded people I knew." This time his voice cracked a little.

After a moment, I said, "What did she complain about in those meetings? Was there something or someone that triggered her rants?"

"It was usually the state of education that got her riled."

"How so?"

"Just how everything in the education system these days is about cutting costs rather than improving instruction. For example, the administration has completely avoided filling Wanda's empty position with a full-time instructor. Instead, they've hired adjuncts on a course-by-course basis, someone who has to find a way to live without benefits. That's why her newest replacement quit last week. His car broke down and he didn't have the money to fix it. It shows just how little we value a student's ability to read and write critically."

"That's so unfortunate," I said.

"It's a little bit like over-development of the environment. You don't really notice the chipping away of the natural world until you wake up one day and you notice something: the sound of no birds singing. Wanda's angst could be interpreted as a totally sane response to a badly tilted world. I guess that's one blessing. Wanda no longer must bear witness to the world's sad entropy."

"That's a very eloquent description," I said.

"The jeremiad, one might say, of a disgruntled English professor."

We both turned to meet the source of the voice. The man was of average build and looked to be early sixties with a graying beard and afro.

"Hello, Samuel," said Roland. "Can I help you?"

"I just wanted to leave something for Wanda." Then he turned to me. "Samuel Aldridge."

"Rett Swinson," I said. "I was a neighbor of Wanda's."

"A terrible tragedy," said Aldridge.

"Samuel teaches African-American literature for us," Roland said. "He's been a professor here nearly as long as Wanda."

"Wanda should still be teaching," Aldridge said. Did I detect a note of tension between the two men? "Excuse me," added Aldridge, "I just wanted to leave this."

He stepped toward the shrine and set up a small, framed photo of himself and Wanda—both looking young and hopeful.

"That's a terrific photo," I said.

"Better days," said Aldridge. "So nice to meet you, Ms. Swinson. I'll leave you two to your conversation." He bowed away and left the office.

I returned to the Wordsworth poem.

"Speaking of 'bearing witness,'" I said. "If I wanted to understand more about the poets Wanda studied and admired, what would you recommend I read?"

He walked over to a massive bookshelf and brought back to

me a slim volume: *Sublime Lives: The Men and Women Behind the Poetry That Changed the World.*

"This book features their biographies alongside their poetry. Understand them, and maybe you'll understand Wanda a little better, too."

I asked, "Did Wanda ever write poetry herself?"

"She did. In fact, she published several poems in the school literary magazine, for which she was the faculty editor until last year, when Professor Aldridge took over. If you like, I'll take you to the magazine archives and you can look up the poems yourself."

I said I would like that. Roland led me into the hallway, around the corner, and down a long corridor to a small storage room. Inside were a number of shelves bearing neatly arranged books and journals. "Here are the copies of the school's literary magazine going back decades."

I was distracted by a strong chemical odor and said something to Roland about it. We followed the smell down the hall to the biology and chemistry labs. Mountains of test tubes and vials sat on the counters alongside glass bottles containing God-knows-what chemicals. There didn't seem to be anyone around. "Remember what I said about staffing?" Roland commented wryly as he closed the door. Sure enough, back in the literary archives, the smell began to dissipate. I thanked him for his help.

"Take your time. Just pull the door closed when you leave." He headed back down the hall to the departmental office and his paper grading.

Each issue of the literary magazine sported a table of contents with titles and contributor names, so it didn't take long to find three issues in which Wanda had published her own work. Still feeling queasy from the chemicals down the hall, I quickly took photos of her poems to look at later.

On my way out I poked my head into the English office to thank Professor Roland again and wish him good luck with the term papers. As I was leaving the building, I passed a bulletin board upon which the college's latest monthly newsletter had been tacked. One headline caught my eye.

Roland to Assume VP of Academics Role in New Year

The short article included a quote by the school's chancellor heaping mountains of praise on the English department chair. "Dr. Roland has never wavered in his commitment to student instruction," the chancellor was quoted as saying.

The chancellor was especially complimentary of how Roland had managed to keep the costs of instruction down "through the creative use of adjunct talent."

CHAPTER 9

THE ARTIST'S LAIR

With most of my day still looming like a long shadow, I decided to reach out—as Jasmine had put it—to "*who* I came from." Problem was, my three closest friends in Raleigh—all successful professionals—rarely stayed still long enough to be cornered for a get-together. So, I was shocked when a quick flurry of texts produced an impromptu gathering with all three of them, the most reclusive of the trio agreeing to host.

Freddy Tate, a college friend with a successful sculpting career, lived just a few blocks from me in a modern home with copious amounts of concrete, stainless steel, and glass. Bald since college, he greeted me at the door, took one look at the two wine bottles in my hand, and produced an expression that might have come off as skinhead-mean if I didn't know better. Freddy had climbed on the sobriety wagon nearly a decade ago and lived a mostly spartan life, rarely dating, totally devoted to his art and healthy lifestyle.

I tried to play off the bottles with a humorous line, but my sassy gay friend beat me to it. "Stop your jabber-jawing and get your Blanche-DuBois-alcoholic ass in here."

I wasn't the first arrival. Resting on the couch was Paige Kirkland, whose catering company Allan and I first engaged back when we were getting our business started. Paige had long since swore off catering, but she was busier than ever as the owner of three of the hottest dining spots in the Triangle. I knew she rarely saw her husband, a partner in the city's largest corporate law firm.

"Don't let us keep you up, Paige," I kidded.

Paige opened one eye. "Hey, Rett. Still recovering from last night. I had several employees at all three restaurants call in sick. I can't recall when I've worked my fanny so hard."

I was popping the cork on the Pinot Gris when Margaret Strand showed up. Good timing, as Margaret was someone I could always count on to clink a glass with me. "Hit me up, girl," she said, my cue to pour.

Like Freddy, I'd met Margaret in college. From the beginning of Swinson Development, she was my go-to interior designer for apartments, condos, and retirement centers. "Inviting someone inside is one thing, but you've got to make them want to *stay*," is how she put it. The maxim described her love life, too. She'd been engaged to three different men but each time had broken off the relationship within weeks of the wedding.

It felt good to be in the presence of these three old souls, who were as messed up as me but somehow managed to get by.

Margaret took a seat on a couch and waved at me to join her. She kicked off her high heels; Margaret didn't go to the drugstore without being dressed to the nines. "I've been worried about you, missy," she said. "Come tell me about this homicide in your neck of the woods."

The word caused Paige to sit up. Buried in her restaurants over the weekend, Paige hadn't learned about the crime. Freddy, absorbed in sculpture making, hadn't heard either, so I had to start from the beginning. Once I'd finished, Paige asked, "How do you sleep at night knowing there's a maniac on the loose?"

"I feel somewhat safer staying with Lydia. Besides, I just don't think this murder was random." Until I said it aloud, I didn't fully realize I believed it.

"And how would you know that, Nancy Drew?" Margaret teased.

I shrugged. "It was very brutal, and there wasn't a secondary crime, such as theft or rape."

Margaret clicked her tongue. "Where was the husband, boyfriend, or ex? You know it usually boils down to one of those three." Where Margaret developed her deep distrust of men was anyone's guess. She had always been tight-lipped about her childhood, though I had to assume it was a privileged one, for she had grown up in one of the mini-mansions near the Five Points area of Raleigh.

I shook my head. "Her ex-husband was on the other side of the planet, and there's been no talk of another relationship." With Freddy right there, I didn't want to come across as assuming everyone was straight by saying "boyfriend." Besides, nothing had ruled out Wanda having a female lover. I thought of Cynthia, never married, deep in mourning.

Maggie asked, "Don't the Norrises still live on your block? Who does Gail think did it?"

"Honestly, Gail and Brad might be suspects." I told her about the Norrises' key role in the makeover gone bad. "Have they said anything to you about the murder?" I asked. "I didn't even know you all were close."

"Not close, but a few months ago Gail came to me wanting help furnishing and decorating their Falls Lake house. I gave her a quote, but they haven't pulled the trigger."

"That's because they don't own the house yet," I explained. "They have to sell their Woodmont home first."

"I'm no detective," Freddy said, "but it seems odd to me that no one would have witnessed a murder in broad daylight. Where were all the trick-or-treaters?"

"Still at the block party," I pointed out. "There was one group of kids from another neighborhood, though, who were cutting through the alleyway around that time. The youngest child told the police she saw someone near Wanda's dressed as a dragon."

"Speaking of police," said Margaret, "tell us about this detective. I watched your eyes when you mentioned his name. You're sweet on him, I can tell."

I felt my face turn red—and not from the wine.

"I find Darryl a doting son and father. That doesn't mean I want to jump his bones."

"It doesn't mean you don't," Freddy needled.

"You should bring him by one of my restaurants," said Paige. "Just let me know in advance so I can be there to get a good look at him."

"I would feel a little weird going on a date while I'm still technically married."

Margaret nearly choked on her drink. "You're no more married right now than I am! Stop rearranging the chairs on the *Titanic*. Grab your lifeboat and find your Leonardo!"

The Leonardo who sprang to mind first was Leonardo Da Vinci — a type who was definitely more after my own heart. Unfortunately, thinking about Da Vinci made me consider all the canvases I wasn't painting. I took a big gulp of wine to drown out the regret.

"It's kind of you to think about my happiness, Maggie," I said. "But I'm still feeling a little burned. Not only by Allan's cheating, but by Stephanie, too." These three were well aware of Stephanie's accusations that I'd been inattentive to Allan's feelings over the years.

Paige said, "Stephanie will see through that skanky ho-bag soon enough. What's her name again?"

Thank you for forgetting her name, Paige. I just wish I could do the same.

"KayLeigh Rider," reminded Freddy. "Think 'Charlotte Hornets cheerleader meets Carolina Hurricanes striker.'" Most people around the country didn't know that Raleigh hosted a professional ice hockey team. It almost made me choke on my own drink imagining KayLeigh compared to one of those toothless brutes on the Hurricane squad.

Margaret put down her glass, stood, and straightened her dress as if in preamble to leave.

"Don't go," I said, perhaps a little too desperately.

"I'm not going anywhere, child. I'm just straightening. As pounds hit the hips, there is an equal and opposite reaction that causes a dress to creep."

"Sounds like Sir Isaac Newton missed his calling as a fashion designer," Freddy said. "I always heard he was queer, so he probably would have been a good designer at that."

I quickly swallowed my mouthful of wine, lest it truly spray out of my nose. "It's just so good to see you all. Honestly, I've lost a lot of friends—or so-called friends—since the separation. Allan wants me to go to an investor soirée on Saturday to celebrate ten years of Swinson Development, and I can guarantee you there won't be a person there who will be on my side."

"Oh, that can't be true," Paige said.

"If it is, at least you'll finally be able to tell your real friends from your real *estate* friends," said Margaret.

"You're right. I find myself appreciating you three more than ever. Is that sappy?"

"Here's to 'sappy!'" said Freddy, as he raised his seltzer.

"Aw," said Margaret. "I'm going to need to wipe my eyes on something, but, unfortunately, our old pal doesn't believe in drapes. Freddy, how do you ever rest your eyes in this green-house of a home? I feel like a winter tomato."

"I rise with the sun and sleep with the moon," Freddy bragged. "How do you think I stay sober? Once you get a swig of real sleep—deep, restorative sleep—you'll never want to go back." Freddy was looking directly at me. I appreciated his Zen calmness since he'd gotten clean, but I worried that giving up alcohol might make me sad and depressed all the time.

I quickly switched back to the subject of my nemesis.

"KayLeigh Rider can eat me," I said, downing the rest of my glass.

"Interesting," said Paige. Forbidden to smoke in Freddy's home, she twirled an unlit cigarette between her fingers. "May I cook something, Freddy?"

"Be my guest."

Paige moved toward the kitchen and asked, "Does Allan have a caterer for this party yet?"

"Who knows?" I said. "Allan was never much on being organized."

"If you do decide to go," said Margaret, "call me and we'll go looking for a new outfit for you."

"Hell, I need a whole new wardrobe," I sighed. "But I hate shopping for clothes."

"It shows." Off my glare, she added, "Back in college you were such the free spirit in your look and style. Our Little Hippie-Dippy Artist Chick."

"Now instead of being a hippie I'm just ... hippy," I said.

"Stop it! You've got a nice figure. It's just that the business attire you wear is so *masculinizing*."

"You're in luck," I said drolly, "because I don't really have a business anymore."

From the kitchen, Paige cried out, "I'm staring into a

Confirmed-Batchelor-Pad Fridge. Looks like it's omelets for supper."

"Watch out, kiddos," Margaret winked. "These will be the best damn omelets that ever slid over your tongue."

"Speaking of masterpieces, what are you working on these days, Freddy?" I ventured. "You haven't talked about a project in a while. Any sculpture commissions?"

"Just one. Something for the newish library at State."

"The Hunt?" asked Margaret. When Freddy confirmed with a nod, she asked: "Interior or exterior?"

"Interior," said Freddy. "Just to the left of the yellow steps."

"Ooh, I *love* those yellow steps!" Margaret gushed. "Though I do wish that foyer could be less bracing. Playful is fine, but I don't think a library should come off as industrial. And it sure doesn't help that robots fetch your books."

"Robots are cool, man," said Freddy.

"You sound like Darryl's little boy," I said. "He loves those Transformer things."

"The folks at State do like their metal and brick," Freddy added. "But since when are you a traditionalist, Margaret? I thought that you were easily bored by classical approaches."

Margaret lifted her nose. "Defy expectations all you want, just please don't stomp them to *bits*."

While the pair talked style and art, I slinked toward the kitchen, staying close to the furniture as the alcohol weaved its way through my limbs and mind. I put an arm around Paige as she cooked our omelets, pretending for a moment that I had a surplus of The Eagles' peaceful, easy feeling.

Moments later we were sitting around Freddy's stainless-steel table and eating those simple yet delicious omelets with none of us saying a word. We were quite the lackluster—make that "lack-lover"—crew. Of my three friends, one was married in name only, another apparently wouldn't be caught dead with a husband, and the third, though out of the closet, was so preoccupied with his art that he might as well be officially celibate.

I adored my friends, but I didn't want a life as a lonely heart. I wanted someone I could count on to be in my corner every single day. I knew I had that sort of loyalty in me. I just worried that no one would think me worthy enough of theirs.

"Has sex ever been as good as this meal?" Margaret asked aloud.

"There was a time I'd have traded sex for food just to make rent." Freddy had lived in the Big Apple for a time after college. Though he'd enjoyed the high life there, it had almost killed him; he ended up returning to the South to get on firmer ground.

As for me, it had been many months since I'd even thought about sex; I was too shy to share my thoughts about it now, even among friends, even with alcohol in my system.

"That was delicious, Paige," said Freddy as he finished his last bite. "You have an open invitation to break into my kitchen and cook here anytime."

"I'd be more likely to break in if you went grocery shopping once in a while."

"I'm too busy looking for components for my sculptures," he said. "Hell, I spend more time looking for parts than putting them together."

"Oh?" I said. "Have you ever heard of Needless Necessities?"

"Yep. Been going there regularly for nearly a year."

"Really? And you never told me about it?"

"I didn't think you'd care." Freddy spent much of the first decade after college urging me to return to painting, to no avail.

I told him how I'd started volunteering at the center. "When were you there last?"

"Late yesterday."

"I'd probably left by then," I said.

"I did run into one familiar face," he said. "Our neighborhood Mr. Fixit, Otis Jones."

My ears perked up. "I only told him about Needless Necessities yesterday. He doesn't waste time."

"Otis seemed eager to unload a lot of stuff—but he made a straight trade for some other material that Sally had piled in the back. Actually, I think he left with more than he brought."

"What do you think he does with all that junk?"

"I know exactly what he does with it. He sculpts."

"Really?"

"So he says. I'm going to his place in the morning to check out his work. He says he's needing some glass, and I happen to have a ton of it left over from my last project. I'm going to trade it for some rubber tubing he said he's got an abundance of."

Margaret raised an eyebrow. "Rubber tubing? Now what would you be needing that for?"

"For the library piece," Freddy said defensively. "Hush!"

"I'd be really curious to see Otis's work," I said. "I had no idea he was an artist."

"You're more than welcome to come along," Freddy said.

"What time?" I was interested in Otis's art, but I also hoped to ask him once and for all what he was up to in my neighborhood the morning after the murder. We made a plan for Freddy to pick me up at nine in the morning.

"Speaking of dates and times," Paige asked, "when did you say that anniversary party is happening?"

"This Saturday, four to seven."

"Are you going?"

I shrugged.

"You should go," Paige said, "just so everyone can be reminded who made that company what it is today."

"I'm sure Allan would find a way to make it about him," I

said. "Why are you so curious about this gathering anyway, Paige?"

"I care about anything you care about. But you didn't really answer me. Are you going?"

"I'm still thinking about it," I said.

My glass was empty. I reached for the second wine bottle, but after noting Freddy's frown, put it down again. This was his house after all. And, I didn't want to stumble and hit my head on his concrete floor.

"I'd like a seltzer with a lime, Bartender," I said. "And make it snappy."

"I'm out of seltzer," Freddy frowned. "And limes."

Margaret shook her head.

"Minimalists," she muttered.

As Freddy pulled his purple El Camino into Otis's gravel driveway the next morning, we caught a glimpse of the three-car garage behind the mobile home that must have once served as his car repair shop. Figuring it for the sculptor's studio, we walked straight to it. One of the garage's three sliding doors had been pulled up. From deep within the building came a percussion of banging.

"Otis, sir!" yelled Freddy.

The banging ceased.

"Speaking!" came a voice.

"It's Freddy, plus a friend."

"I hope it's a friendly friend. *Entrez-vous!*"

We stepped into the gloom, in the process nearly tripping over what Freddy identified as an air compressor. We wove our way past massive stacks of paint cans, jumbles of bungee cords and chains, and avalanches of metal. The floor was alternately slippery with motor oil and soft with sawdust. There was no way to tell where one pile of detritus ended and another began.

We shuffled through shadows in the direction of light until a figure was revealed bent over a large rectangular structure lying prone on saw horses. Otis was arranging and rearranging copper, rubber, and steel objects within a giant wooden frame, as if putting together a gigantic puzzle. Some of the objects had already been fused together.

"You're clearly busy," Freddy said. "We can come back another time."

"No, no," protested the old man. Stooped but spry as he moved around the horses, he was in the midst of swapping out various items, trying to determine what configurations he liked best. "I'm just tinkering, that's all." He nodded in greeting to me and asked, "How is Ms. Schmidt doing today?"

"Better. She's coming home soon," I said.

He uttered a brief "that's good" and bent down again to his work—not antagonistic, but not inviting questions, either. So, while Otis "tinkered" and Freddy observed, I ventured a look around the perimeter.

My eyes soon adjusted to the garage's ambient light, allowing me to see now what hung on the walls: massive, sculptured creations similar in size to the one Otis was working on now, mounted in frames like paintings. The extravagant mixed-media collages featured recognizable objects (a tricycle frame, an old radio, a toaster oven) intermingled with vines of metal tubing, shards of glass, and sundry odds and ends. Some of the pieces were painted; others were in their natural state. The pieces were complex, but not inscrutable. I suspected each piece would tell a story if a viewer spent enough time with it.

At some point Freddy had been drawn to the finished artwork, too. I watched as he aimed the beam of his pocket flashlight at the works on the back wall. "Seamless!" he observed with a whisper. "How does he do that?" To get a closer look, Freddy moved aside a small table and disappeared further into the hardware jungle. I watched his beam of light play like a spotlight around the former auto repair shop. There wasn't an inch of wall that didn't host a piece of art and there had to be at least twenty works in all.

With Freddy preoccupied, I returned to get a closer look at what Otis was working on. I watched him use a rubber hammer to take a wrinkle out of a sheet of tin, then use a large file to dull the metal's edges.

"Do you get all of your metal just from what people throw away?" I asked.

"Yes, but not much is made out of metal nowadays, unfortunately. Mostly plastic. I hate working with plastic. It doesn't look as good and can't be shaped as easily. Usually it just melts away. Smells something terrible." He picked up his hammer again, gave the metal a few more raps, then remarked, "So, Ms. Schmidt is coming home. Good as new?"

"She's conscious but unable to speak. The stroke affected the part of her brain that controls communication."

He shot me a quick look, as if to check whether or not I was joking. Noting my serious expression, he returned to his tin. I took this as an opening.

"Look, Otis," I said, "I'm trying to find out who killed Wanda Hightower. I know I asked you this before, but we got interrupted before you could answer. When you were collecting junk the day after Halloween, did you find anything that might be a clue?"

"I ain't found anything, okay?" I'd touched a nerve.

"Is someone bothering you, Pops?"

I turned to confront the voice's source: a thin, fit Black woman around twenty who, in the dim light, nonetheless seemed luminescent in a white sweatshirt and yellow slacks, reminding me of that old WHAM video in which everyone glowed in the dark. She wore her afro very short. Even in the relative darkness, I could see a pair of eyes none too pleased to be looking at me.

"I'm Harriet Swinson. And you?"

"I'm Augusta, Mr. Jones's granddaughter."

Otis said, "Augusta Shaw Jones was named for two colleges in Raleigh, and she refuses to attend either one of them!"

The granddaughter wasn't amused.

"You never went to college either," Augusta shot back. "And you've done just fine in life."

"I was too poor for school and too young for the war. Then Daddy died. I had to help Mama run the farm." Otis looked at me. "She doesn't have any money, but she won't let me pay her tuition."

"Because you need to conserve your cash."

"I got plenty of money," he retorted. Then, to me, he added, "Augusta is smart. Good with math."

"I won a math contest in the seventh grade—and my grandfather has never let me forget it. I don't even like math. I like computers. They do the math for you."

Otis muttered: "'Com-pu-ters,'" as if they were some mysterious, alien life form.

"And what did you say you were doing here?" Augusta asked me. I didn't like her scolding tone, but it was an honest question.

"Your grandfather has helped me with a million home projects over the years. I'm just here with my friend, Freddy. He's a sculptor who invited me to see your grandfather's work."

"And what amazing work it is," said Freddy, emerging at last from the bowels of the garage. "Hi, Augusta. I'm Freddy Tate. A pleasure to meet you." He turned again to the artist. "Otis, your work is incredible. I have so many questions. But right now, just admiration."

"His family admires him, too," the granddaughter cut in. Turning to me, she said, "Do you mind stepping over here with me for a sec?"

"Okay. Sure." I followed her several steps. When she turned to face me, her words were softer but still direct.

"Is that man an art dealer?"

"No, just an artist. I've known Freddy since college."

"I'll bet he knows a lot of dealers, though. He'll be talking to them, and they'll be coming around here."

"Has your grandfather ever sold his art?" I asked. "He certainly could."

"Oh, yes, he sold some pieces to another artist—a *con* artist. I wasn't born yet, but the way I heard it, some white man came by about twenty years ago and paid my grandfather pennies for a bunch of his work, then sold them for big money in New York. There was a lot of attention back then for so-called 'primitive' artists, especially of the 'colored' sort. You know an artist must be *really* primitive if he's Black, right? Well, I wasn't here to protect him then, but I'm here now. Any swindlers are going to have to deal with me. Pops!" she yelled, standing on her tip-toes. "What are you doing back there? Are you giving away your work again?"

"I'm just talking!" he yelled back. "Freddy is an artist, too."

"So I've heard," she said, frowning. Finished with me, she rejoined the men and proceeded to grill Freddy. "May I ask you, Mr. Tate, where can one find your own so-called art?"

I couldn't see Freddy's expression because he was silhouetted by Otis's shop light, but he managed a polite-sounding response. "I make a living off of my work, if that's what you mean, and I haven't had to steal anyone else's art to do it."

Otis said to Freddy for all of us to hear, "Don't be offended, Mr. Tate. Augusta is one of these twenty-year-old geniuses. Perhaps you've met one or two in your day."

Augusta said to no one in particular, "Gramps treats me like a child. That's because his generation is misogynistic."

Otis guffawed. "Augusta, no need to use words I don't know the meaning of."

"You know what it means," Augusta snapped. "Playing dumb won't work with me."

I couldn't tell if they were totally serious or just having fun with one another. Perhaps a little bit of both. Their affection for one another was undeniable, yet so was the tension.

"I'll go and unload your glass now," Freddy said to Otis.

"After you do that, you can load up that tubing," replied the elder craftsman. "I'll show you where I piled it."

I followed the men. While the pair left to trade the raw materials of their art, Augusta went to her own car and returned with a box of vegetables that she carried into Otis's trailer. When she came out again, she began lighting into him in the yard: "That fridge is empty. When was the last time you went grocery shopping?"

Seems all sculptors shared certain traits.

Otis shook his head. "Ain't got time. The vision must be realized." Augusta, frustrated, went to sit in her car to make a phone call. I stood in the yard and watched the men trade their materials. Judging by Otis's earlier reaction, it wouldn't pay to question him about the murder again, so I kept a distance as Otis finished helping Freddy load the tubing into the El Camino.

When the men were finished, I walked over to Augusta's Mercury to say good-bye. She dismissed me with a quick nod.

"Do you mind driving?" Freddy asked, handing me his keys.

"Sure," I said, going around to the driver's side. *If you're comfortable with a drunk behind your wheel.*

Only when both of us were inside the car did I notice he was shaking.

"What's wrong? Oh, Lord A'mighty, are you having a stroke now, too?"

"No," he said, "but I think I finally know what Eric Clapton felt the first time he heard Jimi Hendrix play guitar. Oh, my! The riffs this guy knows! Otis is a true master. He's so much better than me, Rett."

"Don't put yourself down," I scolded. "You're amazing."

"I'm not jealous. I'm just in awe. When you find art this terrific, it's your duty as a human being to help the world to see it."

I asked him what he was getting at.

"I've got to help Otis get a show," he continued. "People have to see his work. Besides, that way he could sell a few pieces and fix up his place. It's falling apart. He also needs to make room for new pieces. You saw how crowded the walls are."

"A show? Good luck. You'll have to get past his granddaughter first."

"No," he said, "you'll have to."

"Me? Why me?"

"Because you're my BFF, and that's what BFFs do. They blaze a trail."

While I definitely felt honored to be considered Freddy's 'Best Friend Forever,' I confessed to him that I never knew the responsibility that goes with the title.

Freddy didn't answer. He just looked out the window most of the way home while muttering:

"Wow, wow, wow...."

But something else bothered me more. It was something I wasn't ready to share with Freddy, because I wasn't quite certain of what I had seen.

The sculpture Otis was currently working on seemed familiar.

It appeared he was making a dragon.

PART II

POETIC CLUES

I check my thoughts like curbed steeds,
That struggle with the rein;
I bid my feelings sleep, like wrecks
In the unfathomed main.
...
Surely I was not born for this!
I feel a loftier mood
Of generous impulse, high resolve,
Steal o'er my solitude!

—*Letitia Elizabeth Landon, from "Lines of Life"*

CHAPTER 10

A NIGHT-TIME CALLER

As Freddy was dropping me off at my house, I received a text from Darryl saying his mother would be released from the hospital mid-afternoon. Quickly I put together a grocery list. Between my considerable slow-cooker expertise and Lydia's love of 1970s recipes (what couldn't a person do with Cream of Mushroom, a can of peas, and a box of Hamburger Helper?) we would get by.

I worried I wasn't doing enough to solve Wanda's murder. After my shopping trip and putting up the groceries, I picked up the book Gary Roland had loaned me, the one which discussed the poets Wanda had studied and taught.

"Understand them, and maybe you'll better understand Wanda."

Sublime Lives began with Samuel Coleridge, whose "Rime of the Ancient Mariner" still echoed from 9th grade English class. I even recalled the main point of the poem—how the Mariner had become callous, even cruel, and shot the peaceful albatross without any provocation. His disregard for life brought a deadly curse upon the men of his ship and nearly killed the Mariner, too. The experience taught the Mariner to appreciate and bless all life—even ugly life:

He prayeth well who loveth well
Both man and bird and beast.
He prayeth best who loveth well
All things both great and small;
For the dear God who loveth us,
He made and loveth all.

Reading now the biographical information on Coleridge, I learned how he had been born the youngest of ten children, felt lonely and isolated in boarding school, married for status and then divorced, and became an opium addict, which ruined his subsequent marriage. The text described an anguished creature from the cradle to the grave, and his poetry only underscored it, as in "The Pains of Sleep":

But yester-night I prayed aloud
In anguish and in agony,
Up-starting from the fiendish crowd
Of shapes and thoughts that tortured me...

I pulled out my phone to take a closer look at the poems by Wanda Hightower I'd found in the community college's literary magazine archives.

The first of the three poems had been published about fifteen years earlier, around the time of the Hightowers' divorce:

SIGHT LINES

A blind woman says she likes living alone
she knows where everything is

where she put it
where she left it

if you're sighted you find out-of-place
displaced is replaced

where did you put my love?
I have looked everywhere

I could relate to the narrator's confusion, for I wondered when Allan decided he no longer loved me—and what he did with the love I thought I'd shown him. Maybe in this poem about a lonely woman were the seeds of why Wanda eventually became a shut-in.

The second poem, published just a few years after the first, made me think about Wanda's wild yard, especially its ivy-covered porch:

WEBS

When I go out
delicate webs are strung across the path
at face height

it is a season of spiders
what a lovely way to start the day
—a brush with endeavour

The poem expressed a love of nature, getting caught in its webs—an appreciation, like Coleridge's Mariner, of "ugly" life.

The third and final poem, titled "Enough," was the longest of the three. It was published just three years earlier, its opening stanza striking me hard in the heart:

I am old enough to cry
when death snatches away someone I love

Then in the middle of the poem, the narrator (who I assumed to be Wanda) admits to feeling ashamed to cry in public and worries that if she begins to grieve it might become impossible for her to stop:

> I couldn't tell you why
> this urge to hide
>
> why grief must stay inside

The poem ended with her admitting she is...

> old enough to know
> that old is never long enough
>
> that tears will stream
> to sculpt a landscape not in view
>
> grief carries underground
> an echo, not enough of you

Wanda had lost both of her parents and felt estranged from her children to some degree. It would not be outlandish to imagine she had finally had "enough" and decided to shut the world out; that loss would echo through her life.

Could these three sensitive poems be penned by the same woman who told Skip Green to watch his back? It didn't seem possible.

What happened, Wanda?

What happened to you?

I tried to read more, but I must have dozed off. The next thing I knew my phone was vibrating. A text from Darryl: *ON MY WAY HOME WITH MOM.*

My text back: *I'LL MEET YOU THERE.*

I picked up the book, which had fallen to the floor beside me, its pages opened randomly to a poem called "Love's Philosophy" by Percy Bysshe Shelley, the husband of Mary Shelley, writer of the famous *Frankenstein*.

I quickly read the short poem. Two of its verses made me think of Darryl more than I cared to admit:

> Nothing in the world is single;
>   All things by a law divine
> In one spirit meet and mingle.
>   Why not I with thine?—
>   ...
> And the sunlight clasps the earth
>   And the moonbeams kiss the sea:
> What is all this sweet work worth
>   If thou kiss not me?

You're crushing on him, my mirror explained as I quickly drew a wet brush through my hair. *But what would he ever see in you?*

I kept an eye on Lydia's home, and when two cars rolled up, I dashed across the street. As Darryl carefully helped his mom out of the Charger, I walked over to the super-long vehicle parked just behind it, a silver Chrysler New Yorker. A woman stepped out. Unsmiling, grim, she wore her long gray hair in an intricate bun almost like a beehive do.

I introduced myself. "And, you must be Doris, Lydia's cousin."

"No blood relation. But family is family, I suppose."

Trying to maintain my smile and sound nice like my mom would do, I said, "Thank you for helping her in a pinch."

"Glad to help."

But she didn't sound all that glad.

I turned my attention to Lydia. Though weakened by her hospital stay, she was able to stand and walk with her son's help. Darryl saw us waiting for them and held out Lydia's house key for me. Inside the house, Doris wasted no time snatching from the side table the ashtray and pack of Virginia Slims. She took them into the kitchen, where she plopped them both into the trash.

Darryl led Lydia into the house and settled her in her favorite living room chair.

"It's so good to see you, friend," I said with some nervousness. "I was worried about you."

Lydia made movements with her mouth as if to respond, then shook her head in defeat. I traded a knowing look with Darryl.

"Will you come outside with me and help me get the rest of Mom's things?" he asked.

"Sure."

When we were outside, Darryl frowned. "She's so frustrated that she can't communicate."

"It must be awful. Especially for someone as expressive as your mother."

"'Expressive' is the nice way to put it. 'Crabby' is the word I'd use. I'm not trying to poke fun, but she's got a long road ahead. I still think that I ought to move in with her."

"But Charlie has such a good routine where you're living now. You don't want to shake that up, do you? You live so close to his school."

"And his mom. He can see her most every day. She wasn't a great wife, but she's a good mother."

"You don't have to worry. I'll be here to back up Doris."

"You mean *Boring* Doris?"

"Well, the nickname does seem to suit her," I said. *Along with "bitter," "cold," "wretched."*

"I can't thank the two of you enough."

"Lydia is good company for me."

"She'll have rehab most days. Maybe you can get her out occasionally, give her a break from Doris."

"I'll be glad to. If she feels up to it, I'll even take her to Needless Necessities. Trust me, if anyone is going to get your mother talking again, it's those Qrazy Qwilters."

I returned around five with a pot of Mississippi Roast. Doris left to be home before dark. I watched my friend closely. It was excruciating seeing Lydia struggle with language, the words seeming to get stuck even before they got started.

I so wanted to ask her about the morning she had the stroke, especially what happened during that visit from Otis—what, if anything, had upset her enough to trigger the medical event. But posing a question to Lydia right now seemed about as worthwhile as interrogating an infant.

Lydia was ready by seven for bed. Once she had settled, I went downstairs to grab my phone and noticed I had missed a call from Stephanie. I listened nervously to the message, her pained monotone:

"It's me. I wanted to see if you're going to Dad's party. It would really mean a lot to him. Okay, Bye." Though her message dripped with passive aggression, this was the closest I'd gotten to a conversation with my daughter in weeks, and I wasn't going to let an opportunity to talk with her pass by.

She picked up on the fifth ring. "Hey." Like her voicemail, she sounded just this side of comatose.

"Hi, sweetheart," I said. "How's school?"

"Fine, I guess." She cut straight to the chase. "Are you going to the anniversary party?"

"Sounds like you talked with your dad." I thought it was poor form for Allan to use Stephanie as leverage to draw me to the event. "How's he doing?"

"Oh, Mom, don't act like you actually care."

"I was married to your father for twenty years, Stephanie. Of course I care."

"You could have fooled me," she mumbled. I wondered if she'd been drinking. If so, I was in no position to judge.

"Did you get my message about Wanda Hightower?" I asked.

"Yeah, that sounds really messed up," she said. "Do they know who did it?"

"We're still trying to figure that out."

"'We?'"

"Well, the police, and a few of us who have theories about the crime."

"I see." I could almost hear her rolling her eyes.

Feeling a little catty all of a sudden, I asked, "How's KayLeigh? Did she show you any of her new plastic surgery?"

"KayLeigh has the perfect bod, Mom. She doesn't need surgery."

"Good for her," I said. "She didn't have to spend too much money to win a Daddy Warbucks."

"Did you just call me in order to insult KayLeigh? Because that's not cool."

"No," I said. "I really wanted to talk with you." *Insulting KayLeigh was just a bonus.*

"Mom, honestly, it's not like KayLeigh caused the break-up of your marriage. Cheating is a symptom of larger problems."

"For the record, I don't spend a lot of time thinking about KayLeigh's role in all this. Your father is an adult. He knew what he was doing. If he had wanted to work on any of our marital problems, he could have."

"He just didn't see a lot of hope, Mom."

"So that lets him off the hook?"

She was quiet for a second. "Please don't make me have to choose sides."

That stung, for it was plain to me she *had* chosen sides. But the last thing I wanted right now was to show my worst face, which I was totally doing.

"I don't want you to choose sides, Stephanie," I said. "I'm sorry. Maybe we should talk about something else."

"There is nothing else," she sighed.

That stopped me in my tracks for a moment.

"I'm so sorry, Honey," I said finally. "I didn't want this to be your future. But you have to believe me when I say I didn't ask for this either."

She didn't affirm me in that, but she didn't argue with me either.

"I gotta go," she said finally. "Let me know when you decide about the party. I'm going to be there, to support the family business."

"Okay," I said. "Good luck with your classes. Love you."

"Love you," she mumbled, and hung up.

I felt like crying. I felt like screaming. One cancelled out the other, and for the longest time I just stared despairingly at the gas fireplace's low flame.

My cell phone rang. I didn't recognize the number, but I picked it up anyway. Maybe it was a robocall, someone I could cuss at.

"Harriet?" the voice said. "This is Cynthia Roberts."

"Cynthia? Are you okay?" She was breathing so hard, I

wondered if she was having a medical emergency. "You sound agitated."

"I'm sorry I treated you so badly earlier. May I come over and talk with you?"

"Of course. I'm staying next-door at Lydia Schmidt's. Is something wrong?"

Her next words were so loud and manic that I had to hold the phone a foot from my ear. "I just have to talk with someone! I have blood on my hands—and I can't get it off!"

We agreed she should come over right away. After we'd hung up, I immediately called Darryl and left him a voicemail:

"Darryl, this is Rett. Cynthia Roberts is walking over to the house. She called and told me she has 'blood on her hands.' Would you call in the next few minutes to check up on me? Just trying to be careful. Bye."

It had begun to rain, yet Cynthia wore no wrap and under the porch light she looked as vulnerable as a little girl—who just happened to be six feet tall and graying.

"Oh, Cynthia, you're chilled to the bone," I said. I grabbed a blanket from the hallway closet to put around her while she sat on the hearth in front of the warming flames.

"Thank you," she murmured.

"Would you rather sit on the couch?"

Her blonde-gray hair was matted to her scalp, and her fair skin looked as thin as an onion's. She appeared so much older than I remembered her. I would have offered her something to drink, but her call had been so desperate, I was impatient to hear what she had to say.

"I'll be fine." She took a corner of the blanket to wipe the rain off her face. "I need to get this off my chest." It sounded as if a boulder were weighing down her lungs.

I pulled up a chair directly across from her. I wondered if I should open the memo app on my phone. "*Hey, Siri, please record murder confession.*"

"I don't know if you knew this," she began, "but Wanda became my advisor at State when I was a graduate student and she was a young professor there."

I played dumb. "I'd heard she taught there long ago, but I didn't know you were there at the same time."

Cynthia nodded. "Shakespeare wasn't actually her concentration, but the department's only Shakespearean scholar was on sabbatical, and I really needed someone to advise me that year or my Ph.D. would be delayed. On top of helping me, she was teaching a full class-load and advising two other graduate students. She was just a phenomenal scholar and human being."

"I'm sure her death was a shock," I said, more curious than ever as to what was weighing on the veteran professor's mind.

She closed her eyes and took a breath. "I promise this is about Wanda, but first I have to tell you something else that happened." I could hear the pilot light among the fake logs, which sounded like a rocket taking off.

She continued. "There was a party among the graduate students. We were celebrating the fact that one of the graduates had passed her orals. Everyone had left except me and the girl who had hosted the party. I'd had a couple of drinks, so she said I could sleep on her couch. She went upstairs and closed her bedroom door. I fell asleep. At some point later I awoke. There was a man on top of me with his hand over my mouth. I immediately recognized him as one of my fellow graduate students."

"Oh, Cynthia! That's dreadful! Who was this?"

"His name was Dennis Smith. I never liked him—no one

did. He hit on all the female graduate students but none would have him. I guess that night he saw his opportunity. He must have pretended to leave and then hid indoors. After he raped me, he said if I told anyone he would just deny it and tell everyone what a slut I was."

She fell silent and stared past me.

"Cynthia. I'm so sorry this happened to you."

My neighbor closed her eyes, remembering again. "For about a week I didn't tell anyone. I just tried to pretend nothing had occurred. But Wanda picked up that something was wrong. She pressed me until I broke down and told her the whole story. It was painful to bring it into the light, but I was so grateful to be able to confide in someone. I went from feeling like a victim to feeling very angry. Next, I did something that would have terrible consequences. One evening I crept into the graduate student office and—"

"Oh, Lord! You killed him?"

"No—but don't think I didn't think about it. I'd read so much Shakespeare—my thesis focused mainly on *Hamlet*—that I did the next best thing. I stole his manually typed dissertation, took it into some woods, and..."

"And...?"

"I burned it."

"You didn't!"

"I did! His only typed copy. Five years of his precious work, up in smoke! Remember, this was back in the very early eighties before computers and word processors had really come into vogue. Well, it felt satisfying, I'll tell you that. But then the proverbial you-know-what hit the fan. Another grad student thought they saw me take the manuscript, and I was brought before the English department chair. I was standing before his desk, ready to confess everything when the office secretary stepped in and passed him a note. He read it and sent me out of his office. In that moment I had no idea what the note had said, only that I'd been momentarily spared."

I nodded. "Go on."

"Anyway, I had become frightened of what Dennis might do at that point, so I went to the coast and stayed at a friend's house. When I returned a week later, I learned that Wanda had been fired. That's what the note had been about. It was Wanda confessing to having destroyed the manuscript. She told the chairman that the dissertation was so terrible, it just had to be burned."

"Wanda took the fall for you? But that's—"

"Crazy? Yes. Believe me, when I heard she'd been fired, I was shocked, and a little bit frantic. I found her at home, expecting her to be upset with me. Quite the opposite. She was just so serene and at peace with her act—'a grand gesture' as she later characterized it. I told her she couldn't throw away her career like that, that I was going to turn myself in, but she insisted that I should let matters lie. 'You've suffered enough,' she said. '*You've* got a terrific career ahead of you.' Rett, I just broke into tears and thanked her. But why did I let her take the blame?" Cynthia put her face in her hands and sobbed into the blanket I'd given her.

I waited for her to calm down a bit before asking, "But why feel guilty about it now? You said that she seemed at peace with her decision."

"Yes, but what if Dennis finally found a way to get his revenge on her? In that case I'm no better than Lady Macbeth." She looked at her hands. "'Out, damned spot!'"

Now I remembered the words Cynthia had used when I was in her house. "*Out, out!*" She'd been talking to herself—not to me—as if she were a character in one of Shakespeare's plays and had been in the middle of her own psychological emergency when I'd asked her to call 9-1-1.

Cynthia suspected she'd fueled an actual murder, and for

good reason. If I had spent years on my Ph.D. thesis only to have someone destroy it, I would be upset, too—and anyone who raped a woman was definitely capable of killing. Here was the strongest motive yet for Wanda's murder.

"After being fired at State," I asked, "how did Wanda get the job at the community college?"

"She said she had a close friend who vouched for her, and by then she had already won a prestigious teaching award. I went on to finish my degree and landed a position where I was earning more money and acclaim than poor Wanda ever could at a two-year college. Nonetheless, she stayed in contact with me and continually reminded me of my worth. She even called me a few years later when a house came available in Woodmont. She said she would be delighted if I lived near her. Henceforth, we had a nice friendship made up mainly of long walks once a month or so. I guess I felt responsible for her. And, also, I felt safer with her nearby as a friend. But in the end, I wasn't able to keep *her* safe."

"I've been trying to figure out what made her turn so angry last year. Any ideas?"

"We hadn't talked in so long. I spent a sabbatical in England last school year, and we lost touch. When I returned to the States in August, it was a mad dash to get ready for classes this fall. I reached out a couple times but she didn't get back to me. I didn't even know she had become a shut-in."

"You remember the incident with her yard, though."

"Vaguely. I remember giving some money for the cause, but I just—I just didn't have the time to think much about it. Now I wish I had tried harder to see her."

"What about Dennis Smith?" I asked. "Are you sure he wouldn't have figured out who really burned his dissertation?"

"I'm not sure. When I came back from the beach, he had withdrawn from the university. All these years I've been afraid to look him up. If he was still in Raleigh, I just didn't want to know."

"He needs to be questioned as to his whereabouts at the time of the murder," I said. "If he were found, would you want to be notified?"

"I would," she said after a pause. "And if it turns out he hurt Wanda..." Cynthia gritted her teeth and made a face so fierce in the firelight I actually drew back in my chair, "...then God help him!"

CHAPTER 11

CONFRONTATION

Not one minute after Cynthia left, the front door flew open. It was Darryl, who, upon hearing my voice message about Cynthia, had called my phone. When I had not answered, he rushed to check on me in person.

I was touched by his protectiveness. "You didn't have to do that," I said. "I'm so sorry I alarmed you. I got carried away with what Cynthia was telling me and forgot to even look at my phone."

"It's okay. I was headed home anyway," he said. But I could tell he had been worried.

We sat together in the den where I related to him my full conversation with Cynthia, including the fact that she had given me the name of her rapist and, with it, permission to share it with the police.

"Can you arrest this guy and prosecute him for rape?" I asked.

"It would be difficult," he said. "Even though the statute of limitations never runs out on rape, if she didn't report it initially, there isn't a rape kit with DNA evidence that would tie him to the crime."

"Still," I said, "I think Cynthia might be ready to confront her assailant after all these years."

"I'll try to track him down," Darryl said. "Honestly, it's the only decent motive for this murder we've found."

In a word, this detective seemed stumped.

"What are you thinking?" I asked.

"Unless this Dennis Smith pans out as the killer, I'm thinking of this as a random murder. Someone hopped up on drugs or a Devil worshipper who just wanted to kill someone on Halloween."

"Do you run into many Satanists in Raleigh, Detective?"

"No, but there is the proximity to the cemetery, someone spotted dressed as a dragon—or a demon, perhaps." He shrugged. "Otis still keeps popping into my mind as well. I'd still like to know what he and Mom talked about the morning after the murder."

"Does he have an alibi?"

"He told me he was working alone in his shop. So, no alibi."

"It's quite the studio." I told him about my visit that morning. "Deep down you don't actually suspect Otis of murder, do you?"

He shrugged. "His name was scribbled hurriedly on a piece of paper, theoretically by the victim. He was found poking around behind her house the next morning. Now he's evasive whenever we try to ask him about it. It's at least worth noting."

"You were going to meet with Wanda's daughter today, weren't you?"

"She was too tired from her flight back to Charlotte to drive to Raleigh, so we talked by phone again. Angela said her mom had become more secluded in her home over the past few months. She thinks her mother had gone a little crazy—Angela's word—and that her mental health had been deteriorating long before the neighbors' plan to spruce up her yard, even before she was forced to retire. She said Wanda refused to see a medical doctor, much less a psychotherapist. She would call her mom and try to chat, but her mom wasn't that talkative. A couple months ago, Angela just gave up coming to Raleigh at all."

I nodded, knowing quite well how fraught mother-daughter relationships could be.

Darryl continued, "There was one thing Wanda would talk to her daughter about. A few weeks before her death, she really started sounding paranoid and talked about some 'imp' trying to harass her. I asked what an imp was, and Angela said it was a trickster sort of character, a mythical creature who was up to no good. Said her mom was sometimes old-fashioned in how she talked."

"Did she connect this 'imp' to a particular person?" I remembered the sign from the makeover. "What about the neighborhood 'elves' who fixed up her yard?"

"No, the daughter just assumed the imp was part of her mom's paranoid imagination."

"How sad," I said. "The brain sure is a complicated organ."

"Speaking of, thank you for watching after Mom. I don't know what she'd do without you—what I'd do without you."

He looked at me admiringly. Was it platonic adoration, or was there some sexual attraction mixed in? I didn't know how to respond to his praise, and perhaps he read something troubling in my expression.

"How are you doing, by the way?" he asked.

The vulnerable moment I'd shared at the kitchen table Saturday night threatened to come back again in full force. I held steady. "With everything going on, I think it's good for me to stay busy. Working for Swinson Development was a way to avoid so much that was emotionally uncomfortable or difficult. I feel as though helping your mom—and helping with this case—keeps me connected."

And I haven't thought of alcohol all day, I could have added.

Darryl nodded. "Come the weekend you'll get a break. Charlie and I will stay here with her."

I could have told him the truth, that the weekends were the hardest for me. I don't know what caused me to not to share this and so much more. A snatch of Wanda's poem tickled my memory:

> I couldn't tell you why
> this urge to hide...

Darryl said, "Tomorrow Mom has her first appointment at the rehab center. Doris will take her. Maybe you can talk to Mom and persuade her to behave?"

"I'll do my best."

"Your best is better than most."

He stood, prompting me to do the same. I thought we might kiss when he stepped toward me, but at the last second his face turned and he provided a warm, appreciative hug instead. I tried to tell myself that the home of his mother was the last place I'd want a first kiss from a man.

We tell ourselves things like that.

I awoke the next morning with Cynthia's story gnawing at me. I didn't want to wait for Darryl to locate him, so I would try to find him myself.

Googling, I found no English professors in America with his name and age. I called Cynthia and pressed for more details. She remembered one thing. "His grandfather owned a travel agency in Raleigh. Not sure if it's still in business."

Were any at all? Turns out a few still were, with one of them bearing the name of Smith Travel. I put on a long polyester skirt and a white blouse with lots of ruffles, overdid the makeup, and planted my reading glasses on my nose. My diabolical mirror was delighted to portray me at least fifteen years older, a viable contemporary of Dennis Smith.

Smith Travel was empty of customers. I took a seat in front of a desk commanded by a plain-looking female not long out of college.

"I'm so glad you all are still operating," I said. "You don't hear about travel agencies much anymore."

"Yep," she said, dismissively. "How can I help you today?" She spoke super loudly, as if I were hard of hearing. Did I look *that* old?

I told her I was hoping to take a trip to Italy. While she gathered the relevant brochures from a file cabinet, I casually asked, "How's Dennis these days? It's been ages since I knew him in school. Did he ever move back to Raleigh?"

"*Uncle* Dennis?" asked the woman. "Yeah, he moved back a little while ago." Judging by her tone, she wasn't delighted about it.

"I'd love to see him," I said breezily. "He was such a character, that Dennis. What's he up to?"

"He bartends," the niece said. "Just a sec. I'll find out where." She went to the back, presumably to confer with someone. While she was gone, I let my eyes graze over her desk, out of boredom more than anything else. On her notepad, one handwritten note stood out:

Rev. Thompson trip — cancel WH ticket and tour.

The Thompsons seemed like just the type of old-timers who would still reach out to a travel agency for a trip to D.C., which was just a five-hour drive from Raleigh. I wondered why they would skip the White House tour, but even I had to admit that I had lately gotten pretty sick of politics—especially the complaining and rabble-rousing that (mostly) men did over the radio, so-called pundits mercilessly ripping perfect strangers a new one without a second's thought. I wondered if a D.C. trip would feel like a nostalgic escape from all that wretchedness— or if it might land one in the center of that crucible.

The girl returned from the back. "I couldn't remember the name of the place. It's the Pelican. Near the courthouse." The coolness in her voice was unmistakable.

"Do you think he's working tonight?"

"If he's not, he'll probably be there as a customer."

I thanked her for the brochures and told her I'd think about booking.

Back at my car, I paused to phone Cynthia and let her know I'd found the man who had assaulted her so many years ago.

"He's a bartender now?" she said.

"You sound surprised."

"I always figured he had taken his research to another college and reconstructed his dissertation. That's what I would have done."

There was a silence as each of us fruitlessly contemplated what it would be like to be a man who raped women. Finally, she asked, "Are you going to tell the police you found him?"

"I believe I have to."

She became quiet again. Was she reliving that whole terrible experience right now in her mind?

"I want to be there when he's confronted," she said. "I want to look him in the eye."

"Do you expect him to confess to raping you?"

"I'm sure he'll never do that. No, I want to make sure he didn't kill Wanda. I think if I can see his reaction when she's mentioned, then I'll know."

"I'll see what I can do," I said.

I called Darryl and told him I'd tracked down Dennis Smith. He was suitably impressed, but he wasn't crazy about the idea of including Cynthia in an interrogation. "I should question him alone. If he was violent once, he can be violent again."

"But Cynthia is adamant she wants to confront him. I'm afraid she'll try to do it alone if you don't bring her along with you."

He sighed. "I don't like it."

"What if we confronted him in public? Certainly he'd behave himself then."

Darryl thought about it. "I can't keep an eye on him and her at the same time. But if you come along and make sure Cynthia doesn't get too overheated, I'm willing to give it a try. We'll question him at the bar. First sign of things getting out of hand and I'll need you to remove her from the situation. Can you play by those rules?"

"I can. Should we go tonight? Who will stay with your mom while we're gone?"

"I think I can get Doris to stay late just this once. It's driving alone at night she doesn't like, so I'll escort her back home to Garner myself afterward."

"You're a prince," I said.

"I just hope I'm not making the biggest mistake of my career," he said before hanging up.

Speaking of biggest mistakes, I was about to pull out of the travel agency parking lot when a car pulled in beside me. It was Allan, driving his Porsche—an indulgent purchase he'd made right after our separation last Christmas.

We had talked a few times since then but never for very long. I usually became too angry for words and would end the conversation. If he wanted to talk, dropping by my house would have been more direct—but Allan was never direct. He must have really been feeling desperate about me coming to the anniversary party if he was going to take advantage of a chance encounter to confront me like this.

My mind raced through the options. If I did agree to attend the party, it would be half for my benefit. We had not yet decided how to split up the company's assets in the divorce, and it made sense to bring in some additional business in the meantime. But attending might signal approval of his relationship with KayLeigh. That made my stomach turn.

On the other hand, skipping the party would hurt the company my daughter would one day inherit, allowing Allan and KayLeigh to drive even more of a wedge between me and Stephanie. *"See? If your mother really cared about you, she'd help the business,"* and so on.

I'd have to see where the conversation went. We rolled our windows down and spoke from our cars.

"What's up, Allan?"

"I was just driving through town when I saw your car here. Are you taking a trip soon?"

"That's none of your concern." Then I suddenly remembered I was dressed like my mother, which only made me more irritated to be talking with him. "What do you want?"

"Did you get my message about the party on Saturday?"

"I did. And Stephanie called to lobby on your behalf. Thanks for putting her up to that. It wasn't awkward or anything."

He let my sarcasm blow right by. "It would really help if you could be there, Rett. The usual suspects are coming. If they don't see you there, they might not ante up for the over-50 project."

"Maybe you should have thought of that before you made KayLeigh your under-26 project."

"Rett, this isn't about that."

"Everything is about that," I said, borrowing a line from our daughter.

His face reddened. "This is about the business and about the legacy we'll be leaving Stephanie. If you want to dissolve the company—"

"I never said that."

"Well, that's what's going to happen if you don't take some interest in it."

"Allan, I can't do day-to-day business with you anymore. You want me to pretend as though nothing has happened. You might be good at that sort of denial, but I'm not."

Allan looked like a caged animal in his little sports car. He would rather be anywhere than right here, arguing.

"I get it," he said, "but will you just come to this party as a favor to Stephanie? After Saturday, we'll come to terms about the business and figure out what your role will be moving forward."

"Will KayLeigh be at the party?" I asked, knowing the answer.

"Of course. She's the lead agent on the project. But you don't have to talk to her. To be honest, she's not eager to talk with you either."

"I'll bet she isn't."

"Please, Rett. It's just for an hour or two. This is the new reality, whether—"

"'—whether I like it or not.' I know. But why does the reality have to be something that you happen to love and I happen to despise?"

He squirmed in his bucket seat. Just beyond his car, a teenage couple left the fro-yo place that sat next to the travel agency. A quick flash of memory placed me with Allan on our college campus. He was walking me to my dorm after a keg party, making sure I was safe.

How could I ever move on from this sadness?

There was only one way.

"I'll attend the party, Allan. Happy?" *By all means, Allan must always be* happy.

"Thank you, Rett," he said. "It's going to be a nice one. We even got Paige Kirkland to cater it. We'd been struggling to find someone, but she'd heard about it somehow and offered us a great price for old times."

Interesting. I wondered what my restauranteur friend was cooking up.

"See you there," he said. "And thanks. I really appreciate it. So will Stephanie."

He sped off. Only after his car had left the parking lot did it dawn on me that he hadn't said a word about Wanda or expressed a single concern about my safety in our old neighborhood.

In my collegiate memory, I watched Allan from my second-floor dorm room window, walking away.

Prior versions of the Pelican had included an Irish Pub and a generic sports bar. This newest iteration had a 1980s theme, a replica of the world that Dennis would have inhabited when he was in graduate school. I wondered if it also felt to Cynthia like going back in time—to the worst night of her life.

As we entered the bar, I could tell her breathing was already quickening.

We waited just inside the doorway while Darryl went to talk with the manager, a man in his late twenties who was barely old enough to remember the Clinton years, much less the Reagan eighties. Darryl returned a moment later. "The manager is looking up the time sheets to see if Dennis was working Halloween night."

He turned to Cynthia. "Our friend is in the back on break.

Before we go back there to talk with him, I need to search your purse. I saw an episode of a crime show in which . . . well, just let me look in your purse, please."

Cynthia handed it to him. "Don't worry. I've already hurt him sufficiently," she said.

Darryl, finished looking through the purse, handed it back. "Okay. Let's go."

The manager ushered us behind the bar, through the kitchen, and into a small staff room. Sitting at a table drinking coffee sat a thin man with bad skin, a gray-blond beard, and baggy eyes. The man's doleful expression didn't waver when he briefly met my gaze. But, upon noticing Cynthia, the eyes flashed recognition.

The three of us stopped inches from his table. I suppose he could have made a run for it toward the back door, but Dennis Smith seemed like he'd already been sitting there a hundred years.

"I'm Detective Schmidt, Raleigh Police. I guess you can guess why I'm here."

"Nope," he said, his response sounding like a dare.

"A woman was attacked. I presume you know who I'm talking about."

"Lots of women are attacked. It's a terrible thing."

"The woman I'm talking about supposedly destroyed something you had written back in graduate school. You remember that?"

"Oh, I remember *that*." Since that initial glance at Cynthia, he had not looked at her again. But I did. Cynthia's teeth were clenched, her eyes wide and angry, her breath more rapid with every second in Dennis's presence.

"What do you remember, Mr. Smith?"

"That was a long time ago. Why in the world would the law care about that now?"

"Because the woman I'm talking about was killed four days ago on Halloween."

It was nearly imperceptible, but I'm certain I saw Dennis glance at Cynthia as if to double-check she was actually alive. This told me two things: *that he had known for years that Cynthia was the one who burned his manuscript—and that he didn't know Wanda was dead.*

Dennis, quickly recovered, seemed to put the facts together in his mind. "I was working Halloween. My manager can confirm it."

"Time sheets say you were here, but I'll have to call your co-workers to see if they can vouch for you," Darryl said. "By the way, you haven't asked me why these two ladies are here."

Dennis Smith nodded toward Cynthia. "This one has had it out for me for years."

"How dare you!" shouted Cynthia, her voice shaking. "You raped me!"

Dennis snorted. Darryl remained rooted. This situation was highly unusual, and he was taking a big chance to let it play out.

Cynthia practically spat each word that came next: "I was the one who burned your dissertation, as if you hadn't already figured it out! It felt wonderful while I was doing it, and I do not regret it!"

"It don't matter who done what," Dennis said, setting his jaw and looking away. "One crazy bitch is just the same as another." *Had this cretin really been an English major once?* As if pleasantly surprised by what he'd said, Dennis smiled, showing a mouth of bad dental work. "Detective, she just confessed to destruction of private property. Maybe you should arrest her."

"Rape is a thousand times worse," I snapped.

Darryl asked, "Mr. Smith, did you rape this woman?"

Dennis looked Cynthia up and down. "I wouldn't think of touching her."

"A fie upon you!" the Shakespeare scholar roared, taking a step closer to the table, as if in the next move she would try to reach across it and grab him.

"It's okay," I whispered. Cynthia allowed me to back her away from the table, but her body remained wired, ready for a fight.

"Mr. Smith," Darryl said, "I don't work this beat, but I know the officers who do. They'll be keeping an eye on you. We do not abide bartenders who wait for women to drink too much and then take advantage. Do you get my drift?"

Dennis shrugged again.

The detective turned to us. "Let's go," he said.

I put an arm around Cynthia and led her outside. Darryl stayed behind to talk with the manager.

In the parking lot again, Cynthia raised two fists to the sky and shouted to the stars, "Thank you, thank you, thank you! I've been waiting nearly thirty years to confront that beast!" I watched Cynthia's rapid breath blowing in the cold air as she looked up at the stars, her expression radiating bliss.

Darryl emerged from the bar a moment later, frowning. "Cynthia, if you were worried that Dennis had something to do with Wanda's death, I think you can put that worry to rest. He definitely seemed confused when I mentioned Wanda's murder. Plus, I just spoke on the phone with three co-workers who say they worked at the bar with him on Halloween from four until closing."

"I'm so grateful for what you did tonight, Detective," Cynthia said as we all got into Darryl's car. "Thank you a million times over."

"I'm glad you found it helpful," Darryl muttered, clearly still uncomfortable with his decision to stage the confrontative scene.

"You were very kind to do that," I told Darryl once Cynthia

had disappeared inside her home for the night. "That's not something that most women ever get to do safely."

"I may have overstepped my authority," he said nervously. "Honestly, I don't know if I feel good about it. What if he harasses her now?"

"Dennis has long known that Cynthia was the one who burned his manuscript. Besides, I'm quite certain you put the fear of God into him," I said. "At least no one died tonight."

"Sometimes you know just the right thing to say," he smiled.

We were standing just outside his car. Doris, having seen us arrive, was inside gathering her things. Darryl and I might have been sixteen trying to wrap-up a date. The air had grown bitterly cold, but I didn't want the evening to end just yet. *What is all this sweet work worth / If thou kiss not me?*

"Who's your top suspect now?" I asked, trying to draw out the moment.

"Now that Mr. Smith has an alibi? Nobody. Everybody."

"But if you had to wager?"

"Lacking an individual with a strong personal motive, I'm still betting it was a crime of opportunity. Some sadist acting on psychopathic compulsion."

The whisper of sweet nothings...

But I could tell Darryl was distracted by his own frustration with the case. There wasn't going to be a moment tonight.

The cold finally nudged us inside where we found Doris standing just inside the door, wearing her coat and holding her purse.

"Is Lydia in bed?" I asked.

"Since seven o'clock. She was deathly tired."

"Bored to tears" was probably more like it.

"I really do not like driving at night, Darryl," Doris said.

"I'll lead you all the way home, Doris. Thank you for staying late this one time."

As Doris stepped onto the porch, Darryl rolled his eyes for my benefit and followed her out.

The second they were gone, the door to the master bedroom opened and a head peeked through the crack.

I said, "She's gone. You can come out now."

Lydia beelined for her cigarettes, which she'd fished from the garbage and stashed under the cushion of her favorite chair.

"Excuse me?" I said. "No, ma'am." She tried to protest, but when she couldn't get a word out, she gave up and handed me the pack. I felt awful removing this long-held pleasure from her life, but quitting cigarettes had been her doctor's orders.

"I know you're bored, Lydia. Listen, tomorrow I'll come by and take you quilting. You'll be out of Doris's hair for hours."

She clapped her hands and, much like Cynthia had done, raised them high as if receiving God's infinite grace.

A couple of hours later Lydia was long asleep. I was nearly so when my cell phone rang. It was Darryl. He apologized for calling so late, but said he figured I'd want to hear the news. Thanks to leads generated by the newspaper story, police had finally tracked down the person dressed as a dragon who was seen by the young trick-or-treater in our alleyway.

Originally, said Darryl, they didn't know he was the exact masquerader they were hoping to find, but when the cops approached him for questioning, the young man—who is eighteen—made a run for it and tossed some drugs away. They tackled and arrested him.

"His name is Trent Jones, and he's a relative of Otis's. And he's got a bigger problem than a blister pack of Oxycontin. We also matched his fingerprints to some prints that were found in the Hightower home."

The detective's voice was upbeat.

"I think we may have caught our killer."

CHAPTER 12
PRIME SUSPECT

"What makes you think he's the murderer?" I asked.

"We have multiple witnesses who saw him wearing a dragon costume Halloween night, hanging out near his girlfriend's place after dark. The girlfriend says he was with her all afternoon, but she's been picked up for shoplifting a number of times. We think she's covering for him."

"You said he's related to Otis?"

"It's not a close relation—he's the nephew of Otis's first cousin—but he sort of looks up to Otis as an uncle and says he has accompanied him on a few handyman projects."

"What makes you think he killed Wanda? I mean, what could have been the motive for someone eighteen?"

"We think it might have to do with prescription drugs," Darryl said. "Mr. Jones hangs with members of a known ring that breaks into homes and steals opioids like oxycodone, then sells them on the black market."

"Did Wanda even take opioids?"

"We're trying to discover that. We didn't find any after the murder, so they could have been stolen. Maybe she found Dragon Boy poking around in her medicine cabinet. If she was planning to take a shower, that might explain the rubber swim cap. Thinking she recognized him from an earlier meeting, he panicked and chased her to the front porch where he killed her."

"How would they have met?"

"Trent said that Otis took him on some jobs in Woodmont a few days before the murder. Don't know yet if Wanda's home was one of them. I'm going to try to question him some more here in a bit."

"Where did you find his prints? I thought you told me you didn't find any."

"It was after you and I talked that night. They were found the next morning on the fireplace mantle—which, if you remember what Eleanor Foster told us, is carved like a dragon."

I was silent as I remembered how Otis had been working on a dragon sculpture. *Just a coincidence?*

"It may be circumstantial," said Darryl, "but right now, everything points to Trent."

"Are you going to charge him with murder?"

"Our DA would like at least one more piece of strong evidence, something else to tie him to the scene at the time of the murder. We've got a warrant to search his home for the dragon costume—his parents' home, that is, as he's still in high school. Maybe something on that costume will turn up that we can connect to the crime scene. At least for now he's being held on the drug charge. Because he tried to run, bail is set really high, so for now he's still in the city jail."

Darryl added, "Please don't tell anyone about this arrest yet. It could jeopardize the investigation. I just wanted *you* to know in case you were still worried about a killer at large."

I should have been comforted, but somehow Darryl's news made me anxious. It took another two hours—and two glasses of wine—for my mind to settle and allow me to sleep.

About a dozen ladies constituted the Qrazy Qwilters, ranging in age from late twenties to nearly 90. The leader of the Qrazies was a woman named Pleasance Miles, who took over the group when her mother, the group's founder, passed away just a few years ago at age 100.

It was Pleasance who liked to quip: "We Qrazy Qwilters are a tight-knit group."

When Lydia and I walked in the door, it seemed like all the quilters came running our way. They were like Heaven's welcome wagon. Lydia was showered in hugs and kisses. Her normally crabby face turned radiant through the process.

"She's delighted to be back," I told the group. "She just can't tell you so."

"Oh, we can tell!" said Pleasance.

"Lydia doesn't have to say a thing," said another member, Susan. "Pleasance talks enough for all of us."

"Watch it, Susie Q!" warned Pleasance. "I have the power to banish anyone on the grounds of excessive sassitivity!"

"'Physician, heal thyself,'" Susie retorted.

They helped Lydia to her usual seat. Immediately her lap was filled by a moving ball of fur: Q.T. the cat. Q.T. stood for . . . well, there was a perpetual debate about that. Some said Q.T. stood for Quality Time. Others said it was short for "Cutie." The quilting group, of course, insisted Q.T. was short for QuilT. It didn't matter; she was just Q.T. She was primarily white with gray tufts, super soft, and so cuddlesome that you'd need a heart of bricks to resist her kindness. She let you pet her, carry her, cuddle her, set her on your lap. She just loved people.

I intended to go work at the paints station. But, first I wanted to check in with Sally, who I found in deep discussion with Wo, the performance artist.

"I have just one question," Sally was asking Wo in a perturbed voice. "Is this one going to involve menstruation?"

I didn't know whether to keep eavesdropping or run away. But Wo stomped away first, turning on one heel and returning to the register where there was a line of customers awaiting attention.

"What was that all about?" I asked Sally. "Or do I really want to know?"

Sally sighed. "Wo wants to hold another one of her ground-breaking art performances here at Needless Necessities and invite the public."

"What's wrong with that?"

"I guess you haven't heard about the last one?"

"Washington said something about it, now that I recall. But he recommended I ask you for more details. I think he called it a 'girl thing'."

"That's because her installation was a family of mannequins clothed entirely in used tampons and maxi-pads."

"Excuse me?"

"Let me read you the review in *The Independent*. It's on the wall where we keep all the center's news—the good, the bad, and the outlandish."

I followed her to the front desk area. She took a framed article from the wall and began to read aloud: "'*Wo K.'s piece is a commentary on how society puts many aspects of family on a pedestal but denigrates the biological processes that literally give rise to family. Wearing surgical gloves and a mask, the artist rummaged through the trash bins of more than fifty Triangle bathrooms to find her materials for the installation.*'"

"Oh, my."

"'*The result,*'" Sally continued to read, "'*is the bravest exhibit in Raleigh this year, and one that will be near impossible to top for years to come.*'"

"That's good, right?"

"The critics loved it, but many regulars were offended."

"Art does offend people sometimes," I said, remembering my own art education.

"Of course it does, and I'll admit I shouldn't be grossed out by something completely natural like a woman's period. But that's not the point, Rett. I'm afraid what she might do next. I've insisted she tell me, but she doesn't want to give anything away."

"I can understand that, too."

"I can't have the Health Department shutting us down or worse, *quarantining* Needless Necessities. She's at least got to tell me if bodily fluids are involved, and, if so, which ones and *whose*."

Which sounded fair, I said. *And, by the way, were we really having this conversation?*

"Look on the bright side," I said. "She's young and connected to social media. She could attract a whole slew of artist customers to the center."

Sally didn't seem convinced.

"Is this the line for requesting gallery space?" said a familiar voice behind me.

It was Freddy. I guess he wasn't wasting much time trying to get a show for Otis.

"Go ahead, Freddy," I said. "We were just wrapping up."

Instead of heading to the back of the store to work my station, though, I hung nearby to listen to Freddy's conversation with Sally. Impossible not to, as Freddy's voice grew louder by the second.

"But, Sally, do you know what he does when his work piles up and he needs to make room for more? HE THROWS THE PIECES AWAY! How many of his amazing works have ended up in the Wake County dump?" I felt nothing but admiration that Freddy was trying to help another artist's career.

But Sally was digging in her heels. "I'm sorry. We won't have the gallery available till May. It's booked full till then."

"Not the little gallery. That gallery's too small. Otis's works are at least six feet on a side. I was thinking about the space next to the thrift store where you keep donations. We could reorganize the stock to fit half the space and curtain off the other half for the show."

Sally guffawed. "We'll have to staff it, and that's money we don't have."

"How much would it take for just a three-week show?"

"A thousand dollars a week."

"I'll front the money, because I'm sure Otis's work will sell. We can earn that money back and leave some for your center just from the commission."

Uh oh. Now he's gone and said the word.

"Commissions are against policy," Sally said.

"You're kidding me, right?"

"I don't kid."

It was true. Sally didn't have a sense of humor. But I was glad I didn't have to face Freddy's expression right now.

Sally clapped her hands together. "I got it! We'll open the show on the same day as the bake sale and pie contest. In fact, we'll combine the events. Imagine the synergy!"

"When is this bake sale?" Freddy asked.

"The Fifteenth. My birthday."

"That's next week. Too soon. Impossible."

Sally's look was implacable. The stubborn founder...who actually managed to budge, if only an inch. "Get your show ready by the 15th," she said, "and I'll let you charge 10 percent commission. Final offer."

Ten percent was a pittance. I could almost hear Freddy's teeth grinding.

"Fine," he said at last. "I'll talk to Otis and see if we can pull it off."

I watched Freddy leave. Judging by his body language, he was considering the compromise a victory—one that would be filled with considerable stress, but a victory nonetheless.

I should have made myself scarce. Unfortunately, Sally saw me and asked for a pie update. When I didn't have anyone new to add to the list of contributors, she scowled, then found yet another way to scold me. "We missed you on Monday."

I explained that I had been helping Lydia in her return home from the hospital.

"That's wonderful, Rett. You inspire me." She turned on her heel and marched away.

Never had faint praise left me feeling so grumpy.

While I tended my section of the store, I kept one eye on my phone. A little before eleven, I received the text I'd been expecting and went out to the parking lot to greet Margaret.

My favorite interior designer stepped out of her blue Mercedes convertible to the nines in a purple dress, stiletto heels, and a white-pearl necklace.

"You didn't have to get all dressed up for me," I said.

"Not you. I have to meet a client for lunch." She looked around the barren parking lot and dilapidated strip mall. "And what manner of hell is this?"

"My kind of hell," I said.

"I guess no good deed goes unpunished," she muttered. "So, where is this thrift shop of which you speak? I've got twenty minutes to find you something to wear to this party on Saturday. And here I thought you didn't even want to go."

"I *don't* want to go, but if I am going, I might as well look good. And by 'good' I mean different. A whole new look."

"This place is certainly 'different.' Lead on, Virgil."

We stepped into the most popular section of Needless Necessities, a former grocery next to the arts center that had been turned into a sizable second-hand store similar to Goodwill or Salvation Army. Along the walls was some shelving with everything from books to blenders. But the clothing racks in the middle were what we were here for.

Margaret took charge, scanning the racks and tables for things that would wake up my look, which had gone into hibernation decades ago.

"I don't really care that much about clothes," I reminded Margaret, as she pulled one thing after another off the clothing racks.

"Yes, Rett, we know all about your little quirks. That's why I'm here." In rapid succession she held various articles of clothing against me. I said, "You're already frowning, and I haven't even tried anything on yet."

"I'm just concerned there's a very fine line between 'Hippie at Heart' and 'Bag-Lady Bohemian.' Look, I don't have time for you to try things on, so we're going to have to wing it. Just promise me that if this doesn't work out, you'll let me take you to the boutiques of Cameron Village or North Hills and do this the right way?"

Boutique-hopping sounded like absolute torture, but I agreed to her terms. "Okay," I said, "but try to make this work. This place has lots of off-beat options, and it could use the cash."

"Feeling charitable, I see. Now what would Mother Teresa wear?" She gave me a little wink. "Grab a shopping cart, sister. We're going on a tear."

As I wheeled a cart behind her, Margaret picked out corduroys, sweaters, scarves, flannel button-ups, overalls, cargo pants, Birkenstocks, and clogs. She found a few nice knitted dresses, too, and for when the weather got warmer, a number of flower-power sun dresses. "You can wear some of these long scarves as sashes or belts," she said. Over at the jewelry section, she collected numerous hoop earrings, jangly bracelets, and head bands.

"Head bands, Margaret? Really?"

"If you go all Summer of '69 without reining in that weave, you're going to be arrested and tried for witchcraft. Here." She tossed a couple baseball caps and bandanas into the shopping cart. "That should do it. If you don't like something I picked out, I suppose you can just donate it back again."

I considered the burgeoning, bag-lady-like cart. "Thank you, Margaret. Humiliating as that was, it was still my least painful clothes shopping experience ever."

Margaret grunted acknowledgment and looked at her phone. "I've got to rush. Gail Norris and I are doing lunch, then we're spending the afternoon looking at nothing but towel racks."

"Really?" I said, surprised. "For their Woodmont home?"

"No, for the one on Falls Lake. They have a closing date for next week. She dug up my old quote and signed on the dotted line."

"Interesting," I said.

"If you say so." As she went out the door, Margaret announced with her signature sarcasm, "I can't wait to record today's thrilling episode in my diary!"

The second she was gone, I pulled out my phone. I browsed and saw that the Norris's Woodmont home was still listed for sale on the couple's website. Really curious now, I texted Gail to verify that their home was still available.

"It is," she texted back.

"Great!" I responded. *"I might know someone who is interested. I'll let you know."*

I thought about everything the couple had said when Darryl and I interrogated them the morning after the murder. *No one will want to move here now...The downtown homeless population... Guess our move to Falls Lake will have to wait, Brad.*

In short, *"Woe is us."*

Yet it seemed that Wanda's death had given them the confidence to pull the trigger on their forever home after all.

I had just returned to the paints station when I received a surprise customer—Otis Jones's granddaughter, Augusta.

"My grandfather said I might find you here," she said. "You got time to talk?"

She seemed upset about something—and I worried that something was me. We hadn't exactly hit it off the first time we'd met.

"What's on your mind?"

"Can we go somewhere more private than this?"

I suggested the break room. Though just a glorified storage area, it did feature a coffee maker perpetually full thanks to Jasmine the Coffee Fairy.

Augusta chose a mug that read 'I'm Not a Grump, I'm Just Surrounded by Nincompoops.' Mine was a church mug: 'What Happens at Sunday School *Prays* at Sunday School.'

"So, what can I help you with?" I asked, after we'd taken seats at the only table.

"They arrested my cousin Trent yesterday. He says they're trying to pin that murder on him. Had you heard about that?"

"I just found out," I said, "but I probably don't know much more than you do."

"You know the detective that's investigating. Pops said he saw you guys talking the other day." Otis must have seen us together in front of Lydia's house as he drove away so abruptly.

I said, "All I heard was Trent was charged with possession of drugs."

"Trent doesn't do or sell drugs. He was holding some pills for one of his friends."

"You have to admit, that's one of the oldest lines in the book."

"With Trent, it's true. He's never cared about any of that gang-banger stuff. He has a future planned. He wants to go to college for acting. The drug charges are just an excuse to hold Trent until they can pin that murder on him."

"What do you want me to do?"

"Tell them they've got the wrong person."

"I don't think anyone is going to listen to me. I'm just—"

"You got more power than you think. Most white folks do."

I shook my head. "They are going to look at the evidence. If there isn't any evidence tying Trent to the crime scene, they can't indict him."

"Yeah, but they're telling Trent that Pops is hiding evidence and is engaged in a cover up, that Trent needs to come clean so as not to drag Otis into this. My grandfather doesn't have time for such nonsense. All he cares about is his art. He deserves to be left alone."

"Has he told you that he's feeling targeted?" I asked.

"Otis Jones talk about his feelings? Please. That man is so stoic, you could hit his toe with a hammer and he'd ask you if your wrist hurt. No, he hasn't said anything, but I know he's looking over his shoulder."

"So you came to me?"

"When I asked him about you the other day, he said that you're investigating this case, too. I thought if I approached you, you might at least lend insight. He also said you were a nice person."

I felt flattered, but it wasn't clear that *Augusta* thought me nice. Not yet.

I would reveal what I felt I could.

"When a case lacks a prime suspect," I attempted, "minor characters go under suspicion. At least, that's what I've gathered. I'm new to this sort of thing. All of us in Woodmont are new to this sort of thing."

"Right, you live in a 'nice neighborhood'," she said, enacting a Southern white accent. "This 'sort of thing' is more suited for the Black part of town."

"I don't see why anyone deserves to get used to this type of crime," I said.

"Mm-hmm," she said noncommittally and took a sip of her coffee.

It was tempting to write off Augusta as "an angry Black woman" who just liked a fight. Why couldn't Otis's granddaughter be sweet and accommodating like Jasmine? After all, a person could catch more flies with honey than with vinegar. White folks didn't like feeling accused of being racist all the time.

But these days I could identify with an angry female. Augusta's outrage was real. Could I justify my own ire if I couldn't acknowledge that she might have a right to hers? I didn't live inside her skin. If I did, I might be acting the same way.

Besides, it was a much more uncomfortable possibility that Augusta was fighting against—that of her cousin being sent to prison.

If I was going to get to the bottom of this case, I needed to make a real connection with Trent's family. "Tell me about yourself, Augusta. Otis said you were named after two colleges. Was he just kidding?"

"No, he's right. My first name is Augusta, for St. Augustine, and my middle name is Shaw," she said distractedly. Both St. Augustine's University and Shaw University were historically Black colleges based in Raleigh.

I asked, "So why doesn't a smart girl like you enroll in college?" That got her attention.

"I believe in grass roots, not the ivory tower. I can't be wasting time in college while injustice rages outside the walls of the university. Mass incarceration, jobs, healthcare, environmental justice, slavery reparations. But there are other realities that span all of them."

"Like what?"

"Like implicit bias."

"That's a new one to me," I said, wondering if it was similar to being "woke."

Augusta explained, "Implicit bias is prejudice a person shows without even realizing it. Like when a company rejects a resume because it has a Black-sounding name, even when everything else about the resume fits the job."

"That's terrible," I said.

"It's not just race. There was a time when symphony orchestras wouldn't pick women, said they didn't sound as good. Then they started doing blind auditions. When only the music was judged, suddenly women began being chosen for the symphony right and left."

"I'm not surprised," I said. I told her how, as a woman, I'd been witness to sexism more times than I could count.

"Well, if you were a minority, you'd notice racism, too. I've been insulted, snubbed, ignored, talked down to, lectured, and treated differently from white people my whole life. But, when you finally call out a microaggression, you're called a 'snowflake' just to rub salt into the wound. If it happened every now and then you might shake it off, but when it happens hundreds of times, it becomes a cancer."

"Sounds like you've really studied this issue," I said.

"More than that, I've lived it."

"What do you do to pay the bills?"

"Right now I just work part-time at an outfit that refurbishes old computers and resells them."

"That sounds complicated," I said.

"Working with hardware is actually pretty simple. The complexity comes with networking and programming. I'm learning to be an ethical hacker. Just on my own, with YouTube videos and books. It's not easy to learn that way, but it's efficient. I don't get distracted."

"Maybe you got that from your grandfather. His dedication to his art is amazing. He certainly made an impression on Freddy, who has offered to put on a show—right here at Needless Necessities."

Her expression turned skeptical. "I don't know if that's a good idea. I can't bear to watch him be taken advantage of again."

Here was my chance to play my BFF role.

"Freddy is everything honorable in the world," I said. "He wouldn't do anything to harm a fellow artist, especially one he admires as much as your grandfather."

"I'll talk to my grandpa about it," she said, "but an art show is the least of my worries right now. I've got to find a way to help Trent." She thought for a moment. "Would you come with me to the jail to visit with him this afternoon? You just need to talk to him and judge for yourself that he didn't kill anybody."

I'd never been to the city jail—and didn't know if I really wanted to start. I knew I did not hold the sort of power Augusta thought I did. I wasn't even sure how Darryl would feel about me stepping even further into his investigative territory.

I looked across the table at the social justice champion in front of me. Maybe I could borrow some of Augusta's fight to uphold the promise I made to Wanda.

"Okay," I finally said, "should we go to the jail together?"

One of the Romantic poets I'd been reading, Lord Byron, wrote about a prisoner condemned to a dungeon with spiders and rats. The Raleigh City Jail was not so unhygienic as that, but one aspect did seem to mirror the experience of Byron's Prisoner of Chillon:

Dim with a dull imprisoned ray
(A sunbeam which hath lost its way...)

It seemed sunlight was denied the prisoners of every era.

We checked in with the guard at the front desk, then waited in chairs outside a room on the other side of thick plexiglass. Outside the jail I had asked Augusta if she and her cousin were emotionally close. She confided, "He was a snot-nosed little terror to me all our growing up." So I asked her why she was going to such lengths to help him. "It's what we women do for men, isn't it? We come to their rescue."

After what seemed like forever, a guard brought Trent into the sealed-off room. The boy was slim and good-looking with medium length dreadlocks and the start of a beard. Turn his orange jumpsuit red and he could easily be mistaken for a model in a Target commercial.

Augusta introduced us. After a bit of small talk regarding Trent's cell (he had one cellmate, a quiet guy with a drug problem who slept all the time) I cut to the chase.

"I don't have the power to let you out of jail, Trent," I said. "I'm just a normal citizen trying to get answers and find out who killed my neighbor."

"I didn't do it."

"Then if we can figure out who did, you'll be off the hook. Make sense?"

"Yes, ma'am."

"Go ahead," Augusta said to me. "Ask him whatever you want."

I asked Trent if he'd ever met Wanda Hightower.

"Yes, ma'am. Uncle Oats fixed her clothes dryer. I was with him."

"When?"

He shrugged. "Last week. Like, just a few days before Halloween."

"Did you visit the house on Halloween? Be honest."

"No. I wasn't anywhere near it. I swear."

"You didn't visit the alleyway in the neighborhood?"

"No. I swear I didn't."

"The day you were there with Otis, how did you get into the house that day? Through the front door?"

"Yeah, she let us in the front."

"Was the glass in the front door broken?" I asked.

"The police asked me that. It wasn't broken, not that I remember."

I tended to believe him. If the glass had been broken then, Wanda certainly would have said something to her handyman there on the spot.

"And then you went straight to the back of the house to work on the dryer?"

"Yes, ma'am."

"And you told the police you didn't explore any other part of the house."

"Yes."

"But they found your fingerprints on the fireplace mantle, the one that looked like a dragon."

Trent looked down at his hands. "I'm sorry I touched it. Uncle Oats was testing out the dryer after we'd fixed it and Ms. Hightower was upstairs, and I just thought I'd have a closer look." He looked me in the eyes. "If I was there killing her, why would my fingerprints be all over one thing but not other things?"

I knew he could have touched the mantel days earlier, then wore gloves during the murder. But I sidestepped his question.

"Did that dragon mantle give you the idea for your Halloween costume?" I asked.

"Actually, I didn't have the idea. She did."

"Wanda?"

"She came downstairs and caught me looking at the dragon. She wasn't upset or anything. She asked me about myself and we got to talking about theater and stuff. She said when she was in college she would drive to New York and see Broadway shows."

Augusta cut in, "I told you that Trent is an actor."

I turned to him. "Is that so?"

"I was part of a troupe for a while, as a young kid. Raleigh Little Theater."

"Don't you act anymore?"

"I have to work," he said.

It was easy to forget that, unlike my own daughter, kids from low-income families often had to forego after-school activities to earn money for their families.

"You were in that church play around Easter," Augusta reminded him. She turned to me. "It was at one of the white churches. Ardmore."

"Oh, that's Jim Thompson's church," I said. "He's a neighbor of mine."

Trent said, "I got to play Pilate. We only did it a few times though."

"Go back to talking about Wanda. You were saying that dressing as a dragon was her idea, not yours."

"When I told her I liked to act, she told me to wait while she went upstairs. She came down with a box. Inside was a mask, looked like a dragon. Made of wood. Said it was from the Pacific Islands and her father brought it back from some trip. I told her it was cool. Then she said I could have it."

Augusta cut in, "But she gave you that mask, right? You didn't steal it."

"No, I didn't steal it. She gave it to me."

"Did you show it to Otis?" I asked. "If so, he can vouch for you."

He shook his head. "No, I went outside while he was still working and hid it in my backpack so he wouldn't see it. I didn't think he'd let me keep it." He looked at Augusta. "You know Uncle Oats."

"Yes, I do," Augusta sighed.

"Speaking of hiding things," I said, "Tell me about the pills."

"Those pills is what made me run. I panicked. I wasn't thinking."

"The police think you stole them from Ms. Hightower."

"No, no, no. That's crazy!"

"Then where did you get them?"

"A guy I know. He gave them to me. He said they were valuable and I could get some dollars for them. He owed me some money. I didn't really want them."

"Then why did you accept them from him?"

"I thought they were valuable somehow. They weighed on me, but I didn't get rid of them. I should have."

"Trent," I said, trying not to sound judgmental but needing to ask, "why do you hang around those kinds of people?"

"What do you mean? 'Those kinds of people' are the friends I grew up with."

"But they're into stealing and dealing drugs, things that could get people killed. Besides, those things are illegal."

"Lots of things are illegal," he said. "You ever done something illegal? Like, you ever drove over the speed limit?"

"That's quite a bit different."

"Speeding could get someone killed. So, how is it different?" When I didn't reply right away, he muttered, "Mm-Hmm," in a way that reminded me of Augusta and Otis both.

"You make a good point," I said, "but how I drive is irrelevant right at this moment. Right now you're the one trying to get out of jail. Remember, I'm trying to help you."

He nodded.

"What is the name of the boy who gave you those pills?"

"I ain't snitching on anybody."

"Trent," I said, trying to contain my frustration, "the person who gave you those pills can vouch they were from him and not from Ms. Hightower's home. That's huge."

Trent leaned back in his chair and put his hands out. "What's the point? It's just going to get my friend into trouble, and the police ain't going to believe him anyway."

I looked at Augusta. Though we were both frustrated, Trent's argument was, sadly, sound.

"Okay, Trent," I said. "We'll leave the pills part alone for now. I just have a couple more questions. Where were you late afternoon on Halloween?"

"I was with my girlfriend, at her place."

"But the police don't believe her?"

"You might find this hard to imagine," Augusta cut in, "but Trent's girlfriend is Black, too."

Frustrated, I asked Trent, "Are you sure no one else besides your girlfriend can vouch for you?"

"I'm sure."

Trent seemed like a clean-cut kid. His orange jumpsuit notwithstanding, I didn't see a fire-breathing dragon personality in him.

Then again, Trent was an actor. One who was known to play the bad guy.

We locked eyes for a moment.

"I can't promise anything," I said finally, "but I want you to know I'm going to continue to do whatever I can to help the police find Ms. Hightower's killer."

"Thank you," he said softly.

Augusta and I said our good-byes and started to leave, but Trent's words stopped us.

"She was a nice person."

"Who?" I asked. "Ms. Hightower?"

"Yes. She said something funny while we were talking about theater. She said, 'Beauty is truth, and truth is beauty'."

"That's from a famous poem," I said, recalling John Keats's "Ode to a Grecian Urn." I asked, "Do you think she was right?"

He cast a quick glance around him. "Not a lot of beauty here. Not a lot of truth, either, because they're trying to say I did something even though I didn't."

"Hang in there, Trent," I said. "We won't give up."

Coleridge had complained that he was undeserving of his bad dreams. *Such griefs / but wherefore, wherefore fall on me?*

When you see the nightmares some have to live through, it just doesn't pay to complain.

CHAPTER 13

AN ANXIOUS FEELING

D arryl came by the house after work that evening to check on his mom, but Lydia had already gone to bed.

"I hate that you missed her," I said. I asked Darryl if he wanted some leftover slow cooker enchiladas.

"Free home cookin'? Sounds good to me."

While dinner heated up in the microwave, I tried to imagine how I was going to tell Darryl that a few hours earlier I'd interviewed the key suspect in his case.

I noticed he was humming a tune while he checked his email on his phone.

"You're awful cheery," I said.

"I'm just psyched we may have gotten a break in the case."

"You mean Trent." I told him about the visit Augusta and I paid Trent at the city jail.

"I knew you came by," he said with a wink. "We're notified whenever someone visits." He didn't seem upset by it.

"I really don't think he's a bad kid," I said. "Do you?"

Darryl's voice was stern. "Trent has been charged with resisting arrest and possession of a controlled substance without a prescription. We don't know if he was just using or had intent to sell."

Somehow that raised my hackles. "Are you going to charge the drug company for selling those pills in the first place?"

"It hadn't occurred to me."

"Well, they're making plenty of money off addicts, too, aren't they?"

Darryl furrowed his brow. "You're awfully fired up."

I set the food in front of him and went over to the sink to get the ceramic part of the slow cooker soaking.

"I just don't feel good about this arrest," I said. "What about the Frankenstein Freak at the party who was scaring all the women? Why isn't he a suspect?"

"We identified him. He was an employee of Stuart's IT company. I guess Stuart mentioned the block party offhand at a company meeting, and one of his employees just showed up. Kind of a space cadet techie with not very good people skills."

I thought of what Augusta and I had discussed in terms of implicit bias.

"Why not focus on Frankenstein Freak or on the neighbors?" I asked. "Why just Trent?"

"Because it's Trent's fingerprints we found at the crime scene."

"But Trent had been there before, helping his uncle with Wanda's clothes dryer."

"We don't have independent confirmation of that—only Trent's and Otis's word. Otis didn't even mention it until Trent was arrested."

"I just don't see Trent killing someone over a few pills. You said yourself he doesn't have a violent record."

"You'd be surprised how many first-time murderers don't have a violent record. Besides, he ran. He might have had something bigger on his conscience than a few pills."

I didn't have a retort to that. But I could not get rid of my sense that something about this was just too easy.

"If he did do it," I asked, "do you think he got into the house by breaking the glass near the front door?"

"That's one idea."

"Then why wasn't there any glass on the floor inside or outside the door?"

"Maybe he cleaned it up to cover his tracks and dumped the glass in the kitchen, just to throw us off. Look, I'm wondering if talking about the details of this case with you is maybe a mistake. It seems to be upsetting you."

"I'm not upset." But I really was upset—and I needed to calm down. I wasn't going to get anywhere by alienating the lead detective on the case. "We can talk about other things."

I'd finished wiping down the counters. I sat at the table across from him.

Darryl sighed. "I'm sorry I got defensive. You're absolutely correct, until we find evidence that definitely puts Trent at the crime scene on Halloween, he's only a person of interest. But right now, he's the closest we've got to a prime suspect. Even so, I'm not going to railroad him."

"Thank you," I said. But the air in the kitchen was tense. I needed to find a way to defuse the moment some more.

"Tell me," I said, "what got you interested in working in law enforcement in the first place? I never asked."

Darryl went on to share how he had always wanted to become a policeman like his father. "When I was a kid, I used to ride with my dad in his squad car and imagine being his partner. That was during the eighties when there were a lot of cop shows on TV. *Hill Street Blues, Cagney and Lacey*—"

"Those shows were on too late for me. My parents made me go to bed."

"Mine, too, but I'd sneak down after my mother was asleep

and watch them. She slept like a log back then as well. Dad worked a lot of night shifts. I just loved the whole idea of solving crimes. It seemed like fun and rewarding work."

"That was delicious," he said in the next breath, taking the plate to the sink and immediately beginning to wash it—one more thing that Allan never did during our marriage. All housework fell to me. "What about you? When did you decide to go into law enforcement?"

"I guess when I started hanging out with a cop."

"Who would that be?" he teased.

"A real knuckle-dragger," I smiled. "You wouldn't like him."

He laughed. Best I could tell, we were flirting. But there was an added undercurrent of tension, too.

I awoke the next morning with an anxious feeling. The investor party was in just two days. I wasn't having a panic attack, but I needed to talk with someone about it. I had not shared my worries about the party with Darryl, afraid it would just make me look petty.

So I called someone who I knew wouldn't judge me.

When Maxine didn't pick up, I got dressed and went straight to her home. She came to the door. Seeing in my expression that the need was urgent, she led me straight to her home office where I we both sat and got down to business.

"Thank you for seeing me on the spur of the moment," I said.

"Did something happen?"

I told her about my parking lot encounter with Allan and how I'd bent to his pressure to attend the investor party.

"I don't know if I can handle this party," I said.

"Can't you call and say you've changed your mind?"

"I could. But I'd hate looking weak."

"Who do you need to impress?"

"Maybe it's just for my own sake, my own self-image."

"I get why you would feel that way," she said. Maxine was a Buddhist and didn't put much stock in self-image—not when it caused a person to cling to unhealthy thoughts and emotions. "But is it also possible you want to go to this party to face your husband's mistress and put some closure to your marriage?"

"You left out the part about bludgeoning her to death," I said. "Sorry. Poor taste given the present circumstances."

"You've not talked about her much in our sessions. Do you blame KayLeigh for the end of your marriage?"

"Yes. But no more than I blame Allan." She looked at me skeptically. "What?" I said.

"In our patriarchal society, men are entitled to behave badly," Maxine said. "They play the Lovable Rogue archetype— and get a pass—while women are 'conniving,' like Eve. Deep down, we tend to believe that women bear the majority of the blame for sexual offenses."

I listened to the water bubbling in the corner, a small water-fall element that sent water purling perpetually over a stack of smooth rocks.

She continued: "If you could cause a breakup between those two and get Allan back, would you do it?"

I thought about Allan sulking when he didn't get his way with the business, his inability to focus on important details and continually relying on me to steer our company straight. Allan always managed to skate on the surface of life.

I wasn't about to let him skate into my good graces again.

"No," I said. "That's one reason I'm anxious about this gath-ering. I'm worried that he'll try to suck me back into running his company and make me ignore everything else in my life."

"Now that you're fully aware of that, do you think you can guard against it?"

"I don't know."

"Is there any talisman you can take with you to the party?

Some symbol of resistance?"

I looked around her room at the various items on display: a marble carving of a salamander, a rock painted with the message *Peace is a River*, a dreamcatcher dangling from a lampshade. These weren't the sorts of things I could just carry into a party.

My gaze ultimately fell on Maxine's own necklace, a Christian cross.

"Your necklace," I said. "I thought you were Buddhist."

"Some would say Jesus was actually quite Buddhist in much of his teaching. And I take a lot of comfort from Judeo-Christian belief. A person can't read Psalm 23—'The Lord is my shepherd' and so on—and not feel better."

She reached behind her neck and removed the necklace. "Lean forward."

"I can't—"

"Shush." She leaned and placed the necklace around my neck. The cross fell onto my heart. I waited for some kind of change, though I felt nothing immediately. I didn't know what I believed anymore, just that I wanted to believe something.

"How's the wine drinking these days?" Maxine asked.

"Delicious," I answered, quickly adding, "Sorry. I know why I drink."

"Explain."

"I get angry at Allan. Then, to feel better, I drink. When I feel terrible the next day, of course I blame Allan for putting me in such a state. My anger at him rages again. To feel better again, I drink again." My anger was like the water element in Maxine's office: constantly regenerating.

"Anger actually feels very empowering," Maxine said. "It feeds the ego, which has been shattered by Allan and KayLeigh. But you can't ride anger into peace and happiness. Right now you're stuck in the anger stage of mourning your marriage, but I don't think you want to stay there forever. You need to move beyond it."

"Maybe in my next life?" I was being catty. Maxine knew quite well that I didn't believe in reincarnation, for what good are past lives if you can't remember them? She could have defended her belief as she had done in the past, by pointing out that a belief in reincarnation accentuates the importance of growth and maturity and makes every experience count for something.

She absorbed my snarkiness with a gracious smile. "No human transcends anger in this life without intentional discipline. And quiet. Try to be silent for a little while, right now."

For a long time I closed my eyes, felt the cross on my chest, and listened to the purling water of Maxine's little rock fountain.

Suddenly I remembered something.

"Oh my gosh! The hummingbird! How is he?!"

Maxine opened her eyes and smiled. "You mean 'she'? We named her Matilda. We're not sure if her wing is healing, but she's doing okay otherwise. Come have a look at her Disney World."

"Her what...?"

I had pictured the bird asleep in Sheila's sock drawer, but that's not what I found in the couple's bedroom. At the end of their bed rose a miniature yet complex jungle gym of sorts. Plastic ladders, perches, and swings all combined for a veritable amusement park for a bird. In the center of it, the little hummingbird leaned from a plastic perch and sucked from a bottle suspended by a string.

"This is Matilda's play area," Maxine announced proudly. "She has to work for her nectar. But Sheila also finds dead bugs and grinds them up for Matilda's meals. When she's not in torpor—her version of sleeping—Matilda plays and eats. The hard part is someone always has to be around the house to make sure she's safe and fed. Hummingbirds pretty much eat their body weight several times over each day."

Sheila arrived from the kitchen with a plate containing mashed up...something.

"Protein, anyone?" Sheila announced.

Sheila used a tiny measuring spoon to scoop the ground bugs into a small bowl shaped out of tinfoil. The hummingbird took no time at all hopping and crawling from one plastic "limb" to another in order to get to her foil food bowl.

"Sheila, I can't believe what I'm seeing. You're healing this bird!"

"I'm not so sure about that. I had to tape her wing to keep her from trying to use it before it's ready. If I had use of an x-ray machine, I'd be able to tell."

"Why don't you take her to the vet office where you work?" I asked.

"Are you kidding? No vet in their right mind would get involved."

"Aren't there sanctuaries that can help?"

"They aren't equipped to do the kind of care and rehab this bird would require. Imagine if they tried. She has to feed every two hours. If every season they tried to help every injured bird representing more than a dozen migratory species, they'd run out of resources so quickly, they'd have to shut down."

I watched Matilda eat a little more before climbing and hopping from one part of her jungle gym to another.

"Want to hold her?" Sheila asked.

"Can I?"

"Of course."

I put my finger near Matilda, and she immediately hopped on. I cupped my other hand above the bird, as if to keep her from flying away, but the tape on her wing reminded me she couldn't fly even if she wanted to.

"We thought she was blind in one eye," Maxine said, "but Sheila thinks that was just a result of dehydration. She seems to see just fine now."

I put a finger to her chest and could feel her tiny heart beating what felt like a hundred times a second. I put my face close to the hummingbird's. That something this tiny could be so thrillingly alive was simply amazing.

I handed the tiny bird to Maxine, who placed her back in the play area.

Sheila had left the room but now returned and handed me a large ziplock containing several smaller, sandwich size bags.

"What are these for?" I asked.

"If you happen to find any bugs. For Matilda."

"Okay," I said hesitantly, and put the ziplocks in my purse.

I asked how they would feel about Lydia meeting the bird sometime. Both ladies agreed it would be fine, so I asked if Lydia and I could bring dinner to them tonight.

"Sounds peachy," Maxine said.

But I told Sheila *she* could prepare the bugs.

That evening, Lydia and I brought a chickpea curry dish over to the couple's home. The first thing I did was bring Lydia into their room to see the bird.

Her face lit up as she reached a hand toward the hummingbird. "Wan . . . " she attempted.

"You want to pet it?" When I put the little bird in her hands, a peacefulness came over my friend.

By the end of the evening Max and Sheila had promised to fetch Lydia for a walk over the weekend so she could get more exercise and spend more time with Matilda.

There seemed to be magic present when holding a creature that delicate and beautiful. If the magic was real, maybe it could help Lydia, too.

CHAPTER 14

WANDA'S ANGEL

I awoke at Lydia's early on Friday morning, my smartphone beeping. It was an alert from my estate sale app. For years I'd been attending estate sales for affordable ways to decorate my home. What made this particular sale jump out was that it happened to be on my street.

Location: the Hightower residence.

For a sale to go up so soon after a death was unusual. Someone in Wanda's family wanted to clear out the house quickly.

I hadn't been allowed inside Wanda's home right after the murder. A week later, might I find evidence the police had missed?

"Painting is details," Glenda Murlowsky, the most eminent painting instructor at East Carolina University, had always noted. She was a tough teacher, but she was also the one whose words I remembered best so many years later. Though I no longer painted, maybe I could still notice details in the world that others had overlooked.

I heard a rummaging of pans downstairs, a signal that Doris had arrived. Good timing if I was going to get to that sale before others did. I pulled on a pair of clean blue jeans and a sweat-shirt, stepped into some flats, gathered my purse, and even drove the half block to gain a few extra seconds.

Often I would show up at a sale only to find a long line at the door. The most aggressive pickers would arrive hours early to get their names on a list, then catch a few winks in their cars before gaining entrance to the home. However, because this sale had not been advertised until a few moments ago, I would be the first inside.

I noticed some yard work had been done in recent days. What's more, painters had erected scaffolding on one end of the two story home.

Parked beside the Gala Estate Sales truck was a well-preserved white, older model BMW. A Gala sign was stretched across the top of the porch trellis, but it was the real estate sign in the yard that really got my attention. Wanda's home was for sale. Its selling agents: across-the-street neighbors Brad and Gail Norris.

A large tarp covered the front porch. Some might assume it was just there to encourage people to wipe off their feet before entering the home, but I suspected it was there to hide the massive blood stain.

After noting the broken pane of glass had been fixed, I let myself in. Seated immediately to my left, typing on a laptop computer, was none other than Wanda Hightower. Alive! Every-thing had all been a huge prank!

But, no, this Wanda was younger, mid-thirties, and taller, with brown hair drawn into a bun. Her reading glasses made her look older. This had to be Wanda's daughter, whom I hadn't seen since she was a teenager leaving for college.

"Angela," I said, composing myself. "I'm Rett Swinson from just down the street. I'm so sorry about your mother."

Angela looked up from her computer but did not stand.

"Thank you," she replied stiffly. "Mother had a difficult last year. At least she's not suffering anymore."

Professionally dressed, she shared her mother's soft gray eyes, but her overall demeanor seemed stony. "Please look around. If you have any questions, there are workers around here who can help you."

"Thank you. I'll do that."

Almost robotically, Angela resumed typing. I took in the tidy living room with its antique chairs and couch. Those weren't, however, the things that held my attention. The room's real eye-catcher was Trent's tragic obsession—the fireplace mantle made from dark oak, ornately carved in the shape of a Chinese dragon. Doubtless when the fireplace was roaring with flame, one could watch the dragon come to life and appear to breathe fire. I ran a hand along the dragon's intricate, corrugated tail.

"This room is extremely tidy," I said. "Did you have it cleaned?"

"Mother was always OCD about a clean house, but don't let this room fool you. She completely filled my old bedroom with delivery boxes. I took it personally."

"At least you tried to keep in touch with her," I said. "My college-aged daughter rarely reaches out these days." I added: "How did you find out about your mother's death, if you don't mind me asking?"

Angela took off her reading glasses and looked into space. "The police called me. I was on the West Coast with a client." Angela mentioned the company she worked for, a name I recognized as one of the "Big Four" global accounting firms.

"The police said nothing was taken from the home," I said.

"Actually, I learned recently that her murderer stole a curio my grandfather brought home from his travels."

The dragon mask. "I hope it wasn't valuable."

"Not really. Certainly not worth killing for." She went back to pounding on her computer's keys.

"Is Daniel back in town, too?" I thought of the lonesome looking teenager with his dyed purple hair and skateboard.

She spoke through clenched teeth as she typed. "Dan's in Singapore with our dad. They've got a contract playing for some billionaire's daughter's sixteenth birthday party, plus a number of other gigs, and they can't make it back for a while."

"I remember when your parents broke up. You both had graduated from high school." Was I getting too personal, too fast? Possibly, but I also got the sense that this conversation was allowing Angela to let off some long pent-up steam.

Angela stopped typing, took off her glasses, and massaged her eye sockets. "It was a long time coming," she said. "Don't ever let creative types marry one another. It doesn't work. Just look at Hollywood couples."

"I figured your mother to be creative. I know she taught poetry. Did she write it, too?" I didn't mention the poems I'd dug up at the college. That might come across as creepy.

She smiled wryly. "Yes, but she would have had a lot more time to develop her work if she had stayed at NC State, where they allow sabbaticals and actually encourage professors to publish."

"Do you know why she left State?" I knew, of course, but I wondered if Angela did. She frowned. "No, but it meant a drastic pay cut. Daniel got to keep on learning guitar because Dad was his teacher, but I had to quit dance lessons. Mom never could see the true value of money. I had to buy this house from her last year just to keep her afloat."

If Angela ever found out what had really happened—the sacrifice Wanda had made for Cynthia's sake—maybe she would find it in her heart to forgive her mother. Or, maybe she would blame her all the more for their family's money troubles.

Regardless, it wasn't my place to share Cynthia's secret with anyone.

"It sounds like those times were very difficult for your family," I said.

"That's an understatement." Angela closed her laptop but kept talking. "My dad had to go on the road a lot for work, and Daniel wanted to connect with our father so badly. The day he graduated from high school, he joined Dad on tour—and they've been traveling the world ever since. Music is supposed to bring people together. Just not our family, I guess."

"Are your mother's parents still alive?"

"Her father died about ten years ago. Grandma died more recently. That means I'm left to deal with everything."

"The Responsible Oldest," I said.

"Exactly. I haven't had the privilege of living in an ivory tower like Mom, or being a musical gypsy like my dad and brother. I've had to deal with the world as it is, not as I would like it to be."

"I wish I'd known your mother better."

"Oh, Mother was interesting. Not a lot of her life decisions were very logical. Did you know that, even though she was an atheist, she still named me Angel? Go figure that one out."

"Angel is a beautiful name."

"I go by Angela. It's more professional."

"Your mother seems like a fascinating and complicated woman."

"In the past year she really went off the rails. I urged her to get psychological help, but she wouldn't listen. She hated doctors in general, so I guess I shouldn't have been surprised. So stubborn."

"Perhaps she would have seen a therapist eventually?"

"Maybe. We'll never know."

I was touched that Angela had confided in me, but I didn't want to leave this meeting without some tangible lead.

"Did your mom have any enemies that you knew of?"

"Like I told the police, I know that she was at odds with the college. Her department head became a sort of devil in her mind. She didn't like having to attend meetings. I was like, 'Mom, Professor Roland is running a *department*.' But she was irrational about it."

"Anyone else who might have held a grudge?"

She seemed as if she were about to say something, then appeared to think better of it and shook her head. Had she been about to mention The Imp?

"I have a confession," I said. "I was one of the neighbors who tried to do a makeover of your mom's yard. I'm so sorry we did that."

"Don't apologize. There was a time when she would have loved the help. Anyway, after that incident she really withdrew. I don't think we even spoke once in the past month. Sad to say, it's the most peaceful stretch I've had in a while. My job is very demanding, and it was nice to be able to focus. Now, well, it's not so peaceful." She looked at the laptop as if it were accusing her of something terrible.

It sounded like Angela Hightower had reason to be frustrated with her mom. Could she have lost her temper and killed her? But Darryl had already confirmed that she was on the West Coast when the murder happened.

I heard a noise and saw through the front window a pair of pickup trucks parking against the curb. I certainly was not the only one with an estate sale app.

Angela began packing up her laptop and papers.

"Will you be in town long?" I asked. "I haven't heard about any funeral plans."

"We'll have a memorial service in a few months when everyone can get here. Mom didn't leave any instructions. All I know is the house is my responsibility. It's up to me to get it cleaned out and ready to sell. I won't be here long this trip, but I'll be in town from time to time while I work with the agents to get it ready."

I wanted to ask her how she had settled on the Norrises, but couldn't think of a slick way to do that.

"I'm semi-retired and glad to keep an eye on it for you," I said. "Is there a way I can get in touch if necessary?"

She picked up her smartphone. "Give me your number and I'll text you."

～

Angela took the arrival of the new visitors as her cue to leave. It was my cue to begin exploring.

Darryl had said the murder knife may have come from Wanda's kitchen, which, like most of the old homes in Woodmont, was in the rear of the home. The kitchen was small, just enough space for a person to move between the meager countertops. I looked through the cupboards, but they had all been emptied of their bowls, glasses, and plates which had been placed on the counters for sale.

The back door was open, so I pushed the flimsy aluminum screen door which swung out over three narrow concrete steps. A small, scrubby lawn bordered a short, narrow walkway leading to the alley. While this side of the alley backed up to homes, the other side featured a high chain-link fence that lined Woodmont Cemetery. Darryl had said that police looked for signs that someone had bounded the fence but had found nothing, not even a footprint.

Phil and Eleanor had an impenetrable fence of their own, so I walked in the other direction toward Skip's backyard and found the garbage cans where the officer had seen Otis rummaging. The City only retrieved garbage placed in the green plastic bins. The metal can was presumably for rubbish. I lifted the metal can's lid and looked inside, but it was empty.

The house was likely filling up with pickers, so after dusting my hands of rust from the can, I reversed course and headed back inside to explore the upstairs. In the master bedroom were price tags on the side tables and the bed itself. A guitar in the corner was tagged with the notice, "Not for Sale." The master bath, for its part, featured little of note.

The guest bedroom was filled with card tables stacked with clothes, many of them still new and in the factory plastic wrap. Several stacks of boxes in the corner suggested this was where Wanda's many online purchases had been piled. I held up to myself a few of the articles of clothing—mostly flannel shirts, knit socks, sweaters, and hoodies. And gloves—a whole lot of gloves. Many were elbow-length, the type I always associated with Jacqueline Kennedy. White. Elegant.

The rest of the upstairs featured a third bedroom with Christmas knick-knacks, board games from the eighties and nineties, and old linens, while the hallway guest bath was totally bare. I returned downstairs where the initial crowds had thinned out, and I was drawn again to that majestic dragon mantle. No knick-knacks lined it. If there had been treasured heirlooms like photographs, Angela must have already collected them.

Still desperate for a clue, I returned to the main room and focused on the front door. Doorknobs from the early 20th century always seemed a size too small, as if made for tiny hands —this one was fashioned out of smooth glass. The lock's hard-ware appeared original. I closed the door until it latched. To open it again, I found it took both my hands to turn the knob.

While another customer looked through several stacks of books—$3.00 for hardbacks, $1.00 for paperbacks—I got down on my hands and knees to look beneath the chairs and sofa, hoping to find something, anything, that Wanda's assailant may have dropped.

Finding neither matchbook nor business card, I stood and walked over to the dining room table where Angela had been sitting. Bending down again, I did find something along the back wall, but I can't say it thrilled me: several dead bugs of various sorts cluttered around a half dozen moth balls, their chemical reek tickling my nostrils. If I spoke to Trent again, I'd ask him if the preservatives had been packed with the dragon mask in its box.

Finding dead bugs in Wanda's otherwise pristine home bothered me, as they seemed to verify Eleanor's infestation obsession. This I could remedy. I located the front porch broom from my previous adventure there and a dustpan from under the kitchen sink, swept the bugs into the pan, then tipped them into one of the ziplocks Sheila had given me. They grossed me out, but maybe Sheila could make of the insects a nice meal for Matilda.

If Wanda really was as finicky about indoor cleanliness as her daughter claimed, I imagined her feeling grateful for my small gesture.

The books were my final stop. Most were collections by poets I recognized from the *Sublime Lives* volume. I chose *An Anthology of Romantic Verse* and walked it to the adjacent living room where a representative of Gala Estate Sales was sitting at a long fold-out table processing customer purchases.

"What do you do with all the items you can't sell?" I asked the woman as I gave her my dollar.

"It's up to the owner. Sometimes they donate them, some-times they send everything to the dump."

"If there is anything left and Angela is willing, maybe she can donate it to Needless Necessities." I handed her one of the center's cards. "Just call and they'll pick it up. They're a nonprofit that supports artists and recycling. They have a thrift store, too."

She promised to keep the card and share the information with Angela. I took my book and left through the front door, unable to forget the promise I'd made here nearly a week ago, wondering how in the world I was going to keep it.

When I pulled up in front of my home a moment later, Lydia was running across the street toward me, her quilting basket in hand. I rolled down my window and shouted, "What's going on?"—forgetting that she couldn't talk. She ignored me, of course, and continued to the passenger side, letting herself in.

At the same time Doris was emerging from her New Yorker. "Give me a second," I told Lydia. I got out of the car and went over to speak with her cousin.

"Doris," I said, "what's going on with Lydia?"

She spoke through clenched teeth. "I was going to take Cousin to her rehab appointment, but she ran. She needs to come on right now, or we'll be late. Enough of this tomfoolery."

"One moment." I walked back to my car and poked my head in. "Is rehab really that bad, Lydia?"

She pointed past me toward her cousin, grabbed her own throat with both hands, and produced a gurgling sound.

"Let me guess," I said. "You're dying of boredom."

Lydia nodded and scrunched up her face like she was about to cry.

I turned and shouted to Doris, "Mrs. Schmidt seems to be having a moment. Why don't you let me take her to rehab today? I'll take her to quilting as well and then to lunch. It'll give you a stretch of freedom."

"Suit yourselves," she said. "I'll stay here and can some pears."

I thought about the golden pear missing from Wanda's kitchen. And then I had another idea. "Doris, do you think you could make a couple of pies for an event next Saturday?" I quickly filled her in about the fundraiser.

"I don't fiddle with pies," she said, as if pies had done her a great insult. "I only make cobblers."

"Cobblers are awesome!" I said. *Please, Lord, let no one be recording the corny-ass shit coming out of my mouth these days.*

When I got behind the wheel, Lydia wiped imaginary sweat from her brow.

"Lydia, I'll try to find ways to rescue you occasionally when I'm not too busy, okay?"

She took my hand and began stroking it, like a prized pet, over and over.

"Uh, but you can't be doing *that*."

At the rehabilitation center, most of the other patients were visibly worse off than my friend, trying with superhuman effort to get one side of their bodies to respond. But as I watched the speech therapist work with Lydia, I reconsidered that assessment. Not being able to form words, having them get lost somewhere between brain and tongue, was in some ways even more difficult to witness.

Writing, like speech, wasn't going well for my friend either. "It is a language-making problem, not merely a speech problem," said the therapist. "We're going to get good at thinking words again and then we'll get better at saying them." The doctor had told Darryl we would see progress, though he had said it might be slow.

"Thuh...thuh..." Lydia struggled.

The therapist gave her plenty of time before asking, "Are you trying to say, 'thank you'?"

Lydia nodded.

"You're welcome," the therapist said kindly.

∾

The therapy was exhausting for Lydia, but I didn't dare propose skipping her quilting group. Among the Qrazy Qwilters, Lydia was healthy, happy, competent.

While walking to the paints section, I nearly got run over by a large metal contraption on wheels being driven toward the staff room.

"Watch out!" I cried, jumping to the side. I finally saw who was guiding it—Washington Henry, the college-aged janitor.

Wash smiled sheepishly. "Sorry. This thing is hard to steer."

"What is it?"

"One of those gizmos that lifts people from their beds in nursing homes. It's part of Wo's next performance."

"What does Wo need with that thing?"

Washington looked around to verify no one was listening. "She's planning her biggest show yet. There could be a safety issue or two." Washington practically stuttered with nervousness as he talked about it. "I've probably said too much."

I had to admit, I was intrigued. And I'm sure I wouldn't be the only one. After the gushing review for the last show, Ashley Myers—a.k.a. Wo K.—was sure to draw a large audience.

"Have you talked to her parents?" I asked. "I'm sure they'd want to know their daughter was going to try something risky."

"She doesn't have anything to do with them. They don't exactly see eye to eye on things."

"They aren't very woke?"

"Mega *un*-woke."

I hadn't thought about it until now, but I wondered if Wo's art was on some level a means of rebellion.

I said, "I know she's an adult, but I hope you can keep a close eye on her. She trusts you."

"I'll try," he said. "Now, if you'll excuse me, I need to hide this thing in the break room before someone up and buys it."

Shopping activity at the center was pretty brisk on this day. I wondered if most Fridays were like this, with hobbyists making sure they had the supplies they'd need for the weekend. I was feeling a little left out as one painter after another bought their brushes, paints, canvases, and, in one case, a used easel that was a bit smaller but very similar to the one I'd buried in our basement. At some point I took a break and sauntered by the painting class to see what they were up to. Self-portraits, it turned out, were the very last thing I wanted to paint these days.

A text lit up my phone. It was Angela Hightower wanting to meet with me right away if I was available.

A chance for me to learn more?

I texted I'd be back home in about twenty minutes, after my friend's quilting class.

Angela responded in all caps:

IT'S CRITICAL WE MEET OUTSIDE OF THE NEIGH-BORHOOD! YOU'LL SEE WHY WHEN WE TALK!

CHAPTER 15
THE "IMP"

Angela had been staying at the Umstead Hotel, one of the swankiest spots in the Triangle. She suggested Lydia and I meet her at Herons, the hotel's restaurant. We met in the restaurant's lobby, where she asked the maître d' for a table in a corner of the back patio where very few were dining. Tall heating units dispelled the November chill. We all ordered coffee.

When the young man left to get our order, Angela's steely visage melted. Reflexively, I reached across the table and touched her arm. "Girl, what's wrong? You're shaking."

"It's just—this."

With jittery hands she pulled from her briefcase a large book, an art history volume about the Impressionists. Opening its cover, she removed a sheet of notebook paper upon which was scrawled a note crudely written in crayon:

To Wanda H.:
Get yo nasty self out the neighborhood, Bitch!
Or else!

"Where did you get this note?" I asked. "Was it sent to you?"

"No. It was in this book. I'd gone back to the house to meet with Gala when a couple who'd come to the estate sale that morning returned it. They didn't know about the murder. They just thought the note was disturbing and it bothered them enough to bring it back. 'Bad karma,' they said. They didn't even want their money back."

"Why didn't you take it to the police right away?"

"Because I felt ashamed. I had told the police that my mother was crazy and paranoid." Wanda's grown daughter put her head in her hands. "How fearful she must have been. The Imp was real, and I refused to believe her. My poor mother!"

I looked at Lydia. Her eyes, like mine, ached for Angela.

After Angela had seemed to calm down a little, I asked, "What was Wanda like as a mother when you were growing up, before she lost her job at State?"

"A bit spacey," she said through sniffles. "But she was a doting mom. She used to take part in my tea parties as a little girl, with all my dolls and stuffed animals. I remember she'd serve us tea and cookies—'biscuits,' she called them, because she was such the Anglophile.

"She'd have on those fancy gloves she always liked to wear. I'd say, 'Won't you join us, M'Lady?' And she'd say, 'Why, I believe I shall, Wee Lass. It shall do me 'art good,' and she'd sit on the floor and sip her tea with me. She read poetry aloud, too. She had all these books of children's poems that were really cute and funny."

"How did she meet your father?" I asked.

"At Woodstock, of all places. She didn't take drugs, didn't really even take to the music of the sixties, now that I think about it. But her friends really wanted a road trip, so she went along. And in the van was a friend of a friend, this tall, gangly classical guitarist who ended up playing for small groups in the audience. That was my dad. She just thought he was fantastic."

"When was the last time you saw your dad?"

"Over a year ago, in the summer. He and my brother played a couple shows in Charlotte and crashed at my place." She looked wistful as she remembered. "My brother and I came to visit mom briefly. Dan—who has these long arms—took a selfie of the three of us. I thought I saw that photo framed at one point in the house, but I can't seem to find it. I'd really love to have that photo now."

"Maybe you could ask him to send you another copy," I suggested. "Was that the last time Daniel saw your mom?"

"Yes, and I think when he left that last time it was very hard for her. Daniel always called her 'clingy,' which I think is quite ironic, considering how he and my father cling to one another. Anyway, that was about the time she started to act especially strange."

I looked again at the threatening note. It wasn't dated, so theoretically it could have been sent years ago. The paper had a curve down the length of it; a slight breeze caught the lifted edge. I quickly grabbed it before it flew off the table.

"Did your mother somehow offend someone who is Black?"

"I'd be surprised if she did," Angela said. "Mom was the most egalitarian person I knew. Racism disgusted her."

I wasn't convinced. I remembered what Augusta had said about implicit bias, how it was quite possible to act in a preju-diced manner without even being aware of it.

I asked, "Do you recall Otis Jones doing some work for her over the years? Even recently?" Out of the corner of my eye, I saw Lydia lean forward a little.

"He did some work for Mom, and she never said anything bad about him. But the police said he brought his nephew recently to the house and that the boy is the prime suspect. Maybe the boy cased the house that day and then broke in on Halloween. He was seen behind the house the night of the murder, you know."

"The nephew claims your mother gave him the dragon mask as a gift," I said. "She was known as a very generous gifter. Do you think that it's possible she really did give the boy the heirloom, especially if she learned he was interested in theater?"

"I suppose, but after this note—"

Our waiter came. I ordered for myself and Lydia, for whom the menu must have appeared hieroglyphic. Angela handed her menu back without ordering anything.

I looked at the note more closely. "Isn't it odd that a would-be robber would try to get her to move out of the neighborhood?"

"I don't know," Angela said. "What I do know is that my mother didn't deserve to be terrorized."

She pushed back her coffee, which she'd barely sipped. "I've got to drive to Charlotte today, then pack and fly out to Seattle in the morning. Would you do me a favor and deliver this letter to the police? They've got my cell phone number and can get in touch if they want to ask me about it."

I promised I would. She put a twenty on the table, stood up, and released a deep breath. "When I get back from Seattle, I think—no, I *know*—I'm going to find a therapist. I don't have the time, but I can't afford not to."

I said, standing: "I guarantee you it will be time and money well spent."

She hugged me awkwardly, like a newcomer to the form.

Once Angela had gone, I said to Lydia, "I'm calling your son right now."

Darryl arrived about the time our food did. I handed him the note, which he immediately put in an evidence bag. He examined it through the clear plastic.

"What do you think?" I asked.

"We'll see if we can collect any prints from this, and also compare the handwriting to Dragon Boy's. Trent's, I mean."

I asked, "Why would someone who wanted to rob Wanda insist that she leave the neighborhood? Don't people generally take their treasures with them when they move?"

"Criminals don't always think logically. If thieves and killers were highly functional individuals, they might not turn to a life of crime in the first place."

"Darryl, be honest with me, please. Are you going to charge Trent with murder?"

"I think we still need more evidence that ties him to the crime scene."

I mentioned how I'd visited Wanda's house that morning. "But all I found were a few mothballs and some dead bugs."

"We think Otis might have found something." Darryl turned to his mother. "Mother, Otis was seen—"

Lydia grabbed the table and shook her head back and forth so hard the table trembled. A couple seated at a nearby table looked our way, alarmed.

Darryl tried to placate her. "Okay, okay! Calm down. We'll talk about it later."

Lydia stopped agitating the table.

His face red with embarrassment, Darryl turned to me and said quickly, "I'll grab Charlie from Janice's after school. We'll get to the house around five and relieve Doris. No need to worry about dinner. We've got Mom covered tonight and for the weekend."

"Actually, I'm about to go home and put something in the slow cooker," I said. "We can all eat together, if that's okay with you." He agreed that was fine.

Once Darryl had left, Lydia picked up a breadstick from its

basket and snapped it in two. Then she snapped a second one. It seemed I was meant to interpret.

"'Snap'?" I asked.

She shook her head.

I tried again. "'Break'?"

She nodded. Then she stood up and walked around our table once, holding something imaginary in her hand which she pretended to place on the table and open.

I thought of the briefcase that Angela had brought to our meeting.

"'Briefcase'?" I asked.

Lydia put both hands out and then compressed the space between them.

"'Shorter'?" I guessed.

Lydia nodded.

"'Brief'?" I said. She shook her head. "'Case'?"

Lydia's face lit up.

"'Break...Case.' You're going to break this case?"

Lydia pointed emphatically at me.

"Oh ... *I'm* going to break this case?"

She nodded, leaned back in her chair, and feigned complete exhaustion.

"But your son is on this case," I argued. "He even thinks he might have solved it. Don't you think Trent is a serious suspect?"

Her look was unmistakable. I didn't need another charade clue to know that Lydia wasn't buying Darryl's theory any more than I was.

I drove Lydia back to Doris. Before leaving again, I threw some chicken in Lydia's slow cooker with some Cream of Chicken soup and Dijon mustard. I'd serve it over egg noodles—easy.

That taken care of, there was someone else I wanted to visit. I couldn't get my mind off the threatening letter, which I'd taken a photo of before handing it over to Darryl. What struck me the most was how personal it was. The letter had used Wanda's name, and, though it was written in crayon, lacked the feel of a prank. While it seemed to employ Black vernacular, I wanted to be sure I wasn't missing something.

I remembered Wanda's Black colleague at the college. I googled Samuel Aldridge's email address and sent him a short note, asking if I could share with him a letter that might be evidence in Wanda's murder investigation. He wrote back immediately, offering to meet me at his office. When I got there, his door was open. On it were tacked poems by James Baldwin and Gwendolyn Brooks with quotes by Toni Morrison, Maya Angelou, and other African-American writers.

He greeted me warmly. "I have to admit, this was a most unusual inquiry," he said. "I'm not a forensics expert. But I knew Wanda very well, of course. She was a lovely person. She cared about her students."

I heard from him once again all the things that Gary Roland had told me: how she'd been a quiet, steady instructor for decades running, right up until last year when she became difficult to manage and work with.

But Aldridge had no special insight on anyone who would want to do her harm.

I did ask him about Gary Roland and what to make of his recent promotion. "He talks out of both sides of his mouth," I said. "He told me that he doesn't agree with using adjuncts, for example, but his promotion seems to be a reward for doing just that."

The professor smiled patiently. "Gary is my supervisor, so I have to weigh my words carefully. But I'll say this much: Gary is an 'enthusiast.' He can be very passionate about any number of causes—even when those causes seem to contradict one another. He's very enthusiastic about giving the students a good education. He's also very enthusiastic about his career. Make sense?"

"Professor, I was married to an incurable enthusiast for nearly twenty years."

"Then you know what I'm talking about," he said. "Enough said on that. You've got a letter you want to show me?"

"Just a photo of it. The police have the original."

I handed him my phone. He put on his reading glasses and used his fingers to enlarge and move the letter across the screen so he could read it.

"It sounds like a Black person wrote it," I said. "But I'm not an expert on Black vernacular."

"Nor am I, believe it or not. There may be a linguist we could consult, but even then, I don't know that you'd get any special insight. Vocabulary can be rather idiosyncratic." The professor must have detected my disappointment. "Sorry I can't be more help."

"It's okay. It's just that quite a few of us are stumped by this case. I'd hoped this note might break it open somehow."

His eyes seemed to brighten. "I just thought of something."

He began to rummage in a pile of papers on his desk. "Did you know Wanda wrote poetry?"

"I'm aware." I mentioned the poems of hers that I found in back issues of the school's literary magazine.

He said, "There's another poem, one she submitted to the magazine last year, if I can just find... Ah, here it is." He handed it to me:

INVALIDATED

"You are right here on Google," he says. *I am?*

"Yes! Everyone can see
This page describes you to a tee.
Close your eyes, listen: It hums your melo-dy."

Sir, there's nothing "mellow" about me
For my body rages constantly
—though it's no less hurtful to be rendered
"invalid"
in so bland a way.

"Why wasn't it published?" I asked.

"Gary didn't like it."

"Did he tell Wanda she wasn't 'valid?'"

"Even if he never used that word directly with her, perhaps that's how she felt with all the changes going on around here."

I scanned the poem again.

"She uses the word 'rages,'" I said. "Maybe she knew she had an anger management problem?"

He shrugged. "Literature—and life—don't always yield to foolproof interpretation. But enough clues can paint a picture. You seem like someone who isn't going to give up too easily."

Could he tell, like Jasmine, that I was a painter at heart? Was he pulling my leg somehow?

I would give him the benefit of the doubt. I took a photo of the rejected poem and handed him back the original.

"You're right," I said. "I'm not going to give up. Not yet."

I thanked him and we parted ways. Because I was close to downtown, I decided to head back to the jail and try to see Trent again. I was pleasantly surprised when he agreed to see me.

I mainly wanted to ask him about the note. But I didn't want to get too confrontational, so I started off with a different loose thread.

I asked, "When Wanda unpacked the dragon mask for you, were there mothballs in the box?"

He asked me what mothballs were. After I explained, he shook his head. "I didn't see any of those."

Finally, I asked Trent if the police had confronted him yet about a note that was written to Wanda before she died. He nodded. I pulled out my phone and read the note aloud. I asked, "Does this sound familiar in any way?"

"Sorta," he said.

"So you *did* write it?"

"No. I didn't."

"But it seems familiar?"

"Maybe not. No. Not really."

I looked at him. He had retreated behind a poker face. Was this young man playing me?

"I got to go," he said, standing. "Thanks for coming to see me. But I done told you everything I know."

I had a lot to think about on my drive home.

I worried that a simplified reading of the Imp's letter would connect Trent even more directly to Wanda's murder. His cagey reaction to me when I'd read the note worried me further. Yet, I couldn't understand why Trent, if he was going to rob Wanda, would want her to move out of the neighborhood.

However, I did know several people who had wanted her gone. And they all happened to live on my street.

When I arrived home, I pulled out my phone and looked again at the list of those who had helped to redo Wanda's yard. Wanda had told Skip that she had dirt on every single one of the people on this list.

One name stood out for me.

Cynthia Roberts.

I'd been so caught up in Cynthia as a victim, I hadn't given much thought to her as a suspect.

I saw her car was in her driveway, so I called her up and asked if she wanted to go for a walk, which she immediately agreed to.

Perhaps she was still riding high after confronting her attacker, for I could barely keep up with her pace. Once we'd settled into a cadence that allowed me to catch my breath, I started in with questions about Wanda.

I asked her if she knew who Wanda's doctor was. Cynthia shook her head. "The detective called to ask me that, and I didn't have an answer for him. I don't think she ever went to the doctor. If she did, I wasn't aware...wait."

She abruptly stopped walking.

"What is it?" I asked.

"You and I walking just now helped me remember. About three years ago, Wanda broke her foot. Just kind of a random break, landed on it wrong. She had a boot for a month or two. I walked with other people during that time. I'm pretty sure she had to see a doctor for that."

"Good memory. I'll see Darryl at dinner and tell him."

We started walking again. Now it was time to turn the conversation to a more delicate matter.

"You and Wanda used to walk like this often," I said. "I know you've been busy, but that doesn't explain why you wouldn't try to reconnect when you returned from England back in August."

"Like I told you, I did reach out to her, but she kept putting me off."

"Why do you think she did that?"

"I don't know. Wanda was a private person. Even on our walks we rarely talked about private matters. We mainly discussed literature."

I told her about Wanda's bold statement to Skip about having dirt on the people who contributed to the makeover. "Did Wanda ever threaten that she'd tell NC State about what really happened so long ago? That really you were the one who burned Dennis's dissertation?"

She stopped walking again. "Why would you suggest that?"

"Tell me the truth, Cynthia."

She paused, her expression inscrutable—until it broke wide open. "I wrote a whole book about Shakespeare's view of truth in *Hamlet*, so I suppose I owe you the truth now." We started walking again, but more slowly. "A few days after the makeover, Wanda did call to berate me for giving money for her yard. She said all she had to do was place a phone call to the chair of my department and my career would be through. I was shocked. It was so out of character for her. I knew immediately that something terrible had happened to her mind within the time I'd been away."

"Why didn't you say something to Darryl about it? To me?"

"I didn't see what good could come of it. Her whole life, Wanda was a lovely woman. I didn't want her behavior in her final few months to define who she was. She had done so much for me, Rett. She saved my life, when you think about it. I could never do very much for her—I certainly couldn't save her from being killed—but this one thing I could do. Can you possibly understand why I'd want to preserve a positive narrative of her life, so others could know who she really was at heart?"

We looked into each other's expressions for the answer.

"I can," I said.

The rest of our walk was made up of small talk. When we got home, out of shared habit, we each stopped at our respective curb-side mailboxes—and simultaneously screamed.

In each of our mailboxes was tucked a bloody mound of fur.

~

Darryl responded to my phone call within minutes. Wearing surgical gloves, he quickly ascertained that both squirrels had been stabbed in the back, just as Wanda had been.

"The mail hasn't come yet today," I said. "They could have been placed in the mailboxes last night."

After bagging each squirrel as evidence, Darryl rushed to deliver them to the crime lab before he was due to pick up his son from school—the bizarre, bifurcated life of a police detective.

Noticing the hubbub, several who lived on the block stopped by or texted to ask what had happened. Those with mailboxes reported relief at finding them free of roadkill. Cynthia and I had been the only recipients of the gruesome deliveries.

"Who does something like this?" I asked Cynthia once we were alone again. We remained talking in the street, trying to make one another feel better.

Cynthia said, "Dennis. That's who."

Of course it was Dennis. He'd even made sure to kill the squirrels the way Wanda had been murdered, just to make us think that Wanda's killer had returned to the neighborhood. Just to scare the living daylights out of us.

Sure it was Dennis—with a message meant mainly for Cynthia.

Or maybe this had been done by someone else.

With a message meant mainly for me.

CHAPTER 16

THE BATTLE

Darryl returned with Charlie an hour or so later to begin his weekend shift with Lydia. At the last second, I begged out of dinner. Darryl pleaded, "Please stay and eat. You cooked it, after all."

But all I could think about was the investor party, now less than 24 hours away. I didn't want to get into the details of that, so I let Darryl think that the afternoon's squirrel scare was to blame and that I was just emotionally exhausted, which wasn't far from the truth.

I went home, drank wine alone, and stayed up late watching old episodes of *Downton Abbey*, trying to keep my mind from the next day's challenge. Why couldn't I be more like Allan, for whom avoidance came naturally? Why did I have to drink myself silly to achieve distraction?

I awoke the morning of the party feeling terrible, so I took some ibuprofen and slept some more. At least I remembered to call Needless Necessities to tell Jasmine I wouldn't be volunteering today. Around two in the afternoon I finally felt human enough to get out of bed. I needed to shower and get dressed, but I stalled. I reached for *Sublime Lives* and read to myself the last stanza Lord Byron allegedly ever wrote:

> *If thou regret'st thy youth, why live?*
> *The land of honourable death*
> *Is here: — up to the field, and give*
> *Away thy breath!*

It was time for me to prepare for my own battlefield. I took a long shower and donned a stylish but low-key hippie ensemble, wondering if it really did communicate "Bag Lady Bohemian" more emphatically than it should. At the last minute, I decided I wouldn't risk it and changed into business attire—navy dress skirt with matching kitten heel pumps and white blouse. Margaret wouldn't be there to see my regret, but damn if I didn't think Lord Byron was somewhere out there judging me.

The party started at four. I wanted to be fashionably (translation: passive aggressively) late, so I headed out around 4:15. Allan and KayLeigh's pretentiously named neighborhood, The Rills of Innesfree, consisted of too-small lots, sapling trees, and gleaming white concrete curbs. The 4,000-square-foot home was done in a style I like to call Modern Mishmash, with a half dozen or more historical motifs thrown together—a couple of Corinthian columns, a stone wall, red metal roof, and two front porch gas lamps flickering at 4:30 in the afternoon like something a thirteen-year-old boy might design for *Dungeons & Dragons*.

The impeccably manicured front lawn looked spray painted green. I got the sense that not a single leaf dared drop, lest it be severely scolded.

Distant laughter flowed from the pool area in the back of the home, but I let myself in through the yellow-painted front door. There was no one there to greet me, and that was fine with me. I took in the home's decor. There was little in the way of antiques, just the artificially distressed Pottery Barn fare that some called "Shabby Chic." But there was nothing shabby about this home. A lot of dollars had gone into furnishing it.

Everything. Was. Perfect.

I ducked into a side room which turned out to be KayLeigh's office, small yet charming. Maybe I would find something incriminating—say, a letter from her mafioso boyfriend. Instead, my eyes settled on something much worse.

Lying in a neat column along one side of the desk were cards from several popular high-end, home furnishing stores. They weren't advertisements. They were personalized cards, each containing a login for KayLeigh to go online and choose the components of her wedding registry.

North Carolina law required a couple to separate for a year before their divorce could proceed. My divorce from Allan couldn't go through until December at the earliest.

But KayLeigh seemed more than ready for the day. *Her* day. And she was already planning for it.

After some tears and more than a few calming breaths, I escaped to a sitting room where I ran into Joe Archibald, the financial planner. Archie, as he was known, was relaxing in a chair in the corner of the living room tipping back a short glass of brown liquor. Though he wasn't himself an investor in large-scale developments, many of his clients were.

"Hi, Rett! Good to see you." He stood up to give me a hug. "Congratulations on the company anniversary."

I appreciated the squeeze. "You do know that Allan and I are separated?"

He nodded as we both sat down. "Yes, I heard. I didn't want

to bring it up if you didn't want to talk about it."

"Thank you. If you don't mind me asking, how did you hear?"

He looked to make sure we were alone.

"Brad and Gail Norris told me."

"Really? Are they your clients?"

Archie chuckled. "They *were* my clients, until about two months ago. They didn't like my financial advice, I guess." He finished his drink and set the glass down.

"Oh? Were you advising them to invest in Florida swamp-land again?" I teased.

"Actually, I was advising them to slow down. They were way over leveraged. I suggested they unload some land—lots of it, actually—to improve their cash position. But they insisted prop-erty prices were going to keep going up and they just couldn't bear selling anything."

"Except for their home in Woodmont," I suggested.

"Yes, that's one they'd like to get out from under. 'Too many liberals and queers moving into Woodmont,' as Brad put it."

"That's a terrible thing to say."

"I guess he forgot that my sister came out of the closet a few years ago. Politics is one thing, but I can't excuse homophobia, not if you're an educated adult who should know better. Kind of glad to be rid of that guy, if you want the honest truth."

I said, "I think things are looking up for the Norrises" and shared as how their Woodmont home was likely to sell very soon—due to the recent death of the person whose home was an eyesore. "She was murdered on Halloween."

He let out a low whistle. "Interesting—because I saw Brad and Gail downtown the very next night, and they did seem pretty light on their feet, now that I recall."

"Where?"

"My wife and I were walking along Hargett Street and saw

them entering The Rabbit's Hat. They were practically skipping down the sidewalk. I thought, 'That must be how you feel after you fire Archie as your family's financial advisor.'"

"Behave! One would only experience long-term remorse and regret."

He shrugged. "More power to them." He looked at his watch. "I better go."

"You shouldn't drive. I can run you home."

"I'm fine. Been here quite a while and just the one drink. I already congratulated Allan. I just wanted to make an appearance anyway."

After filing away yet another reason to suspect the Norrises of something nefarious, I found myself hungry, so I headed for the hors d'oeuvres table. Catching my eye along the way was a scale model of the condominiums that were being planned by Swinson Development. I suppose I should have taken more interest in my own company's project, but I just walked on past.

The table of food held much more appeal. What an assortment! I filled my plate and tasted several of the finger foods, each one more amazing than the last. I looked for a menu that described what I was tasting but found only a table tent:

Join the Group Toast and Menu Reveal at 5 p.m.
Please enjoy the Food and Drink in the Meantime

That's odd, I thought. Since when was a menu "revealed?" As the hottest chef in Raleigh, I suppose Paige could do what she wanted. I also made a mental note to ask Paige if she had seen the Norrises on Saturday night. The Rabbit's Hat was the most popular of Paige's three restaurants, and more often than not she could be found working its kitchen.

More laughter erupted from deep in the home. I wanted to leave—but I couldn't now. If I was going to provide assurance to the investors, I needed to stick around for the group toast. And that would likely mean having to face KayLeigh.

Better to be predator than prey.

I spotted her through the French doors, standing by the backyard pool and holding a glass of wine as she chatted conspiratorially with the third installment wife of one of our investors. As expected, KayLeigh looked superb, wearing a black cocktail dress cut so as to show off her evenly tanned legs. Matching her long and straight silky black hair were exquisite black pearls. Her large brown eyes were professionally lined, tasteful in a way that didn't overpower her naturally glamorous features. Was her background Italian? Greek? Armenian like the Kardashians? I felt I needed to know.

Fortifying myself with a big gulp of wine, I headed with my glass to the patio.

She didn't see me—or more likely had pretended not to. I decided to make her sweat a little, by taking a detour to one of the tables in the shade of a tiki bar where Allan was lounging and talking with two men I knew.

"Hello, Allan," I announced flatly.

"Howdy, Rett!" he responded with old-time cheeriness. "You know Doug and Frank."

"Hello, Gentlemen," I said. "Y'all sit back down. It's just me."

"Hi, Darlin'!" said Doug Lane, a nice enough guy who owned a successful engineering firm.

The other man, Frank Carter, saluted me with his beer glass. With his lovely white hair and tanned skin, Frank looked like a retired professional golfer. He had made his fortune in manufacturing in the 1960s and '70s, but got out in the '80s when the getting was good. Frank was the type of big fish Allan would want to land for this project. Shrewd, he would be looking for assurance that this new development was going to be well monitored.

Trouble was, I was pretty sure I *didn't* want to monitor the project. For now, though, I'd act like everything was business as usual.

In the middle of my conversation, I saw KayLeigh shoot into the house like a bottle rocket. As Allan had predicted, I wasn't the only one anxious about an encounter. I excused myself and traced her path into the house, then positioned myself with a replenished wine glass right outside the closed door of the master suite.

"Hi, KayLeigh," I said cheerfully when she stepped out.

"Oh, hi!" KayLeigh said, her smile wide and forced.

I knew she couldn't get around me in the narrow hallway. The moment felt private, but if voices became raised, someone would certainly hear us.

"It's sure been awhile," I said. "I think we last met a couple years ago in Midtown. Is that where you met Allan for the first time?" It wasn't entirely a trick question, but if she admitted knowing him any sooner than that open house, it might suggest they'd begun their affair a lot earlier.

"I'm not really sure," she evaded. We'd begun a variation of the staring game, only with smiles. I was at a slight disadvantage, because I'd never entered the type of beauty pageants where a girl learned the art of endurance grinning.

"How are you doing these days?" she asked with exaggerated sympathy.

"Oh, I'm terrific. Light as a feather. I'm sure if you ever get divorced, you'll understand exactly what I mean."

She responded, "I suppose," while her tone communicated: *I aim to keep my man.*

"You'll see," I responded, as in: *Your man and my man are one and the same, honey.*

KayLeigh was acting all innocent and sparkly, but I

suspected she was far from either. She was manipulative and diabolical, and I aimed to confirm it.

"Heard you're planning a wedding," I said as a took a sip of my drink.

Surprise flashed across her face. "Oh, really, who told you that?"

"If it's true, what does it matter who told me? Is it?"

She frowned at me, as a teacher might confront a hapless teenager with a lackluster future.

I said, "You realize that Allan is still married."

"Oh, Harriet, you knew a long time ago that your marriage was over. You just didn't want to admit it."

"Really? No one told me it was over."

"Allan told you many times he was unhappy, but you didn't listen."

"He actually didn't tell me any such thing. It's not like Allan to be so direct. You're right, though. I got the message eventually. I only had to read his text exchanges with you. I thought Allan was too old for 'sexting,' but I guess I was wrong."

KayLeigh lifted her chin. By God, this modern woman was bound and determined not to wear the scarlet letter.

"Are you finished?" she asked. "I think I should rejoin my party."

"Sure, but first you need to apologize," I said, "for helping to ruin *my* marriage."

"Your marriage was already a disaster. I just helped Allan salvage a life for himself." She smiled, pleased with her pithy comeback. "I hope you'll find a way to move on and be happy. I really do."

"Oh, I've moved on," I lied. "But, you, on the other hand, have just gotten started. I got the best years of Allan Swinson. All you're getting is a hand-me-down." Judging by her new home's sparkling décor, secondhand rarely sat well with KayLeigh Rider.

Her fury was palpable. "Are you done finally?"

"Right," I said. "Back to your party. By all means."

I began walking away, KayLeigh right on my heels. I said over my shoulder to her, "I might as well have some of the food that *my company* is paying for."

"It's delicious," she said. "Peg is just the best."

"'Peg?'" I asked, as we reached the table.

"Oh, sorry, Paige Kirkland. I'm sure you've heard of her. James Beard nominee and all that."

"Ah, Peg *Kirkland*." Paige fucking hated whenever people called her Peg. I'd have to ask her about that later. In the meantime, I'd play along.

"You and Peg must be super-duper close," I said, "because I hear she almost never does catering gigs anymore. Her restaurants are just so busy. But you must already know that, because you're on a nickname basis."

"I suppose so," she said, as she stopped at the long table of food and took an infinitesimal bite of one of the carrot cake petit fours. "By the way, have you seen Steph yet? I thought she'd be here by now."

My, my, KayLeigh. You and I really do hold similar dance cards these days.

"I haven't seen my daughter," I said. "But if you see her first, please tell her I'm eager to hear how she's doing. And tell her that there are fried oysters with pimento cheese here. That girl loves her some seafood."

"I know. She's so awesome. We're BFFs, you know."

"Why, that's so cute!" I said, as in: *So cute that you think so.* Could KayLeigh be a suspect in Wanda's murder? Because here was someone who really knew how to shove a blade into someone's torso and ever so slowly twist it.

There was a silence as we both sampled the food and thought about our next lines. Our stand-off was made permanent when the front door flew open and in strode my only child. The first thing I noticed were the dangly opal earrings she had bought in Australia on her senior trip there with me—our last hurrah before Allan's affair was discovered. I never told her that while she and I were having our little walkabout in the Land Down Under, her father was shacking up at our beach house with his 25-year-old sheila.

Steph had a breezy, casual way about her that drew others her way. Her straight, dirty-blond hair and sharp nose were just two of the physical features I'd always envied. (I always thought my nose looked a little squashed.) When she saw KayLeigh, her smile lit up and her arms opened wide.

"You are adorable," KayLeigh said. "I love that belt!"

"Your dress is stunning," Steph reciprocated. "Hi, Mom," she muttered at me over KayLeigh's left shoulder. I wondered if the Devil was taking notes from this party on how he could make Hell more hellish.

"Hi, Hon," I said. "How are you?"

She walked over to me and, in lieu of a hug, grabbed a glass of wine. At least a penchant for inebriation was one bond we shared.

Before I could say anything more, I was accosted by Anna Walker wiping her hands on her apron. Anna was Paige's right-hand for everything; she had managed each of her three restaurants at some point. I wanted to ask her why Paige had decided to cater this gig, but she was already lifting an empty wine glass and tapping it with a spoon. Others of her staff must have already been fetching guests from the pool patio, for soon the food table was totally surrounded.

KayLeigh and Steph went to stand near Allan. I tried to step away from Anna to join the flank of the crowd opposite my relatives, but she grabbed my arm.

"Stay next to me," Anna whispered. Reluctantly, I remained with her at center stage.

Once everyone had gathered, Anna began a speech. "This won't take long. I know you are here for business as well as pleasure, but before I turn the floor over to Allan, I wanted to share a bit of a secret. Paige Kirkland, while she rarely caters events these days, jumped at the chance to service this event for one very special reason: she has known Allan and Rett for many years and considers them dear, dear friends. As a businesswoman herself, she knows what a challenge it is to deliver excellence again and again, project after project. This is Swinson Development's tenth anniversary. Let's give the company a huge round of applause!"

There was a round of boisterous clapping. Anna continued.

"In honor of the occasion, Paige has put together a special menu, which I shall reveal to you now."

Anna's worker bees had been distributing small copies of the menu through the crowd. While Anna donned a pair of reading glasses, I quickly skimmed the menu—and nearly choked on my wine.

Oh, Lord, she didn't.

Oh, yes, she did.

Anna began reading the menu aloud:

"Fried North Carolina Oysters on Pimento Cheese and *Rett's* Cracker..." (Laughter. A splattering of applause).

"...*Rett*-White-and-Blue-Fin Tuna Bites..." (More laughter. More applause.)

"...1970s *Rett*-ro Spam Sandwich..." ("I love Spam!" someone cried out.)

"...and topping it all off: Care-*Rett* Cake Petit Four Squares!"

Full applause. I glanced in the direction of KayLeigh. My

nemesis had been eating from a small plate, but now it appeared is if she might lose her lunch. She swallowed quickly and put on a perfectly adequate smile.

My face was so red (so *Rett!*) I felt like fainting. Meanwhile, the staff were busy passing around wine glasses to everyone and filling them.

It seems that Anna—and Paige, her boss—wasn't finished.

Anna continued, "Paige wishes she could be here herself, but I'm going to read you a note in her own words:

'Dear Friends,

These four 'Rett-cipes' were inspired by my best friend, Harriet Newsom Swinson, whom we all know simply as 'Rett' and whose brilliant work helped to build an amazing company over the past decade. As they say in the restaurant biz, many may try to make their company's dough to rise, but not very many succeed. Please raise a glass with me in celebrating our friend Rett's singular contribution to the legacy of Swinson Development.'

The applause was overwhelming. As I found myself showered with hugs, I thought everyone might put me on their shoulders while singing *For She's a Jolly Good Fellow*.

In all the excitement I glanced in the direction of KayLeigh. She wore her plastic smile like a pro, and, aware that others were stealing glances at her, assumed the picture of good sportsmanship.

But I'd already spied her initial mortification, her reflex pain. And it had been *delicious*.

"Last but not least," Anna continued, "today's featured wine is a 2014 Thessalonian 'Rett'-sina. This is a special release retsina with a custom label by a friend of Paige's in Greece who has a winery in the Northern part of the Peloponnese. And guess what? Each of you may take home a bottle at the end of tonight's affair."

There were considerable oohs and ahhs as I tried to show everyone how touched I felt—by the recognition, of course, but also by Anna's use of the word "affair," intentional or not. For whenever my divorce was finalized, Allan's affair would officially be over, too.

"To Swinson Development," toasted Anna, "and especially to Rett."

"To Rett! Hear hear!"

"Hear hear!"

The feelings swirling inside me were so extreme, and in some ways so diametrically opposed, I felt I might explode. Combined with the wine I'd consumed, my reality seemed surreal. But I publicly thanked everyone and even managed to put in a good word for the over-50 project—the whole reason I was there, after all.

Allan spoke next, standing close enough to me that we might have been mistaken for a couple. He thanked everyone for coming and managed somehow to act as if the indirect insults aimed at his mistress had already been forgiven and forgotten.

Once the speeches were over, I looked over at Stephanie. I guess I had hoped for some support, at least a nod and smile, but she was still focused on KayLeigh, distracting her with compliments about her home, her dress, her hair. Allan was shaking hands with guests he hadn't had a chance to speak with yet. Tonight, I'd receive no expressions of affection from the humans who once had loved me most.

I'd done my part; I didn't feel like fielding any questions about apartment layouts and mixed-use development. Allan could do that—or maybe he'd already prepped KayLeigh to be the public-facing sidekick so he could start to focus on the more tedious financial details. I didn't much care.

I got out of there with my hide and pride intact. But you can bet I took with me some of my namesake wine, two bottles in each hand. How does one manage that, you may ask?

Why, you grab them by the neck.

CHAPTER 17

THE CONVERSATION

I beelined it for The Rabbit's Hat, a (mostly) vegetarian restaurant that made believers out of even the most loyal carnivore.

Like all of Paige's restaurants, the dining room of The Rabbit's Hat smelled magical. I worked my way to the belly-up bar where patrons had a front row view of her culinary artistry, then let myself into the kitchen where I found my friend pulling a tray of puffed-up pita bread out of a stone oven.

"Paige! What the hell did you just do to me?"

My friend put on a mask of innocence. "Wha-aaatt?"

"You know exactly 'wha-aaat!' You named that whole menu after me. Even the Spam!"

She wiped her face with her apron.

"Well, you did say at our last gathering—and I quote—'Kay-Leigh can *eat* me.'"

"Okay," I said, remembering the conversation now. "But I didn't say she could *drink* me, too."

"I couldn't resist that touch. Wasn't that Greek vintage just wonderful?"

"Yes, but I don't think KayLeigh enjoyed it. She looked like she'd swallowed a bug."

"Then I'll consider the evening a rousing success."

"After that little stunt, you may never get hired to cater ever again."

"Good. Because I *hate* catering."

"You mean you manipulated KayLeigh and Allan into hiring you just for me?"

She put her pinky to the corner of her mouth, Dr. Evil style. "*May*be."

"And who told KayLeigh you liked to be called Peg? You hate being called Peg."

"I know—and all my friends know it, too. So, when she name-drops around town—"

"—everyone will think she's lying about knowing you!"

"Precisely."

I launched into a cathartic belly laugh. "I can't believe—"

"Girl, you need to calm down—and I need to catch a breath. Follow me."

I matched her steps to the back of the kitchen, through a storeroom, and past a walk-in freezer to a door that led into pitch dark. When she flicked on a light, I realized I was standing in the equivalent of a loft apartment.

"Where am I?" I asked.

"This is where I unwind. You think I want to sit in the dining room and get harassed by my customers?"

"Are you saying you're a misanthrope?"

"If that means 'sourpuss,' you'd be spot-on."

She bade me sit on the comfiest sofa ever and plopped straight across from me.

"Now tell me everything. Did KayLeigh choke on an oyster and Allan had to give her the Hiney-Licky Maneuver right then and there?"

I gave her a play by play of my conversation with KayLeigh, Stephanie's inhospitable entry, and the magnificent job Anna did embarrassing the hell out of me.

"That's Anna," Paige said. "Always on task."

Then I related something else from the party: learning from Arch about Brad and Gail's recent night on the town. "I wish I could have been a fly on the wall for their conversation. Of all the suspects in Wanda's murder, I still feel they are the most suspicious."

Paige rose and poked her head into the kitchen. "Mitch? Could you ask the wait staff to come back here for a second, please? And will you ask Vanessa to bring me one of those real estate guides from the lobby? Thanks, Hon."

"You don't have to go through all this trouble, Paige," I said.

"Please, Harriet—call me Peg," she said with a wink.

Paige's voice turned serious a moment later was we were joined by two waiters and two waitresses. "Did any of you serve a couple here last Saturday who looked like this?" She held up a picture of Brad and Gail from the homes and land guide. "They're kind of famous. You've probably seen their billboards."

One of the waitresses raised a hand, "They were in my section. Did they complain about their service?"

"Not at all. Okay, you, Alissa, stay. The rest of you can go."

Once the others had left, Paige asked Alissa conspiratorially, "What did you observe regarding this couple. Were they having a good time?"

"Having a ball."

"What did they order?"

"The prime rib and scallops."

"Really?" Paige flashed a raised brow of intrigue at me. "The evening's token *carnivore* entree." She returned her attention to Alissa. "Did you hear them talking about anything in particular?"

"Um, am I going to get into trouble?"

"Why would you get into trouble? Alissa, you're the best server I have—just don't tell the others I said so."

"I'll be sure to. Yes, I did hear them talking while I was serving the next table over."

"You can do two conversations at once?" I asked.

"It helps. That way I always know if another table is needing me to come by, and I look like I'm reading their minds."

"Impressive," said Paige. "Please remind me to bump up your base salary."

"Will do."

"Now tell us what they said."

"Well, the woman said, 'Death happens to the nicest people sometimes.'"

"Oh, my," Paige observed. "And...?"

Alissa paused. Paige frowned. "*Come on, Alissa...*"

"Sorry," said the waitress. "I'm just trying to remember. And then the man said, 'I just had to make sure that the timing was right.'"

"And *then*..."

"And then she said, 'My dear, you acted not a moment too soon.' And then they clinked wine glasses."

Paige's eyes became wide. "What did you think when you heard that?"

"I thought they were just sharing some sort of inside joke."

"Sounds devious to me," Paige said.

Me, too. I asked, "How did they act as they left? Did they seem nervous in any way?"

"A little self-conscious maybe. The guests at one or two of the tables recognized them and said hello."

"How did they tip?" asked Paige. "Just curious."

Alissa shrugged. "Not great. About fifteen dollars on a hundred-twenty-dollar meal."

Paige smirked, "I guess some real estate agents think because they only get six percent, maybe everyone else should, too."

"A twenty dollar entree isn't the same thing as a million dollar home," I said.

"That entree was thirty-six," corrected Paige.

"Beg your pardon," I said.

It didn't matter. If a couple can murder a neighbor, they can certainly stiff a waitress.

Back home I played back every moment of the party in my head. I wish I could have been quicker with comebacks, but I was secretly delighted with myself for having confronted KayLeigh in the first place.

I was also invigorated by what The Rabbit Hat's waitress had remembered of Brad and Gail's private conversation. Added to the other detail I'd discovered—their final purchase, according to Margaret, of the Falls Lake home—I thought it fitting to call Darryl and inform him.

"I'll confront them about it in the morning," he said after my blow by blow. "Maybe they'll slip up and say something incriminating."

In the meantime, Darryl had another detail to report. One of his officers called the three largest orthopedic practices over the weekend. The police submitted Wanda's name and found the practice that had treated her broken foot.

"Her records show she was prescribed Oxycodone. The pills in Trent's pocket were produced around the time Wanda was prescribed them. You can tell from the blister pack."

Another potential nail in Trent's coffin.

"What about the threatening letter Angela found?" I asked. "Were you able to connect it to Trent?"

"The letter didn't have any usable fingerprints. And we couldn't match it to Trent's handwriting. That doesn't mean he didn't write it."

"It also doesn't mean *I* didn't write it," I said. "I still think you're barking up the wrong tree."

"Show me a better tree," he said, "and I'll gladly hug it."

I hung up with Darryl feeling grumpy—but extra motivated. I turned to my laptop and googled the Norrises. I even paid forty dollars to see their criminal records, but all it revealed was a pair of speeding tickets, years old.

I went through the same process for the Fosters and for Skip Green. Nothing. I concluded that if Wanda really did have dirt on the people who had invaded her lawn, the Internet probably wasn't where she found it.

I googled Wanda, too. The first listing to pop up was a website that students used to rate their professors. Wanda's scores and comments from students were all over the map, from "boring as a hell — who cares about this English potry stuf??" to "such a kind and supportive teacher. Best class I've had at Tech."

I noted that the most recent entries were consistently grim. "Continually AWOL from class, and when she's there, constantly berates students. Don't even bother with this one!" and "What a horrible person. What rock did she crawl out from under?" The scores for her final semester of teaching were in the basement.

The comments basically tracked what everyone else had testified to: a personality that had come apart, a disintegration.

I went to YouTube and did a search. After many dead ends, I finally found a video from a symposium on Romantic poetry from five years earlier, a panel discussion that Wanda was part of. The topic: "Are the Romantics Still Relevant Today?"

The moderator was a personality from a local public radio station. His first few questions were fielded mainly by the other two panelists who produced an impenetrable jargon. I had to remind myself that these were experts in their field who were presenting to other scholars, not to a general audience. Even the radio host—older, perhaps less enamored of literary theory—seemed to be getting a little frustrated as he turned to Wanda for the first time.

Moderator: Let's back up a little. Why do we think Romanticism saw the success it did, when it did? Ms. Hightower, we haven't heard from you. Any thoughts?

Wanda: Thank you. I'll try.

Wanda was poised, calm, pleasant. She wore her signature elegant to-the-elbow gloves. Shyly, she pulled the microphone closer to herself.

Wanda: In early 18th Century England, unless you were landed gentry, you probably lived on a farm. You didn't own the land your family lived on, but you worked it. You probably couldn't read very well, and, even if you could, you didn't have the time to read very much. In terms of what you chose to believe, you likely looked outside yourself for your opinions—to Church leaders, or to the educated owner of your land, because your own education was extremely limited.

However, late in the 1700s, factories began luring more and more people to the cities. Education for the average person became easier to come by. By the end of that century, books began being published at an amazing rate. Prior to that, authors would typically write from some authority—referencing Scripture, what passed for science, or citing the wise thinkers who came before them. The Romantic poets, however, shifted the central point of reference. They followed their own hearts and minds to see what they could discover. Appalled by the 'dark Satanic mills' of London, they looked for meaning in Earth's natural beauty, in the mythologies of Greece and Rome, and in childhood innocence. In short, they searched for a purity in this world that they could locate and express through beautiful language.

Moderator: You make them sound almost religious.

Wanda: Not particularly religious, but certainly spiritual. The Romantics were the opposite of unbelievers. In fact, they were idealists almost to a fault who longed for connection to Spirit. As a result, we get John Keats's shepherd-chief hero, Endymion, who chases a Greek goddess through four thousand lines of poetry, and a different sort of seeker, Mary Shelley's Doctor Frankenstein, who attempts to bring a corpse back to life. In both cases, there is a strong curiosity about the supernatural and a fervent attempt to connect to something that transcends our suffering world. "Poetry as prayer," you might say.

It might be helpful to remember that life two centuries ago was way more of a struggle. The average life expectancy in England in 1800 was forty—half of what it is today. Those who did live long lives invariably saw dozens of close friends and family die. Who wouldn't wish to transcend such grief?

Moderator: I understand what you're saying, but, honestly, I grew up thinking about the Romantics as sort of hippies before their time. You know, free love, opium, revolution...

Wanda: Yes, there was plenty of that, but I think theirs was a more legitimate impulse than the hippies. I mean, the 1960s bacchanal couldn't last, right? Yesterday's hippies have 401Ks today. The Romantics, however, sought a much more sustainable radicalization of the mind and spirit.

Moderator: Carpe Diem. "Seize the Day." Seize every day?

Wanda: Yes, and experience eternity—by fully apprehending the world we live in.

The other panelists fielded the next few questions, but I found myself skipping ahead to Wanda's next opportunity to speak...

Moderator: This symposium asks us to find the relevance of the Romantics in our modern era. But if everyone today is already an individualist, do the Romantics offer us anything today that we currently lack?

Wanda: I don't agree that everyone today is an individualist.

Moderator: (laughing) I don't see how you can hold that position, what with confessional blogs, incessant tweeting. Selfies.

Wanda: Taking selfies doesn't make you an individualist. In fact, I'd say the opposite, that the people who do that are strongly lacking a sense of self.

Moderator: Can you elaborate?

Wanda: The tyranny of advertising and franchising has created a group-think and a terrible sameness. The Internet has collapsed into echo chambers, some of them diabolical. The advanced speed of media has destroyed reflection. Our comfortable lives have disconnected us from the Earth, idealism is scorned as naive, and anti-intellectualism has banished literature and philosophy to remote corners of our culture.

As a result, we don't know how we feel, and when we do feel some-

thing, we work very hard to numb it with drugs, sports, sex, or some other distraction. We allow others to nurture in us a single emotion—anger—as a proxy for feeling alive. Absolutely we need the Romantics—today more than ever. We need them to help us feel fully human again and to inspire us to give expression to a range of feelings. We need them to wake us up to ourselves, because everything that is not acknowledged is lost.

The panel ended soon after that with more cryptic commentary by the other panelists.

Seeing and listening to a once very much alive—and so very well-spoken—murder victim saddened me. It also reminded me that I was no closer than before at understanding what had happened to Wanda in the last year of her life, much less what had caused her to become someone's target. What was I missing? I listened to Wanda's comments a couple more times before copying the webpage address and emailing it to Angela in case she had not seen it.

Everything that is not acknowledged is lost. I went over in my head all my conversations with those who had known Wanda, especially those who had been burned by her wrath. Surely the Norrises stood out. But I couldn't totally rule out anyone else either—even Trent (the actor, the dragon) who had so much circumstantial evidence pointing his way.

I told myself to rest, but my mind refused. In our real-estate business, while Allan always schmoozed the investors, I would be the one who paid attention to the details, still following Glenda Murlowski's painterly advice to apprehend detail, but in a radically different context. I might be out of practice, but I didn't need Darryl's pen and notebook to keep up with the details of this investigation. The picture was in my head. I went over that picture again and again, trying to find something that would crack this case.

It was past three in the morning before I managed to sleep. As if returning from another trip to Australia, I slept all the next day, leaving the bed on Sunday only to pee and eat. I awoke refreshed on Monday without a thought in my brain, as if newly born. Was this the sobering sleep that Freddy talked about?

I walked across the street where I found Lydia in her backyard attempting to garden for the first time since her stroke.

"Where's Doris?" I asked, half expecting her to pop out from behind some bushes.

I expected some sort of hand gesture. "In...side," Lydia said, haltingly but clear as day.

"Lydia! The therapy is working!"

Blushing a little, she returned to her task. I saw she had dug up a lime tree to put in a large pot. I remembered when she had planted the tiny tree this past spring as a birthday present for Charlie.

"In...side," she said again.

"I'll help you." I brought the pot closer and helped her lift the tree inside it. Once I had done so, she said a third time, "In...*side*" and pointed to the house.

"Okay. I can help you carry it, but what about the worms?" I'd noticed that several wigglers had clung to the roots of the little tree and were now in the pot with it. Would they survive in that cramped space all winter?

As I lifted the tree again, Lydia bent down and carefully pulled the worms from the roots, placing the creatures back in the hole they'd come from. I thought again of the enterprise Lydia and I had helped to fund: a team of do-gooders going into Wanda's yard, tearing it apart before replanting. Wanda, who had tried to explore Buddhism with Maxine and seemed to connect with the Romantics' embracing of all life—even ugly life—might well have viewed our favor to her not only as an insult, but as a considerable violence against the nature in her yard.

Was a weed unworthy of life? And what of the many worms that cling to that weed's roots? An experience like that might be traumatizing, especially for someone whose mental state was already quite fragile.

Inside, while Doris knitted in the front room, I hung out in Lydia's kitchen a little while, putting together an easy pulled-pork slow cooker meal. I got the cooker started, then stood for a while just staring out the window, watching Lydia's wiry, stubborn arms lifting mulch from a wheelbarrow and placing it around shrubs and flower beds to keep their roots warm. Watching her work relaxed me.

The speed of media has destroyed reflection.

My eyes came to focus on the window sill and a dead fly. Without thinking, really, I pulled a ziplock from my purse, brushed the fly into it, and zipped it up.

"Curious," said a familiar voice.

I turned. "Darryl! What are you doing here?"

"I'm just someone who likes to people-watch. Folks do the craziest things, don't you think?"

"I don't know what to say."

"Let me guess, this has something to do with someone who wouldn't hurt a fly?"

"Sheila's making another insect collection," I blurted, "using insects that are already dead."

Darryl raised an eyebrow. "Really? I watched her when she and Maxine came and got Mom for a walk on Saturday. Sheila was holding something in her shirt—something, judging by the look on her face when she saw me, that she's not supposed to have."

"Okay," I said, backed against the proverbial wall. "Maybe

she's breaking a rule or two trying to nurse a wild animal back to health."

"What sort of animal?"

"Just a little hummingbird. Are you going to turn her in?"

"No, but I'm wondering if someone else threatened to report her—someone who said she had dirt on everyone in the neighborhood before she was murdered."

"But Sheila and Maxine weren't even involved in Wanda's lawn makeover."

"Maybe Wanda was confused."

"They didn't even find the bird until the morning after Wanda was killed," I explained.

"That's what they told *you*."

"I believe them. They didn't even have a place for the bird to sleep when you and I showed up that morning. And they certainly hadn't built its Disney World yet."

"Its *what*? Never mind." He smiled and shook his head. "Look, I can understand why you didn't report Sheila to the bird cops. I don't care about that. I was just curious what she was hiding, and now I know." He opened his little notebook, turned to a page, and made a mark.

That little notebook was getting on my nerves.

"You really don't like being left in the dark, do you?" I asked.

"I'm afraid of the dark," he said. "Always have been."

I chuckled to myself, for I doubted that Darryl was afraid of much.

"By the way," he said. "I just confronted the Norrises about what that waitress overheard."

"Really? Did you tell them who told you?"

"I just said it was someone at the restaurant. For all they know it was another diner. Anyway, they acted very puzzled. Gail suggested maybe they had been discussing an episode of

Game of Thrones. I don't watch the show, but I gather from what others say that it's pretty brutal, lots of killing."

"So, they aren't suspects in your mind?"

"Oh, everyone's still a suspect. But I'll need something stronger than overheard conversation to tie the Norrises to the crime."

Fortunately, I had just the idea for how to do it.

CHAPTER 18

A CLOSER LOOK

After Lydia came in from gardening and had washed the dirt off her hands, I whispered to her conspiratorially, "Want to have a little fun?"

She raised an eyebrow. I beckoned her to follow me into the living room where Doris was still in her chair, knitting.

"Doris," I said, "I was just thinking. It might be really nice if you could live a little closer to Lydia, don't you think?"

She didn't look up. "What do you mean 'closer?'"

"Close enough to walk to Lydia's instead of having to drive all the way from Garner."

Lydia pinched my arm. Hard. I gave her a wink. *Play along.*

Doris still hadn't lifted her head from her afghan-in-progress. "I like Garner fine. Not so busy. Not so *crime-ridden.*"

"Humor me, Doris. There's a house for sale I'd like you to look at. It's just down the street."

She looked at me with suspicion. "I hope you're not referring to that *murder* house."

"Oh, no. The house way on the other side of the street. The nicest house on the block, in fact."

"Not interested."

But I kept on until she finally agreed to come with us to look inside the Norris home.

$\sim$

Their for-sale sign listed an app which—once I had the okay from Gail to show the house to Doris—opened a lockbox containing a key.

"What do you think?" I asked as the three of us stepped inside.

"Too hoity-toity."

Doris somehow managed to be a snob even about snobs.

I knew Doris was a human Eeyore, but I needed her to show some real interest in case the Norrises' rooms were being monitored by hidden cameras. I tried to muster excitement any way I could:

"There are built-ins here in the living room where you could keep your knitting supplies..."

"I have several paper bags with handles from the supermarket that work just fine."

"...and, look at this big, modern kitchen with the island for all your pickling jars...and these huge windows—"

"I don't like people looking at me."

"—can be covered with heavy window treatments. Remember, you'll be filling the home with your own furniture." *Giving it, Doris, your signature 1960s funeral-home look.*

"Hmph!"

"I'll take lots of pictures on my smartphone so you can look at them later," I said, snapping away as I walked. "And here's an office where you can pay your bills each month. My, have you ever seen such a pretty oak desk?" I casually took pictures of the desk and its various papers from several angles.

Doris sneered. She was like that little silver-medal American gymnast from a few years back: *Unimpressed.*

"I pay my bills at the kitchen table," Doris croaked, before turning and stomping out of the room.

Somehow we were able to lead Doris through every room in the house. There were no severed heads in the open—but plenty of places to hide incriminating evidence.

"Let's go to the garage," I said finally.

"I don't need to see the garage."

"We need to see if the garage is big enough, Doris."

"It's a two car garage. I only got one car."

Yes, but your Chrysler is longer than the Santa float in a Christmas parade.

"Just be a sport," I said. "It's the last thing to see."

The garage was orderly, with enough shelving to hold various hardware and holiday decorations. Doris was showing signs of a meltdown—as if she had someplace else she needed to be!—when a small package on the edge of a shelf caught my eye.

I looked at it more closely. The package was addressed to "Dr. Wanda Hightower."

I doubt they would have a camera in here, but I still made as if I was taking pictures of the garage's impressive shelving as I excitedly snapped a photo of the package, trying hard not to let my hands shake.

"Can we go now?" Doris pouted.

"Sure," I said. "I can't wait to sit down and hear what you think of the place!"

The package came from Rumlin Health Industries in Toronto, Canada. According to the company's website, Rumlin sold a large variety of pharmaceuticals, but only to licensed medical professionals. That seemed fishy. Wanda's doctorate was in English literature.

I really wanted to open that box, and there was only one legal way to do it. I called Darryl and told him what I'd seen.

"What do you think?" I pressed. "Can you get a search warrant?"

"Shouldn't be necessary. I'll ask the Norrises about it. Did you see a postmark date on the box?"

"Hold please." I zoomed in on the photo I'd taken. "October 21. Just a couple weeks ago."

I could hear him scribbling in his little notebook. "If it got delivered to them by mistake, it seems odd that they wouldn't have returned it."

"That's what I was thinking."

"But if they stole it, it also seems odd they would keep it visible to the world whenever the garage door is open."

"They aren't very discreet," I said. "Remember their restaurant conversation?" *Game of Thrones* my buttocks!

"But if they stole it, why wouldn't they open it? You said the tape was still on the box."

"That's true." Stop it, Darryl. Stop trying to ruin my clue!

"I'll ask them about it," he said, "but it probably means blowing your cover."

"Maybe you could just ask them if they ever received any of Wanda's mail. Just say you understand that she may have ordered drugs illegally, and you're trying to get to the bottom of that."

It didn't take more than an hour for him to call me back.

"Dish," I said.

Darryl had spoken with Brad first. He told Darryl that the package came to their address by mistake a couple weeks ago, and he placed it on Wanda's porch that same evening. But then he found it in his driveway again early the next morning on his way to his car. He was in such a hurry to meet a client, he said, that he stuck the package on the shelf in the garage to deal with later. Then he forgot about it.

"He apologized for not remembering the incident the other times we'd talked," Darryl said. "He sounded pretty convincing."

"Did you talk to Gail, too?"

"She said she didn't know about the package. It wasn't necessarily something her husband would find notable enough to tell her about. Again, pretty convincing."

"Did they give you the package?"

"They did. And that's what's really interesting." According to Darryl, scrawled in black magic marker on the bottom of the package—which Brad swears wasn't written there the first time he saw the package and which he didn't notice the second time the package arrived—was the message: HOW DARE YOU TRY TO POISON ME!

"Wanda wrote that?" I asked.

"I'm assuming so. We dusted for fingerprints and found Wanda's prints as well as Brad's—that's all. Then we opened the package. Inside was a prescription hand cream for dry skin. She definitely ordered it herself. She paid for it with a signed personal check that she mailed to the supplier. And she'd been a customer for over nine months, beginning in January. Best guess is she was trying to get the wholesale price by being listed with the company as a physician. We confronted the supplier who apologized for the oversight. They have a very good reputation overall, no civil or criminal lawsuits filed, so I doubt it was intentional, but we reported it to the Canadian authorities anyway."

"If she ordered it, why did she reject it?"

"I don't know. Sorry, Rett, but this doesn't seem to be a smoking gun—or knife. And, I wouldn't go snooping in anyone else's house again under false pretenses. It makes me nervous. At least, if you do it again, please don't tell me."

"Okay," I said grumpily. "I won't."
Tell you, that is.

Maybe Darryl was right. Perhaps I'd been focusing on the Norrises when there were other neighbors who had more in the way of motive and opportunity.

I visited the Fosters again on the pretense of reminding Eleanor about Saturday's bake sale and pie contest. She answered the door looking all healed up. After seating me and fetching some sweet tea for us both, she began praising Wanda's daughter for bringing in a painting crew, which had radically transformed the home's ratty exterior with a tasteful gray finish.

"It looks like a whole new house," she said. "Maybe the next owners will actually take care of it."

I needed to change the subject.

"Where's Phil?" I asked casually. I took a sip of my tea and watched her closely.

"What do you mean, 'Where is Phil?' At work. Where he always is."

"Always?" I said. "That's what I used to think Allan was doing. Working."

"Yes, I heard how Allan did you wrong." *Raw-ONG.* "But you know, men will stray. It's in their natures."

"Oh?" I said. "I thought they also had something called free will."

She laughed. "The first time Phil had an affair I acted just like you. I was devastated."

I tried not to choke on a homemade ice cube.

"The *first* time?" I sputtered. "Oh, Eleanor, just how many times are we talking about?"

"I can't keep track. Oh, don't look at me like that. It's only about the sex, an animal urge. Women want kids, men want sex, and they really aren't very picky. It's as simple as that."

"But how can you—?"

"We have an agreement. No sneaking around. He always has to let me know who-with. That way I don't get embarrassed at any of the events I cover for my newspaper column. You can relate. That investor party you had to attend with Miss Rider cannot have been pleasant, but it would have been worse if you found out *after* the party that she was Allan's mistress."

I couldn't believe it. Was I an honorary member of the Wake County Club for Cheated-On Women without knowing it?

"And you?" I asked her. "Are you allowed to cheat, too?"

"I suppose. But I love Phil. He's always been the only man for me."

If there was such a condition as Irony Detection Disorder, here was a textbook case. But it got worse. She added, "You might think twice about letting Allan go. The older a woman gets, the harder it can be to find a single man who isn't seriously damaged."

I was going to throw up in my mouth if I didn't redirect the conversation immediately. I asked Eleanor flat out, "Did Phil have an affair with Wanda?"

She laughed. "Heavens no! But she still wanted to humiliate me. After that disastrous makeover, she threatened to tell everyone on Planet Earth that Phil was a serial cheater."

"What did you say to her?"

"I told her to go right ahead, that most people already knew I was married to the most desirable man in town—and I wasn't afraid for everyone else to know it."

Never had I known a woman to be prouder of her husband's infidelity. "Eleanor, be honest. If you found out that Phil had an affair with Wanda, wouldn't you be upset?"

"He knows what I think about that house. What if he

brought back some bugs in his clothing? He'd have to answer for that!"

The rest of our conversation, compared to the beginning, was completely forgettable.

I didn't know what to think—except that I could scratch Eleanor off my list of likely suspects.

She was a nut. But she wasn't a killer.

I headed in the direction of home, but decided on a whim to stop at the Thompsons. I'd been meaning to ask them if they remembered Trent from the Passion play held at their church.

The three of us sat around their kitchen table where I filled them in on the fact Trent was being investigated for murder: how he hung out with youth associated with break-ins and drugs, had allegedly been spotted near Wanda's house at the time of the murder, how his fingerprints were found in her house, and that his alibi wasn't being believed. "I don't think he did it, but the circumstantial evidence is piling up."

Jim confirmed that Trent and another Black teen had joined the Easter production, which had toured several other churches as well. "I remember Trent. A very convincing Pontius Pilate. *'What is truth?!'* For some reason the audiences got a chuckle over that line the way he delivered it. I was impressed he was able to play Pilate for a laugh." Jim mused, "Will our teenage Pilate be tried and convicted for murder?"

Nancy remarked, "Ha! Now that would be ironic, wouldn't it?"

"I sure hope not," I said. "Who was the other Black boy in the play with Trent? I might want to talk with him, especially if he knows Trent's friends who are suspected of breaking into houses."

Jim said, "The other boy played Simon of Cyrene, the man who carried Jesus's cross. I don't remember that boy's name. He didn't have any lines. Do you remember him, Nancy?"

"I remember him, but I don't remember his name either."

"You could call the boys' church," Jim suggested, and he gave me a contact number. I thanked the Thompsons for their help. As I left, Nancy walked me to the door and asked, "If this Trent boy didn't kill Wanda, who do you think did?"

"Could be someone who lives in this neighborhood," I said.

Nancy's jaw dropped. "Please don't say that. I like where I live. I do not want to move!"

"I could be wrong," I said. "I hope I am."

I called the other church and was told by its secretary the name of the other boy: Barry Watson. When I told her I was working to help the family of Trent Jones, she gave me Barry's parents' number. When I dialed it, Barry picked up.

He told me he was well aware of Trent's plight and wanted to help. We arranged to meet outside one of Raleigh's landmark fast food restaurants, Snoopy's, near the Meredith College campus. I ordered one of their famous chili dogs and some onion rings and paid for Barry's chili burger and fries.

We sat across from one another at the restaurant's only patio picnic table. Barry was shorter and stouter than Trent and wore thick glasses. I thanked him for agreeing to help me help Trent.

"How well do you know Trent?" I asked him.

"Pretty well. We're in drama class together at school and see each other at church, too."

"Do you consider yourself good friends with him?"

"More like professional associates. We don't socialize, but we're both into dramatization."

"Does Trent have a good reputation at school?"

"Reasonably. He's somewhat quiet. Introverted, until he gets on stage. Then he really comes alive."

I filled him in on Trent's situation, including the prescription drugs angle and the friends he was known by the police to hang out with.

"Did you know that Trent was in trouble?" I asked.

"I'd heard at church about the drug part, not about the murder though."

"Does the murder part strike you as plausible?"

"No. Not the drug stuff either. Trent's not like that."

"Do you know these other friends?"

Barry frowned. "I think I know who they are. Most of them already dropped out of school, so I don't see them much."

"Trent won't say who gave him the pills. Do you know the names of these other friends?"

"Now you're asking me to name names. That's too risky." I tried, but nothing I could say would change his mind.

I asked him how he and Trent got involved with the Passion play.

"Brother Lawrence said a white church was looking for someone else to be in their play. He asked me and Trent, and we said okay."

"Do you want to become an actor like Trent does?"

"Actually, I want to be a screenwriter. I wrote a movie. I'll show you."

He reached into his backpack and pulled out a thin, tattered stack of papers and handed it to me. The cover page bore a title: *The Hustler*.

"You wrote this?"

"Yep. It's going to be a blockbuster. I'm going to show it to Tyler Perry. It's about a guy who hustles and hustles until he hustles the wrong people. Then he's on the run, because they want to kill him."

I flipped through the pages quickly, noting a plethora of exclamation points, curse words, and all-caps words like POW!

BAM! BOOM! It seemed like something that Hollywood would love, but not like something I would enjoy.

"Impressive," I said, as I tried to hand it back.

"Keep it," Barry insisted. "Read it."

"Are you sure? What will you show Tyler Perry?"

"I printed out a ton of copies. You never know who might read it and share it with somebody in the business." He smiled. "Just you wait. Tyler is going to love it."

Youthful optimism. Something that Trent, if he was innocent, should be allowed to experience, too.

Before I left, I gave Barry one of my old Swinson Development business cards, just in case he thought of anything else later that could help Trent.

Doris took the day off on Tuesday to attend a Veteran's Day ceremony, as her late husband had fought in the Korean War. I took her place and made Lydia listen to a recap of all the evidence and the theories I'd explored in the case. She wasn't surprised to hear about Eleanor and Phil's open relationship. I had to conclude the Qrazy Qwilters were tapped into that bit of scuttlebutt.

I read Wanda's poems to her, starting with the ones on my phone that I had photographed in the archive. Lydia wasn't a poetry person any more than I was, but the way she closed her eyes, I could tell Wanda's words held power for her, too. Lastly, I pulled out from my purse the unpublished poem that Professor Aldridge had given me. The poem slipped out of my hands, floated, and hit Lydia in the ankle. She picked it up and tried to decipher it herself, her expression forming a question mark.

"This poem is quite the puzzle," I said. "Let me read it to you."

She handed it back to me, but then she held up a finger as she readied her smartphone and clicked the memo app to begin recording. I cleared my throat. "*'Invalidated*, by Wanda Hightower.'" She had me recite the whole poem, then began playing it back. "I can't stand the sound of my voice," I said, ashamed the moment I spoke the words. At least I had a voice; my friend didn't. Lydia remained focused, deep in concentration. After playing the poem once, she played it again. And again...

It was too much to bear. Which words were getting through, and which ones were becoming stuck in endless eddies within her brain? I went in the kitchen so she wouldn't have to see my pity.

I spent some time googling slow cooker recipes for dinner. We needed a few things from the store, but we could stop at the Food Lion after rehab. I didn't mind being a help, but I wondered if I'd made the right decision. Would I soon become like Boring Doris, best known for "sitting" with the older generation? Whenever I saw Lydia resting in her Lay-Z-Boy, I saw myself, too. For a long time, Allan had been my Lay-Z-Boy for whatever growth I might have otherwise done. Without him in my world, how would I fill my days? Such had been the question hanging over my in-limbo life these past many months.

In the next room I could hear my voice on repeat:

Everyone can see
This page describes you to a tee...

Maybe this exercise was good for Lydia somehow.

...my body rages constantly...

Wanda's rage hitting a fever pitch when she saw what the neighbors had done, clearing away the wildness, delivering order to her yard's chaos. Inadvertently destroying the spider webs that usually greeted Wanda in the morning.

I knew a little about rage, too. I thought about my face-to-face with KayLeigh, the wedding registry cards I'd seen in her office, the urge, quite frankly, to do serious harm to her perfect world.

"'You are right here on Google," he says. *I am?*"

"'Am,'" Lydia shouted. "'Am!'"

I returned to the den.

"Good job, Lydia!"

She didn't acknowledge the praise. She just pressed play again, my awful voice:

"'Yes! Everyone can see...'"

She paused the recording again. "'See.'"

"Keep going," I encouraged.

"'This page describes you to a tee.'"

"Tee," said Lydia. "Tee!"

"Good, Lydia. You're doing great!"

"'Close your eyes and listen: It hums your melo-dy.'"

"'-dy,'" she echoed. I tried to smile, tried to stay positive. "Mel-o-dy," I intoned slowly, hoping she could say the whole word.

She shook her head emphatically.

"'-dy!'" she repeated. "'-dy!'"

I looked at her hopefully. She looked at me like I was an idiot.

She rewound the poem once more:

"'Close your eyes and listen.'"

"'*-dy!*'"

"Oh!" I said, the lightbulb going off. "Do you mean D? The *letter* D?"

Relief washed over her face as she played the poem's first four lines again, stopping the recording at the end of each line and repeating each final sound. I finally realized what she was trying to say:

Not 'am,' but M.

Not 'see,' but C.

Not 'tee,' but T.

Not '-dy,' but D.

She put the phone aside and looked at me expectantly.

"'MCTD' isn't a word," I said. "I'm sorry, Lydia. I don't get it."

Clearly annoyed, she picked up her phone one more time, rewound, pushed play AGAIN...

"'You are right here on Google—'" She paused the poem there.

"Fine," I said. "I'll google it."

And that's how we both learned about something called Mixed Connective Tissue Disease—MCTD for short.

"Holy crap," I said. "Wanda didn't just feel invalidated."

Lydia smiled.

"She felt like an *IN*-va-lid. Or, at least, like she was being treated like one."

The rest of our day, when we weren't running errands, I was on the computer learning about the diagnosis that Wanda appeared to have been none too happy with. MCTD was an auto-immune disease that carried a whole host of symptoms that can appear gradually over decades, making it difficult to diagnose. Muscle and joint pain. Rash. There was no known cure.

If her body raged, that could mean she was angry.

But it could also mean she was in *pain*.

What's more, the websites said that most people with MCTD also experienced cold fingers and toes as part of a condition called Raynaud's Phenomenon. Which would explain the gloves Wanda constantly wore. Not an attempt to be dainty or stylish, but an effort to keep her hands warm.

According to her daughter, Wanda didn't have a doctor. Then who was the "sir" in the poem who was giving Wanda her "invalid" diagnosis?

On a hunch, I went back to the Internet, and, after surfing for a while—and coughing up another forty dollars—found what I was looking for.

"You're a genius, Lydia," I said.

After Lydia's rehab and before hitting the Food Lion, we took a little detour back to Wake Tech. There we found Gary Roland in the same spot I'd left him, still grading term papers.

He seemed surprised to see me.

I put Wanda's poem on the table in front of him.

"Care to explain this?"

He barely glanced at it. "It wasn't up to her usual standards. Are you really taking me to task for failing to publish a poem in a community college's student literary magazine?"

"This poem was personal, wasn't it, Dr. Roland? Doctor—as in M.D.—not Ph.D."

He looked at Lydia. I explained, "This is Lydia. She's my crime-fighting partner."

Roland looked back at me. "How did you find out?"

"That you used to be a medical doctor in California but lost your license due to stealing drugs from the hospital where you worked in the ER?"

"I had a problem. I've been clean for over fifteen years."

"But Wanda threatened to expose your past, didn't she?"

A beat. "Yes."

"And that's why she wasn't fired last semester, even though she skipped meetings and missed classes."

Another beat. "It is."

"I wonder if what she knew got her killed, too."

"No. She got her full retirement. That seemed to appease her." He added, "I actually tried to help her, you know."

"By diagnosing her?"

"Wanda didn't like doctors. She said—"

"Let me guess: that medical science took all the mystery out of the human body—the same way that religion tamed God and that psychology had spoiled the mind's mystery?"

He smiled sadly. "Something like that."

"How did you diagnose her?"

"There were her gloves—always the gloves—and the long sleeves even in the warm months. Initially I asked her if she was battling a drug problem and needed help. That wasn't it, but she did admit she hadn't been feeling well. I got a little more information out of her. About the chilliness in her fingers—the Raynaud's. The pain in her muscles. I threw out some possibilities for her to consider."

"MCTD being one."

"Yes, but it's not like I insisted on that being her diagnosis."

"But she trusted you, because you weren't a *doctor* doctor. And you helped get her the steroids."

"Steroids are a reasonable first line of defense."

"They must have worked to some extent, because she used them a lot, didn't she?"

He sighed. "Yes. A lot more, I think, than she should have."

"Which explains her temper tantrums," I said. "When did you realize you'd created a monster?"

"You have to understand, she wouldn't see a physician. I showed her how to order the drugs—then it was in her hands. And then she decided at some point she was done with me. She was irrational at that point."

"When she wrote this poem."

"Right. I didn't publish it, only because I didn't see why the world had to read what was, essentially, hate mail directed at me alone."

"Or a cry for help."

"Wanda was brilliant, but she couldn't get out of her own way. She never learned that sometimes you can be your own worst enemy." Spoken like someone who would know. The recovering addict, never fully recovered.

I looked at Lydia, and she shook her head.

Roland wasn't the one.

I said, "You're a bundle of contradictions, professor. On the one hand, you probably harmed Wanda by playing armchair physician. On the other, I know you thought you were helping her."

Roland shrugged. "I figured she would eventually hit bottom with the steroids and then do what she needed to do to get healthy." We all participated in a moment of depressed silence.

Lydia and I stood to leave. About the time we reached the doorway, Roland added by way of reflection: "You know, after I lost my license to practice, I pivoted. I went back to school in English and got my Doctorate in Education. I was so much happier after that. Didn't miss medicine for a second. Maybe I'm like Wanda, in that I enjoy a good mystery. But don't most people? Don't *you*?"

CHAPTER 19

"CLUCK"

That evening I called Darryl and told him all about Gary Roland's secret past, as well as what he had revealed to me and Lydia regarding Wanda's medical situation.

"That would at least explain the gloves she was wearing when she died," he said.

I asked, "Will you investigate Roland, given the fact he used to be a drug addict?"

"If what he says is true, he's put that behind him. But, yes, I'll run a complete background check on him. And I'm curious if he knows where else Wanda was getting her medicines."

"Why does it matter?"

"To see if she was getting her hands on painkillers, too."

Wednesday was frigid. Lydia wasn't feeling well and begged out of rehab as well as quilting. I went alone to the center where in the parking lot I noticed (who could miss it?) Freddy's purple El

Camino and, to either side of it, Otis's pickup and Augusta's silver Mercury sedan.

Inside the expanded area near the thrift store I found Freddy emerging through a gap in some hanging black curtains.

"We're about ready for Otis's show on Saturday. Even the art labels have been placed. Otis said it would be okay if staff got a sneak peek today. He and Augusta are already inside." Freddy turned to his sometime assistant, a young man named Ricky. "Will you go invite whichever of the staff is available to come and take a look?"

"Certainly," Ricky said.

As Ricky went on his errand, I asked Freddy, "Did Sally budge on the commission?"

He frowned. "She would only go as high as ten percent."

"At least it's something."

"It means more dollars in Otis's pocket, but the commissions will barely pay for the space, even if every one of his pieces sells."

"Sally expects her bake sale to be the big money-maker," I said.

"Don't even get me started," he muttered.

While we were still waiting for Ricky to return, Augusta came out of the exhibit room looking upset. "That man is impossible!"

"Who?" I asked. But I knew who. Otis.

She abruptly changed the subject. "I almost called you. Trent's still in jail. They are keeping his bail high saying he's a flight risk."

"I guess I'm not surprised," I said.

"What are you hearing? Are they going to charge Trent with murder?"

"I'm not sure." What I thought I knew, and didn't say, was that the police were not looking seriously at any other suspects.

We were interrupted by the arrival of several Needless Necessities staff who had come over to check out the installation. Sally, Jasmine, and Wash didn't know what to expect, for within our small group only I had seen samples of Otis's work.

Together we moved through the curtains into what felt like an open airplane hangar. The space was quite dark, but each piece was well-lit, creating the initial effect of a stage production. Already impressive under the fluorescent bulbs of his shop, Otis's pieces really popped under the museum-grade halogen lighting.

"What do you think?" Freddy asked after I'd had a moment for my eyes to adjust.

I didn't know what to say. The sculptural elements of the works jutted out of their frames, defying gravity. Imagine being an ant on a thickly layered Van Gogh. That's what it felt to wander among Otis's work.

I felt like the luckiest bug ever.

"This is really something, Freddy," I said.

There were twelve pieces in all—five along each side, one above the entrance, and an especially massive piece on the far end—the one called *Jazz* which featured two actual tubas in addition to what seemed like every other instrument imaginable, all exploding in visual sound.

I didn't see the piece he'd been working on, the one I could have sworn resembled a dragon in progress.

Everyone was walking around openmouthed, like they'd landed on a different planet.

"*How...? What the...?*"

"*Oh, my my my my.*"

"*Cool!*"

Augusta turned to her grandfather. "You see?" The pair stood off to the side of the entrance, almost in shadow. "Everyone loves your work. You aren't charging near enough. You can't just give them away."

Otis's said, "What's a few extra dollars? I need to make room for more work. If they don't sell, I'm just going to throw them away."

I stepped toward the placard next to one of the works. After comparing what I saw there to the pieces to either side, I confirmed I wasn't just seeing things.

Otis was selling each of the pieces for a mere thousand dollars.

I caught Augusta's eye. *Your grandfather's not charging enough!*

Her eyebrows narrowed. *I know—and it makes me furious!*

"Judging by these prices, what we've got here is just another bake sale," I whispered to Freddy.

My friend shrugged. "Otis won't listen. Part of it is he doesn't know his worth. The other part is he doesn't care about the money that much."

We became aware of another presence. The artist known as Wo, wearing a secondhand ivory-white gown and a black wig, floated into the room looking like some little lost angel of gloom. Without a word to anyone in the group, she approached Otis's first piece, *Birth*. After a moment of contemplation, she burst into a baby wail. Like the piece itself—red and bulbous, suggestive of the womb—her sound was primal.

Then, just as suddenly, Wo stopped her wailing and moved to the next piece: *Bully-1955*, where remnants of a jungle gym snaked across the canvas, enveloping and strangling a boy-like figure in the center. Wo closed her eyes and fell to the ground, her lungs heaving at some vision or memory, "Fairy-ass artist! Lesbo Dyke! Get out of our face!" She lay crumpled and stricken for several beats before calmly standing again and moving to the next piece.

I searched the faces of the others to see what they were

making of this. Otis was staring at the ground, his expression impassive. By contrast, Augusta's gaze was laser-locked onto Wo, watching, waiting. If she wanted, in a heartbeat she could put a stop to all this nonsense.

I was nervous. If Wo was going to react so dramatically to each and every one of the paintings, I wasn't sure those of us watching could endure it. Mercifully, she quickly scanned several of the sculptures and ended at the room's far end where the exhibit's most complex work, *Jazz*, held court.

Looked at from one angle, it was a celebration. Regarded another way, it seemed gruesome, like a cadaver. The effect was similar to when I first saw Michelangelo's *David* in person in the great Duomo in Florence, Italy. From a distance, the shepherd boy appeared brave and noble; up close, he looked absolutely terrified. To me it was what embodied the best of all art: an ability to capture complexity within a startling unity.

Wo slowly opened her arms, as if to receive the imagined sound of *Jazz*. She turned slowly, as if showering in the work's aura, her face rapturous. She finished by lowering herself into a lotus position directly facing the piece.

The rest of us went back to the pieces we had already viewed, making sure we hadn't missed something the first time around.

At some point Wo began revisiting all of the works, pressing very close to each of the pieces' object labels—though it was unclear exactly what she was doing. Was she missing her glasses and needing to read them up close?

Having completed her enigmatic task, Wo walked over to Otis, bowed, and said, "Thank you, sir. 'Tis a marvelous show."

"You're very welcome, Child."

Wo handed Augusta a sheet of paper and disappeared through the black drapes in as dramatic a manner as she'd arrived. Wash rushed to catch up with her.

The whole time Wo was in the room, Augusta had maintained a skeptical expression. I went up to her. "What did that crazy girl hand you?"

Augusta looked at the paper in her hands. "Pricing stickers, looks like." Otis's niece stepped forward to examine the object label for *Birth*. Confused, she stepped over to the next piece, then reported back. "Ghost Girl placed a zero near each of the price tags. Just what is she up to?"

I checked the next two paintings and confirmed it. Wo had placed a tiny zero sticker above each of their $1,000 price tags. Was a zero her "Zorro" mark, and she was somehow claiming these paintings for herself? That would be unusual, if not downright insulting.

Jasmine, who had been following our investigation, rushed to the far end of the hall, checked something else, then rushed back. "She placed *two* zeroes on the label for the largest painting."

Confused myself, I looked at Augusta—and was surprised to catch her smiling. "I see what that girl did. Pops," August said, grabbing her grandfather's shoulder, "she's saying you should charge *ten* thousand for most of the pieces, but a *hundred* thousand for *Jazz*. Are you gonna be alright with that? You won't take my advice, so will you take the advice of another ar-TEEST?"

Otis took his time thinking about it.

"I guess so," Otis finally said.

"Praise Jesus!" cried Augusta, acting like she'd won her first argument ever with her grandfather. "Then that's what we're going to do! Where's my man Ricky?"

Freddy's assistant stepped out of the shadows.

"Ricky, we need to update the pricing on these paintings right away."

The young man looked to Freddy, who nodded assent. "I'll get right on it," Ricky said.

The others congratulated Otis on his show before returning to their jobs at Needless Necessities. While Ricky tended to the pricing, Freddy and I lingered to talk.

"Wow," I said, "now the whole lot is priced at over $200,000."

"I guess the bake sale won't be necessary now?" Freddy said.

"Knowing Sally, she'll still have it. But, if even just one these paintings sells, it might start a new sustainable trend at Needless Necessities."

Freddy said, "Let's just hope the public shows up—and appreciates the level of genius that's on display here."

"And if they don't..." I let out the mock sound of a baby's wail.

Augusta was waiting for me outside the pre-show area, looking troubled.

"I just got off the phone with Trent," she said. "He's starting to feel hopeless. I'm beginning to worry about his mental health. He acts tough, but he's just a kid."

"Are you still convinced that he has nothing to do with this crime?"

"In my bones," she said. "Some trick-or-treater saying they saw someone dressed like a dragon? Something that lame could get my cousin charged with murder? And some people wonder why Black people run from the police."

I had a thought. "If only I could get in touch with those trick-or-treaters again; I'd like to ask them some more questions. Maybe they saw something they didn't think was important. Or maybe they were too scared to tell the police everything they saw."

Augusta asked me to describe the group of children and what names I remembered. She got on the phone with a family friend, shared the same information—and then gave the grapevine time to do its work.

About a half hour later Augusta found me in the paints section.

"You still want to meet with those kids?"

"I do. Do they live far?"

"No."

"Then I'll leave my car here and ride with you."

Along the way we were forced to stop at a light. *KayLeigh Rider: "Your Real Estate Friend"* stared down at me from her billboard perch.

"Bitch won't stop following me," I muttered.

Augusta's gaze snapped to her rearview mirror. "Who's following us?"

"No, the girl on the billboard," I said. "She happens to be my husband's mistress."

Augusta hunched down so she could see.

"I can already tell I would not like her," she said.

"Why not? She's very pretty, very charming. And, any day now, very wealthy."

"Home Girl wants to take the vacation without the baggage. She wants to look Black, but she's no better than those bronze-faced, plumped-lipped influencers."

"I would never have thought of her as Black," I said, surprised. "Do you really think she is?"

"No. She's just using that Egyptian Queen look to her advantage. See, Miss Exotica can shed that when she wants, but it gets the rest of us arrested."

~

The houses in the children's neighborhood were strikingly small, 1970s era, back when people's ambitions weren't so grandiose and the mortgage interest rates were ten times higher. These were the types of homes all but gone from the wealthier parts of town, torn down to make way for the sort of garish monstrosities KayLeigh and Allan preferred. I knew better than most, because for years I'd rented the wrecking ball.

We parked in front of one of the houses. Shauna's aunt, the woman I'd last seen holding a pink tutu, was waiting for us on the front porch.

"Hello again," I said nervously. "I'm Harriet, but you can call me Rett."

"I'm Tameka. But you can call me Meka."

That released some of the tension as we both chuckled.

"Come in," Meka said. "The boys are playing. Tameisha's not here. She's at a friend's."

"What about the little one, your niece?" I said. "Is she here?"

"Shauna's here. But she's scared. She didn't like talking to the police."

"I'm not the police," I said. "I hope she knows that."

We stepped inside the home's foyer. The house was loud with children running and yelling. A Nerf Gun battle was in play.

Meka led us into the den, where Shauna, the five-year-old, was sitting on a sofa with a number of dolls and stuffed animals. She was cute as pie. Pretty brown eyes. Pudgy cheeks. Her hair had been made into several pigtail braids with colorful beads.

"Hi, Shauna," I said. "I almost didn't recognize you without your cute ballerina costume." She remained still and looked at me askance. "My name's Rett. How are you today?"

"Good," she said softly.

"She's usually pretty quiet," Meka said. "Let me get them boys so you can talk to them, too. Isaiah! Curtis! Come on in here!"

Their play only got louder.

"Y'all stop the horseplay and come sit down! This nice lady wants to ask you some questions."

The play noise sputtered and the boys ran into the den, racing to get the prime chair—the leather recliner. When they both couldn't fit, they decided to share the loveseat instead.

I sat in a chair across from Shauna and the boys. Augusta took the recliner, while Meka continued to stand sentinel.

"So," I said, "I don't know if you all remember me, but we met Halloween night when you came to my friend's front door for candy. Do you remember? I think it was one of the last houses you might have been to. We talked about why the police were in the neighborhood."

"I remember," said Isaiah, the slightly older of the two boys, the Pee Wee football player on Halloween.

"I remember, too," said Curtis, the former pirate. "A lady was stabbed!"

"Yes, that's right," I said, "though I didn't tell you that. You must have learned that on your own."

"People was talking about it," Curtis said.

"The next day," clarified Isaiah.

"I just wanted to ask you about that night. What do you remember seeing? Go back in your head to that afternoon, to the moment you entered the neighborhood. What do you remember?"

Isaiah: "There was a party."

Curtis: "Yeah, there was a party."

Isaiah: "We wanted to go to it, but Tameisha wouldn't let us. Said it was for white folks, not us."

I wanted to point out that not everyone at the party was white. But most of them were, so it probably would have looked like an all-white party to the children.

"Start at the beginning," I said.

Curtis said, "Mama dropped us off, and we kind of, you

know, went down that little street behind the houses. But there weren't any front doors."

"Just back doors," Isaiah said.

"You were in the alley," I said. "Did you stop at any of the back doors?"

"No," said Isaiah. "Well, we stopped once, because Shauna was laggin' way behind. She was always laggin' behind while we trick-or-treated."

"I wasn't laggin'!" Shauna jumped in.

"Yes, you were," Isaiah argued.

Meka entered the fray. "Isaiah, enough. Go on, Rett. Keep asking questions. Augusta said that you might find out something to clear that boy, Trent Jones. His grandmama is a friend of my mama's. They go way back."

I asked the boys, "When you stopped, or even before that, did you see anybody?"

"No," Isaiah said. "I guess everybody was having fun at the party."

Curtis: "Might of been nice to go to that party."

"I'll make a deal with you three, and with Tameisha, too," I said. "Next year when Halloween rolls around, all four of you are going to be my guests at that block party, okay?"

They looked at their mother. Curtis pleaded, "Can we go? Can we go?"

"We'll see," Meka said. "That's a year away. You'll forget all about it by then."

"No, we won't!"

"We won't!"

"Now," I said. "Think. Who, if anyone, did you see in that alley way?"

The boys looked at one another, scratching their heads.

Curtis asked sweetly, "If we didn't see anybody, can we still come to the party?"

"Of course," I said.

"Good," Curtis said, "because I didn't see nobody."

"Me either," said his brother.

"I saw him," said the little girl slowly, softly.

Everyone in the room turned to face her.

"Who, Shauna?" I asked. "Who did you see?"

The girl was taking her time, milking it. With two rowdy older cousins, when did she ever get this kind of attention?

"Cluck," she said, soft as silk.

"'Cluck?'" I repeated. Now here was something I didn't expect. Had I stepped into a knock-knock joke? "Who is 'Cluck'?"

The little girl's eyes started to wander to her right until her head turned and she was glancing over her shoulder at a bookshelf where also a number of several family photos were lined.

"Is the person's picture in this room?" I asked.

She looked at me and nodded her head.

I cast a glance at Augusta. What if the girl was about to implicate a relative? Were we ready for such a development?

Augusta shook her head slightly, her expression a tense mixture of hope and skepticism.

I asked, "Will you show us who you saw, Shauna? Please?"

The little girl looked at her aunt.

"It's okay," Meka said soberly. "You can show her."

The girl stood, slowly and deliberately, and approached the bookcase. I expected her to reach for one of the family photographs. Instead, she pulled down a large book and walked it back to her original seat among her dolls and animals.

The book took up her entire lap. Augusta and I leaned forward so we could read its title: *Civil Rights in the South, 1945 to 1969.*

We exchanged confused looks, then watched as Shauna

opened the book and began turning the pages, slowly, as she watched our eyes.

"Do you know anything about this book?" Augusta whispered to Meka.

"That's her Paw-Paw's book. He looks at it sometimes."

"Did your Paw-Paw show you this book?" Augusta asked Shauna.

"Yes." She was still turning pages but looking at us, as if we might stop her at any point, like a human Ouija board. When she finally stopped turning pages, we looked where she landed.

We were staring at a full-page photo of a group of Ku Klux Klansmen, all wearing white hoods and robes. One of the men's garb seemed more important than the others. It was this particular hooded figure, the one on the far left, that the little girl finally pointed to the photo's cutline identifying him as the "Grand Dragon of the Ku Klux Klan, 1955." In wizened hands, the man held a staff of some sort.

"There he is," she said in the softest whisper. "Cluck...*the Dragon!*"

Augusta was the first to say it aloud, "Dang! That looks nothing like a real dragon. If anything, that Klansman looks like a ghost!"

Meka said, "Her Paw-Paw calls them old racist white folk the 'Klu Kluck.'"

And this 'Cluck' was a clue. I pointed to the photo of the man and asked Shauna, "Is this definitely the sort of person you saw? Someone with a sheet like this?"

She nodded.

I looked at the picture again. The only visible skin, the only sign that it was a human being at all, were the Grand Dragon's hands.

"By any chance did you see his hands?" I asked.

She nodded.

"What color were they?"

"Brown," she said.

In the old photo, the hands were shadowed, dark. I wondered if Shauna was aware that the men under those sheets were white men who believed themselves superior to Black people in every way.

"Where exactly did you see him?" I asked.

"Behind the garbage can," she whispered.

"What color was the garbage can?"

"Brown," she said again.

Which could have been Skip and Stuart's big rusty can; the city receptacles were green and blue.

I asked Shauna: "What did you do when you saw Cluck the Dragon?"

"Ran," she said.

"That must have been a scary moment. Did Cluck try to hurt you?"

She shook her head.

"Did he say anything to you?"

Again, she shook her head.

"So, you just ran and joined your cousins?"

Shauna nodded.

"And that's when we found the front doors with candy," Isaiah cut in.

"Yeah," said Curtis. "So it all worked out!"

"My, my," I said to Augusta a few minutes later, once we'd spoken our thanks to Meka and walked to the car. "This means that the police have a lot less reason to suspect Trent. Heck, they wouldn't have even found him if they had interviewed the little girl properly in the first place."

"You got that right," Augusta said.

I called Darryl on the way home to tell him what we'd discovered, that the littlest had seen someone who reminded her of a figure she'd seen in a book her grandfather had shown her—a Grand Dragon in the Ku Klux Klan, someone in a white sheet. Not a *dragon* dragon, but a KKK dragon.

"'Klux' sounds like 'Cluck' to a little girl," I said. "That picture must have sure made an impression."

Darryl was silent for an agonizingly long time.

"What are you thinking?" I asked.

"I don't know what to think," he said. "Something doesn't add up."

"Exactly. You shouldn't have been looking for someone in a dragon costume at all. You should still be looking for someone in a full ghost costume. Good luck with that. Could a Halloween costume get any more generic?"

"We know Trent's been in that house, because his prints are there. He ran. There is the matter of the pills. And no reliable alibi."

"All circumstantial. Like you said, nothing to tie him to the crime scene."

It reminded me of people who held on to the stock of companies that were doomed for bankruptcy. They just couldn't bear to sell at a loss.

Release Trent now, Darryl, and take the loss.

Darryl said, "I will keep the child's new testimony in mind, I really will. Look, no one is going to go to prison for murder unless we can prove beyond a doubt that they committed it."

"Wrongful convictions never happen?"

"I didn't say that. They just don't happen in *my* cases. Please trust me here. I'm not a bad guy who prosecutes innocent teenagers. And neither is our D.A.," he added, though not as confidently as I would have liked.

"I know you're not a bad guy," I said.

"Okay," he said. "Give my best to Mom. I'll see you both before long."

We hung up, an unsteady energy in our wake. Yes, I believed Darryl was a good man. But that probably wouldn't make Trent or his family feel any better about the cloud of suspicion still hanging over the boy's head.

And, right this second, I didn't feel good about it either.

At home, I quickly freshened up. Moments later I was walking over to Lydia's for my evening shift when I heard someone calling my name. It was Nancy Thompson. She looked upset. When she caught up to me on the sidewalk, I learned why. With shaky hands, she showed me a note written in a familiar crayon scrawl:

Who ask y'all to get involved? Back off, Punks!

PART III

REVELATIONS

The person who looks into the mirror to reflect on themselves has already changed.

—*Seneca*

CHAPTER 20

FIREPROOF

Come the next day, Thursday, Lydia was feeling well enough to quilt again. As I worked the paints department, I reflected between customers on the recent occurrences in Wanda's murder case.

And I was more confused than ever.

Nancy Thompson had found The Imp's latest message in her mailbox. Jim was furious, his normally calm demeanor rattled. "Does whoever this is really think we're going to stop talking to our neighbors? No!" I had immediately called Darryl, who collected the note the same way he'd taken in Wanda's note as evidence. We had not yet discussed it, but he had to be just as frustrated as I was. Trent, still in jail, could not have delivered the message. So, who? Presumably someone who had seen me talking to the Thompsons on Monday.

One might theorize the note was from one of Trent's unsavory friends suspected of stealing narcotics. But why would my own investigations make them nervous, considering that I was trying to find evidence to clear Trent, not convict him?

It didn't make sense. And maybe that was the point. Perhaps the note was just meant to throw me off the scent. I didn't like that it ramped up the fear in my neighborhood—especially among the oldest and most vulnerable.

As I ruminated, I tended to an inordinate number of customers. Meanwhile, Wash kept pacing in my vicinity, angling for conversation.

"For Pete's sake, Wash," I finally said during a break in customer traffic. "What's wrong?"

He led me to the break room, where he closed the door behind us.

"Wo's show is happening tonight," he said, "and I'm a mite worried about it."

I took a deep breath. Ever since Sally had refused to sanction Wo's next performance, I'd wondered about the artist's plans. When I'd asked Sally about it later, she had erupted, "I don't know what she's planning—and I've decided I don't want to know!"

Now I asked Wash, "Who knows about tonight's show?"

"Everyone. She announced it on social media this morning, and she asked me to pull together the rest of the materials. Take a look."

He handed the list to me:

- *Steel frame and twin mattress from thrift store (use my credits)*
- *Donated quilt from Qrazy Qwilters*
- *Strawberry Shortcake Doll or similar (credits!)*
- *Books (in box in staff room)*

I scanned the staff room and saw three large boxes of books labeled with Wash Henry's initials. But the list continued—and here's where things started to get scary:

- *Tiki torches*

- *Five gallons of kerosene*
- *Small blow torch*
- *Women's Size Small Flame Retardant HazMat Suit*

"Kerosene?" I asked.

"I'm supposed to soak the books in it for three hours."

"That could explain the fireproof suit. Have you known Ashley to have a death wish? Be honest. What's her state of mind these days?"

"Hard to predict."

"I notice, Wash, that you don't use the word 'odd' or 'weird' when you talk about Ashley. I suspect most people do."

"Most folks just don't understand her."

"And you do?"

"Okay, maybe I don't *understand* her exactly. Maybe I just—"

Adore her? Love her?

"—appreciate her." He must have noted the skepticism in my expression. "Don't you see? A country boy like me is becoming the rarest creature on the planet. I don't feel like I belong in college, Miss Rett. But Ashley tells me I do belong. She makes me feel worth something." He gulped. "I don't want her to hurt herself tonight. Please. Can you help somehow?"

I suspected that getting Wo to postpone her show or alter its elements would be out of the question. But I had an idea.

"What time is the show?" I asked.

"Nine."

"Okay. Here's what you can do to prepare for tonight." I told him my idea, and his face lit up.

"Great idea, Miss Rett! I knew I could count on you!"

~

That night during dinner with just the two of us, Lydia said something that sounded like a full sentence. I was excited, because while she'd been using subjects and verbs together, much was still left to interpretation.

"IT'S...all...up...here." To emphasize, she lifted the slow cooker recipe book and rapped on it with her knuckles.

"Are you saying that everything you had before the stroke—everything—is still in your brain?"

She nodded.

"I'm glad to hear that, Lydia. You'll be reciting the Gettysburg Address in no time."

The whole exchange made me recall something else. After Lydia became settled in for the night—in bed by seven-thirty since the stroke—I emailed Gary Roland at Wake Tech:

Professor,

Do you still have that photo of the stack of books that Wanda sent to the department in place of a headshot? If so, may I see it? I'm just curious to see what books Wanda might have identified with the most. Her daughter might be interested to know as well.

Sincerely,
Rett Swinson

I knew he wouldn't ignore me now that I knew his secret. An hour later, he emailed me a photo of, sure enough, a stack of a dozen books. I looked at the titles on the spines. Most were related to Wanda's field; titles like *The Lake Country Poets of England* and *Words of Worth*. No surprises there.

However, at the very top of the stack—the "head" of her self-portrait—sat a different type of book: *The Spy's Briefcase* by Andrew M. Ion.

I googled the title. A summary from a publishing industry website read: "A scribbled note with the code word 'BOMBAY' and the theft of an Allied spy's briefcase together prompt a hunt for the foreign agents who would use the information against the free world." The summary was followed by a brief announcement that the book had been nominated for this year's "Selfie"—one of three novels nominated for the category of Best First Spy Novel by the Kelley Self-Published Writers Network.

There was no accompanying author photo. I googled the author's name, but nothing came up there either.

I ordered a copy; delivery would take a week.

Wanda didn't seem like someone who would read spy novels —or place one in her self-portrait. The book seemed significant, but on what level, I had no idea. I texted Angela Hightower:

Sorry to bother you. I was just wondering what happened to the books that didn't sell at the estate sale. Did you keep them?

A response came right away:

Gala Estate Sales donated them to some local charity. I have the receipt for tax purposes. Stand by.

I didn't have to wait very long. Her next text came back a minute later:

A charity called 'Needless Necessities.'

I tried to imagine what would have happened to those books after the donation. One had to assume they'd been routed to the thrift store. If so, there was no telling how many had already been sold.

Unless someone who worked there had set them aside for another use. Why, just that morning I'd seen a box of books that Wo had bought with her store credit, a box labeled WH for her quasi-boyfriend, Wash Henry.

Or Wanda Hightower.

Wash: "I'm supposed to soak these books in kerosene for three hours."

I looked at my watch. Wo's show would have just begun. I looked out the window and saw a light on in the room where Cynthia often read at night. I called her landline and asked if she could come sit at the house with Lydia while I ran a quick errand.

Four minutes later I was pulling into Needless Necessities, heading straight for the ring of tiki torches in the center of the otherwise empty parking lot. Flames danced around the heads of a large crowd who had gathered to watch the spectacle.

A reviewer writing in *The Independent* would later describe the scene:

A young girl's bed served as the centerpiece of the show. On the bed was a layer of books, perhaps representing the future education of a young girl, who, played by the artist, wore a pink flame-retardant hazmat suit. Holding a doll, the artist hovered above her bed of books, suspended by a nursing-home lift machine. A young male dressed as Father DreamTime used a pump spray to douse the girl with a gelatin-based goo that smelled distinctly of strawberries. (The pump's canister was labeled, "Innocent Dreams.") Then the Slum Lord (dressed in all-black) approached the bed with one of the tiki torches, poised to incinerate the bed of books before the girl was lowered to the bed and her presumed doom.

By the time I arrived, Wo was already suspended above the bed, pretending to cry out in her sleep. "If we have to leave our home, Ma, I don't want to wake up!"

I paused on the edge of the crowd and watched as Wash, robed all in black and looking like the Grim Reaper himself, used a torch to light the bed on fire. Flames went up with a "WHOOSH." The crowd collectively stepped back.

"Wait!" I shouted, drawing nearer, my hands outreached, blocking the bright light.

"Mother?" Wo's character cried out, as the tips of flames licked her pink suit. "Is that you?"

The crowd parted as I presses forward. I peered into the fire but couldn't make out a single thing amidst the smoke.

"Can someone please help!" I yelled.

"Stand back, everyone!" commanded a man's deep voice. Everyone else did as they had been told as blasts of fire extinguishers from multiple directions covered the bed in a white foam. The crowd acted unsurprised to see the fire fighters, as their pink helmets signaling they must somehow be a part of the show.

Purposely unmindful of the risk, I leaned over the smoldering bed and began using my hands to make sense of the foamy mess. I must have leaned a bit too far, for I toppled onto the bed face-first, covering myself in the foam. What's more, the contraption that was supporting Wo gave way, sending her into free fall. Tiny Wo didn't feel so tiny as she landed with a wet slap between my shoulder blades.

All at once my back felt the coolness of Wo's pink slime.

Wo stood up on the bed and straddled my primordial body as she ad-libbed to the crowd, "Matriarchy has sacrificed herself for the next generation! There will be no consuming fire tonight! Loving sacrifice has instilled new hope!"

I craned my head sideways. "Darlin', I don't want to ruin

your performance any more than I already have, but can I please get up now?"

With Wo's assistance, I was able to sit up on the edge of the charred bed. Someone handed me a rag, allowing me to wipe some of the foam from my eyes. I looked around and saw dozens of faces staring back at me in the torchlight. Hopefully this wasn't the part where the townsfolk began stabbing the monster with pitchforks.

I stood up, ready to run if I had to.

"Mother Queen!" Wo intoned. "I love you!" She gave me a giant hug, sliming the front of my body with even more strawberry-scented goo.

The crowd burst into applause. It seemed that I was meant to do something, so I took a squishy little bow. *This better be worth it*, I thought, as I frantically stirred the books on the bed, at last putting my hands on the title I was looking for.

Then I slogged out of there under the watchful eyes of the fire fighters. I could have paid a fee to any old fire station to have them stand by during the performance, but they would have stuck out terribly. Wo wouldn't like that. My sizable donation to Station Number 23 had been a way to help those firefighters in their breast cancer research fundraiser, but it had really been an indirect gift to a lovestruck college boy. Pink-clad firefighters would fit right in—and be on hand whenever Wo's performance got a little too hot.

I was eager to examine the book I'd salvaged, but I needed to clean myself up first. The reddish goo made me look mortally injured, while the fire extinguisher foam made me appear frozen solid. The expression on Cynthia's face was priceless. "You look like something out of *Macbeth*," she said. I had to reassure her multiple times I was perfectly fine so she would return home.

I stayed under the shower for the longest time without feeling the least bit cleaner. Then I remembered how seabirds had been tidied up after an oil spill, so I puddled my way to the kitchen to grab a bottle of dish soap. That made a big difference, actually. I toweled off, put on a robe, and made my way downstairs again where Andrew M. Ion's book awaited me.

I was nervous. Had I overhyped the chances that this genre novel harbored an important clue? The front cover image depicted a male hand holding a briefcase, the man's wrist handcuffed to the handle. On the book's title page, charred but still readable, was the following inscription:

Wanda,
Thank you for helping me pay attention to the secret troubles of those around me and not to be afraid to walk through dark valleys in search of a story.
Sincerely, "Andy"

The rest of the book, unfortunately, had been destroyed. It must have soaked up quite a bit of the kerosene before being set aflame.

I looked again at the Kelley Self-Published Writers Network website. The group's 2nd annual awards banquet was coming up in December, to be held in New York City. That's where "Andy" would be receiving his award. I supposed I could crash the party in hopes of meeting Mr. Ion and ask him how he knew Wanda, but the event was still several weeks away.

There wasn't a phone number for the writers' network on the website, but there was a contact form.

I filled it out—making sure to state that my request was in connection with a homicide investigation.

CHAPTER 21

COMPLICATIONS

I had left several voicemails with Stephanie since the party on Saturday; after Wo's show, I left one more. I guess I was naive to think that at least some of the appreciation shown to me by others that night would have rubbed off on her.

On Friday morning, I went with Lydia to her rehab session. This time Darryl met us there. Surprisingly, in this session she didn't demonstrate the progress she had exhibited at home. Full sentences eluded her, and she stumbled over every word. If anything, she was backsliding.

"I sure wish she'd heal faster," Darryl told me in the waiting room as Lydia wrapped up her session. "Besides the fact that I want her to get her life back, I need to ask her some more questions about Otis's visit. But every time I bring up the subject, she acts like she's going to have another stroke."

"What is Trent's status, by the way?" I was trying to sound casual, but I was keen on hearing Darryl's answer. I felt like time to help the boy was slipping away.

"The chief is considering asking for a search warrant for Otis's property. But we have to know what we're looking for." He looked more than frustrated. He seemed almost anguished.

"What's wrong?" I asked.

He shook his head. "I can't tell you."

I knew this was his homicide case, but I'd taken on a responsibility, too. I asked, "Are you sure you can't talk about it?"

"I'm sure. It's just...complicated."

Like relationships.

I didn't reach out a hand. I wanted to.

I took a walk around the neighborhood, trying to marshal my thoughts. I'd drawn what I thought was a more accurate picture of Wanda. The persistently cold hands, a constant, raging pain that, in combination with the steroids, could have made her stark raving mad. But I didn't have a sketch of her killer, surely nothing to compete with the evidence surrounding Trent, even when the dragon costume connection was put aside.

I dropped by Nancy's to see how she was feeling since the note, and to make sure she was still on track with her pies for the next day. Jim, appearing restless, politely stood up from his desk to let me in.

"I'm afraid I've interrupted your work, Reverend," I said.

"Jim's been working on a book of daily devotionals to present to his church when he retires next year," Nancy offered from her own nearby desk. "He's been working so hard on it." Nancy, for her part, seemed in the middle of penning a letter. Did people still do that? One of the reasons I enjoyed visiting the Thompsons is that each visit felt like a step back in history.

Jim shrugged. "What Nancy means is I'm *trying* to write a devotional book."

His wife smiled. "All you have to do, Honey, is draw from all those years of terrific sermons."

"Sounds like a book with best-seller potential," I teased. "No pressure."

Jim chuckled and asked what prompted my visit.

"I just wanted to verify that your wife is still on for the pie sale."

"Of course!" said Nancy. "In fact, I baked three pies this morning. I didn't want to feel rushed tomorrow." Then her face fell as she added. "It's been a nice distraction from all the madness around here." From his desk, Jim reached a comforting hand over to Nancy, which she took.

"I'm so sorry you two received that note," I said. "I feel responsible. I'm pretty sure that the dead squirrels left for Cynthia Rogers and me were also because of my sleuthing."

"We won't be intimidated," Jim said, giving Nancy's hand a final loving squeeze before letting go.

While we had been talking, I became aware of a photograph above Jim's desk of a Black sailor. I hadn't noticed it the last time I was here. I asked Jim about it. "That's Dorie Miller, a hero of Pearl Harbor. He received the Navy Cross that day. Dorie was one of my idols when I was growing up."

"You really are a World War buff," I said, noting again the various war curios peppering his desk. "You could probably write a book about *that*."

"It's a nice hobby, but it's not the kind of thing that calms the heart," Jim said, with a knowing look at Nancy. "I think I'll just focus on finishing the devotional book."

I apologized again for interrupting his writing.

"Not at all," he said. "God bless you, Rett."

I started to leave then, but something stopped me. All the anxiety of the previous days just kind of hit me at once.

"Actually, Reverend, I wonder if I could share something with you."

"Sure thing," he said. "Come, let's sit down."

"I can leave the room," Nancy announced, standing. "I have some things to do in the kitchen."

"No, please stay, Nancy," I said. "It has to do with the investigation, and that applies to everyone in the neighborhood. Though I'll understand if you don't want to talk about it."

"I'll be fine," she said. "If it means getting us closer to finding the killer, I'm definitely interested."

Jim led me to the sitting area of the den. He and I sat across from one another, while Nancy stood behind her husband's chair.

"So, what's troubling you?" asked the pastor.

I told him about the investigation and how it continued to focus on Trent, the teenager, and on Otis Jones, whom we all knew so well. "Now the police think Otis is protecting his relative somehow," I said. I didn't mention the possibility of a search warrant; that seemed like insider information.

Jim listened, his expression somber. "Regarding Trent—just how do they think he committed the crime?"

"They think he broke the glass near the front door and used that to reach inside and open the door. Maybe he was upstairs looking for drugs when Wanda saw him. She ran and tried to escape through the front door. Thinking she had recognized him, he killed her. Or maybe the sound of glass breaking alerted Wanda from the outset. She came out to the porch to see what was going on and he jumped her. The boy then went inside to steal the pills and left through the back door where he was spotted by a trick-or-treater. That's their theory, anyway."

I continued, "There are so many problems with it. The biggest issue is that we know now that the girl didn't actually see someone dressed as a dragon, which was Trent's costume that night. We think she saw more of a typical ghost in a white sheet."

Jim nodded. "Surely they'll drop this line of thinking if they can't find more evidence, right? Then they'll leave the boy alone?"

I frowned. "I wish I believed that. It seems like whenever a door closes, they grasp even tighter onto the other threads, however thin. I never thought about the human element in solving crimes. I thought everyone focused only on the facts."

"Suspicion supplies its own evidence," Jim remarked, almost offhand. He looked over his left shoulder at his wife. "I've got to tell her, Nancy."

"Yes, you do, Jim."

"Tell me what?" I asked.

Just closed his eyes and took a deep breath. "That I'm the one who broke the window next to Wanda's front door."

"Excuse me?" I said, flabbergasted. "What?"

Jim nodded. "Remember how I told you how Wanda became a shut-in and how her mail and papers just started to pile up on the porch? Every morning I'd walk the dog past her house and just become more concerned. Well, the night before Halloween, my worries got the best of me. I went to her porch and peered through that little window. It was dark inside, but I thought I could see her lying on her couch. I banged on her door, and, when she didn't stir, I knocked hard on the glass. It broke. I started yelling through the window for her to please come to the door, just to please come talk to me and let me know she was okay."

"Jim is a man of action," Nancy said. "He doesn't just stand around."

"I think that's why I admired Dorie so much," Jim said.

"The Pearl Harbor sailor?" I asked.

"Yes. While everyone else froze with their jaws on the ground, Dorie actually did something. He manned the anti-aircraft gun for a while. Then he performed critical first aid on a number of the wounded."

"I see," I said. "So did Wanda respond to your voice?"

"To my relief, she did. I got her to realize who I was. After I apologized for breaking her window, she actually let me inside, and we talked for a little while."

"Your dog, too?"

"Ben stayed on the porch."

"How did Wanda seem?"

"Bad off. She confessed that she was depressed and..."

He stopped.

"And what?" I asked.

"This is why I didn't want to say anything to the police. She said she had some pain pills she'd been experimenting with. She said she planned to take the whole bottle of pills that night. I asked if she would let me take her to the hospital to get some help, but she refused. But I insisted she at least give me the bottle, which she did."

I was elated, because if we could show the police the pills that were leftover from Wanda's foot surgery, it would let Trent off the hook as having taken them. "Do you have the pills?"

Jim shook his head. "I tossed them in the garbage. They're gone by now."

I was crushed. "That's too bad. What happened next?"

"I made Wanda promise me she wouldn't hurt herself. I offered to pay for the broken window, and she said she'd get in touch with Otis and send me the bill. She also said she was going to have Otis fill in the mail slot and put up a real mailbox at the street. But just before I left, she removed the tape and cardboard that been covering the slot from the inside. I took that as a good sign that she might just turn a corner."

"That's probably why we saw Otis's name written on a notepad," I cut in. "And it also explains why the officers didn't find any broken glass near the front door. She probably cleaned it up herself that night or the next morning. But she never got a chance to get those things fixed, because the next day she was murdered."

"When I left her house, she was very much alive," Jim said. "I wanted to tell the detective all about that conversation, but I'm not in the business of telling people's darkest secrets. She wouldn't want the world to know that she'd been suicidal. Honestly, when I heard she was dead, my first thought was, 'How did she stab herself?' Crazy, I know. The whole thing is just so tragic."

Nancy laid a shaky hand on Jim's shoulder and asked me, "Do you think the police will suspect Jim had something to do with Wanda's death?"

I shook my head. "I seriously doubt that a retired minister is going to become a stronger suspect than a wayward teen with illegal drugs who ran from the police."

Jim said, "I guess I didn't technically lie to the detective about the last time I saw Wanda. After I left her house to finish walking the dog, I did notice Wanda's upstairs bedroom light flick on and saw her silhouette. However, I was deceptive by not sharing the full story, and, if others are being suspected due to something I've done, that's unacceptable. I'll call Darryl today and tell him all about it. Do you suppose that will take some of the heat off this Trent boy and Otis?"

"I'm beginning to doubt much of anything, short of a signed confession from the killer, would actually get them to stop suspecting the Dragon Boy, as they call him."

Jim hung his head. "If you don't mind, Rett, I'd like to take the dog for a walk now and clear my head." I watched him stand and find the old dog's leash before leading Old Ben outside.

Once they had gone, I stood and turned to Nancy. "Don't worry too much about Jim. Darryl reminded me that he's not in the business of convicting innocent people of murder."

"I can't help but worry. Jim just cares so much about helping others."

I said, "Enough to break down a door if he has to, just in order to help?"

"He would do that for you, too, if he thought you were in trouble."

I suspected she was right. I thought about the moment I barged in on Cynthia, and how different this world would be if more of us took a fierce interest in the well-being of our neighbors.

She put a hand on my arm. "I'm glad Jim shared about breaking the window. I was worried about that. You said you were anxious about this case. Do you feel better now after talking about it?"

"I do, thank you," I said. "And I feel even more convinced than ever that Trent is not the killer—and that I need to keep doing what I can to find out the truth."

I'd been so caught up in thinking about the case that I hadn't made it to the store. I asked Nancy if she had any beans I could have for some chili I was planning to put in the slow cooker for dinner. She seemed to welcome the change of subject and went to the kitchen to check. "Sorry. None."

A thought occurred to me. "No dry beans either?"

"Zilch," she said. "But if even if you had the dry beans, you'd have to soak them overnight for your chili."

"You're right," I said. "Thanks anyway for checking."

As I was walking from the Thompson's house, a car pulled up. It was Gwen, the parishioner from Jim's church I'd met the last time I'd visited the Thompsons. Before she could get out of the car, I made a motion for her to roll down her window so I could let her know that Jim was out taking his dog for a walk. She thanked me for letting her know.

"We sure are going to miss that man when he retires," she added. "And to think, we almost let him go after just one year."

I asked her what she meant.

"Brother Jim's sermons were terrible when he first arrived. I mean, they were just dreadfully boring. But he prayed on it—we all prayed on it—and the Holy Spirit gave him a new voice! Soon everyone was asking their friends to come hear our spirit-inspired preacher. We doubled in size in less than two years."

"That's amazing," I said.

"That's the power of Jesus!" she said. "'He walks on heaven's pavement and talks brotherly to divine powers.' Have a blessed day!" Then she zoomed away.

As I left the home and reflected on the visit with Jim, I couldn't help but feel more and more unsettled. By the time supper rolled around, I had decided something.

I was adding Jim Thompson to the list of suspects.

CHAPTER 22

THE INVESTIGATION BEARS FRUIT

A ll through dinner I was dying to talk with Darryl about the case. When Lydia and Charlie went to watch *Wheel of Fortune*—cheesy game show doubling as language therapy—he and I stayed behind to clean up the kitchen together. It was a routine I could come to enjoy.

"Did Jim call and tell you about the broken window and the pills?" I asked.

"He called me." Darryl had not been pleased to learn that Jim had held back the information; however, "the pastor doesn't have a motive," he added.

"Actually, he might." I shared how I had interrupted Jim struggling to write a devotional book and how one of his parishioners said he was a terrible sermon writer when he first arrived at their church. "We know he delivered inspirational Christian books to Wanda. What if she was writing his sermons for him all these years, then suddenly refused? He's so close to retirement. Might he have gotten angry at her refusal and snapped?"

"But she was an atheist, Rett. Hard for me to believe she'd ever help him write a church sermon."

"But we know she was still spiritual to a large degree and a poet besides. She struggled with money. Maybe he paid her something for them. It doesn't matter what their arrangement was. He broke that window, and he didn't say anything about it to you for a long time. That tells me we can't trust him completely."

"It is troubling," Darryl said.

"At least now we know Trent didn't break that glass," I said. "And we can probably rule out that Trent got his pills from Wanda. You said the ones Trent had were in a blister pack. If Jim is to be believed, Wanda's were in a bottle."

"At least that's what Jim said," Darryl reminded.

"But you couldn't connect the Imp's note to Trent. And then there's the matter of his costume."

"I admit that not a lot here makes sense, but the chief has lost patience with the Hightower investigation. He wants something to happen." Once again a worried look came over Darryl's expression. "He's asked a judge for a warrant to search Otis Jones's property."

"To look for what?"

"Evidence Otis may have found when he was collecting rubbish in the alleyway."

"But he often collects junk there."

"Yes, but he acted suspiciously when a policeman showed up."

"Since when does having a cop on your heels not make a person nervous? And it sounds like Trent also had good reason to run, because of the pills. I'm not meaning any offense, Darryl, but the chief just seems determined to connect these two somehow so he can close the case."

"I know it's not much, but it's the best we've got."

"It's going to take hours to search Otis's packed studio, you know that. And it's going to upset Otis terribly."

"It can't be helped," Darryl said, appearing torn. "I probably shouldn't have said anything. Don't tell anyone. It might not happen anyway."

I had promised Augusta to keep her informed of what I knew regarding Trent's case. I couldn't in good conscience run to her now, but I would compromise. I would tell Augusta about the possible search warrant *after* tomorrow's show. I didn't want to put a damper on her grandfather's biggest day yet as an artist. His day.

Which made me think of KayLeigh Rider and *her* day. And that helped me remember to do something else. At home I opened my phone's photo stream and found the pictures I'd taken of KayLeigh's wedding registry information. I went online, curious to see what she'd registered for.

Anything and everything, it turned out. Hundreds of items ranging from the very small—a ten-dollar spatula—to a two-thousand-dollar bed frame. Where did she plan to put all this stuff?

Call me a glutton for punishment, but I poured myself a glass of wine and meticulously began scrolling through every one of her bridal registries.

I wasn't halfway through the first glass when one item in particular stood out from the others. I stared at it long and hard. The longer I stared, the more excited I felt.

I could share my discovery with Darryl. Either he'd be super impressed and see me in a new light—or he'd wave it off and consider me a silly fool. I needed to keep this one to myself, at least for now.

If only I could figure out what it meant.

Around midnight I was awakened by police lights flickering through the windows. My first thought was that some harm had come to Cynthia. Had Dennis struck again? Loud voices from outside drew me down Lydia's stairs to the front room, where I looked outside and saw two police cars parked—not in front of Cynthia's house—but in front of Skip and Stuart's.

Lydia was still sound asleep, so I put on my robe and stepped outside. One policeman—tall, super skinny—was tidying up his notes from talking with Skip, while a second, huskier cop was looking around the front yard with a flashlight.

"What's going on, Skip?" I asked.

"They caught some guy going through my Triumph looking for pocket change. He's in the police car wearing handcuffs right now."

"He threw something when we drove up," the note-taking cop said. "Might have been drugs."

Which would explain why the other cop was kicking around leaves in Skip's front yard.

"I don't know why we're even bothering with all this," Skip said. "People come through here checking cars for valuables all the time. It's why I leave the car doors unlocked."

The cop looked up from his notes, surprised. "You leave your car unlocked? Why would you do that?"

"If I keep it locked, someone might take a knife to the soft top in order to get in. This way they only take the little bit of change I keep on the center console just for this reason."

The policeman interjected, "Looks like they rummaged through your glove compartment, too."

Skip shrugged.

"But, Skip," I said, "aren't you the one who called the police?"

"No. The police said someone driving by did."

I looked up and down the block. The only house with a light on was the Thompsons. Was that Jim's face peering through their front door window?

"Found it!" announced the cop who had been searching in

Skip's yard. I turned to look. The cop shined a light on what he held. Resting in his blue latex glove was a piece of fruit with a bite taken out of it.

"A pear?" the thin cop asked.

"A golden pear!" I said excitedly. Though it might be difficult to verify, I couldn't help but think we were looking at the missing pear from Wanda's kitchen. Though a couple weeks old, it had held up well. It must have been barely ripe to begin with.

The beat cop clearly wasn't aware of the pears as a crime-scene detail. Before I could begin to explain, Darryl pulled up in his Charger.

"I heard the commotion on the scanner," Darryl said, stepping out of his car. "I was at the precinct. What happened? What's that?" He looked at the pear, which appeared especially squishy in the cop's hand. "Where did you find this?"

"In the leaves. We saw the suspect throw it when we drove up."

Darryl said, "Bag it for the lab. Where's our guy?"

"In the back of the car."

I followed at a safe distance as Darryl went over to speak to the individual, a strung-out-looking white man in his 20s. "Hey, where did you get that piece of fruit?"

The man shrugged.

"That's a powerful piece of evidence. It tells me you may have killed a lady on this block two weeks ago."

"What? No way! I found that pear in the little car just now! In the glove compartment. I swear! I found it just now and I took a bite. I was hungry. Seriously."

"Hang tight," Darryl told the man, and he walked over to confront Skip.

"He says he found the pear in your glove box."

"I've never seen it before," he said. "He must be lying."

"Who else drives this car? Does Stuart?"

"I don't let anyone else drive it. Even Stuart."

"Has anyone else had access to it that you know of?"

Skip thought a moment, then snapped his fingers. "I'd almost forgotten. I was trying to get to an event the other day, but it just wouldn't turn over. So, I flagged down Otis, who was driving by on one of his junk salvaging runs. I knew he used to be a mechanic, so I asked him to take a look at the Triumph."

"What day was this?"

"Why, it was the day after the murder. Saturday morning. Around ten. I had to go to a brunch event in which a number of candidates for state office were speaking."

Darryl asked, "And did Otis fix the problem?"

"He did. He had some tools in his truck."

"Did you watch him the whole time?"

He shook his head. "I went inside at one point to get my coffee."

"He could have planted it then," Darryl muttered. Before I could challenge him, Darryl turned to the other two policemen. "Book our friend. Get the pear tested. Run a DNA test where someone took a bite. Dust for prints—the works."

I looked at Skip. Could he be lying, implicating Otis in order to throw the scent off himself?

Darryl walked me back to his mother's house.

"You may suspect Otis of planting that evidence," I said, "but most anyone can get to that glove box given that Skip always keeps his car unlocked."

"True. And I haven't ruled out Skip killing Wanda and keeping that pear as a memento."

"I can think of much better mementos. Even a crispy golden pear is going to spoil eventually. A few more days and that thing will be a soggy mess." Bring in Doris the Mad Canner!

I asked, "What if that vagrant had something to do with the murder?"

"We'll interrogate him. He isn't going anywhere for at least a day. We'll charge him tomorrow with trespassing and theft."

"Who called the police, by the way?" I asked.

"Didn't leave a name. Dispatch said they were driving by and saw something suspicious. Deep voice. Probably a man's."

"You look nice, by the way," he said once we'd arrived at Lydia's porch.

"Are you kidding? I'm not even wearing any makeup."

"A natural beauty doesn't need it," he said.

"Maybe you're just feeling generous with your compliments because you may have gotten another break in the case tonight."

"Maybe," he smiled.

I considered my appearance, which included a bulky robe worn over pajama pants. No matter what Darryl might think, I felt frumpy and unattractive right now.

"It was good to see you, Darryl," I said. "Have a good night."

I left him on the porch.

I hoped he felt a little disappointed.

Inside, I poured a glass of wine and took it up to my bed. I already regretted not raising some additional questions with Darryl about the pear. For example, if Otis had found the pear in the alleyway, why would he go and plant it in Skip's car, only to return again to the alley? He'd have to know such behavior would appear suspicious.

But it was no use speculating. If I was going to help Otis and Trent, I'd have to present real evidence to back up my alternate theories.

On the bedside table was the short stack of books I'd collected during the case. Among them was the burned-out copy of *The Spy's Briefcase*. If only I could speak to Andrew M. Ion, what might he tell me?

I raised my glass of Pinot Noir. "A toast, to Andy M. Ion!" I was about to take a sip, but stopped myself:

Close your eyes and listen: It hums your melo-dy.

Perhaps I couldn't speak to Andy.

But maybe he could speak to me.

I tracked down the book of Romantic poetry I'd bought at the estate sale and hurriedly turned to the long section on John Keats. Introducing Keats's poetry was an essay by the book's editor that spoke glowingly of the young Englishman's amazing talent. The introduction included words that Keats's good friend, the poet Percy Bysshe Shelley, had penned after the poet's death:

"John Keats, died at Rome of a consumption, in his twenty-fourth year, on the 23rd of February 1821; and was buried in the romantic and lonely cemetery of the protestants in that city.... The savage criticism on his Endymion, *which appeared in the* Quarterly Review, *produced the most violent effect on his susceptible mind; the agitation thus originated ended in the rupture of a blood-vessel in the lungs; a rapid consumption ensued, and the succeeding acknowledgements from more candid critics, of the true greatness of his powers, were ineffectual to heal the wound thus wantonly inflicted...*

"You, one of the meanest, have wantonly defaced one of the noblest specimens of the workmanship of God. Nor shall it be your excuse, that, murderer as you are, you have spoken daggers, but used none."

So, Shelley blamed a literary critic for the death of John Keats, whereas everything else I'd read attributed his death to tuberculosis. I skipped over the Keats poems that I'd already read and landed at the opening stanza of Keats's longest work, the poem I hadn't yet had the courage—or stamina—to tackle.

The young bard's four thousand line epic about a Greek shepherd named Endymion, a name that must have inspired someone else's choice of a pen-name: Andy M. Ion.

Endymion's first line read: "A thing of beauty is a wonderful thing indeed." Only about three thousand nine hundred and ninety-nine lines to go. I could almost hear Darryl's voice saying how this line of thinking could not lead to anything at all that was relevant. It was crazy to think that reading such an old-fashioned poem could shed a single ray of light on this confusing murder case.

So be it. Call the gesture absurd. Tonight, to me, it was a needless necessity.

Reading the poem took me all night and put me in a sort of trance. When I had finished, it was like I had been shown every detail about the case—or nearly everything. I walked outside where light was dawning, or as the young Keats might put it:

> ...'Twas the morn: Apollo's upward fire
> Made every eastern cloud a silvery pyre
> Of brightness so unsullied, that therein
> A melancholy spirit well might win
> Oblivion, and melt out his essence fine
> Into the winds...

I looked down the street at Wanda's home, the rising sun lighting up her porch.

Oblivion, here I come.

CHAPTER 23

THE BIG REVEAL

Otis's show opened to immediate buzz. Early arrivers went on their cellphones to tell their friends what they were missing. In Raleigh one was within fifteen minutes of anywhere else in the city, so just in the first half hour the crowd at the show grew exponentially.

The heads of the NC Museum of Art as well as Raleigh's Contemporary Art Museum were already present when Lydia and I arrived. Would at least one of them purchase something for their respective institution's permanent collections?

I'd invited a few others—among them Brad and Gail Norris. They were art collectors, and, according to Archie, at least, didn't mind spending money—even money they didn't have. I had hoped they'd come, because I wanted to watch them and, hopefully, listen in on their conversation. I had a theory about the case, but I needed to be sure I wasn't leaving something out.

I had asked Darryl if I could plant a microphone in exhibit tour headsets that the Norrises might wear. "Sorry," he informed me, "but you're not allowed to plant a bug on them without their knowledge." Somehow I'd have to get close to them on my own.

I found Otis and Augusta on the periphery just taking in the scene. Otis looked dapper in a gray wool suit and red tie. Augusta wore black slacks, pumps, and a vibrant orange long-sleeve blouse.

Augusta did a double take when she saw me. For this arts event I was wearing some of the clothes Margaret had chosen for me: a Renaissance-like blouse with a colorful vest and a long, purple skirt that fell over amazingly comfortable brown leather boots.

"I almost didn't recognize you," Augusta said. "You look sharp!"

"Look at your spectacular self!" I said, energized by the compliment. "And don't you look handsome, Mr. Jones."

"Thank you, thank you."

"The heads of two museums are here," I said. "So are a number of well-heeled collectors."

"It's a free country," Otis said, playing it off, trying to mask his pride.

"Let's meet some of these VIPs," Augusta urged her grandfather. "They need to know who created all this."

"You know how nervous I get in crowds, Augusta."

"Here," she said, "I'll hold your hand." She sweetly led him to the center of the room where some who had already made a tour of the pieces were mingling near the refreshment table. The appearance of the wrinkled gentleman garnered polite greetings until someone ventured the question, "Are you the sculptor?" The displays of admiration that followed his answer were effusive.

Sally had insisted that the dessert station be placed in the dead center of the gallery on a long table, next to several racks where a few of the Qrazy Qwilters showed off their magnificent work. I had watched Lydia go to hang out with the ladies, but it was only after she had made the rounds of the room to examine Otis's art. I'd watched her act like she was going to approach

Otis, but at the last second she changed her mind. Was it embarrassment over her condition, or something else that made her pause?

On the middle dessert table were the submissions for the pie contest, a couple of dozen in all. Placed to either side of those were pies and cakes for actual sale. At least Sally was smart to turn the event into something with a bit more suspense. Each baker would bring identical pies—one to be sold in a silent auction, the other to be judged for the contest.

Ricky, Freddy's assistant, worked the cash box for the pies and art alike. I'd already given instructions to the dessert judges —Jasmine, Wo, and Wash—on how to record their ratings. "I hope you're hungry," I said to them, as I gave them their forks. "There were at least twenty pies submitted."

"Oh, I can eat a lot of pie," Wash confessed. "We'll pick a winner. No problem."

I found Freddy near a table where wine was being served. I'd seen him working the crowd in an effort to gauge the show's impact. "Everyone is impressed," he reported. "Ricky has already sold two of the smaller pieces." As we talked, I watched Ricky leave the pie station to place red-dot stickers next to the sculptures that had already sold.

"That's encouraging," I said. "Have you told Otis, yet?"

"I was on my way to do that."

"But you saw me heading for the wine and thought you'd ambush me first?"

A twinkle appeared in his eye. "Guilty dog barks."

I moved away from the alcohol to set his mind at ease. Besides, I'd been up all night and was too tired now to drink.

I saw Brad and Gail standing off by themselves regarding the largest piece, *Jazz*, and engaged deep in conversation. So I sneaked over and planted myself just behind them where I could listen. They were each a little tipsy and spoke a little too loudly for their own good.

"But Brad, it will look so fantastic at the lake house, right in the living room."

"I still think it's too—busy."

"It's an investment! Do you see how fast these pieces are already going? Outsider Art is hot again. Did you see Reginald Byers just walk in? If we don't snag it, he will."

"I don't really care what that fat faggot buys," Brad said.

I'd been warned by Archie about Brad's homophobia, but it was startling to actually hear it in action.

In the next breath, Brad softened his tone. "You really want this crazy thing, don't you?"

"Yes. And now that we know we're getting a windfall, we can go out on a limb and buy it."

"Thanks to Aunt Lucy."

"Thanks to *you* for making sure she updated her will before she entered the nursing home. And making sure you visited her every day while it was being rewritten. Your kindness didn't go unnoticed when it really counted. You deserve all that she gave you, because that was more love than that son of hers ever showed her."

So that explained the couple's euphoria the day after Halloween. Apparently, it had little to do with Wanda and everything to do with a timely bequest from a wealthy relative.

"Aunt Lucy was a bitch, but she was a *rich* bitch," Brad said drunkenly. "Most miserable week of my life, but it paid off. Cousin Leon ain't gonna like it, but he's always been a snot. I hope I can be there to see his face when he learns that most of his inheritance is going to me."

Brad gave his wife a sloppy kiss on the cheek. "What the hell. Buy the painting. I'll enjoy watching Flaming Reggie freak out when he sees that red dot appear."

As Gail darted to find Ricky and make the purchase, I saw Darryl enter the gallery. I could tell him what I'd heard from the Norrises and give him my final thoughts on who had done the crime, but the excitement I felt at seeing him was undermined by the appearance of two additional officers he'd brought with him. I rushed over to meet the detective and his men.

"What's going on?" I asked.

"I need to talk to Otis," Darryl said, all business.

My heart sank. "Why now?"

"There's a new urgency to the case," Darryl said. "One of Trent's friends has disappeared."

"One of the bad elements he was hanging out with?"

"No. An acting friend of his. A boy named Barry Watson."

Darryl must have seen my face go pale. "Do you know him?"

I nodded grimly. "What do you think happened?"

"He didn't come home from school two days ago, so his parents filed a report yesterday. We don't know if his disappearance is connected to this case, but we don't have any more time to waste. We need to catch this killer. Otis might hold the key."

"Okay," I said, "but please don't approach him in the exhibit hall. Let me get him for you. You can talk outside the curtains."

Grudgingly, Darryl agreed. I was on my way to fetch Otis when Wash stopped me.

"Miss Rett! It's an emergency!"

"What's wrong?"

"We can't choose a winner. It's a two-way tie."

"I don't understand. There are three judges."

"Wo refuses to pick a winner. She decided it's wrong to hold a beauty contest for fruit tombs."

"'Fruit *tombs*'?" I exclaimed, hitting my limit of exasperation. "Don't tell me Wo thinks pies have rights, too. Just give me the three ratings sheets and I'll take it from here."

Feeling like the Angel of Death, I approached Otis, who had

warmed up to the admiring crowd. I hated to be the one to tell him that the police were here to speak with him, but I had no choice. I led him and Augusta through the crowd to just outside the showroom where the police were waiting.

Turns out I'd started a sort of parade. Freddy followed me through the gallery's black drapery, Wash and Jasmine right behind him.

"We saw you leave the show quickly," Freddy said. "Is everything all right?"

I put my finger to my lips.

"Otis," said Darryl. "We have reason to believe you may be withholding evidence from this murder case, perhaps to protect your relative. I've got with me a warrant to search your property for specific items detailed in the warrant. Officers are searching your home and studio as we speak."

"You won't find nothin'," Otis said defiantly.

Darryl continued. "We also have the authority to examine and, if necessary, tear apart as we search each and every one of these art pieces here today. Do you have anything you want to tell us before we do that?"

I couldn't believe what I was hearing, and I wasn't the only one appalled.

"Destroy this man's art?" said Freddy. "Why, some of these pieces predate the murder by a decade?"

"Besides, you're too late," Augusta added. "Several of the pieces have already sold—including the largest one, which someone just bought for a hundred thousand dollars. People have to take my grandfather seriously now."

Darryl shook his head. "No one can take any of these pieces out of this hall, even if they have been purchased."

Our small group looked at one another, stunned. Destroy Otis's art, in order to find some piece of evidence that may not even exist? If the pieces were destroyed, Otis would surely have to give back every cent he'd been paid for them. And there would be none of his art left for posterity.

"Mr. Jones," said Darryl, "I need you to tell me what you know."

Otis's stoic reticence seemed to waver. "I—"

"No!" came a cry.

We all turned. Lydia, who had followed us out of the hall, had been listening to the whole conversation.

"Mom?" Darryl said. "What's going on?"

Lydia, on the verge of angry tears, spoke in halting cadence. "Don't...you...bother...Otis!"

"She doesn't want you to destroy Mr. Jones's art," said Wash, assuming his default role as artist translator.

"That's clear enough, son," said Darryl, very red-faced and frustrated with the way this whole warrant serving was going.

Lydia trembled, "I...killed...Wan...da!"

"Lydia!" cried Otis. "What foolishness is this? Officer, I can explain—"

"Hush, please, everyone!" I shouted.

I knew what was going to happen if I didn't intervene. More people were going to say things they'd regret, and we'd be no closer to the solution of this mystery. There was only one way that I could keep my various promises to Darryl, Augusta, and Wanda all at once. The path forward was a huge gamble and might not work, but I had to try.

"Detective," I said, "I believe I can get you the evidence you need to close this case, and we won't have to destroy a lick of this man's art in the process."

He looked at me hard, a look that said: *I can't, Rett. Not this time.*

I persisted. "Please. Give me two hours. Not even. An hour and a half. Keep one of your officers here so he can make sure no one tampers with the art. If in ninety minutes you don't have enough evidence to make an arrest, then you can go through with your warrant."

Everyone was looking at Darryl.

"Fine. Ninety minutes," Darryl said. "After that, a search of the art goes forward."

The air in the group was still tense, but somewhat less desperate. After some doubting looks in my direction, most everyone filed back into the show, leaving just me, Darryl, and one of the two officers.

"Now," Darryl said, "what the hell do you have in mind?"

I explained my idea. Grudgingly, he agreed to my plan. He and the one officer returned to their police vehicles, while the other officer remained to stand guard inside the gallery.

I dodged into the gallery again and beelined it for Nancy Thompson at the pie auction table. I'd enlisted Nancy to help with dessert sales, but there had been a lot more interest in Otis's art (surprise, surprise). Several times during the show I'd looked over and noted her bored expression. At least the arrival of police was providing some welcome excitement.

"Is everything okay?" she asked. "What did the police want?"

"I need your help," I said. "I've got to leave in a second, but do you think you can shut down the pie contest for me, go get your husband, and meet me at Wanda Hightower's house in exactly half an hour? And here." I quickly scanned the ratings sheets that Wash had handed me. "Bring with you pie entries Number Six and Number Eleven, a half dozen plastic forks, and half a dozen Dixie Cups."

"Okay," she said tentatively, "but can you tell me what's going on?"

"I need you to help me break a pie tie," I said, "and catch a killer."

CHAPTER 24

ONE STANDS OUT

Brad and Gail were still congratulating one another over their purchase of an Otis Jones masterpiece when I dashed right up to them and put on my most innocent face. "Gail, if I can reach Angela and she doesn't mind, would you let me into the house? I told her a while ago that I wanted to get a photo of that beautiful dragon mantle."

Gail smiled. "Of course. When you have her text me, I can just let you in remotely with the app on my phone."

"Thank you," I said. "By the way, congratulations on buying that huge painting. It's super amazing."

Brad and Gail traded a smile.

I added: "Reggie Byers shared with me that, although he doesn't think it's the most valuable piece in the show, it's definitely one of the most impactful!"

I got out of there just as the wind was leaving their sails.

~

"We came as quickly as we could," said Nancy about a half hour later when I answered Wanda's front door to her and Jim. "At first, Sally didn't want me taking away the finalist pies. She said she was in charge and that 'all the pies *stayed*.'"

"So what did you do?"

Nancy patted her pie basket and whispered conspiratorially, "I took them when she wasn't looking."

"Come on in, you tricky thief!"

As I led them into the living room, Jim asked, "What's going on, Rett? Nancy said I was needed to help judge your pie contest and 'catch a murderer.' I'm not sure I'm qualified for either."

"You're just as qualified as I am. Come and sit down around the coffee table. Our primary suspect will be here shortly."

I began spooning samples of the two pies into four cups each. The first finalist, pie six, looked to be Doris's peach cobbler, while pie eleven was a traditional apple pie.

There was a knock on the front door. It was Skip Green looking very puzzled. "Hi, Rett. Your text said to come right away, but I don't really understand what this is all about."

I shot Jim and Nancy a quick, cautionary look over my shoulder.

"Come on in, Skip," I said in a friendly manner. "Sit down with us. We need a professional dessert taster, and you're our guy."

"I have worked hard to develop my palate over the years!" he said, patting his considerable midriff. "Why are we meeting here, by the way? Kind of gives me the creeps."

"My house is a mess," I said. "Besides, I was going to be here anyway. Angela Hightower said I could get a photo of this wonderful dragon fireplace mantel before someone buys the house."

There were polite greetings all around as we all got settled around the small coffee table. Even without a fire in the fireplace, the dragon seemed ferocious, alive.

"Here's your fork, Skip," I said. "Nancy and Jim each have

one. I've got one, too, though I won't vote. Let's first each take a bite of the cobbler and compare notes."

Everyone tasted the sample in their cups. After a moment, I asked, "Nancy, what do you think?"

"Passable," she said politely. "A little on the sweet side, maybe."

"I was going to say the same thing," said Skip. "The sugar has caramelized. No offense to the baker. Whose work is this?"

"Lydia Schmidt's cousin, Doris. She used canned peaches—perhaps not as good as fresh." I handed out the next round of Dixie Cups. "Now, for entry number ten: an apple pie." After everyone had tasted, I said, "Skip. Your thoughts?"

"I can't say anything critical. This pie is lovely, right down to the firm-yet-flaky crust. Extraordinary, really."

"I've always liked a classic apple pie," Nancy said.

"Nancy's just being humble," I said. "This is her entry."

"I wasn't going to say anything," Jim said. "I'd know that crust anywhere."

"I'm not surprised, Nancy," Skip said. "You always provide just the right touch of cinnamon and brown sugar. Are these Honey Crisp apples?"

"They are."

"I never miss!" Skip bragged. "I wouldn't change a thing, unless you decided to cook it a wee bit longer to make sure the fruit releases its maximum juice."

"A fair critique," said Nancy.

"Skip," I said, "thank you so much for helping us to pick a winner. But, before you go, I was hoping you could clear something up."

"Oh?"

"Remember how you told me and Darryl that Wanda didn't have any dirt on you? I don't think you were being truthful."

"I don't know what you mean."

"She worked with you to organize the Woodmont Chocolate Fest five years ago, correct?"

"Yes. Everyone knows that. So?"

"So I think you should come clean as to why she wouldn't work with you anymore after that."

He blushed. "Fine. I'll tell you. I left all the chocolate in my car, and it melted. Wanda saw all the bees buzzing around the Triumph and investigated. I had to replace thirty pounds of expensive chocolate with money from my own pocket."

I said, "But you didn't buy the same kind of chocolate, did you?"

"Does it really matter? I found a cheaper brand that tasted the same. No one was able to tell the difference."

"But Wanda knew, and you needed to make sure she stayed quiet about it. After the makeover when she threatened to tell everyone what happened—"

"I didn't kill her, if that's what you're saying!"

"I'm not saying you did. Just that you had a motive. If they found out about the chocolate, people would have felt cheated. You might never be allowed to organize an event in Woodmont again. That would have been devastating to you."

"Think what you like. You don't have any proof of anything."

He threw his fork on the table and stormed out of the house, slamming the front door in the process.

Jim asked, "Rett, do you really think Skip Green killed Wanda?"

"Well, you saw how defensive he got," I said. Working quickly, I took out a ziplock from my bag and added Skip's fork to it, then sealed it and wrote his name on the bag in black marker.

"What are you doing?" Nancy asked.

"Collecting his DNA so we can link him to the crime scene. Now," I said, "I'm famished!" I spooned a large clump of Nancy's pie into my Dixie Cup. "I think I'm going to eat the rest of your pie right now."

"Okay...," said Nancy uncomfortably.

"I'm going to become truly fat, and I don't even care! I'm tired of living by convention, tired of having to please everyone. Don't you ever feel that way? Don't you ever want to cut loose and just —live?"

"I suppose," but Nancy seemed pained watching me stuff my face.

"One thing I learned about Wanda," I continued, "is that she wasn't wedded to convention. What made Wanda unusual was how she thought about and looked at life."

"I'll say," Nancy muttered.

"She was an expert in the great Romantic poets. Not romantic as in love and sex—though those are part of what the Romantics were about. I mean romantic in the broader sense in terms of understanding one's feelings, harkening to one's senses, just grasping life and allowing oneself to feel wonder and awe."

"Self-centered, you mean," said Nancy. "Everything that goes against the Christian way of life."

"Now, now, Nancy," Jim said.

"It's true!" she said. "That family always thought they were too sophisticated for God. Romantics? We all know Jesus Christ died a virgin." She cast another glance at the wreckage I was making of her pie. "Are you quite done with that, Rett?"

I put my fork down and reached into my purse.

"I know the police told you about the note Wanda received, the one that was a lot like the one The Imp put in your mailbox. I printed out a copy." I handed the copy to Jim.

The pastor sighed. "This is so cruel. What must Wanda have thought after reading this?" He handed it to Nancy, who clicked her teeth.

"There was something interesting about the original version

of that note," I said. 'It was found in a coffee table book, but it wasn't in the book long enough to flatten it out. The note still had a curve its entire length, as if it was originally folded in something else. I think whoever wrote the note didn't want to be seen delivering it to Wanda's front door, so they put it in her newspaper, which Jim likely placed in her mail slot."

"Jim would never write a letter like this," Nancy said.

"You're right," I said. "Jim didn't write it. Someone probably planted the note in their own paper and then switched them before Jim did his morning walk. I'm thinking this happened when he was still recovering from the flu and he was sleeping a lot more, allowing someone else to get to Wanda's newspaper before he did.

"The letter was one of the last straws for Wanda. That's when she taped up her mail slot from the inside and stopped going out except to get her packages. She must have thought the whole world was against her."

"Did she think I wrote it?" asked Jim, appearing wounded.

"I doubt it. After all, you were always so encouraging. You delivered books to her—self-help books from a Christian perspective. But she didn't include any of those books in the self-portrait for her department's website. Instead, she included a different type of book you gave her, Jim, one she really did treasure—the one you wrote yourself: an espionage novel called *The Spy's Briefcase*."

Nancy laughed. "A spy novel? Written by Jim? That's crazy."

"It's okay, Nancy. You don't have to cover for him anymore. Judging by the inscription in the book, Andy M. Ion had to be a former student of Wanda's, someone who credited Wanda with helping him find his muse. Jim, yesterday I bumped into Gwen, the parishioner who you are counseling. She recited a Bible quote that she had certainly learned from you, something about Jesus 'walking on heavenly pavement' and 'speaking with divine powers.' But that's not from the Bible. It's a line from John Keats's poem, *Endymion*. I know that because I read the entire poem last night, thinking it just might be important.

"This morning I emailed Gary Roland and he confirmed that you enrolled in one of Wanda's classes more than twenty years ago. Taking her class must have worked. Your sermons improved, and you kept your job."

Jim nodded. "My parishioners would never have understood how I could learn to write a sermon from a non-religious college professor, but that's exactly what happened. Wanda taught me to 'go toward the trouble.' She said it was the Romantics who really figured out you had to wrestle with what scared you. Each week I found a new worry or concern to explore in my sermons. And, guess what? I became known as a preacher's preacher. And I owed everything to Wanda."

"Yes, Wanda saved your career," I said. "But at some point you grew bored just writing sermons. I could tell by your body language yesterday when I interrupted your work, just how much of a chore it felt to you."

Nancy pursed her lips. "I don't know why he wants to write silly spy books. All those *secrets*. Trash!"

I stood up for him. "They aren't necessarily silly, Nancy. Plenty of people who love history just need a good yarn to help them remember it. And, your husband is obviously very good at it, because he won an award for his first book. He wanted you and Wanda both to join him at the awards ceremony in New York. That's the real reason Jim broke the glass in her front door. There was no other way to get the invitation and the plane ticket to her, especially after she taped up her mail slot."

Nancy turned to Jim, "Did you tell Rett—?"

"Jim didn't tell me about Wanda's ticket," I said. "I stopped by the travel agency to do some other research and saw a notepad with a reference to your trip with the reminder to cancel the

'WH tour and ticket.' At the time I thought WH meant 'White House,' but later I realized it meant Wanda Hightower."

I turned to Jim. "What was the tour in New York that the note referred to?"

"The Tenement Tour in Brooklyn," Jim said. "I thought it would be something we'd all enjoy. Of course, after Wanda passed away, there was no reason to keep her plane ticket or the tour tickets."

"But you didn't cancel your and Nancy's trip to New York."

Jim was emphatic. "I still want to go to the awards ceremony. Wanda would have wanted that, too."

"But there was a problem," I said. "If the police found evidence of Wanda's New York trip and connected it to you, you'd have even more explaining to do beyond the broken window. Your itinerary needed to change slightly. That's why you booked flights to DC and changed your original tickets to leave for New York from D.C."

"That was Nancy's idea, to make it seem we were only going to D.C.," Jim said. "For some reason, Nancy wanted—"

"—to protect your *reputation*," Nancy said sharply. "What if someone found out Wanda was flying to New York on a ticket you bought her? And not to mention staying in the same hotel. What might people think?"

"I don't care what they might think, Nance," Jim said impatiently. "You were going along on the trip, too, after all. Look, I'm done living under a microscope. I'm not trying to be anyone's lord and savior. I'm just one man—Jim Thompson."

"And 'Andy M. Ion,'" Nancy added, almost mockingly.

Jim said, "I'm sorry I disappointed you, Nancy. I promised I would make it up to you and write that devotional book."

While the couple were having it out, I cleaned up a bit, collecting everyone's forks and Dixie Cups and putting them into ziplock baggies that I labeled and placed in my purse.

All this conversation had been interesting, but there was still a lot to be unraveled, many more details to be sorted out. I had asked Darryl for ninety minutes. I had barely twenty left.

"Now it's time to talk about the murder," I announced.

"I'm not in the mood for this anymore!" Nancy said abruptly, and she started to gather her things.

I reached across the coffee table and put a hand on her arm. "I don't think you'll want to leave, Nancy. I think you'll want to learn what I know, because that's why you came here in the first place, isn't it?"

"You don't know anything," she said, pulling her arm away. "Jim wouldn't do what you're suggesting. He's a good man. Besides, you already figured out that Skip is your killer. He's a sneaky little guy, and he absolutely hated what Wanda did to all that marvelous landscaping. He took that darn pear and kept it in his car as a morbid souvenir."

"There's a problem or two with the theory of Skip as the murderer," I said. "One has to do with Skip's hands. In fact, hands are important to this entire case."

"What do Skip's hands have to do with anything?" Nancy asked.

"I believe the killer left the house through the back door. One of the trick-or-treaters says she saw someone near the alleyway dressed as a dragon. But she didn't see a *dragon* dragon. She saw someone who resembled the Grand Dragon of the KKK in a photo from the 1950s. I don't think it was just the white sheet the person wore that reminded the little girl of that photo. That KKK member in the photograph had an old person's hands. The hands of the killer probably looked old, too."

I saw Jim instinctively look down at his own hands and flex them. They were large, wrinkled. To a young girl, they would appear ancient.

I said, "This is the clue that actually makes me doubt that

Skip was the killer. Skip has soft, pudgy hands, thanks to the fact his husband does all the yard work."

"Well, that eliminates one suspect," Nancy said sarcastically. "We just need to check the hands of all the other million old fogies in the city."

"Fortunately," I said, "we don't have to. We can just check the DNA evidence we find on the gloves that the murderer wore. It's easy to deduce that the murderer wore gloves inside the home, because there aren't any prints on the knife or anything else for that matter. Yet we think the little girl saw the person's hands. Likely there was blood on at least one of the gloves, and the murderer didn't want to be seen with them on. So the killer quickly ditched them in Skip and Stuart's trash can when the children showed up.

"I figure those gloves must have been what Otis found the next morning while he was looking for scrap. Think about it. He reaches into Skip and Stuart's trash can and pulls out a pair of bloody gloves; at the same time he spots a cop car patrolling the alley. Now that he's touched the gloves, how could he ever prove they aren't his? As a Black person, he doesn't feel he's going to get the benefit of the doubt. He panics, speeds off, thereby casting suspicion on himself for the entirety of the case."

"How do you know they aren't his gloves?" Nancy snapped.

"We'll be able to check the inside of the gloves for DNA. If the killer was an older person, their hands would likely be dry enough to leave skin cells on the inside of them. I care for Lydia Schmidt, who has to use a ton of lotion every evening on her hands due to cracked skin."

"So where are these mysterious gloves?" Jim asked.

I reached into my purse and held up another large ziplock.

"Why, they're right here."

CHAPTER 25

FINAL JUDGMENT

"How did you get those?" Jim asked.

"Otis gave them to me in secret at the end of the show," I said. "He knew he couldn't hide them anymore or his art was going to be destroyed."

"Why didn't he just give them to the police in the first place?"

"Because he doesn't trust them," I said. "Why? Because he knows the police don't trust *him*."

"So the police will just have to test the inside of those gloves and they'll know who killed Wanda?" asked Nancy.

"Yes and no. In order for there to be a match, the murderer's DNA would already have to be in the criminal database system. If we think the murderer is someone in the neighborhood, the police can ask neighbors to voluntarily provide a simple mouth swab, then test those samples looking for a match."

Nancy cringed. "Blech! I wouldn't agree to that. I don't know who would."

"You don't have to. Fortunately, I've got this." I held up the forks we'd used for the pie tasting, each one sealed in its own separate ziplock and labeled with the owner's name.

"Like I said," Nancy protested, "Jim would never commit murder."

"I'm not as interested in Jim's fork as I am yours," I said.

Jim's eyes bore into mine. "What are you insinuating, Rett?"

"Nancy had motive. She hated the way you did little favors for Wanda, like delivering her newspaper and giving her books of encouragement. Those things were bad enough. But when you invited her to the awards ceremony in New York, that's when her imagination really ran wild. That's when—how did you put it? 'Suspicion provided its own evidence.'"

Nancy shook her head. "It's his prerogative. If he wants to bring to the big city some hussy—"

"Now, sweetheart, don't—"

"'Hussy?'" I asked. "Would you even go so far as to say Wanda was 'nasty?' I figure you sent Wanda that impish note right after Jim bought her plane ticket to New York. To mislead the police, you stole lines from young Barry Watson's gangster screenplay, one of the many copies he must have handed out while he acted in that Passion play at your church. You consulted it again in writing yourself a threatening note, to keep me from suspecting you."

Nancy pursed her lips. "I didn't write any notes, but it's true Wanda had men. Probably Philandering Phil next door. Maybe even that Black janitor. Perhaps Otis was the jealous one. Did you think of that?"

"It's not his DNA that will be on the inside of these gloves, Nancy."

"How dare you try to implicate me! Have you gone completely insane?"

"I'm not insane, but I will make you a deal. Answer my remaining questions, and I might just look the other way. I don't like to see elderly women go to prison for a crime of passion.

Won't you answer just a few questions in hopes of getting your DNA back?"

She screwed up her face and looked at me hard. "Whatever makes you happy, Little Miss Busybody."

"Did you go to the front door or the back originally?"

"Oh, come now..."

"You weren't at the party in the very beginning. You had time to commit the murder, return home, and pull a dessert out of the oven. I think you went to Wanda's back door, dressed as a ghost, pretending to trick or treat. But Wanda would not have had candy ready in a bowl to give away, so after opening the door, she turned to come up with a treat in her kitchen, and you followed her inside. Meanwhile, she did find something to give you: a single golden pear that she was getting ready to slice up for a snack. The moment she bent over to put the fruit in your bag, that's when you jumped her and—"

"Really? That's when I stabbed her?"

"No—it's when you the poisonous treat bag over her head and pulled the draw strings."

Nancy sucked in a breath. "But how—?"

"How did I know? Those dead bugs and moth balls on the floor in the corner of the living room. I didn't understand their relevance until I saw those very same kind of moth balls on a wedding gift registry. Only they weren't moth balls. They were ceramic pie weights for baking crusts. Dried beans are what most of us use, but some perfectionist bakers—those who always have a tool for everything—use specially-made pie shell weights, little ceramic balls that closely resemble moth balls.

"You soaked your ceramic pie weights in liquid cyanide, the same chemical that's used by biology students to make an insect kill-jar. I figured you must have taken an entomology class when I saw that photo hanging near your desk of you and some class-mates holding butterfly nets. I called Sheila this morning to ask her how a kill jar is made, and it's just a jar with something in the bottom that has absorbed the poison. You couldn't make a giant kill *jar* for Wanda, but a kill *sack* would do.

"Because all your pie shell weights had been soaking overnight in poison, you couldn't use them for your signature Halloween pie. That's why we received an apple *crumble* instead of a pie at the block party. A crumble is basically a pie without the shell. I happened to ask you yesterday if you had any dried beans for a recipe. You had none, yet you had already managed that very day to make not one, not two, but three pie crusts for your fundraiser pies. Skip just confirmed for all of us that your crust was perfect. Which means you must have bought some replacement pie weights after the murder. I'll bet if I found that trick-or-treat bag—way more trick than treat—I'd discover a bag with an inner lining sewn into it, with some of those cyanide-soaked pie weights still between the layers.

"Those extra wrinkles I saw around your face at the party? That wasn't old age taking its toll. They were caused by the gas mask you wore for safety under your costume. The gas mask that was certainly one of Jim's many pieces of World War memorabilia."

"I do have one of those," Jim said. "Nancy, is any of this true?"

Nancy didn't answer, for she was too preoccupied with glowering at me.

I continued. "For better or worse, cyanide gas doesn't work very quickly, certainly not as quickly as you had expected. Wanda wasn't as easily killable as a bug in entomology class, and your cotton gloves were slippery. She managed to jerk the bag away from you and run into the den while ripping the bag off her head. There she was, running toward the front door. She was going to get away!

"You could have left the scene then, Nancy, retreating

through the back door and returning home. You could have hidden your costume and resumed your identity as the charmingly saucy wife of a preacher man. You might have done that, but something caught your eye on the kitchen counter: a selfie photograph of Wanda with her two children. You didn't like Wanda looking happy, and all of a sudden you imagined Jim in that photograph as the husband and father—one big happy family.

"So while Wanda with her terrible MCTD struggled with the front-door knob using her unresponsive hands, you improvised. You grabbed the knife Wanda was going to use on the pear, and, just as she finally managed to open the door using the rubber shower cap she kept nearby—it's the only explanation for the cap being there that makes sense, and I know I had trouble turning that glass doorknob myself—you rushed forward and plunged the knife into her back."

"Only because she deserved it," Nancy said.

Jim cried, "Nancy! For the love of God—"

"It was the Lord's will, Jimmy. Why, He had placed the knife right there for me, right on the edge of the counter."

Jim just looked at his wife, completely speechless.

I wasn't quite through. "Wanda fell face down on the porch —too mortally wounded to make much of a sound, but if she did manage to cry out, the noise just blended in with all the other Halloween sound effects on the block. This manner of death you hadn't planned for, Nancy. But you didn't panic. You immediately noticed that one of your gloves—the knife hand glove—was soaked in blood. Remembering that Jim's fingerprints might be on the doorknob from his visit the night before, you wiped the knob clean with the clean glove, the one on your left hand.

"Then you returned inside, locked the front door, and spent a moment tidying up the scene. In the process of Wanda getting away from you, the outer layer of the sack had ripped and a number of those deadly pie weights had fallen out. You gathered the ones you could see, but several of them had rolled into the various corners of the room. And there was no way you'd ever have time to collect them all. You knew you had better leave and get to the party, fast.

"You saw Wanda's plane ticket to New York on a side table, dropped that into your treat bag, and headed for the back door. Just before leaving, you grabbed the framed family photo and smashed it on the counter, creating the broken glass near the back door that confused investigators. You dropped the smashed photo and frame into your bag and slipped out the back.

"It was still light outside. It wouldn't do at all to be seen wearing a bloody glove against your perfectly white costume. When you heard some kids entering the alley, you quickly ditched both gloves in Skip's trash can and hid behind it. What I thought at the block party to be cinnamon on your hands was actually rust from the can lid.

"The three bigger kids didn't see you when they passed by, but when you stood up, the little girl who was straggling behind did see you. After she ran away scared, you didn't try to retrieve the gloves. You figured that having them in Skip's trash would be a good way to steer suspicion toward him. The next day, when you saw Otis working on Skip's roadster, you got the idea of planting that pear in Skip's glove box. Homeless men checking Skip's roadster for change was nothing new. The next time it happened, you disguised your voice and alerted the cops. It didn't really matter who got blamed for the killing—a homeless person, a gay neighbor, a Black handyman—so long as suspicion was deflected from you."

"Now, about those gloves," Nancy said, standing. "I need you to hand them over to me right now. Along with my fork."

"Okay," I said, remaining seated, "but first please explain one thing more. Did you actually think your husband was having an affair with Wanda?"

"He's a good man, but he's still a man. That hussy would have found a way to seduce him in New York. And I couldn't let him be put in that position. Not after all he had worked for all his life."

"No, Nancy," I said, "you mean all *you* had worked so hard for. You knew the darkness in your soul, and you thought that by making your husband seem perfect to the world it would provide you some cover. I totally get that, because I know what it's like to want to live in the aura of a spouse because you feel you're so inadequate inside that no one could possibly love you."

"I have no idea what you're talking about," Nancy said. But I looked at Jim and saw his expression alter, like a dawn rising in his eyes.

"Wanda fought you," I continued. "She was stronger than you thought. Maybe she was stronger than any of us thought."

"She was nothing but a hairy, hunchbacked, unbelieving monster!" Nancy cried. "Now, give me those gloves." When I didn't budge, Nancy reached into her purse and pulled out a small, snub-nosed pistol. "I'd like them right now, please."

"Nancy, that's my gun!" Jim cried.

"Stand aside, Jimmy," she said. "This isn't about you."

There was some commotion elsewhere in the house. A second later, Darryl was in the room, his own gun drawn.

"Give it up, Mrs. Thompson," said Darryl. "It's over."

Nancy clenched the pistol more tightly and pointed it at Darryl. "Where did you—?"

"This whole time he's been in the next room listening to our conversation through this," I picked up my phone from the far end of the coffee table. "It's the baby monitor app I used with Lydia when she first came back from the hospital."

"Another sneaky spy trick," Nancy said, swinging the gun in my direction. "And here I thought you were a good person."

I froze. Was this the end of me?

Jim shouted, "Nancy, please, think about what you're doing!"

Nancy kept the gun trained on me while she responded to Jim. "You were going to make a big mistake in New York, Jimmy. I couldn't let you do that. You'd worked so hard your whole life to be a godly man. Why, you're the last soft heart in the world. Why did you have to bring secrets—and that nasty woman— into our perfect, Christian home?"

"I'm sorry I broke our rule and met with her alone. Nothing happened, I promise. I was just trying to comfort her."

"You could never know what it was like in my home growing up. You'd never think people could hurt one another like that, that people could tell so many lies, until their whole life was one big lie! I worked so hard to make our home different from that. But I guess in the end the secrets won."

Suddenly she turned and dashed toward the back of the house and into the kitchen. Darryl, giving chase, tripped on the coffee table and lost his balance briefly, but caught up to her just as she opened the back door. Jim and I rushed into the kitchen, too, and got there soon enough to see Nancy reach with her free hand into her purse. In the process she dropped her gaze for an instant, allowing Darryl to take the gun from her while immobilizing her. But, she pulled away, causing her to fall backward against the kitchen's screen door. While she was falling, I saw her place something into her mouth and bite down hard on it.

Jim asked frantically, "Nancy, what was that?"

"It looked like a pill," I said.

Nancy was sitting on the floor now, leaning against the screen door, her eyes closed and her breath heaving.

Darryl turned to me, "Call 9-1-1." I realized I had my phone in my hand and began to dial. As I did so, Nancy opened her eyes again and spoke to her husband with ever quickening breaths.

"We both know it would hurt you too much to see me in prison, Jimmy. But don't you worry about me. I know where *I'm* going. I'll wait for you there, Dear Love..."

Then we all watched in horror as the aluminum screen door gave way and Nancy Thompson's limp body fell backward onto the home's rear steps, into the cold, November air.

CHAPTER 26

TOO CLOSE FOR COMFORT

With her husband at her side, Nancy was rushed to the hospital in an ambulance. Darryl met them at the emergency room so he could ask more questions if Nancy regained consciousness, but she never did. Preliminary cause of death: suicide by cyanide poisoning.

While we waited for Darryl to come home, Lydia paced her living room, begging for a cigarette.

"I'm d-d-dying," she said.

"Good thing," I said, "because your son is going to kill you."

I suppose I should have been upset by Lydia's exaggeration of her stroke's aftereffects, but, in light of everything else that had happened that day, it was small potatoes. Besides, the brain is a mysterious thing. She still slurred some words and had trouble starting others, so I knew that she hadn't totally made up her symptoms; she had merely hidden from us the full progress of her rehabilitation.

But why?

"Tell me about your relationship with Otis," I insisted. "It's more than just handyman and client, isn't it?"

She finally stopped pacing and sat down on the couch next

to me. "Oh, it's n-n-nothing like that, though I do c-c-care about him." She confessed how, three years after her husband died, she tried to seduce Otis, hiring him to do one fix-it project after another around the house. Nothing worked; he was all business. Finally, she flat out asked him if he had a girlfriend and, if not, if he was interested in a love affair.

"Now that's the direct Lydia I know," I said. "What did he say?"

"He said his late w-w-wife had been the only w-w-woman for him and he just w-w-wanted to be f-f-friends." Lydia smiled. "He w-w-wasn't kidding. We became great f-f-friends."

The two shared one love in particular. Even though Otis was too busy with his art to tend a garden, he'd grown up on a farm and knew the names of most native trees, bushes, and vines.

She was about to tell me what happened the morning after the murder when Darryl showed up.

"I'm glad to see you, Mom—and glad to see you're speaking again."

Lydia trembled, ready for an interrogation. But it seemed that Darryl could only contend with one mystery woman at a time.

He turned to me. "I haven't really had a chance to congratulate you. That was pretty damn impressive."

I did the dorky thing I always did whenever I received a compliment: I blew a puff of air on my right-hand knuckles and rubbed them on my shirt.

He added, "I've just got one question: those weren't the actual gloves Otis found, were they?"

"No, they weren't." I explained how, immediately after leaving Otis's show, I had dashed over to the thrift and art stores and bought a pair of white gloves and rust colored paint. "It was a reasonable calculation, for I figured that at least one bloody glove existed somewhere."

"Oh? Whatever gave you that idea?" Darryl cast a suspicious glance at his mother.

"Lydia didn't say anything to me, if that's what you're wondering," I said. "I had to deduce the existence of the gloves, just like I had to deduce most everything in this case."

Lost in a moment's thought, Darryl scratched his chin's signature five-o'clock shadow. I grabbed the moment to ask, "Did your colleagues search Nancy's house yet? Did they find cyanide?"

"A bottle of it in granular form was found in Nancy's little gardening shed, where Jim said he never went. She had her own mini chemistry lab in there."

"Whoever runs the lab at the community college needs to do a better job of keeping that stuff under lock and key," I said. "But what I want to know is, how did she get a *capsule* of cyanide? I doubt the chemistry lab had those ready-made."

"I wondered about that, too." Darryl leaned back in his chair. "We're quite sure she tried to poison Wanda with cyanide capsules in the days leading up to Halloween."

This was a surprise. "How? When?"

"Probably not long after she wrote her threatening note to Wanda. She must have worried the note wouldn't be enough to scare her off. Meanwhile, Jim was beginning to recover from his flu, which meant she didn't have much time. So, she steals one of the Canadian drug company packages from Wanda's front porch, takes the package home, and replaces one of the capsules from a bottle of steroids with a cyanide pill. She returns the package to Wanda's porch, goes home, and waits. A couple days later, Nancy notices the package appear on Wanda's porch again. She knows she probably shouldn't return to the porch to retrieve it, but she can't help herself. She gets a surprise: Wanda has written on the package, 'You can't fool me!'"

"Just like the package Wanda later gave the Norrises!"

"Right. Not wanting anyone else to see it, Nancy brings the package home. We discovered it in her garden shed laboratory. Thank God for tamper-resistant packaging that alerted Wanda someone had been meddling with her pills. That kind of packaging wasn't even a thing until the Tylenol murders—which, incidentally, happened in the Chicago area at the same time that Nancy was living there with Jim as he was earning his theological degree."

"Do you think—?"

"—that Nancy Thompson committed the Tylenol murders? No, but I think it's where she got the idea. Those murders were never solved, so maybe poisoning seemed a safe approach to her. Speaking of poisoning, I had a vet look at those dead squirrels. Yes, they were stabbed, but only after they'd eaten poison peanut butter."

"Nancy's poisonous intimidations didn't work," I said. "Against me or against Wanda."

"No, but they did manage to get Wanda to stop taking medicine through the mail. Including her steroids. We found over a year's worth of past orders for corticosteroid pills from another company in Canada. It's illegal to import prescription drugs from Canada or anywhere else, but our government looks the other way."

I thought about Trent's drug dealing friends. They could only hope the U.S. justice system would go just as easy on them.

"That confirms it," I said. "Wanda suffered from a version of 'roid rage.' Why didn't the medical examiner catch that?"

"We asked him that. Judging by the amount of medicine she ordered and when, he thinks she didn't take steroids all the time. She would go on and off the medicine for stretches to avoid the major physical side effects, things that would be noticed in an autopsy. But that seesaw approach would play hell with her mood. She'd experience pain relief and maybe even euphoria and mania, followed by depressive episodes whenever she abruptly stopped the medication." The coroner told Darryl that Wanda's bloodwork would likely confirm low cortisone levels— a sure sign of steroid use.

"Then when the pain became unbearable, she'd do it again," I said. "But why didn't you find any steroids in the house?"

"After about October 20th, when she found the tampered bottle, Wanda didn't place any more orders for drugs. She probably trashed any steroid pills she did have, because we didn't find any on the scene. When that last order of prescription cream to treat her dry hands was mistakenly delivered to the Norrises, she must have seen Brad place it on her porch and just assumed he was part of the conspiracy. By then she would have been off the drugs for several days and in a pretty bad way. She would not have been thinking straight enough to call the police."

"I see. Then Nancy turned to Plan B, deciding to poison Wanda in person with her kill sack on Halloween. Did you ever find her ghost costume?"

"Folded and placed on a shelf in her laundry closet under a mountain of window dressings."

"What about her toxic treat bag?"

"Buried in her garden."

"And inside the bag?"

"A plane ticket to New York and the shattered picture of Wanda with her children."

I felt vindicated. Most of my theory had been deduction, but I'd actually painted an accurate picture of the murder after all.

The three of us sat there for a moment, thinking about our neighbor and all she must have gone through.

"What about Trent?" I asked suddenly. "Is he still in jail?"

"We dropped the charges against Trent. All of them."

Darryl started up the stairs, but stopped on the first step, testing its solidness with his foot.

"Oh, my gosh!" I cried. "That broken first step! But...I guess I was too tipsy that night of the murder to remember it later. You obviously noticed Otis had fixed it, so why didn't you just—?"

"—open up the step and grab the evidence? Think about that for one minute, and *then* tell me what you think of the idea."

"Well," I began, thinking aloud, "you must have figured that important evidence existed beneath that repaired step, evidence which could implicate the killer. But, you also knew that you couldn't be the one to find it. Doing so might look like you set someone up, and a jury might let the accused go free. You'd have to take yourself off the case first and let someone else find the evidence"—which finally explained the silent anguish I'd witnessed in Darryl over the past two weeks.

Darryl said, "I don't like giving up cases."

"But I also know how humble you are. You'd give up a case in a second if you knew it was the right thing to do. I think you didn't want to give up *this* case because you couldn't guarantee another investigator would be as fair to Trent as you would try to be."

Darryl met my eyes. "I work with really good people."

"But you know I'm right. That's why you tried to get Otis to confess as to where he hid the evidence. The search warrant of his art was just a ruse to get him to speak up."

Darryl nodded. "However, someone else spoke up, too, and put a wrench in that plan." He looked accusingly at Lydia, who reacted by holding a throw pillow in front of her face.

I stood up for Lydia. "But me cornering Nancy and getting the confession was much better, because there's no guarantee you would have ever gotten a DNA match from the evidence anyway. And, now it wouldn't make sense to dig up that evidence at all, because what if it accidentally implicated the one who originally found it and held it—namely, Otis Jones?"

Darryl nodded again. "I think we've got a closed case. And now I'm going to go upstairs and take a nice long nap." He looked sternly at Lydia. "Mom, I don't have the energy to question you tonight. I guess I'm just relieved that you're talking again. Besides, I figure if I make you sweat a little more, maybe —just maybe—you won't pull a maneuver like this ever again."

"F-f-fine, Son. You w-w-win." Lydia hid her profile with a hand as she gave me a sly wink.

After a roll of his eyes, Darryl climbed the stairs and disappeared behind the guest room door. I turned to Lydia. "You pretended to be mute because Otis showed you the gloves and you didn't want to implicate him, didn't you?"

"That wasn't the only r-r-reason. You and Darryl sure have g-gotten a chance to know one an-n-nother the past couple w-weeks..."

Perhaps over and above everything else, my friend had been orchestrating a devious game of matchmaking. I gave her a stern look. Pretending to flee my wrath, she shuffled over to the stairs as if to head up to her own bedroom, but not before she, too, stopped thoughtfully on the step that Otis had made a hiding place for the evidence he'd found.

I said, "When he showed up that morning with those gloves, didn't it give you pause? Didn't you suspect him of something ghastly?"

She shook her head. "W-w-when you n-n-know s-s-someone, you just *n-n-know*," she said. "We just n-n-needed time for the t-t-truth to come out. Thank G-G-God you f-f-found the truth in time, because I don't th-th-think I could have kept my m-m-mouth shut another d-d-DAY!"

∼

I needed some time to relax and wind down, so I headed across the street to do just that. I was nearly there when Skip came running out of his house at me, waving a piece of paper in the air.

Skip had done a great acting job at Wanda's house, helping me to divert Nancy's suspicions so I could gather her DNA. The chocolate story had been real—I was one of the few people who had known about the fiasco—but his indignation had been a show. My plan was to thank him, but one look told me now was not the time.

"What's wrong, Skip?"

Gasping for air like he'd just run a marathon, Skip handed me a notecard. I read it silently:

A Poison Tree
By William Blake

I was angry with my friend—
I told my wrath, my wrath did end.
I was angry with my foe—
I told it not, my wrath did grow.

And I watered it in fears,
Night and morning were my tears;
And I sunned it with smiles,
And with soft deceitful wiles.

And it grew both day and night
Till it bore an apple bright,
And my foe beheld it shine,
And he knew that it was mine,

And into my garden stole,

When the night had veiled the pole;
In the morning glad I see
My foe outstretched beneath the tree.

I looked up at Skip. His face was red and clenched, this time from emotion rather than windedness, and he was struggling to say something. "Read the back," he managed. I turned the note-card over.

My anger, Skip, has run its course.
Thank you for caring about me.
Will you please tell the others I appreciate them
And together, soon, we'll plant a tree?
—Love, Wanda

"When did you get this, Skip?"

"All our mail gets thrown in a drawer until Stuart sits down to pay the bills, which he does religiously on the 15th and 30th of each month. I think Wanda must have delivered her note to our mail slot the day she died—the 31st. Stuart only came across Wanda's note today. And here I had thought so badly of her. Rett, I'm a terrible person."

"No, Skip, you're just...a person."

"If only it all wasn't so difficult, you know?"

I wanted to tell him I sympathized, that—whether we wanted to admit it or not—in every person's body is hidden a soft heart.

I asked, "Will you tell the others about the note?"

"Yes. I'll tell them all."

And, he walked off, looking a bit like the Ancient Mariner.

∾

Skip's display of emotion stirred something in me. Instead of returning to my empty house, I headed down the block to Sheila and Maxine's. Sheila let me in; Maxine had been lying on top of her made bed and reading while Matilda, the little lame hummingbird, played on her jungle gym.

I told them what we'd learned about Wanda's last days, including our theory that she had gone repeatedly on and off steroids to treat her pain, making her irascible, out of her mind.

"Those drugs are powerful," Maxine said. "Sometimes it's hard to know where the chemicals end and one's real feelings begin."

I nodded. "I think Wanda eventually realized she'd been fooled. Her anger didn't come from her heart. It wasn't who she was or who she wanted to be."

Maxine asked, "What are you feeling right now?"

"Something of Wanda's pain," I said. "Until now, I think I avoided dwelling on it." I imagined Wanda's last moment, her mad rush toward safety halted before she could reach the friendly spider weaving its strands across the front of her porch.

"What does this feeling make you want to do?" Maxine asked.

"In the past, I'd want it to go away. Drink it away. Anything but to be feeling this."

"And now?"

I looked over at the hummingbird, struggling to get from one apparatus to another, just doing her ever-living best to get by.

"I want to feel existence again, Max. I just don't know if I can bear it."

∼

At home, standing in front of my mirror, I found myself wondering how John Keats—how anyone, really—could equate beauty with truth, truth with beauty.

A thought occurred to me. Maybe when you call someone ugly, you've denigrated them, made them something below you. You've made an idol out of yourself, and, in so doing, you've created a lie, a tacit untruth.

Maybe to see something truly was to see its beauty.

Beauty was what Keats lived for. He was in love with the world and the world behind this world, a land of gods existing just below the surface of existence. The beauty that poked through, making everything—the pain, the suffering, the regret —worth the trouble.

Finding beauty in the non-obvious. The old. The wrinkled. The age-spotted.

Not just the pretty in Skip's yellow Triumph, but the genius in Otis's spray painted pickup. The coins in the console; the scrap in the bed.

Until Augusta suggested it, it had not occurred to me, even for a second, that KayLeigh Rider's elegant coloring could stem from ancestors who were African.

And this. For the split second I thought that KayLeigh might be Black, I was delighted. Because it was a gotcha. Because it was something I could look down on her for.

Whether KayLeigh really was part Black was beside the point. The point is, it had been baked into me that Black was not beautiful. I was that racist.

As if God ever made junk. As if God wasn't just like Otis Jones, forming beauty from the throwaway, sculpting humanity out of mud.

I didn't pretend that I could shed racism's ugly, invisible skin —not in me, and not in our society, with a justice system that gave few people of color the benefit of the doubt.

Suspicion supplies its own evidence.

What I could do was a better job of searching for the beauty in others—starting with my mirror's reflection. I was never one of the popular girls, but that's not the beauty Keats was talking about, what any of the Romantics had in mind. I needed to stop measuring myself against the thin wash of color that somehow constituted the glamour of our day.

Beauty could be many things, but it often presented as thick layers. "Painterliness" as Glenda Murlowsky had called it. The trials that scarred us, the friends who dressed us.

I never was able to penetrate the veneer Allan showed the world. But I could learn how to let go of my anger toward Allan, KayLeigh, and everyone else, so I could begin to see their humanity.

I could stop killing the proverbial albatross in my life with every word and every thought. Every breath.

When Darryl told me about Barry's disappearance, my mind had raced to understand what could have happened. I couldn't come up with any theories in the moment with so much going on, but since then I had come up with a theory. Could Trent's gangster friends have been involved in his disappearance? In my last conversation with him, Trent had clearly recognized the Imp's letter to Wanda as coming from his friend's screenplay. It's why he'd been so cagey with me. If Trent had somehow sent a message to the gang that Barry was involved in this mess, they may have retaliated by kidnapping Barry—or worse. I couldn't help but feel partly responsible. I'd met with Barry out in the open where anyone could have seen us. What is more, I'd given Barry one of my business cards to keep.

I called Darryl right away to tell him my worries. He listened patiently—then began chuckling.

"Why are you laughing?" I demanded. "This boy is in trouble! He's been kidnapped by a drug-trafficking gang and he might even be dead for all we know!"

Darryl said, "Calm down. Barry is fine. He decided to leave school one day and drive to Hollywood. He had left a message for his parents, but they didn't find it until after they'd alerted the police. Turns out he was able to meet with some director and sell his script. Craziest thing I ever heard. Who does something like that? How does someone that young have the out-and-out balls to do that?"

Someone like Barry Watson, a modern day John Keats, that's who.

~

I waited several days before approaching Jim Thompson's front door. When no one answered, panicking a little, I pushed open the unlocked door and shouted his name. It was well into the afternoon. He should have been up by now.

Jim was coming down the stairs. He seemed careworn but his cheerful greeting made it clear he was grateful for a visitor. At his invitation, I followed him to the kitchen, where he turned on the radio and poured us each an iced tea.

We sat at the kitchen table as cool, late November light played on the checkerboard tablecloth.

"Nancy would rarely talk much about her childhood," he said. "I do know her parents abused one another as well as Nancy. I think she was attracted to me because I seemed harmless. Recently she started to distrust my thoughts and motives, the only man she had ever trusted. All the old feelings she experienced in her childhood started to come back. I think they just overwhelmed her."

"The ticket to New York," I said. "Are you sure there was no romantic intent?"

"I've had plenty of opportunities as a pastor, and, yes, I've been tempted from time to time. But long ago I made the decision never to cheat."

"So, it was basically an irrational jealousy on Nancy's part?"

He nodded. "But Nancy had no idea..." His voice trailed off.

"No idea of what?"

"I didn't want to tell this to the police either, but Wanda shared some other things with me during that final conversation. Now I wish I had told Nancy, because it might have prevented her from doing what she did. I'd like to tell you now, if you can keep it under your hat. It's weighed on me."

I nodded. "Go ahead."

"When I visited with Wanda that early morning, right before I left I asked if I could pray with her. She said she didn't believe in prayer. I asked her if she believed in God at all, and she said she didn't. I asked her if she believed that things sometimes happened that we just could not explain. In other words, I asked if she still found life to be full of wonder, and magic, and soul—all the things the Romantic poets believed in. She admitted that a part of her still did.

"Can you imagine, Rett? Even after all that this woman had lost—her marriage, her parents, her health, her friendships—she was still what she always referred to herself in class as a *hopeful* Romantic."

Jim continued. "She asked me if I still had perfect certainty in my faith. I admitted that I often didn't understand God and that I couldn't control God, and that after all these years I found the Bible more puzzling than ever and God's decision to act or not act in certain situations utterly baffling. That's the truth, too.

"Well, she seemed to appreciate that. She said that if a minister like me was willing to believe that praying might *not* make a difference, then she was willing to believe that it might. I told her I'd take that deal. 'Then get to it, sir,' she said."

"So I put my hand on her back and prayed aloud for her healing. I prayed that she might experience peace. I prayed for her soul and for God to accept her into His care. I asked her if she would let God love her and, if she felt His love, if she would receive that love into her heart. She said, 'If I ever feel love again, I promise not to turn it away.'

"Rett, I think that Wanda opened her heart to God that night, because when I saw her silhouette in her bedroom window, I'd almost swear she was kneeling at her bed, praying.

"And then, less than twenty-four hours later, she was dead—at the hands of my own wife. I feel responsible. If I had not gone into that house, I might not have fully unleashed Nancy's anger and jealousy. If I'd stuck to that one simple puritanical rule not to be alone with a woman, Wanda might still be alive today."

"However," I said, "if you had not gone into that house, you might not have given Wanda the hope she needed to survive another night."

Jim looked at me with uncertain, aching eyes. I could see why a woman like Nancy would put so much stock in him, but right now his face looked as old and tired as God's. We were both quiet for a moment. I finally noticed the radio playing, the country song long finished, a man now spitting fire:

"...*trying to destroy this country. Why, they hate America. It's true! If they can burn the flag they can burn the Constitution, too. They have to be stopped, Ladies and Gentlemen. These so-called neighbors? They are your* enemies!"

"Jim," I said, "what are we listening to?"

"...*next it could be your neighborhood that's being burned and looted...*"

339

He went over and looked closely at the radio.

"Odd. This isn't the Christian station." He turned the radio off.

We looked at one another amidst the silence, each asking ourselves the same thing: how long had Nancy been listening to such poison?

Shaken, but also sobered, Jim sat down at the table again. I asked him what came next for him.

"I reached out to Otis Jones yesterday and apologized for what my wife did. He was gracious, as always. Then I called Trent. I told him I wanted to help him in any way I could. We agreed I could help him with his college application process. Also, now that Barry has gone Hollywood, their acting troupe needs a new playwright. I agreed to try my hand at some new plays. I want to work with Trent's pastor to see if we can expand our theatrical outreach work beyond church walls, get at-risk young people like Trent's friends involved. I think he may go for it."

"Looks like you're going to be plenty busy in retirement," I said. "No plans at all to cut loose a little?" I thought about Dorie, the Pearl Harbor hero. It was hard for me to imagine Jim being selfish even for five minutes.

He chuckled. "You know, I could probably stand to do some travel, but I don't have the appetite for anything too risqué. It's amazing what you lose the taste for if you focus on other things."

Did he mean that last statement for me? Was my drinking habit that obvious?

I raised my iced tea. "Here's to new habits."

CHAPTER 27

GRAND GESTURES

"Mother, I'm glad you have your voice back, but I'm going to worry sick about you having another stroke. Cousin Doris has said she'll move in with you permanently. I caught her in a generous moment. She was all bubbly after finding out she'd won that pie contest."

Lydia gave me the evil eye.

"Sorry," I explained, "but we sort of had to disqualify Nancy." I turned to Darryl. "Are you sure Doris is okay with moving here? I thought she didn't like downtown Raleigh with all its 'crime.'"

"She said she's not afraid now that we caught Wanda's killer."

Lydia muttered at me, "Th-th-thanks for that, t-t-too." She looked hard at her son. "Doris is b-b-boring!"

"Yes, but she's doing us an incredible favor. I'm not sure you can look a gift horse in the mouth."

"A b-b-boring horse!"

Darryl was looking at me for help.

Wanda believed in the grand gesture. The question was, did I?

"Doris won't have to move in with Lydia," I said. "I'll live here with her. That is, if Lydia will have me."

Darryl shook his head. "That's really kind of you, Rett, but we need a long-term solution."

"I am talking long term," I said. "You forget, I live alone in a big house, too. And I don't feel comfortable there anymore. That's not the word, exactly. I don't feel *complete* there." I looked at Lydia. "Besides, it's for sure boring living alone."

"Don't you want to t-t-travel?"

"Darryl can spell me for the periods I need to get out of town," I said, turning to him again. "Won't you?"

"Sure, but—"

"I accept," said Lydia. "I accept, D-D-Darryl!"

Darryl took a deep breath and held it for a second. When he realized that neither of us was going to change our tune, he finally relaxed.

"Okay. Well, now that that's decided, I need to get to work."

I needed to get to work, too.

The second week in December, our year of separation complete, I called Allan and told him my final terms for the divorce. I reminded him that I owned half of the business and, if we didn't come to an agreement, I would continue to receive half of all profits until the end of time, as well as remain on his board and be part of every business decision indefinitely. I pointed out that neither of us wanted that.

I proposed a different idea: have the company buy back most all of my shares. It would only cost the company half of its $20 million nest egg. "Just think," I told him, "no one will fight you anymore over each year's profits. You can triple your salary overnight."

That's all he needed to hear.

"I'd still like to keep five percent of the business," I added. "Call me sentimental, but I don't want to completely walk away."

"Five percent?" he said over the phone. "What good is that?"

It wasn't sentimentality, actually. Keeping a tiny part of the business would give me access to the company's financials. This way I could monitor the health of the company and intervene in time if I ever needed to help preserve our daughter's legacy.

While Allan was still feeling flush, I dropped the final shoe. I needed him to sign over to me his halves of our Woodmont home and our vacation home at Emerald Isle, NC. He hemmed and hawed, but after talking with his lawyer, he agreed. His counsel likely reminded him that, because there was evidence of his infidelity and, given my prominent role in the business, I could probably fight for a much larger buy-out. I had my own lawyer look over the papers and within two weeks they were signed. By Christmas Day our marriage—and our business relationship, if they were ever mutually exclusive—were finally over.

And I was independently wealthy. I thought I'd feel different somehow, but I didn't. Like Claire Foy, the star of "The Crown," told *The Guardian*, even when your situation has changed, you're still the same person. Or, as she bluntly put it in the interview, "Ultimately, all the same old crap is going on."

I knew what else I needed beyond financial security, even beyond a housemate. I needed my tribe—and to know my tribe was safe.

As I stepped into Needless Necessities, I found Sally "Not the Actress" Field scurrying around like a mad woman. "Jasmine is out with a cold!" she practically screamed at me before I could say the first word. Also, there was a leak in the quilting room, which meant the Qrazy Qwilters had to cancel. (This I already knew, and Lydia had not been happy about it at all.)

Also, there had been a truck shipment of donated metal

scrap, but the frat boys from Shaw couldn't be reached to help unload it. It had gone to a scrap yard instead.

The only thing going well was that Wo was on time to work the register.

"Hi, Wo," I said.

The artist didn't answer, didn't even look up.

"She doesn't answer to that name anymore," came a voice.

I turned to find Wash with his mop.

He explained. "The name 'Wo' has East Asian overtones, and someone pointed out that could be interpreted as cultural appropriation."

"I see. So, what should we call her now?"

"Ashley is going to crowd-source a new name through SnapChat."

"But don't those texts disappear after a few seconds?"

"That's the whole point," Washington explained. "Ashley says each of us is...um..."

"*Ephemeral*," the performance artist whispered, her high-pitched voice surprising me just as it always did, so rarely did she use it.

"That's right. 'Ephemeral.' Meaning 'everything disappears'."

"Except art," I said. "That's it! Maybe we should call you Art, Ashley."

Both students stared at me, blank faced.

"Well, you can't live without a name," I insisted.

Just then Q.T. the quilting cat came a-purring. *Cutie. Quality Time.* Perhaps the beast triggered a thought in the girl.

"'W. O.,'" said the performance artist. "Moving forward, I shall be known as: WithOut."

"She will be known as WithOut," Washington echoed.

"That means I can't work this job anymore," she said, stepping out from behind the counter. "And, as WithOut, I won't be able to have you as my voice, Washington. Thank you for your service, kind sir."

The pair shared a friendly hug, then a European-style kiss on both cheeks, followed by high-fives and fist bumps. Next, WithOut located Sally and told her she was quitting. Only when she'd finally walked out of the store did the reality of what had just happened seem to register in Wash, who rushed to the break room so we wouldn't see his tears.

"Have you ever seen a boy so desperately in love?" asked Jasmine, who had walked in late with a box of Kleenex after Sally begged her to come in even though she was sick. "Wash is enthralled with her, and she doesn't even see it."

I said, "I suspect Little Miss 'WithOut' is too busy continually re-inventing herself to notice the faithful souls around her."

"Those artistic types," Jasmine mused aloud, as she gave me a special wink. I knew what she was insinuating, but there's no way I could think about taking up painting again with so many other things going on in my life. I gave her a defiant look.

But she wasn't done teasing me. "How's your detective, by the way?"

I blushed. "Darryl is fine. He's been really busy with work and with his boy."

"Maybe you should catch up with him, see how he's doing?"

"Are you and Lydia determined to connect everyone in the world with a life mate?" I asked. "You know, not everyone wants a significant other. I just got divorced this week, for crying out loud!"

Just saying it caused me to break down a little. Jasmine held out her tissue box for me, and I readily took one.

"Have you ever thought about becoming a therapist?" I said through my sniffles.

"I'm better than a therapist," she said. "I'm a *friend*."

"Please don't change a thing," I said.

Pulling myself together, I tracked down Sally and told her I needed to talk with her privately. She was rifling through stacks of donated items, trying to organize them into piles.

"I guess I'll just have to stay after hours to do this," she muttered as she led me through the break room to her office.

"Here's the deal, Sally," I said, as she sat down behind her desk and I closed the door behind us. "I want to be on your board. In fact, I want to be Board *Chair*. You can still run the day-to-day operations, but I think I can steer the overall strategy to make Needless Necessities profitable. We both know that we need to expand in order to make the organization financially secure."

"We did make over $20,000 on the bake sale and pie contest..."

"...with most of that from the commissions on Otis's art," I added.

I'll give her credit, she decided not to argue with that.

"Go on," she said.

"I have a few ideas. First of all, we can start hosting kids' birthday parties. They are money makers and they are an awesome way to introduce parents to the place, too. Also, we need to add a coffee shop and get Jasmine to agree to run it. Coffee is a high margin business. Free coffee for cops and other first responders means you'll never have to pay for security."

"I like that," she said. "What else?"

"We can use the larger gallery area that we borrowed for Otis's show to create a theater space. If you get the theater crowd here, you'll develop a night business for the coffee shop. And—"

"Okay, okay," she said. "I get it. You've got ideas. But what will I do if you take over? I might as well just retire. I'll have no purpose."

"*You* built this, Sally. You created this marvelous place where people can express themselves and create so much beauty. But right now, I don't see you having very much fun."

She nodded. "That's an understatement. Ever since Lydia had that stroke, I've worried that I'm next. Just making the rent each month is stressful enough."

"Just leave Mr. Simms to me," I said.

I met with Simms and made him an offer he couldn't refuse.

Yep, I bought that old strip mall.

It wasn't a lot of money, but it was more than twice what Simms paid for the property just ten years earlier. First thing I did was lower the rent and provide a six-month reprieve so the center would have the cash to build out the coffee shop and theater.

After the board's vote to install me as chair passed, Sally "Not the Actress" Field came to work looking like someone who had finally gotten a good night's sleep.

I didn't dare tell her, but she looked fresh and perky.

Just like America's Sweetheart.

Returning home, I noticed a familiar car parked along the curb.

Stephanie.

My heart skipped a beat. Had she already heard from her father about the divorce settlement, which was just a few days old? There weren't many secrets between those two.

We both got out of our cars. I braced myself for a true tongue-lashing in the middle of the street, but then I could see she had been crying.

"What's wrong, darling?" I asked, walking quickly to meet her.

"KayLeigh called and said you robbed them blind. She called you a gold digger."

Here it comes.

"Now, Stephanie, I—"

"Who does she think she is? I mean, you were dad's wife for twenty frickin' years before she came along! You helped build the business, and, oh, by the way, you're tons better at real estate than Dad is. And KayLeigh's complaining to me that you took all 'their' money? What the fuck? And why did she ever think she'd get any sympathy from me?"

Because you fawned all over her. Because you worshiped her like a Kardashian. Because...

I opened my arms and was instantly rewarded with my daughter's embrace.

"I admit I'm surprised," I said, as we relaxed our embrace. "You were so angry with me for so long. Can you help me understand why?"

"I don't know." She turned and faced the house where she'd grown up. "Maybe it was just easier to believe you'd been a bad wife than to believe my father is a bad person."

"Your father isn't evil, Stephanie. He just made some really bad decisions." Even as I said it, I knew it would take a while for me to truly believe those words, too.

Stephanie shrugged. "Either way, they're both on my shit list right now. As your daughter, *I'm* allowed to be mad at you, but no one else is going to trash-talk Mama and get away with it. No, ma'am! They'll be lucky if I go to the wedding, which, by the way, they've already set for June. 'Thanks for waiting tastefully after the divorce to make the announcement, people!'" I had to laugh a little: You really *can't* take the Eastern North Carolina out of the girl.

I felt vindicated by Stephanie's change of heart, but also a little sad that it took having a shared target for our anger to bring us back together. Sad, too, that there was now a wedge between Stephanie and her father. I'd been given a head start on learning how to release KayLeigh from my anger, not give her so much power in my life. If I'd learned anything, it's that sometimes you have to name your hate and work through it, or the hate will bubble over and consume you. Nancy Thompson, who had lived a life of denial and appearance, was proof of that.

Stephanie, if she was going to find peace, would have to work through her feelings. I was determined to help, if she'd let me.

∽

We had a routine, Lydia and I.

Each night, I'd say, "Goodnight, Sunshine." And she'd respond with, "Good...night...Loony...Moonie..."

I'd never thought of myself as loony, but once I'd moved in and took stock of the past few weeks and months, I wondered. Had I gone a little bit bonkers? So be it. I felt more alive, more vital, more myself than ever.

There was just one thing missing.

Lydia had already gone off to bed when Darryl dropped by to say hello. I invited him in. He'd already delivered Charlie to his ex-wife, as he was going to have to work the long New Year's weekend.

"I'm sorry I missed seeing Mom," he said. "Another hit-and-run case on Capital Boulevard. Want to hear about it?"

"Not right now," I said. "There's something I want to get out of the way."

"What's that?"

"This."

I moved into him, and, as I thought he might, he opened up, accepting my New Year's Eve kiss and wrapping his long arms around me. I'd surprised him, and that's probably why this first kiss didn't last very long.

"What sparked that?" he asked.

"I wanted you to know that I was paying attention. To all the nice things you've done for me, for your mother, and for your son. You really know the meaning of serving and protecting. I've not met many men who do. In addition to being kind, you're also kinda cute."

"You're the cute one," he smiled. "I'm merely tall, dumb, and handsome."

We looked into each other's eyes for a little while before kissing again. It wasn't going to go any further than kissing tonight. I made that a certainty when I changed the subject.

Radically.

I asked, "Why didn't you shoot Nancy Thompson?"

He smiled slightly. "I could see her gun wasn't functional. It had a plug in the barrel."

"You waited long enough to figure that out," I said. "Don't police say these things happen in a split second? That there's no time?"

"Often there's not. This time there was."

"But in the time it took you to figure out the situation, she could have killed you, me, and Jim."

"I suppose you're right," he said.

"Rather than shoot and risk being wrong, you made sure. Why?"

He shrugged. "I didn't really think about it."

I told him what Augusta had shared with me about implicit bias. When I was done, Darryl was silent. Had I gone too far?

"You know one thing I like about you?" he said. "You give me a lot to think about."

"You're already the smartest homicide detective I know," I said. "Now, go do your thing. We'll continue this conversation on our next date."

"And when will that be?" he asked.

"Oh, sometime next year."

He shook his head. "You'll forget me by then."

"Not on your life, detective."

A few weeks into the new year, I got a phone call out of the blue. It was Margaret. She wanted to know if I'd seen Gail Norris lately.

"No," I said. "Why?"

Margaret's voice turned dark. "She's avoiding me. We were supposed to go to High Point last week to prowl some furniture showrooms, but she cancelled at the last minute. Now she won't return my calls."

"Stand by." I hung up with Margaret and called Joe "Archie" Archibald. I'd filled him in earlier on what I'd learned about Brad's inheritance from his Aunt Lucy; now Archie agreed to try to find out the latest. It wasn't an hour later that I got a call back from him. He sounded amused.

"You remember how Old Lady Lucy Norris changed her will to cut out her son and write in Brad instead? Seems the son lawyered up and got that new will nullified. Lucy wasn't running on all gears at the time, and the law protects people from manipulation. Anticipating the inheritance, Brad and Gail had been spending on lines of credit—now they're scrambling for cash. One of my clients is a pretty avid art collector, and he tells me he just bought an Otis Jones piece from the Norrises for a song. He was pretty proud of himself."

"Let me guess. Reggie Byers? Good for him."

I hung up with Archie and called Margaret back. "I figured out what happened. Let's just say Gail is really, really house poor right now. I don't think she's going to be able to decorate her lake house just like she wants."

"That totally bites," Margaret said. "That account was going to help me redecorate *my* place."

"Don't forget Needless Necessities," I said.

"I'm not *that* desperate yet," she said, adding, "but maybe I will see you at the next estate sale."

Later that same day I saw some activity at Wanda's house and went to investigate. Angela's car was out front, but the door was answered by a man in his early thirties. Back in the day he'd been a skater dude with purple hair that had covered his eyes, a concert t-shirt a size too big for him, and lack of eye contact whenever you approached. Now he wore his dark hair neatly trimmed and looked at me steadily with warm, gray peepers that reminded me so much of his mother.

"Hi, Daniel," I said.

Angela asked from the back of the house who it was and insisted her brother let me inside. She greeted me warmly, with a hug instead of a handshake. "We're going through the house one last time. There is a closing tomorrow. Then Daniel is on to Europe for another tour."

"More Dueling Guitars?" I asked.

He sighed. "Yes, though this is the last tour." He looked at his sister. "I've got to break out on my own and get out from under our father's personality."

Angela walked over and squeezed his hand.

A real change had come over Angela since her mother's death. Her rigid exterior had softened, making her seem younger, happier.

"Cynthia Roberts came by yesterday," Angela said. "She told me what happened so long ago to cause Mother to leave State."

"You have every right to be angry," I said. "What Cynthia did caused your mother lose her job. You lost out on so much after that."

"I choose to look at it another way," she said. "Cynthia's tragedy set about a chain of events that ended with my mom being really heroic. I am so proud to be her daughter."

She put a hand on her brother's shoulder. "I feel like there was so much about our mom's heart we didn't know. I wish I'd tried harder to understand her."

Daniel put his arm around his sister. I looked behind them, where on top of the mantel leaned a photo of the siblings with their mother, its new frame and glass replacing the one that had been shattered by Nancy.

"There is one thing I always wanted to ask about this house," I said, stepping closer to the fireplace. "This beautiful mantle work—where did it come from?"

In a kind of trance, Daniel stepped closer to the mantle. "There's something I kind of remember. Here." He touched the dragon's mouth and traced its teeth, then pushed two fingers down its throat.

A panel in the center of the mantle dropped open, causing Angela to jump. "What in the world?"

Daniel explained, "Mom and I used to hide things for each other when I was young. I was so little, I hadn't even recalled it until just now."

"She never showed me," Angela said, a little hurt.

"You two were already close, and Dad demanded so much of me, I think this was one secret Mom and I had together."

"I wonder what this hidden compartment was for," Angela mused.

"Eleanor Foster said this house had the reputation of being a speakeasy during Prohibition," I explained. "Even if that's just a rumor, most people of means needed a place to hide their liquor in case the police showed up. See, the space inside looks big enough for a bottle."

Angel reached her hand inside the compartment. "This could totally hold a bottle," she said. "Wait. I feel something way in the back..."

She withdrew her arm. In her hand was a small notebook.

"Goodness," she said, looking at the cover. "Could this be more of Mom's poetry?"

On the cover in large letters was written: "To the Queen of my Heart." Later I would google those words and find a poem of the same name by Percy Bysshe Shelley, which included the following lines:

> *Those boiling waves,*
> *And the storm that raves*
> *At night o'er their foaming crest,*
> *Resemble the strife*
> *That, from earliest life,*
> *The passions have waged in my breast.*

"She wanted you two to find her work," I said to Angela. "It doesn't take a detective to figure that out."

Later as Angela was seeing me out, I asked if she'd ever witnessed her mother in the act of writing a poem.

"She usually wrote at night," Angela said. "She'd kneel down beside her bed with her notebook and scribble away."

I remembered what Jim had seen as he was leaving Wanda's house early Halloween morning, a kneeling silhouette in her bedroom window. Jim took that as a sign Wanda had become a Christian. I wasn't so sure. I think she had another way of connecting to worlds beyond this one.

Poetry as prayer.

There were a million things to be done at Needless Necessities. Starting in the new year I was there practically every day, all day, working with Sally to plan its expansion. Jasmine had jumped at the chance to manage a coffeeshop. But on this particular day, it was something else that got her excited when she saw me.

"You can finally meet Russell! He's with the painters, working on his creative side. I keep telling him he needs to start a portfolio for his college applications."

Finally, I'd get to meet the boy Jasmine wouldn't shut up about. Perfect in every way—star athlete, hardest worker ever, college bound. I guess I was a little jealous, not because her son was clearly more exceptional than Stephanie, but because I didn't have as close a relationship with my child as she obviously had with hers.

We walked over to the painting class which, today, served about a dozen adults all working with the instructor on painting an old barn with two horses and some free-range chickens. Jasmine led me to the back, where somewhat off to the side facing a single easel and canvas were two young men, their backs to me, one slight, the other very buff.

"Aaron," announced Jasmine, "this is my friend Rett I was telling you all about. She wants to finally meet Russell."

The beefy one, the one I assumed to be Jasmine's son, turned in his seat and found me with his eyes. He stood out of politeness and took the hand I offered.

"I'm Rett," I said.

"Nice to meet you. Aaron."

"Russell?" said Jasmine, addressing the one still seated. "Can you please say hello to Rett?"

Aaron looked down at Russell. I looked at him, too, or at the back of him, at least. I still had yet to see his face, but from what

I could tell of his build, nothing about the young man screamed "weight lifter" or athlete in any way. The boy didn't respond. He was moving his paint brush on the canvas very slowly, painting a muddy, gray inkblot that was so thick it had started to drip down the canvas.

"He's focusing," Jasmine said cheerfully. "Maybe if you sit down beside him he'll notice you, and the two of you can converse."

Aaron, who I now took to be a sort of paid companion to Jasmine's son, stepped away from his own chair and presented it to me for my use. I sat next to Russell, who wore glasses with super thick lenses. He was painting, but he didn't seem engaged. Clearly, he had a disability of some kind, exactly what type I couldn't yet tell.

"Hi," I said. "I'm Rett."

"HI," he said in a flat affect, plus much too loudly given that he was sitting right next to me.

"Do you like to paint, Russell?" I asked.

"IT'S OKAY."

"That's good."

"I'M A GOOD PAINTER." Now I could see that Russell had mixed together all the colors on his paper plate, producing the river-muck color.

"I'm glad you're a good painter," I said. "Because I'm not. In fact, I haven't painted in years and years."

"IT'S EASY."

"Easy for you to say."

"GRAB A BRUSH. I'LL SHOW YOU HOW."

Nervous around this loud and damaged boy, afraid that I might say the wrong thing and set him off, I rose and went hunting for a brush. I was nervous to look at Jasmine, afraid she'd see my surprise, or worse, some sort of judgment.

Aaron, thinking ahead, had procured for me an easel and

canvas. I found a brush and a paper plate with the colors being used by the group. I also put my hands on a wet sponge for us to wipe off our bristles between colors. We were too far behind on the instructions to catch up with the rest of the class, and I was feeling terribly anxious.

"What are you painting, Russell?" I asked as I sat back down.

"A DOG."

"Oh, a dog."

"NO. A DUCK." I hadn't misheard him. He had simply changed his mind.

"A *duck*," I repeated. "That's great. Want to paint something new together?"

"WHAT SHOULD WE PAINT?"

I finally looked over my shoulder at Jasmine. She was smiling cheerfully as ever, and I knew immediately that she was delighted with what she was seeing unfold. I knew, too, that she hadn't orchestrated this moment for Russell's benefit. She'd done it for me, to get me painting again.

And I was grateful. I told Russell, "Let's paint your mother, shall we? Because she's such a neat person."

"HEY, MAMA! WE'RE GOING TO PAINT YOU NOW!"

"Be sure to get my good side," Jasmine said. "I can't wait to see it!"

~

Winter waned. April bloomed.

Angela knew there would be a good number of former students who would want to come to her mother's memorial, so she approached N.C. State's JC Raulston Arboretum to host it. Paul, Wanda's ex-husband, didn't show; Angela said he was angry at Daniel for pulling away from their band to go solo.

He wasn't missed. Daniel played his solo guitar so beautifully, there wasn't a dry eye in the audience.

Two former students read poems they had written. The former English Department Chair, now VP of Academics, Gary Roland, read a poem by Wordsworth that contained the memorable line: *She sleeps in the calm earth, and peace is here.* He also mentioned something I hadn't noticed in my reading of the Romantics, that John Keats—poet of goddesses and nature—had been born on Halloween.

The final speaker, Angela, through tearful sniffles, recited from memory the last poem her mother had written in her notebook, left in the soft heart of the dragon:

Making Ready

Somebody's baby comes into the world
as somebody's beloved leaves
birth, death, life in-between
put to good use and wasted

I'd cradle you as gentle as a newborn in my arms
all tenderness restored
as if the long impossible good-bye
could be a welcome home.

Finally, a willow tree was planted in Wanda's honor in the gardens' British Isles section, its dedication simple: "For Our Dear Friend and Neighbor, Wanda Hightower — The Woodmont Neighborhood Culture Committee."

A guest I was especially glad to see, Otis Jones, had come alone. He wore a brown suit and brown Stetson hat with a black ribbon.

"I didn't see your trusty pickup in the parking lot," I said.

"She gave up the ghost," he said. "I bought a new one—and a Buick, too."

"Good for you, sir. You finally got the recognition for your art that you deserve."

He smiled shyly. "I think I got the recognition that Augusta wanted me to get."

"She just thought you got snookered by that dealer years ago."

"That gentleman bought my work, so what do I care what he sold it for? I was glad for it at the time. Made me believe I was on to something."

"I think she just wants you to be treated fairly."

Otis looked stricken. "'Fair?!' I'm afraid of fair—for I have taken much more from life than I have given. But I'll happily take *kindness* any day of the week. I don't deserve that either, but I will take it."

Before I could let Otis walk away, I had one more question for him.

"When I visited your studio, I saw you making a new art piece. It looked to me like a dragon. Was I seeing things?"

He smiled. "I guess, on the one hand, that dragon was inspired by Ms. Hightower's fireplace, and she certainly had been on my mind. But I was also thinking about the Great Smaug, that fierce and terrible dragon from my favorite book when I was a boy, *The Hobbit*. Know it?"

"Of course. I never read the book, but I think I saw the cartoon version at some point."

"You know, I always wanted to be invisible like little Bilbo wearing that magic ring. I thought that would make me so powerful. Turns out I really was invisible to a lot of people for a long time. Flew under the radar, I guess. But now, I think I like being noticed a little bit. It feels different out here in the sun, but it's all right."

He briefly looked up at the sky, then snapped his fingers. "I need to get back to my studio. 'The vision must be realized!'" After tipping the brim of his Stetson to me, he turned and walked with purpose toward his new Buick.

Over Christmas I'd run into Otis's granddaughter. Augusta had come into Needless Necessities to get some fabric for a costume she was making for a play Trent was in.

"I suppose you want me to tell you how grateful I am," she said, half kidding, half not. "I hate that I have to feel that way. I'd sure like a day when I can be selfish and just *expect* things to work out in my favor, rather than be shocked and surprised. Tell me, what's that like?"

"Maybe some people feel that way," I said, "but if I ever did, I must have forgotten."

She didn't look convinced.

I said, "Look, I'm not trying to say my life is harder than yours, because I'm sure that it's not. I'm just saying I think you're made of stronger stuff than me. That's all."

She nodded. "I'll take that."

I'd always wanted to plant and tend a flower garden myself, but I never knew how. In the days after the memorial service, Lydia began pointing out the plants in her backyard: hellebore, grape hyacinth, green-and-gold, and anemones, plus a plethora of snapdragons she'd planted recently.

Though most of her yard looked carefully laid out, Lydia insisted on keeping one corner of the yard completely chaotic. Wildflowers lived there, even a number of plants that some might consider weeds.

A pretty Saturday afternoon such as this normally would have been an occasion to break out a bottle of wine. This

Saturday I broke out something different: a dusty, clunky, wooden easel, still functional enough after two decades of storage to balance a 12-inch-by-12-inch canvas.

If I was going to stop drinking for good, if I was going to allow myself to experience the full force of feelings again, I was going to have to find a new way to weather my emotional storms. Painting, I suspected, was the way I'd get through.

I figured I'd paint those standout snapdragons in their bright, orange glory. But the edge of my eye kept being drawn to the more subtle beauty of the wild plot, so I relocated the easel there. As a breeze blew, I tried to recapture my old form, a hand that used to trace the strokes in my mind's eye. I was all elbows, revealing myself to be a beginner again. I immediately thought about giving up.

Instead, I decided to laugh at the rough marks on my canvas, call it a clumsy walk through a spider web, my own "brush" with endeavor. It worked. Before long I became lost in the painting zone, an intoxicating space I hadn't expected to visit again.

At some point I noticed Lydia standing off to my right, just taking a break from her own work to breathe in the afternoon air. I was about to say something about the loveliness of the day when something buzzed near my ear.

"Bee!" I yelped. I hopped back and put my brush out like a sword. But it was no bee.

It was a hummingbird.

Several houses down, a great commotion was stirring. I was too preoccupied at first to figure out where the shouts were coming from, for I was fully focused on the creature in front of me. The bird spurned the snapdragons and was now indulging its little beak in one blue wildflower after another. My brain at last caught up to the moment, and I finally recognized the cheering as coming from Sheila and Maxine, who were striking their back-porch gong over and over again in celebration.

"It's...it's..." Lydia sputtered. She still got stuck on a word occasionally. My eyes, the clearest they'd been in years, apprehended the image of the whirring creature better than any Polaroid. This tiny bird would become the central figure of my painting, was insisting on it.

"You're right, Lydia," I said. "It's Wanda. Just look at her fly!"

The End

ACKNOWLEDGMENTS

Sincere writerly thanks go out to the following:

The Scrap Exchange in Durham, N.C. A nonprofit with a mission like few others, this art center values the re-use of materials we normally throw away and provided the inspiration for Needless Necessities.

The folk artists of Alabama, including Lonnie Holley and Charlie Lucas, who shared their time with me in the mid-1990s and whose art never ceases to amaze me. Also, the Gregg Museum of NC State University, for hosting an exhibit of Tilden Stone, inspired carver of whimsical furniture not unlike Wanda Hightower's dragon mantle.

Poet and Professor Clare Brant, who introduced me to the Romantics three decades ago and who I am honored consider a close friend to this day. In addition to "Sight Lines," "Webs," "Enough," and "Making Ready," more of her amazing lyrics can be found in her collections: *Entering Sleep Mode, Accidentals in the*

Main, *Dark Egg*, and *Breathing Space* (www.shoestring-press.com).

The subject-matter experts: Elizabeth Hall, who shared some of the technical context of painting (www.sporastudios.com); Noelle Schofield, who tried her best to correct my many gardening gaffes; Matthew Brown, who shared the rich history and background of Raleigh's historical Oakwood Neighborhood; retired Homicide Detective Andre Watkins, whose real stories are so much better than anything I could make up; real estate professional Rye Honeycutt, who gave some veracity to how I wrote about Rett's former profession; and Dr. James Weaver, who helped dream up medical possibilities.

Brave readers of early drafts, including Delsey Avery, Donna Barton, Reva Bhatia, Carol Engel, Susie Larson, Becky Pickle, Cathy Pratt, Katy Reynolds, Carolyn Schendel, Teresa Wilder, and Leigh Ann Wilson.

Those who have encouraged my writing over the decades, beginning with a bevy of English teachers in Florence, Alabama, especially Joan Dorris, Judy Jenkins and Sandra Murray; college writing professors Elizabeth Cox and Melissa Malouf; generous writers Laura Durham, George Ivey and Jeff Jackson; friends Robert Baggett, Charles Eaton, Julie Freeman, Laura Ivey, Patrick Jordan, Dave Kumar, Dave Parrish, Snow Roberts, and Kristen Wall; insightful Triangle Siblings in Crime, especially Kathleen Heady, Kate Parker, Pamela Raymond, and E. Santeio; and, of course, my editors for this book: Laura Engel, Barb Goffman, Jordan Porter-Woodruff, and Brent Winter.

Finally, the one who reads my first and last drafts, she who is my beginning and my end — my wife, Marian.

HOW YOU CAN HELP PROMOTE "SOFT HEARTS: A RETT SWINSON MYSTERY"

We hope you liked *Soft Hearts*! If you did, please **text a friend about it, post something on social media,** and/or take a moment to do the following:

- **Write a short review on Amazon.com (or wherever you bought the book).**

- **Add some kind words to Goodreads.com.**

- **"Like" and follow his Facebook Page: Eric Lodin Mystery Author.**

- **Visit www.EricLodin.com and sign up for his e-newsletter to learn about special promotions.**

- **Pre-order *Slumbering Beasts*, the second installment in the Rett Swinson Mystery Series, coming in early 2022.**

THANK YOU for your kind attention and support.

ABOUT THE AUTHOR

Author Eric Lodin has been playing with words on paper since the third grade. Over the years he has tinkered with several novels and screenplays, trying to improve his craft one sentence at a time. He lives in Raleigh, N.C., with his wife, children, and a mischievous Havanese named Duke. *Soft Hearts: A Rett Swinson Mystery* is his first mystery novel.